The Botticelli Angel

Also by Harry Cauley

Bridie and Finn

The Botticelli Angel

Harry Cauley

MICHAEL JOSEPH
LONDON

MICHAEL JOSEPH LTD

Published by the Penguin Group
27 Wrights Lane, London W8 5TZ
Viking Penguin Inc., 375 Hudson Street, New York, New York 10014 USA
Penguin Books Australia Ltd, Ringwood, Victoria, Australia
Penguin Books Canada Ltd, 10 Alcorn Avenue, Toronto, Ontario, Canada M4V 3B2
Penguin Books (NZ) Ltd, 182–190 Wairau Road, Auckland 10, New Zealand

Penguin Books Ltd, Registered Offices: Harmondsworth, Middlesex, England

First published 1995

Typeset in Monophoto Sabon
Printed in England by Clays Ltd, St Ives plc

A CIP catalogue record for this book is available from the British Library

ISBN 0 7181 3872 4

To Marte and Bill Slout for
all the years of love and support

Acknowledgements

I wish to thank the following people who were instrumental in my writing this book. Fanny Blake for her encouragement way back when it was merely an idea; Erica Spellman-Silverman and Sappho Clissitt, my agents, for making things happen; Richenda Todd for her considerable taste, judgment and finesse in editing; Bill Slout for his willingness to share his tent-show expertise; Dick Bolks and Ron Harris for their musical know-how and correctness; Suzanne McNair for bringing the Iowa of the 1920s to life for me and all the family and friends who light my way.

Just as I Remember It

March something, 1935

I'm putting all this on paper because I know some people blame me for what happened to the Angel. The truth is, nobody, including Celine and me, really knows what happened to him that night in Los Angeles. Of course, I have my own theory. I suppose a lot of people do. But I thought it was time I set the record straight and tell as much of the story as I do know. I'm telling it exactly as it happened and whoever reads this can believe it or not but it's the truth. It's been a few years now and it eats at me like acid that I'm being blamed for something weird, so I just have to put it all down the way I remember it. Maybe these pages will never be found but if they are, and anyone still remembers him, it might help to explain some things.

To begin with, I want to say that I liked him. No matter how peculiar and hairy things got, I liked him. Anybody who saw the two of us together can tell you I only wanted what was best for him. Celine can back me up on that. She was there to see what went on. Not all the time because we didn't meet her until we hit Iowa and got mixed up with Cyril Blythe. *The* Cyril Blythe of the Cyril Blythe Comedians. But from Iowa on Celine was there to see I always looked after the Angel as best I could. His wellbeing was all I ever wanted. Shit. I'm lying already. I said I was going to tell everything exactly the way it happened so I have to admit that sometimes I cared more about me than him and I did some things that when I look back, I'm not very proud of. But nobody's perfect, for Christ's sake. I used him once in a while but using people is the name of the game when you've got somebody like the Angel. It's called exploitation for the good of all parties concerned. Anyway, we all exploit each other. You live past the age of puberty and ten will get you twenty you exploited a couple of people. The truth is, I liked him even though, a lot of the time, he made my life a pure and miserable hell. I don't want to sound like some damn Christian martyr, but it wasn't a picnic, I can tell you that much. I had to work my behind off just to keep food in our mouths. Sometimes it got so bad I even thought about getting a real job. Celine can back me up on that, too. But he was full-time work and that's no lie. Just finding a place to spend the night could take a solid day's planning. Not to mention money for gas. That's what happened that night with the couple from St Louis. We didn't even have money for gas and we needed a place to sleep and, even though it was a crazy thing for the Angel, my back was against the wall. You get desperate when you don't know how you're going to get through the night. We hadn't eaten anything to speak of for a couple of days and here was this couple from St Louis and they made the offer and I just couldn't turn it down. But I don't want to get ahead of myself or I won't be able to tell it all the way it happened and make sense of it.

My name is John Carroll Tree. I'm 5′ 11″ tall and I have brown hair and blue eyes and straight teeth. My build is pretty good and I'm not bad looking. At least that's what the women have always said. I've got a small scar in my left eyebrow where Violet Pennaman hit me with a rock when we were kids and I called her a smelly pig. She was a smelly pig. I also have a scar on my left cheek from chicken pox. I like music and I like to sing. I'm not real partial to manual work. My favourite food is toast.

I was born in Pittsburgh, Pennsylvania four days after the start of the twentieth century. My parents got a free month's rent from the landlord because I was a boy and maybe that's why I grew up expecting a free ride and thinking there was something great in my destiny, something special and different and above what the average man does in his lifetime. My mother was a skinny, undistinguished woman who damn near killed herself taking care of the family and one day, without saying a word to anyone, took off with a Polish insurance salesman whose name nobody could pronounce. My father, indifferent and big, bordering on fat, worked in the steel mill and drank homemade beer every night with his friends on the South Side and didn't notice my mother was gone for months. Her absence had little or no effect on him. I had two sisters and a brother who I didn't like much but they don't figure into this so I don't have to talk about them. Except, of course, my sister Aggie, who was pretty and sweet and played the piano. I like her.

In school, I learned faster than any kid in my class and if I didn't get a subject right off the bat, I figured it wasn't worth studying. I liked math best. I was a whiz at it and won every mathematics prize in the whole Pittsburgh school district. I generally got good marks because I was smarter than everybody else and because it was so easy to worm my way around those stupid teachers who believed any damn thing I'd tell them. I graduated from high school, which is more than I can say for most of the boys in my class, and when it came time for me to follow in my father's footsteps and go to the mill and sweat until I was an old man before my time, I got the hell out of town. The only thing I was sure of was I liked money. Money, money and money. In that order. And I intended to have as much of it as I could. But somehow it always slipped through my fingers. Women were easy but money was something else.

How I Met the Angel in the First Place

It all started because the Board of Education wouldn't listen to my side of the story even though Millie lied to cover up for me. Millie Quick, that is. She was the wife of Police Chief Albert Quick and, of course, they were going to believe him even though Mrs Quick cried and carried on and was so convincing she almost made *me* believe I was innocent. Also, I was from out of town; out of state, for that matter, and Albert Quick was born and bred in Lowell, as was Millie. They had been high-school sweethearts and everybody in town knew them and thought they were the perfect couple. I taught their daughter, Glinda, in the seventh grade, and from Get Acquainted Day on Mrs Quick had an eye for me. She was always finding a reason to drop by after school, usually when I was alone, and she never missed an opportunity to touch me or rub up against me in some provocative or seductive way. It wasn't the first time it happened, either. Two other schools had asked me to leave for the same reason. Lewd conduct with the mothers of students. But, God knows, it wasn't my fault. Just like Mrs Millie Quick, those other two women were just begging for it and they finally wore me down and I gave in out of pity for them. After all, I'm only human. The truth is, I wasn't sorry to leave Lowell, anyway. Those mill-town people weren't up to my standards. In fact, I wasn't sorry to leave

Massachusetts. Of course, I didn't have any choice once they discovered I wasn't really a qualified teacher. The whole town was ready to ride me out on a rail when they found out I had never been to college even though the kids said I was the best damn math teacher they ever had. But that didn't make any difference, especially with Chief Albert Quick egging them on, so they gave me twenty-four hours to pack up and get out of town. Since it was April and near the end of the school year, I asked for severance pay but Dr Waldo Converse, the pot-bellied principal who always had food stains on his shirt front, said I was lucky they weren't cutting off my balls and threw me out of his office. And, and this is hard to believe, Mrs Millie Quick snuck up the back stairs to my room in Pinabaugh's Boarding House and we fooled around right there on my unmade bed, with everybody, including the mayor, right out front in the street, ready to tar and feather me. It was like their shouts were cheering us on or something and, of course, all that danger just made it so much better and I knew it would be a cold day in hell before I ran into a woman as hungry and willing as pretty Millie, so we did it twice. I finally managed to tear myself away and hightailed it down the back stairs with my faked, framed diploma and my falling-apart cardboard suitcase and threw them in the trunk of that old Willys-Knight I had, with the motor damn near falling out, and I hit the road for Pittsburgh. Kids were running and screaming behind my car and dogs were barking like I was the circus leaving town or something. Hell, all I needed was a marching band and an elephant. Millie watched from Pinabaugh's window, her dark hair falling around those white, round shoulders and I almost turned around and went back up the stairs. God, the thought of her, neglected and needy and full and rich with the juices of life, brings a smile and makes the blood rush in me. I never will forget Millie Quick and I'd make bet on her not forgetting me either, and if she put into practice the things I taught her, as true as I'm sitting here with a pen and a bottle of ink, Police Chief Albert Quick is still seen on the streets of Lowell, Massachusetts with a smile as wide as Pawtucket Falls.

Even though a cold, spring rain had started, I decided to drive straight through to Pittsburgh because it costs money to stay at a guest house and since the Board of Education had taken my 1200-dollar-a-year job away from me and I lost the only money I had ever saved in a crap game with two Italians who worked in a shoe factory, I knew I had to watch every meagre penny I had. And I didn't have any choice but to keep going because if the damn car broke down I was a dead duck. But about nine o'clock at night, when I was somewhere near Tamaqua, Pennsylvania, which was way the hell off the beaten path and I have no idea how I got there, I had to stop because the Willys-Knight started to boil over. It happened every so often so I knew it wasn't too serious but I also knew I had to stop and let it cool down. The motor might have been hot but I was about ready to freeze to death and I thought if I sat there too long the police would find my stiff, cold body in the morning. The rain was coming hard and straight, with no angle from a wind, and the night was as black as a tar pot, but I could see a light about fifty yards off the main road so I walked along the shoulder until I found a mail box and started up a lane running thick with soupy mud. As I got closer I could make out a house and a light moving from one room to another and from the orange yellow of the glow I knew someone was walking around with an oil lamp. Even in the blackness, as I went up the steps, I knew the place was falling apart. I tried to look in the windows but there were thin curtains, made of flour-sack cotton, drawn tight, and I thought to myself there could be anybody in there, crazy people or murderers, but my clothes were drenched through to the skin and I couldn't stop shivering and I knew if I didn't get in someplace warm I was going to get the pneumonia or something and die, so I knocked. The muscles in my jaw were starting to cramp from trying to stop my teeth from chattering and I was so hunched against the cold I thought I'd never be able to stand up straight again. It felt like I was there for an hour before the door opened.

'You finally got here. Praise God Almighty.' It was a woman, almost too small for a grown-up but too old for a child. She looked to be about mid-forties, with a long, thick, grey braid hanging over her shoulder and she was dressed in a ratty, chenille bathrobe and worn-out work shoes. As soon as I saw her I hoped there was a mister around because I didn't want to have to fool around with a little woman in men's shoes who was expecting something from God. 'You're the messenger, aren't you? I had a feeling in my soul all day that tonight was the night God would send you.' She held the oil lamp up to get a good look at me. I could smell a mixture of wood smoke and kerosene fumes and feel the warmth of the house and I had to get inside.

'We're all messengers from God,' I said, hoping it was the right answer as I stepped over the threshold.

'Amen to that, and praise the Lord.' She looked at me standing there, dripping all over the faded linoleum in the hallway. 'I don't know why I expected you to arrive in glory. I been looking for a blaze of light and listening for the trumpet of Gabriel. I thought maybe you'd arrive on a cloud like a steed from the heavenly pastures. But you look just like the other bums that stop by here, looking for a handout.'

'Maybe they're all messengers from God, too.'

'That's why I always feed them. You just never know. Come in, come in.' She closed the door behind me. 'What's heaven like?' She smiled warmly and all the teeth were missing on the left side of her mouth.

'Heaven?'

'Yeah. What's it like?'

'Real nice.'

'I always knew you'd come for him in a storm when the world was washed clean. It just seemed like the right time to me. Every time it rains I get him ready. I've been doing that almost twenty years now. Almost twenty years.'

There was a fire in the front room so I pushed past her and almost ran, taking off my dripping overcoat and kicking off my soaked shoes. 'I hope you don't mind if I get myself warmed up? Jesus, it's cold out there.'

'You're taking the name of the Lord in vain.'

'Oh, no. No, I'm not doing that. I'm sort of talking to him. You know like you might say to a friend, Herbie, it's cold out there.'

'Then you know Him?'

'We all do.'

'Of course, you'd have to.' She picked up the shoes and coat. 'Do you eat?'

'Yes, I do.'

'So does Michael. He eats like a horse sometimes. I didn't think you would. You know what I mean? I didn't think you'd have to.'

'Well, once in a while . . .' I didn't know what in the hell she was talking about.

'I got sauerkraut and potatoes. No meat. And bread and chicory coffee.'

'Sounds like a feast.' She started out of the room. 'Thank you, ma'am.'

'You don't have to thank me. How about a hot bath?'

'That would feel real good.'

'You want to see him first?'

'Uh . . .' I didn't know what I was getting into but I figured I had to go along with her if I wanted to eat and warm up. 'I guess maybe I should see him first.'

'Praise God,' she said and led me up a rickety old staircase that looked like it was ready to fall off the wall. Somewhere on my way up I got a picture of some dead somebody that she'd been dressing for twenty years and it about scared the shit out of me. I kept telling myself that I was a grown man and she was just a little crazy woman and I could handle anything that happened but it didn't do a damn bit of good. As we started down the hall I saw glaring light spilling out of one of the rooms and brightening the dirty, worn carpet and it occurred to me that this strange woman might be some kind of witch or something, leading me to the fiery doorway to hell. I knew my imagination was running wilder than usual but knowing it didn't do anything to stop it.

'He's in that room, isn't he?'

'Waiting for you. He's been waiting all these years.'

'Is he asleep?' I asked, hoping she wouldn't say he was dead.

'Oh, yes. But he's ready to go.' When she got to the door she stood aside to let me go in first and I thought if I took one step in there I would drop off the edge of the earth. As I turned the corner I squeezed my eyes shut, afraid of what I might see.

'He's come for you, Michael,' said the little woman and I

opened my eyes a slit. The brightness almost blinded me. There must have been a hundred candles burning and the walls were covered with white sheets and I had to squint to see what was there. The only furniture in the room was a bed and on it was a boy dressed in a long white gown as clean as the rest of the house was dirty. He was a big fellow, I figured near twenty, and his brown wavy hair came to his shoulders and was combed out all nice on the pillow. His hands were folded on his chest like a dead person's but I could see him breathing and I damn near fainted from relief.

'How long has it been since you last seen him?' The woman was standing next to me, smiling at the boy.

'Uh, well . . .'

'Did he grow this big in any of his other lives?'

'That's it. That's why I didn't recognize him. He never did grow this big.'

'He's beautiful, isn't he?'

'Yes, he is. He's real pretty.'

'You want to see how nice his wings are growing?' Her eyes were so bright they looked like they could flash light.

'He has wings?'

'Don't you all have wings?'

That's when I knew the little woman was really crazy. Not only did she think I was a messenger from God, she thought I was an angel. People have thought a lot of things about me in my lifetime but nobody ever, in the farthest reach of their imagination, thought I was an angel.

'We don't need our wings all the time.' I was thinking so fast my head was beginning to spin.

'You want to see his?'

'I guess,' I said, expecting her to go out and bring back a set of homemade paper wings or something.

'Sit up, Michael.' She touched his arm and he opened his eyes and it scared me so much I jumped back, almost knocking the little woman over. He sat up, staring straight ahead, like we weren't even in the room, and I felt like I was going to see something I shouldn't be looking at. She undid the nightgown and pushed it down off his shoulders.

'There,' she said, and I couldn't believe my eyes. Coming out of his shoulder blades were these two things that looked like the start of wings. They were pink and sore looking, sort of like embryo wings or some kind of appendages in the process of being born. They were about a foot long and looked a little like really big hands without thumbs. It was something a person might see in a freak show at a carnival or in the circus. 'The boy with four hands', I would have called him but I could see how somebody who was religious, and crazy to boot, might think they were wings.

'When does he get his feathers?' she asked.

'Well, that's different with different angels. Sometimes it takes a lot of years.'

'I thought so. Those are just pin feathers, aren't they?'

'Yeah, I guess you could call them that.' The boy just sat there, flattening those wing-like things against his back and then sticking them straight out like he was flapping them.

'And what is your name? I never even asked.'

'John.'

'Angel John. You're not mentioned in the Bible, are you?'

'No. Some of us didn't make it.'

'I named him Michael after the archangel.'

'That's nice. Michael's a real nice name.'

'Are you going to take him tonight?'

'Well . . .' I didn't quite know what to say.

'You got to. It's time he went back to heaven.' She said it slowly and emphatically so there would be no mistaking what she wanted. 'I did my duty taking care of him, didn't I? It's not that I'm complaining but I didn't ask to birth an angel. All these years keeping him from the prying eyes of people. I been a prisoner here. A damn prisoner.' She looked heavenward. 'I'm not complaining, God, but you been promising me for almost twenty years that you'd send somebody to take him back to his heavenly home. Please, God, it's not easy looking after an angel. You gave me the burden and I been carrying it all these years without hardly a complaint. But I'm sick of just scraping by selling eggs and horseradish and piccalilli. I hate piccalilli. Now it's time You called him home so I can have a life of my own. You hear what I'm saying, God?' She looked at me with cold mean eyes. 'You are going to take him, aren't you?'

'Of course I am. That's why I'm here, aren't I?' I had the feeling she'd go for my throat if I said anything else.

'Well, good.' Her face softened and she smiled with great relief as she pulled up the gown and covered the wing things. 'I'll go fix your bath and you two can get to know each other. He used to talk but he stopped about eight or nine years ago. Maybe he'll talk to you.'

'He doesn't say anything?'

'Not a single word,' and she hurried out of the room. He looked like some kind of statue sitting there with his long hair hanging down and not moving a muscle. Like a pale, white statue of Jesus.

'Well, Michael, I never met anybody like you before.' He didn't respond. He just sat there staring straight ahead. He didn't move a hair or blink an eye but he seemed to be shivering like he was afraid or something. 'Can you hear me?' But there still wasn't any response so I thought he was deaf and figured if he turned to me so he could see my lips he might understand me. I tapped him on the shoulder and said, 'Look at me.' He flinched and startled both of us but he turned and looked me right in the eye. We were nose to nose, me looking into those black eyes and him staring without the slightest sign that he was seeing anything. He was, without a doubt, the handsomest fellow I had ever seen. And it was right then, like a flash of lightning, it hit me. Sitting there on the side of that bed was my destiny. The chance of a lifetime. The opportunity I had been waiting for since the day I was born. I had something nobody in the whole world had. I had an angel. So what if he wasn't a real angel, just some freak of nature with an extra set of whatever they were growing out of his shoulder blades, he was as close as anyone was ever going to get to an angel and he was all mine for the taking. The little woman was asking me to take him off her hands. Hell, she was demanding I take him, threatening me if I didn't. I had no idea, not the foggiest, what I was going to do with him but I knew if I didn't take him with me I would regret it the rest of my life. It was meant to be. Deep down in my bones I could feel it was my destiny. I just knew that boy was the making of my fortune. Little did I know what the hell I was getting into.

When I went down to the kitchen, a steaming bathtub was sitting in the middle of the room and the little woman was at the stove stirring a pot.

'Did he say anything to you?'

'Not with words he didn't.'

'You didn't need words, did you? You spoke in the language of angels. I wish I could hear the language of angels.' She was all sweetness now that she figured I was taking him away. 'You better jump in before the water gets cold.' She made no move to leave.

'Are you going to stay?'

'Why?'

'Well, I'm sort of shy.'

'I'm not going to look, for Lord's sake. Just get in.' She turned back to the stove and I got out of my clothes and slipped into the hot tub. I was still chilled to the bone and it felt damn near as good as sex. Just as I got settled, the woman came over and peered down into the water.

'You got man parts, too. Just like Michael. I wouldn't think angels would need them.'

'Yeah, well . . .' I said, covering myself, 'man is made in the image of God. Right?'

'That's what the Bible says.'

'And angels . . .' I was thinking as fast as I could. 'Angels are made in the image of man.' Damn, I was getting real good at instant religious philosophy.

'The image of man,' she echoed. 'Now that makes perfect sense, don't it.' Satisfied with the explanation, she went back to the stove.

'Where's Michael's father?'

'He don't have one.'

'Oh, I'm sorry. Is he dead?'

'No. He never had one. He was immaculate born.' She turned to me. 'Aren't you all immaculate born when you come to earth?'

'Not all, but most.'

'You don't think any of them thick-headed miners I used to see on Saturday nights down at the dance hall could have been a daddy to an angel. They was all big and smelly and grey from the coal dust in their skin and they only wanted one thing and when they got it they went and told the others and sometimes they'd line up. They all wanted me 'cause I was so little. Just like a little Kewpie doll. Half of them didn't even speak English. They was all from Hungary or Poland or some of them other countries over there near Russia. But believe me, that was one thing they knew how to ask for. Course, all that was before the light come into me and I have to admit, I liked it. All that attention from all them men.' She poured water in the coffee pot. 'But not one of them nasty things was the daddy of Michael. He grew in me a couple of months after I stopped seeing them. After I made friends with the Lord.'

'I see, ' I said and wondered if some big, grey, Hungarian coal miner in Tamaqua, Pennsylvania knew he had a son who was damn near sprouting wings.

After I ate, I told the little woman to get Michael out of his angel dress and into regular clothes so he could be ready for the trip.

'He don't have much. Work pants and a few shirts. He's a real good worker though. He'll do whatever you tell him. Course,' she said with a smile, 'I don't expect there's too much work to do in heaven.' She chuckled to herself as she left the room.

'But don't forget to pack his angel dress,' I called. I figured as long as I had an angel I might just as well have all the trappings and trimmings that go with it.

'I will,' she answered.

Now, I don't like admitting this part but I said I was going to tell everything just the way it happened. Not that I think there's anything wrong with taking advantage when an opportunity presents itself but I did feel a little strange about what I did. The little woman's pocketbook was on top of the ice box and when she was gone I went through it. Of course, there wasn't much to go through. There was just a change purse inside a bigger change purse inside the pocketbook. Rolled up in a ball were eight dollars and there was forty-two cents in change. Her piccalilli money, I suppose. I left the change and one of the dollars and put the other seven in my pocket. If I was going to take care of him until I decided how I was going to make my fortune, I needed some money and I figured she wanted me to take him off her hands so I was doing her a service and there was no reason why I shouldn't be paid for performing that service.

'Can I go with you?' She was standing in the kitchen doorway with Michael who was dressed in an old work shirt and overalls that were so small they looked like they were choking him in the crotch. He was holding a dirty old sack which I presumed to be his belongings.

'You still have some work to do for the Lord.'

'I don't have to birth another angel, do I?' Her eyes twitched nervously.

'No, no, the Lord has other plans for you. And if you went to heaven who would do the work?'

'I'm uncommon selfish, aren't I? Lord, forgive me my selfishness.'

'He forgives you.' I was as magnanimous and pious as I could be.

'Amen and thank you, Jesus.'

'Amen.'

She stood on her tippy-toes and kissed Michael on the chin which was as high as she could reach even with him bending down. 'You go with Angel John,' she said and he obediently came to me and took my hand like any good little boy would. It gave me the creeps and I tried to slip my hand out of his but he had a grip as strong as a vice. He was only about ten years younger than me but he was at least four inches taller and I thought to myself, we make a strange pair standing here holding hands, and for a quick couple of seconds I thought about shaking him loose and running down to my car and getting the hell out of there but that little voice, telling me that this was too good a thing to pass up, was louder than ever.

'Why don't you turn your back and kneel and pray us back to our heavenly home?'

'You mean I can't even watch?'

'Some things aren't meant for human eyes.'

'The ways of the Lord?'

'Exactly.'

She nodded her head and looked at the Angel for one last time then turned and knelt. She closed her eyes and started saying her prayers and we took off down the hall and through the front door, down the dilapidated stairs, slipping and sliding in the mud as if the Devil himself was after us. I shoved the Angel in the car and slammed the door and got behind the wheel and my heart was beating so hard I thought it was going to burst right out of my chest. And why not? For Christ's sake, I was kidnapping him! I don't know how far away we were before I calmed down but when I did, I noticed the rain had stopped and the biggest, brightest moon I had ever seen was shining down on us and Michael was looking up at it and his face was all aglow like . . . well, like the face of an angel.

Pittsburgh, Aggie and Frank

We didn't see many cars on the road as we drove through the night on our way to Pittsburgh. Having the Angel with me wasn't exactly what I planned when I left Lowell but I didn't know where else to go and I needed some time to think things through and come up with some kind of plan. And, of course, I needed to borrow some money. As if explaining to my sister and her son of a bitch of a husband, Frank, why I wasn't teaching any more wasn't bad enough, now I had to explain what I was doing with this strange person with growths on his back. He just sat there next to me, eyes bugging out at the light spreading over the highway and it occurred to me that he had never been in a car before. Maybe he had never been away from that old farmhouse in his whole life? Maybe he had been born in that house and would have died in it if it hadn't been for me coming along and taking him away? Maybe it was all planned? Like providence. The car boiling over at exactly that spot on the road and the light in the window beckoning to me like I really was some messenger of God coming to save the Angel from withering up and dying on the vine. Maybe it was all preordained? But who cared? I didn't put much store in preordination but it would make a hell of a good story for the newspapers when they asked how I found him. I would paint myself as some kind of hero or saviour guided through the stormy night by the hand of the Lord. The public ate that shit up. The more I thought about it the more excited I got and wanted to talk about it and wished the Angel could talk back and after about forty miles I started talking to him anyway, not expecting an answer, just to keep myself company. Like people talk to their pets.

'How are we going to do this? That's what we have to figure out. We have to come up with something great. Something spectacular. Hell, boy, you're better than anything P. T. Barnum ever had in his circus. So, he had a few midgets and the Siamese twins. He never had an angel, did he? Imagine what he would have done with you! Well, that's what we have to do. Think like Barnum. You just wait and see. We are going to be living on easy street. All the money we want, all the women. God, I never thought about that. You probably never saw any woman except your mother. Well, Mr Angel, you are in for a real treat. They're not all little with missing teeth.' I laughed out loud and when I looked over there was the trace of a smile on his face. 'You liked that, did you?' And he looked right at me like he knew what I was saying. A rabbit darted out in front of us and he sat up straight as if he was keeping an eye out for anything else that might run out of the darkness. I was feeling full of piss and vinegar and riding high so I just relaxed and started singing. 'Bye, Bye, Blackbird', as I recall, and I wasn't into the song more than a few bars when he started humming. It was such a shock I damn near drove the car off the road. He wasn't humming 'Bye, Bye, Blackbird' but at least he was making some noise. I stopped singing so I could listen to him but as soon as I did, he stopped.

'Go on, keep singing. It sounds good.' He smiled and

right then I knew he understood every word I was saying. 'Go on, sing.' It was tentative at first but he started humming a song. It was this really pretty wordless melody, that sort of universal song that little kids sing to themselves when they think nobody is paying any attention, and his voice was as sweet as any voice I ever heard on the radio. Thank you, Jesus, I thought to myself. Things were just getting better and better. Not only did I have an angel, I had an angel who could sing like one.

It was a few hours later when he spoke his first word to me. He had fallen asleep and when he woke he sat up straight, looked at me and without batting an eye said, 'Outhouse.' I had to pull over and stop the car, I was that shaken.

'What?'

'Outhouse.' It was just as clear and understandable as any word I ever heard.

'By Christ, you can talk!'

'Outhouse,' he said again, urgently, and started to squiggle around in the seat. I figured he had to go to the toilet so I went around to his side and opened his door and he got out.

'There isn't any outhouse. You can just pee right here.' And he unbuttoned his pants and did exactly as he was told and peed all over my shoes. 'No, no, no. Go over in the bushes.' And he did, peeing all the way, all over his own dirty old work boots. It was clear, from that moment on, that I had to be extra careful of what I told him to do.

By the time we got to Pittsburgh we were having a regular conversation. Well, actually, I was asking a lot of questions and he was throwing in a 'yes' or 'no' every once in a while. It took him a few days to warm up and become conversational. He hadn't talked to me because he had never seen anyone but his mother up close and even though he knew an angel would come for him some day, he was afraid. As near as I could figure out, he hadn't talked in all those years to his mother because he didn't have anything to say. She told him when to eat and when to take a bath and what chores to do and he apparently didn't think any of it warranted discussion. He couldn't read or write and the closest he came to anything in the outside world was sitting on the porch, hidden behind a trellis, watching the cars go by on the highway. The only entertainment he had was his mother reading to him from the Bible which I later discovered he could quote with what I expect, not being a Bible student myself, was absolute accuracy. During the day, if anybody came up their lane, he was told to hide until they went away. At night he went to bed, usually when the sun went down, except on rainy nights when his mother prepared him for the heavenly visitor who was going to come to take him back to meet his Father. Me. It sounded like a pretty miserable life and I thought, no matter what I did with him or where I dumped him along the way, he was going to be a hell of a lot better off than before I came along, so I didn't have a thing to feel guilty about, taking him away from his mother under false pretences. When I asked if he thought he was an angel he responded with an emphatic 'yes'.

'You certainly are,' I said, knowing it was going to be a hell of a lot easier selling an angel who was convinced he really was one.

About fifty miles from Pittsburgh, I noticed the gas indicator bobbing on the E and started watching for a gas station. But it was five o'clock in the morning and I knew we'd never find one open and I had visions of us curling up by the side of the road until the sun came up. Well, as it turned out, there must have been something wrong with the gauge because we drove all the way to Pittsburgh on empty.

The minute we were in the door, my sister Aggie's kids took to the Angel like he was some big toy or something and he obviously thought they were a wonder. He had never been around kids before and right away there was this weird, special connection between them. I never was fond of children, especially when they were like those two with their rheumy eyes and red, snot-encrusted noses. I don't know why but they never seemed to change or grow. They were stuck in some disgusting, foul-smelling quicksand of childhood and I would have sworn they were never going to get out.

'Who the hell is he?' asked my brother-in-law Frank Orlansky who disliked me as much as I disliked him and who was not only unhappy to see me but put out because we interrupted his breakfast.

'His name is Michael and he's a poor unfortunate boy and I'm taking him to the Mayo Clinic.' I thought a mission of mercy was my best way of explaining why I was travelling with the Angel and at the same time might soften Frank's hard heart when I hit him up for money to get to wherever it was I was going.

'What about your job?' I knew it would be the first thing he'd ask about.

'Well, for the time being, there isn't any job.'

'What'd you do this time?' There was a sneer on Frank's face, making his piggy little eyes look even meaner and slittier.

'Nothing. The school burned down.'

'Did you start it?'

'No, I did not start it.'

'Was anybody hurt?' asked Aggie.

'Luckily it happened on a Saturday afternoon and the school was empty.'

'Why don't you sit down and eat.' Aggie put plates on the table for us. Frank just made a kind of annoyed sound in his throat and moved his fingertip from one square to another on the checkered oilcloth, like he was thinking of something important to say. I never could understand what my sister saw in a man like Frank, gap-toothed and pinched-faced with his skinny shoulders and fat ass, who thought he was better than everybody else just because his uncle was a chauffeur for one of the Pittsburgh Mellons. Frank had been inside the mansion house twice and he bragged about it to anybody who'd listen, making it sound like he had a personal relationship with the Mellon family itself and they had asked him to tea or something. But what he always failed to mention was that he had only been in the servants' quarters. Not that Frank had anything to be ashamed of. He was a successful butcher with his own shop near Market Square. They could afford better but they still lived on the gritty South Side of Pittsburgh even though Frank had been planning for years to move to one of the tonier neighbourhoods. He had all kinds of plans, including a political career.

'Can't he eat out on the back porch? He's got hair like a girl and he stinks. Come on, kids, you might catch something.' He almost yanked their arms out of the sockets getting them away from the Angel. I thought if anybody was in peril it was the Angel, from catching a contagious disease from those two runny-nosed kids. 'Get him out of here.'

'I like him,' said Verna, snorting snot back up into her

sinuses, as she strained to get away from her father. Aggie kept her kids immaculately clean but with her thin, dish-water hair streaming down her back and her pasty complexion and thick-lidded, lacklustre eyes, Verna always looked like she needed a good bath.

Little Frank, better known as Squirrel, for some long-forgotten reason, pulled free and went to the Angel. Like his sister, he was dull and soiled looking and on the verge of being repulsive. He had a very bad stutter and agonized so much over people watching him agonize over every syllable that he rarely talked. In fact, he never talked to people. Only to dogs. He wanted a dog desperately but Frank thought they were dirty and wouldn't let Squirrel have one so he only talked to neighbours' dogs. If the family wanted to know what was going on in his congested little head they had to be lucky enough to be around when a neighbour dog happened by. Aggie tried to get him to talk to a cat that was always hanging around their front porch but, apparently, cats didn't speak Squirrel's language.

'Now, Frank,' said Aggie, 'you heard what John said. There's something wrong with him.' She turned to me. 'Is he a dummy?'

'Not quite. He talks every now and then.'

'That's just what we need. Maybe he talks to dogs, too.' Frank shook his head, disapprovingly.

'But he's dimwitted, right?' Aggie was dead set on figuring out just what was wrong with the Angel.

'I'm not real sure. That's why I'm taking him to the Mayo Clinic.'

'Well, we have to have pity on the poor boy.' She put some pancakes on his plate and without waiting for butter and syrup, he stuffed them into his mouth and started chewing.

'My God, he's like a wild animal.' Frank knocked over his chair as he got up.

'His manners do leave something to be desired, don't they?' I squeezed a fork into the Angel's hand. 'You better use one of these,' and he looked at it like he was holding a snake.

'I'll be goddamned if I'm going to eat breakfast with a disgusting thing like that sitting at the table. Jesus, it's enough to make a person sick.'

'Watch your language in front of the kids.' Aggie picked up the chair.

'Don't tell me what to do. Never. You hear what I'm saying?' He started out of the kitchen. 'I'm going to work.' He turned to Aggie, 'I want them out of here by the time I get home. Out! This is my house. I let you live here but I don't have to put up with your goddamn family. It doesn't look good for a person in my position to be socializing with people who aren't up to snuff. You know what I'm talking about, Aggie. It's bad enough I got to live with the stigma of marrying beneath me. I got my reputation to think of and a breath of scandal could ruin me.' Aggie didn't say a word. I suppose she was used to him talking to her like that. If I wasn't going to try to hit him up for money, I would have punched the bastard right in the mouth.

'Well,' I said, 'it might be good for your reputation, you know, people seeing you be nice to some poor unfortunate person. Helping them out, so to speak.' He just looked at me like I was speaking Greek. 'You know what I mean?'

'Well, for God's sake, I don't have to import a dimwit from out of town if I want one. Pittsburgh's full of them.' He leaned in as if he was going to tell me some important confidence. 'I'm going to be mayor of this town someday. Maybe even the governor of the state.' He was almost nose to nose with me and I could smell the coffee on his breath. 'And nothing and nobody is going to stop me.' The front door smashed shut as he left and it was dead still for a moment before the kids started climbing all over the Angel.

'He's campaigning to get on the City Council.' Aggie cleared Frank's dishes. 'To hear him talk, you'd think he was a threat to President Coolidge.'

'Hold on,' I said to the kids. 'Michael is going to have a lesson in table manners.'

'The poor thing is like something out of a side show.' There was no end to Aggie's compassion. 'The Wild Man of Borneo or something like that.' She put some more pancakes on the Angel's plate and we had our first lesson in being a civilized human being. It wasn't half an hour before he was using his utensils instead of his fingers. If I had any doubts about how smart he was, they were put to rest when I saw him sitting there pushing food in his mouth without sticking a fork through his lip. And I noticed his mother was right on the button when she said he ate like a horse. It was more like a team of horses.

'Why, he could have dinner with the Queen of Sheba.' Aggie smiled proudly, like she was fussing over one of her own kids.

'Maybe we could stay just a couple of days. What do you think?' Aggie had always been easy to soft-soap.

'Maybe. Maybe by the time he comes home from work he'll have settled down a bit. Plan on staying at least tonight. One of you can sleep in the kids' room and one on the couch in the front room.'

'I'll take the couch.' I wasn't about to spend a whole night in the same room with those two disgusting children and worry the rest of my life about scratching something sinister and untreatable that I caught from them.

It was hard to drag him away from the kids but once I did, my sister ran a tub and the Angel dutifully took his bath and washed his hair when I told him to. He never was any trouble doing what he was told. Aggie gave him an old shirt and a pair of Frank's pants from back before his ass started to spread and he looked quite presentable when he was all spruced up and smelling good. She wanted to cut his hair but I thought it might take away from trying to sell him as a real angel so I talked her out of it by saying whenever anybody touched his hair he threw a mean tantrum fit. Instead, she pulled it back and tied it at the nape of his neck with a black ribbon and he looked like a young Thomas Jefferson or somebody else whose picture was on paper money. Nobody knew about his wing things and I didn't know what to do about telling them. As long as he kept them flat against his back you really couldn't see much if he had a shirt on. He just looked a little round-shouldered.

It wasn't until late in the afternoon, after the Angel and I had had a snooze and after Aggie had done her housework and washed down the steps and the street in front of the house, as she did every day of her life, that I brought up the subject of money.

'Two hundred dollars!' My sister's pretty blue eyes opened wide and she looked just like our mother. 'Where would I get two hundred dollars?'

What I really wanted was a hundred but I had learned a long time ago that people don't mind nearly as much giving you half of what you ask for so I asked for two hundred. 'Frank's got money stashed away. You know he does.' I thought I'd better ask her before Frank came home so she'd have time to figure out how she was going to wheedle it out of him. Aggie had never failed me in the past.

'Yes, but he's not going to give you any more money. Besides, you hate each other.'

'What's that got to do with anything? I'll pay you back.'

'Sure! We've yet to see a penny of the money we've loaned you.'

'Well, I've had a run of bad luck.'

'I'll say. Since the day you were born.' Those were harsh words coming from Aggie and I knew, this time, it wasn't going to be easy getting the money. 'I'm not your only sister, you know. Why don't you ask Grace? Or Thomas or Pa? Why's it always me?'

'Because you're my favourite. And I don't even talk to any of them. You've been like a mother to me.'

'Well, I'm not your mother. I'm younger than you, for Lord's sake. Sometimes I think the smartest thing Mama ever did was run away with that Polack. Mr what's his name.'

'Come on, Aggie. It isn't my fault I lost my job.'

'You're always losing your job.'

'I told you, the damn school burned down.'

'How come you're not being paid to take Michael to the Mayo Clinic?'

'Well, I am. But I don't get the money until I get there. That's how I'll pay you back. I just need money so we can sleep and eat on the way.'

'You're so full of shit, John, your eyes should be brown.' She was peeking through the curtains on the back-door window, watching the Angel playing with the kids in the grimy back yard and I could tell she was starting to soften. 'He really gets along with the kids.' She smiled. 'Too bad he's like he is, being so good looking and all. Why, any young girl would go crazy for him. Tall as he is and handsome as sin with those broad shoulders. He's enough to make a girl go weak in the knees. And he'd make such a good father.' She turned to me. 'Is dimwittedness inherited, do you think?'

'I don't know.'

'Are his parents dimwitted?'

'I only met the mother. She's just little and sort of strange.'

'What a pity. He'd have such good-looking kids. I'm afraid Verna and Squirrel won't be much to look at when they grow up. What with having Frank and me for parents.'

'What are you talking about, Aggie? You're a very pretty girl.' And she *was*, even though she was starting to fade. She'd had a sweetness about her ever since she was a baby and, no matter what, she never seemed to lose it.

'Girl!' She giggled. 'It's been a coon's age since I was a girl. Besides, I don't keep myself up. Doesn't seem to be any reason to. Frank and I never go anyplace. Oh, *he* does. He goes places where he thinks it will do him some good. You know what I mean. Politically. But he never takes me with him.' She turned away from the window and looked at me. 'I'm going to say something even though I know I shouldn't. I'm sorry I married Frank. I know he's the father of my children but still, I'm sorry I married him. Lord knows, I wouldn't give up the kids but the truth is I never loved him. Never. I married him to get away from home. After Mama left and Grace took over . . . well, she was a terrible tyrant. Even Pa was afraid of her. But he only came home to sleep. He was always with his drinking friends. And you were about gone by then. You and Thomas. I would have married the Boogie Man to get out of that house.' She turned back to the window. 'No, I never loved Frank. Now I don't even like him.'

I hated to see her looking so sad so I changed the subject.

'Why don't you play us a few tunes on the piano. Come on, that always made you feel better.'

'What piano?' There was a wistful little smile on her face. I hadn't even noticed. The piano was gone.

'What happened to it?'

'Frank said it drove him crazy. I was teaching Verna how to play. She really has a knack for it, too. He sold it.'

'That son of a bitch.'

'I loved that old piano.'

'God, Aggie, why don't you leave him?'

'And do what? Move in with Grace or Thomas? Lord I'd rather stay with Frank. And Pa's got some Ukrainian woman living with him and I never even met her. I don't even know her name.' Something caught her eye in the yard. 'Oh, my heavens! Come over here and look at this.' I went to the window but all I could see was the two kids and the Angel.

'I don't see anything.'

'Squirrel is talking to him. I don't believe it.' And, sure enough, that puny little kid was sitting on the Angel's lap and it looked like he was talking a mile a minute.

'Maybe a dog got in the yard.' We went out on the back porch.

'Couldn't be. The gate is closed. Squirrel, honey,' she asked as we went down the steps, 'were you talking to Michael?'

'He was, Mama,' answered Verna. 'He was talking just like a regular person. He was telling Michael all about Papa's shop and what the guts of a pig look like.'

'Won't you talk to me?' But it was too late. We must have waited there for ten minutes but Squirrel seemed to have said all he wanted to about the entrails of that pig.

*

It was getting dark and I thought it was best the Angel and I were out of the house when Frank came home so Aggie could have some privacy when she tried to soften him up so I told her I was going to do a little sightseeing with Michael and we'd probably grab a bite to eat someplace downtown. I was afraid to use the car, it being in shaky condition and the hilly streets being so narrow and all, so we took a couple of streetcars and went up Mount Washington so I could show him where the Monongahela and the Allegheny rivers came together to make the Ohio. Whether or not he was impressed by the geography of Pittsburgh, I don't know, but he was damn near giddy looking down through the smoke from the mills at the lights of the boats as they meandered up and down the rivers. He had never even seen a river before, not to mention a city glittering in the night with boats and automobiles and the red glow of the furnaces in the mills. And never in his life had he had a vantage point like that, right between the river and the stars and he couldn't make up his mind about where to look and his head kept bobbing back and forth until I thought it was going to fall off.

'*There is one glory of the sun,*' he was staring up into the sky, '*and another glory of the moon, and another glory of the stars: for one star differeth from another star in glory.*'

I had never heard him say so many words all at the same time. 'What's that?'

'I Corinthians. Chapter 15, verse 41.'

'Oh, yeah. Right.' I didn't know one Corinthian from another.

'*When I consider thy heavens, the work of thy fingers, the moon and the stars, which thou hast ordained . . .*'

'II Corinthians?'

'Psalm 8, verse 3.'

'I knew that.' The fact is, I don't know shit about the Bible. The only times I ever touched it was twice when I was holding it in my hand and swearing to something. As I recall, whatever it was I was swearing to, I lied about.

He changed his focus to the river. '*And a river went out of Eden to water the garden; and from thence it was parted, and became into four heads.*' He didn't wait for me to ask. 'Genesis 2: 10.'

'That's one of my favourites.' I couldn't believe he was spouting the Bible like that.

'*By the rivers of Babylon . . .*'

'OK, OK, that's enough. How much of that stuff do you know?'

'Most all of it.' He fixed me with those black eyes. 'Don't you, Angel John?'

'Yeah, sure I do. But I don't go showing off about it like some people I know.' He looked at his feet as though he had been scolded. 'And I don't think you ought to call me Angel John. People get a little nervous when they know they're around angels. You know what I mean? Just call me John.' He nodded his head. We started back to the streetcar stop. 'So, you can quote the whole Bible! Jesus! It's hard to believe you can't even read or write.'

We ate in a diner downtown and I used up over a dollar of the money I took from the Angel's mother. The waitress, a chubby woman who looked to be close to eighty, had marcelled hair the color of an Irish setter and lip gloss as red as blood. She had thin black lines for eyebrows and just the slightest trace of a moustache. The Angel couldn't take his eyes off her when she was taking our order.

'What was that?'

'What do you mean? She's a person. A waitress.'

'I don't like her.'

'Well, she does look a little like a drunk's nightmare, but she's just trying to look young.'

'Why?'

'Because. People get to a certain age and some of them try to look younger. Especially women.'

'Why?'

'I don't know exactly. Hell, nobody wants to get old. I guess it's because when you get to old age you start thinking about dying. Maybe if you fool other people about your age you can fool yourself, too.'

'Why do they want to fool themself?'

'Jesus, you ask a lot of questions. I liked it better when you were a dummy.' I wasn't in the mood to be a teacher. I left all that behind me when I hightailed it out of Lowell, Massachusetts. 'Nobody likes to think about dying because it's scary. Old age is scary. It's all over. It's the end. Let's just let it go at that.'

'But when a person dies they go to heaven.'

'I'm not going to talk about heaven because then we'll start talking about hell and I don't want to ruin my appetite. So just forget about it.'

He didn't say any more until the waitress was serving our food. '*And thou shalt go to thy fathers in peace; thou shalt be buried in a good old age*. Genesis 15:15.'

She stopped serving and looked at him. 'What?' she asked flatly.

'When you die you go to heaven.' He was all smiles.

'That's right,' she said and went on with what she was doing, putting a plate of beef stew in front of him. 'And the Easter bunny shits coloured eggs.' She mumbled something about religious nuts minding their own goddamn business and went back into the kitchen.

The Angel looked at me for some explanation but I was hungry and wanted to end any further Bible quotes and discussion of the implications of the hereafter and Easter bunnies shitting coloured eggs so I just said, as firmly as I could, 'Eat!'

We left the diner and walked around to kill some more time and the Angel looked at everyone as if they were visitors from some other world. Especially if they were slightly different. A little too tall, too fat, too short, whatever, and he followed them with the curiosity of a kid looking at freaks in a sideshow. And the peculiar thing was, he was probably the biggest real freak in the whole city. When he saw his first coloured man he about scared him to death. He stood right in front of him and stared hard in his face. Luckily the man was good natured and must have figured the Angel was some kind of feeble-minded person and just smiled at him hoping like hell he'd leave him alone. I know if I hadn't grabbed Michael's hand and pulled him away he would have reached out and touched the poor fellow and probably given him a heart attack.

The store windows were full of so much for him to look at it took us close to half an hour to walk one block. A pretty dark-haired girl in a yellow dress with a white flower over her ear was playing the latest tunes on a piano in Volkwein's music store and when the door opened we could hear snippets of the songs and without even looking to see if I was tagging along he went right in. There was a group of maybe twenty people standing around the piano listening and he pushed his way through until he was standing right next to the girl. She smiled at him and I noticed his wing things were twitching. It looked like there were a couple of small animals on his back, fighting under his shirt. I suppose he had never heard music of any kind before except for the wordless little songs he made up and my rendition of 'Bye, Bye, Blackbird' in the car or whatever singing the little woman did. His eyes were as big as a kid's on Christmas morning and he just couldn't believe the magic of the piano. She started playing a ragtime tune and he got carried away, swaying back and forth and before I knew it he was dancing a wild little jig as though he was alone in the place and there wasn't a soul there to see him. I wanted to get him away from there before people noticed his wing things which by then were keeping time to the music, but I couldn't get near him. Everybody started laughing. It wasn't mean. I'm not saying they were making fun of him, they were simply carried away by his exuberant spirit and the next thing I knew they were all dancing right along with him. A nice-looking young couple was the first to start dancing together, then an elderly man and woman and soon everyone was pairing off, complete strangers, old and young, women with women or men with men, it didn't matter, and in no time at all the music store looked like a dance hall. The Angel, seeing everyone having such a good time, got wilder and wilder until I thought the wing things were going to come right through his shirt. Well, I wasn't about to break the news to the world that I had an angel and he was dancing in Volkwein's on Liberty Ave, so I made my way through the revellers and took hold of his arm and, clearly against his will, dragged him the hell out of there.

He was still dancing around to the music in his head as we walked away from the store.

'Is this heaven?' he asked when we were halfway down the block.

'Heaven! Hell, no. This is Pittsburgh.'

'Heaven can't be any better than Pittsburgh.'

'That sounds like a slogan for the Chamber of Commerce.'

'What's that?'

'Never mind. You wouldn't understand.' Passersby were getting a kick out of him because he was spinning around like a little kid. 'Boy, calm down now. You know, you're going to have to learn to control those wings of yours.'

'Why?'

'People will wonder what you've got under your shirt. You don't want them to know you've got wings. Not yet, anyway.'

'Why not?'

'Because.' He was still dancing around and it annoyed me. 'Now stop that when I'm talking to you. You're making me sick with all that jumping and spinning. Christ, act your age.' He finally stopped to catch his breath. 'I told you before, people get nervous when they know there's an angel around. It's human nature.'

'What's human nature?'

'Nothing angelic, I can tell you that much.'

'What do you mean?'

'Never mind. Some things you don't need to know.'

'Why?'

'Just because.'

'Why?'

'Jesus Christ! Will you shut up and stop asking questions.' Just like that I lost my temper and shouted at him and anyone would have thought I had slapped him across the face. He looked like he was going to collapse and I realized that he had probably never had anybody yell at him in his whole life. The little woman was convinced she had given birth to an angel. She believed the Lord had entrusted him to her care and she wasn't about to be mean to him without risking the wrath of Jehovah. I reached out to try and reassure him – 'Hey, now, I didn't mean to yell'– but he pulled away and I knew, from the look in his eyes, that he was scared to death of me. If there had been anyplace in the world he could have run to I was sure he would have. But he didn't have another soul but me. I hadn't thought about that before and I didn't like the way it made me feel. 'I'm sorry, OK?' The apology didn't do a damn bit of good. He just stood there, a safe distance from me, looking like a frightened rabbit. I knew no amount of talking was going to change the way he was feeling towards me at that moment so I moved on and he followed a couple of paces behind as if he was waiting for my next violent outburst.

We must have been walking for fifteen minutes or so without saying a word when we came to the Aldine Theater where they were showing a moving picture and I stopped to read the billboard. It was an all-talking, -singing and -dancing picture, *The Broadway Melody*, starting Bessie Love, Charles King and Anita Page. I wasn't much for the moving pictures and had never even seen a talkie but knowing how much the Angel liked music I thought it might take his mind off my yelling at him so I went to the booth and bought two tickets. Our funds were dwindling but it was worth spending the money if it smoothed things over between us. Besides, I was confident that Aggie would get some money out of Frank.

'You missed the first ten minutes,' said the woman behind the glass as she put her movie magazine down and made change for the dollar I had given her. She was dressed like a bellboy and the strap under her chin was too tight and cutting into her fleshy jowls.

'I don't care. As long as there's music.'

'Oh, there is. It's just wonderful. I'm crazy about Bessie Love.'

When I gave the tickets to the doorman, Michael hesitated

and for a minute I thought he wasn't going to go in with me. 'Well, come on. You don't have to sit next to me if you don't want to.' The doorman, also dressed as a bellboy, gave us a funny look.

'The usher will show you to your seat. The picture's already started.'

'Yeah, I know.' I turned to the Angel. 'Come on, come on. Nobody's going to hurt you.' He followed me and another bellboy met us.

'This way, please.' I could see, the moment we walked into the lobby, the Angel was starting to forget my losing my temper because that wide-eyed look of wonder was on his face as he was confronted with yet another marvel. And I must admit, when we were seated and I saw the actors up there on the screen, their mouths moving and words coming out, I was pretty flabbergasted myself. I think the Angel and I were sitting there in the dark with our jaws down to our belly buttons. Whenever the actors started singing and dancing I could feel the vibrations of his wing things and I'm sure everyone else in our row of seats could too.

And then, by God, it hit me. It was like a lightning bolt coming right out of the movie screen. The place for the Angel was Hollywood! Hell, he was twice as good looking as any of the men in the movie. And he could sing better, too. Being as smart as he was, I was sure he could learn songs and dances and a fool could see it didn't take any brains to be an actor. He was a goddamn natural. And, last but certainly not least, there was the big plus. He was, for all intents and purposes, an angel! I could see his name up in lights in front of theatres all over the world . . . Angel Michael! Hollywood had that dog, Rin Tin Tin, and Rex the Wonder Horse; it had about a million cute kids and Charlie Chaplin and Mary Pickford, heroes and villains and vamps and everything else a person could imagine. But it didn't have one goddamn angel. Nobody had an angel but me.

Aggie was standing in the front window when we came up the stairs and from the look on her face I could tell the news wasn't going to be good.

'Frank wants you out of here first thing in the morning. I tried, John. I really did. He said hell would have to freeze over, thaw and freeze over again before he'd give you a plug nickel.'

'Where is he? I've got a business deal for him. He'll change his mind about the money when I tell him what I'm going to do. I know he will.' The Angel was still smiling from the excitement of the moving picture and I was about to boil over, just thinking of going to Hollywood.

'If I were you, I'd just get a good night's sleep and get on the road first thing in the morning. I mean it, John. He's not going to give you any money.'

I started upstairs. 'I've got to tell him something.'

'He's not up there. He has a meeting with his campaign committee at the butcher's shop.'

'Then I'll go down there, take him out for coffee when the meeting's over and offer him the deal of a life time. Trust me, Aggie, he'll give me the money.'

'What on earth are you talking about?'

'About everything working out. About me and Michael and the big pay-off. I can't explain now but if Frank is any kind of businessman he'll want in on it. I've got to see him.'

'John, don't. I have a little money hidden away. It's not much but I can let you have it. Please. He'll go through the roof if you show up down there. And he'll take it out on me for telling you where he is.'

'Don't worry so much. You'll get lines in your pretty face. Everything is going to be just fine.' I kissed her on the cheek. 'Michael, you stay here with Aggie until I get back.' I went to the door and he was right behind me. 'No, no, stay here. I'll be back in a little while.' But he wasn't about to be left behind.

'You can't walk out and leave him like that. He's like a child. What guarantee does he have that you're coming back?'

I looked at him and he had that scared-rabbit look on his face again. 'OK, OK. Come on.'

'You're wasting your time,' called Aggie from the porch as we went down the street.

My mind was going a mile a minute as we crossed the Smithfield Street bridge. The Angel wanted to stop and watch the boats but I kept telling him how great it was going to be when he was a big movie star and we had all the money we'd ever need and all the fancy cars and all the fancy women.

'I thought we was going to heaven.' He looked a little confused.

'Yeah, well, we are. Hollywood's kind of like heaven. We'll call it a stopover on the way. OK?'

'If you say so, Angel John.'

'Just John. Remember?'

'Oh, yes. John.'

'You're going to like Hollywood. And Hollywood is just going to love you.' And I started again on a rundown of the good times we were going to have. I'm sure he didn't know what the hell I was talking about but my enthusiasm was contagious and he seemed to be as happy as a kid going to a picnic.

I knew, if I was going to cut Frank in on the deal and give him some small percentage of what I made as the Angel's manager or whatever, that I was going to have to tell him about the wings and everything else. I thought I'd best downplay the kidnapping part although, knowing what a greedy bastard Frank was, nothing short of murder would make a difference as long as there was something in it for him. Once I laid out my plan, there was no way Frank was going to turn me down.

When we got to Market Square it was empty except for two men sweeping the street and a truck unloading into a dairy store. The only light in Frank's shop was coming through a curtain separating the back from the counter and display cases. I didn't want to bang on the door and barge in and disrupt the meeting or anything stupid like that so I thought we'd just slip in and wait until the meeting was over. But when I tried the door it was locked.

'We'll just have to wait out here,' I said to the Angel who was bouncing from one foot to the other like he was cold. 'You want my jacket?'

'No.'

I tried the door again. 'Damn. It's getting late, the meeting can't go on much longer.' I wandered out to the kerb, watching the fellow unload the truck.

'Angel John?'

I turned to Michael and he was standing by the open door. 'How'd you do that?'

'I tried it and it just opened.'

'Ssh, we don't want to disturb anything.' We went in and I listened for a bit but I couldn't hear a thing. There was no meeting going on as far as I could tell. Then I heard Frank moaning, then a woman moaning, and I knew exactly what kind of meeting it was. I motioned to the Angel to be quiet as I pushed the curtain aside and the first thing I saw was Frank's big fat bare ass, as white and soft looking as bread dough, pumping away. His pants and drawers were down around his skinny ankles and from where we were standing all I could see of the woman was a leg on either side of Frank, with stockings falling down and her bloomers around one calf and a high-heeled shoe hanging off of one toe. He had her laid out right there on the butcher block where he cut the meat. Well, he was cutting the meat, all right! She started moaning and groaning and it got louder and louder and the Angel stood there watching, his brows knit together, wondering what the hell was going on.

'Is he killing her?' he asked out loud and just about scared Frank shitless. He turned and at the same time tried to pull up his pants and he got all tangled up and went ass over tea kettle, flat down in the sawdust on the floor. We got our first look at the girl then, lying there in such shock she couldn't move, her legs spread wide, taking our picture. She had a lot of make-up on but I thought it was to try and make her look older than she was.

'What the fuck are you doing here?' said Frank, struggling to his feet.

'I don't have to ask what you were doing, do I, Frank?'

'How'd you get in here? The door was locked.'

'Apparently not.' I smiled at the girl. 'Put your bloomers on before you catch a draught.' She scrambled off the butcher block and got herself pulled together. She was a tall girl with an upturned nose and big eyes and brown hair. The Angel was fascinated with her. 'My name's John and this is Michael.'

'How do you do.' She was very polite. 'I'm Cindy.'

'Don't tell him your name, you stupid little bitch.' Frank was looking every bit like a cornered rat.

'Well, I'll say this for you, Frank, you don't play favourites. You're as sweet to this young lady as you are to your own wife.' And without missing a beat I said to her, 'How old are you, my dear?'

'Sixteen.'

She said it before Frank could stop her. 'Oh, fuck!' he screamed, scaring the Angel who was still trying to figure out what was going on.

'Frank,' I smiled, 'you ought to watch your language in front of the children.' Then I felt it. That tingle way down in the pit of my stomach, the tingle that only comes when you know you're going to win. When the horse you bet on is four furlongs ahead of every other horse in the race, or when you have a poker hand that could only be beaten by a royal flush and from the looks on the faces of the other players you just know they don't have shit, or when you can feel the dice in your hand and there's no doubt about it, you're going to roll a seven. Well, the feeling I had watching Frank trying to get his shirt-tail out of his fly while he buttoned up was all of that and more. I had just hit the jackpot.

'Get out of here,' he yelled at Cindy. She threw her head back and with the dignity of a queen, started for the door.

'It was nice meeting you,' she said as she passed.

'Likewise,' and I smiled again. 'By the way, where can I get in touch with you if I wanted to?'

'Oh, you can usually find me someplace around the Square.' She stuck out her tongue at Frank and turned to me. 'In case you were wondering, all that moaning was just play-acting. I'm real good at play-acting.' She patted Michael's cheek as she passed and left.

'Get out of here. Take that thing,' he said, indicating the Angel, 'and get out of here.' He was red in the face and huffing and puffing and it occurred to me he might have a heart attack before I got what I wanted out of him.

'Now, Frank, just take it easy. We can make this transaction as painless as possible.'

'What transaction? I told Aggie, you're not getting a penny out of me. This doesn't change anything between us.'

'Oh, I think it does. We have two people here who witnessed you committing adultery with a minor.' Well, that's all I had to say. Adultery was the magic word and the Angel was off and running.

'*Whoremongers and adulterers God will judge*. Hebrews 13:4.'

'You tell him, Michael,' I shouted. 'Take him down.'

'*Now the works of the flesh are manifest, which are these; Adultery, fornication, uncleanness, lasciviousness*. Galatians 5:19.' Frank was dumbfounded.

'Hit him with the whoremonger again,' I said, getting carried away with the spirit of the Lord. The Angel was starting to get carried away, too. I could see the wing things going at it under his shirt.

'*Ye know, that no whoremonger, nor unclean person . . . hath any inheritance in the kingdom of Christ and of God*. Ephesians 5:5.'

'Amen,' I shouted.

'What the hell is he?' asked a stunned Frank. 'A holy roller?'

'Maybe, brother, maybe.' I felt like an evangelist and I wanted more. 'Give him something on doing it with a woman who isn't his wife.'

Without batting an eye Michael said, '*The mouth of strange women is a deep pit: he that is abhorred of the Lord shall fall therein*. Proverbs 22:14.'

'How do you turn the son of a bitch off?'

I hated to stop Michael when he was just warming up but I was in the mood to do some horse-trading. 'OK, Michael, that's enough. That was real good. Real good. You just go out in the front of the shop and calm down and wait for us. We have business to discuss.'

After he was gone, Frank turned to me in a rage. 'You bastard, you know this is blackmail!'

'You bet your big fat dimpled ass it is. You hog. If I wanted to, I could ruin you in this town. In the whole damn state for that matter. Not only would you not be able to run for office, I could fix it so you couldn't sell a damn pork chop.'

'You son of a –'

'No, no! Don't you say another word, hog. I'm doing all the talking now. Sit down and make yourself comfortable. This might take a few minutes.' He took out his handkerchief and started mopping his forehead. 'First off, if you ever treat my sister with anything less than the respect she deserves or if you say one more nasty word to her or the kids you'll be in jail for statutory rape. Cindy is only sixteen, you asshole. And even when she's thirty, if you aren't doing exactly what I tell you to do, I'll write to every newspaper in the state and give them the story. You know how clean we all want our politicians to be. Just the hint of scandal, even if nobody can prove a thing, is all anybody needs to drag you through shit. Hell, when I finished with you you wouldn't even be able to run for dog-catcher let alone City Council. And you *should* run for office, Frank. You've got everything you need to get elected. You're mean and sneaky and small minded.' He knew I had him exactly where I wanted and he would have killed me if he thought he could have gotten away with it. 'Now . . .' I said it with all the aplomb of a businessman. 'I'm not going to be greedy. I'm going to let you give me three hundred dollars. And I said *give* not *lend*.'

By the time we got back to the house, with Frank chauffeuring us in his almost new Ford, which I did think of asking for but decided it might be pushing things, we had worked out most of the details of our deal. Frank agreed to give me the three hundred dollars and also to get a piano for Aggie and Verna. And if they wanted to practise all day and all night he wasn't to say a word. Little Squirrel was to have a dog of his choice which could live in the house and sleep in Squirrel's bed if that's the way he wanted it. Frank was to buy Aggie and the kids some new clothes and he was to take Aggie out to dinner at some nice restaurant at least once a week. And, most importantly, he was to act as though he loved her more than anything in the world and he was to treat her like a lady. So what if she didn't love him? Feeling loved was better than nothing. And he would accept the charges when I called collect no matter where I called from. That was so I could check on things and make sure he was sticking to our agreement. I promised, on my honour, which Frank suggested I didn't even have but I said he'd just have to take my word for, that if he stuck to the terms of our deal I'd never tell a soul that he had slipped the sausage to sweet young Cindy. I made Michael promise, too, although I think he was promising never to tell anyone that Frank had tried to kill her. He still didn't have the foggiest idea of what went on. I knew I was going to have to have a serious talk with the boy. And I told Frank that if he slipped just once I would come back to Pittsburgh and castrate him. At first politically, then I'd think about it and if I wanted to I'd actually do the deadly deed. Frank was scared of me and I knew it. That was one of the happiest days of my life.

It was hard for Frank to smile with his teeth clenched so tight but somehow he managed when he told Aggie she could have a piano. Her eyes filled up and the tears started streaming down her cheeks.

'Hey,' I said, putting my arm around her, 'Frank's going to get you a piano. You heard him. That's no reason to cry.' Aggie wasn't used to affection and I could tell how much she enjoyed the feel of another person holding her. Even if it was her brother. 'He's going to get you the best piano there is. Isn't that what you were saying, Frank?'

'Yeah,' he mumbled with a little growl thrown in.

'Oh, Frank,' was about all Aggie could say.

'I heard a piano tonight,' said the Angel.

'You did, Michael? Did you like it?'

'Oh he liked it all right. He turned Volkwein's into a dance hall.'

'I'm feeling a little sick.' Frank did have a peculiar green cast to his skin.

'You want me to fix you a cup of tea?' Aggie went to him.

'No,' he said gruffly and I gave him the eye. 'I mean, no thanks. I'm just going to get some aspirin.' He started for the kitchen.

'Hey, Frank,' I stopped him. 'You forgot to tell Aggie about the dog.'

'Oh, yeah,' he said feebly. 'Squirrel can have a dog. Any dog. Any damn dog he wants. I don't care.'

'Oh, Frank, he'll love that.' Aggie turned to me. 'I just can't get over it. What's going on?'

'Nothing,' Frank jumped in. 'Can't I buy my boy a dog if I want?'

'One more thing,' I called as he started for the kitchen again.

'What now?' There was a kind of whimper in his voice. A defeated, sad desperation.

'Since tomorrow is Sunday, Frank thought it would be fun if we all went to Kennywood for the day.' Kennywood is an amusement park out by Homestead near the end of the streetcar line. I had always wanted to go as a kid but had never had the money.

'Good God, is there no end to this?' Frank sounded downright mournful.

'Kennywood!' Aggie's face lit up. 'Wait until I tell the kids!'

'Fine. Kennywood. Tomorrow. What difference does it make?' And he mumbled his way back to the kitchen.

'How was the meeting?' asked Aggie as he went but all she got was a sickly groan. 'I don't understand any of this,' she said to me. 'Are you going to tell me what happened?'

'Nothing happened. Frank and I had a little talk, that's all. I told you everything was going to be OK.' I kissed her on the cheek and pushed Michael ahead of me up the stairs, leaving a very bewildered Aggie watching us go.

The next day, as perfect a spring day as anyone could ask for, we piled into Frank's Ford and went to Kennywood. We rode the rollercoaster three times, screaming our guts out with each breathtaking drop, and we dared each other to stand up on the Ferris Wheel and we raced around and around on the carousel. Frank didn't go on any of the rides because be said he felt sickly. He *did* still look a little green around the gills. It was an obvious effort on his part but he was being nicer to Aggie and the kids. They were all too busy having the time of their lives to pick up on the murderous glances Frank gave me every time I suggested doing something else that he had to pay for. And, of course, the Angel didn't notice anything. He was overwhelmed by the sparkle and the noise and the music. Twice he asked if I was absolutely sure Pittsburgh wasn't heaven. Aggie was still thoroughly confused but smart enough not to ask any questions. She knew something had happened between Frank and me but she was enjoying the turn of events too much to say or do anything that might threaten it. I suppose she never expected to see her kids so happy and several times I caught her watching them with the glint of a tear. And the children never stopped smiling. Their eyes were bright and they had colour in their cheeks and their sinuses opened and all of a sudden they were two of the cutest kids I had ever seen. They wouldn't let go of the Angel and the three of them raced around the park, carrying on and laughing like there was no tomorrow. It was a day we'd remember for a long, long time. The day everything changed for all of us. Even Frank. And Squirrel talked. He stuttered his little head off, mostly about the dog he was going to get, and he didn't give a damn about how he sounded. In fact, he was still talking when he fell asleep in the Angel's lap on the way home.

When we left the South Side the following morning, Aggie and the kids were in front of the house to see us off. Frank was down at the butcher's shop so I didn't have to deal with saying goodbye to him knowing he hoped the Willys-Knight would blow up before we got halfway down the block. Aggie, who had packed us a lunch, thanked me over and over for whatever I had done or said to Frank. I told her to forget about it and just get on with enjoying her life. The kids, still aglow from their day at Kennywood and looking fresh and clean and better looking than I ever imagined they could, were all over the Angel, not wanting him to leave. He didn't want to leave, either.

'The kids love him,' said Aggie.

'I know. I think it's mutual.'

She came to me and hugged me once more. 'Good luck.' She turned to the Angel and put her arms around him to say goodbye but before she could, she squealed and jumped back. I knew she had felt the wings. 'My God, what is that?'

'A little deformity. That's all. Get in the car, Michael.' He did as he was told.

'He's got wings, Mama,' said Verna. 'He showed them to us. He's an angel.'

'I'm sure he is, honey.' Aggie looked a little pale. 'The poor thing. Is that why you're taking him to the Mayo Clinic?'

'Exactly.'

'I have to apologize, John. I didn't think you really were taking him there. I didn't know what you were doing with him but I didn't believe you.'

'Aggie, don't you trust your brother?'

'Not as far as I can throw you. Are you really going to the Mayo Clinic?'

'You never know,' I said, 'you just never know.' I kissed her and got in and started the car.

'You keep in touch.'

'You can count on it.'

I pulled away from the kerb and the kids were shouting and the Angel was waving and I felt like I was on top of the world. I had three hundred dollars in my pocket. More money than I had ever had at one time in my whole life. And I had a foolproof plan to make my fortune. But the best part of it all, I thought as I made my way down the narrow hilly streets, was that my son of a bitch of a brother-in-law was a beaten man and I was the one who was holding the stick. I looked over at the Angel who was hanging out the window, still waving goodbye long after the kids were out of sight, then I headed for the Lincoln Highway and Hollywood.

The Last Man in Paradise

That first night on the road, it was almost dark when we stopped and rented a cabin. It was in some little burgh between Lima, Ohio and Fort Wayne, Indiana. I wasn't even sure which state we were in. There were about eight or nine cabins, all freshly whitewashed for the coming summer season, looking like oversized chicken coops with blue curtains in the windows. The little flowerbeds lining the walks to the individual cabins had been turned over and topped with manure and were ready for planting and the whole place smelled like a damn barnyard. Whoever was in charge of keeping the place neat and tidied up was doing a hell of a good job.

Aggie had made enough sandwiches for an army so we ate the last of them for supper along with some soda pop I bought from Vernon, the bald man at the desk in the office.

'You'll be the only guests we have. It's still kind of early for the tourists. We're just getting the place readied up. Where you headed?'

'California.'

'Someday the wife and me want to go to California. In the winter. I hate the snow. And every year it seems to get worse.'

'Well, you have a nice place here.'

'It's too much work. My wife's always after me to do

some goddamn thing. Fix this or clean that. I don't think she knows Lincoln freed the slaves! She's enough to drive a sane man crazy.' He shook his head in disgust then laughed about it. 'There's a shower bath down behind the last cabin on the left. If you want hot water it's ten cents extra and you have to tell me ahead of time so I can turn on the gas.' Vernon handed me the soda pop and the change and I noticed he had two fingers missing on his left hand. 'I lost 'em when I was a baby. My uncle's dog bit 'em off. He swallowed 'em, too.'

'Jesus!'

'It never bothered me none. Three fingers was better than no fingers. That's the way I look at it. And I was real partial to that dog.'

'Didn't they shoot him?'

'Hell no. He was a good bird dog. You want the hot water or not?'

'Sure,' I said, the three hundred dollars burning a hole in my pocket. 'We'll shower before we leave in the morning. Hot water for certain.' I leaned across the desk and whispered. 'Hey, Vernon, you got any whiskey?'

'Whiskey! Of course I don't have whiskey. Where you been, mister? The moon? Alcoholic stuff's illegal!' He said it loud enough to be heard in the next county. He looked over his shoulder into the living quarters and cocked his head as though he was trying to hear something but the only noise was a radio playing. When he was certain no one was paying any attention to us he pulled me aside and said in a low voice, 'Watch what the hell you're saying, young fella. My wife is the head of the Temperance League in town. If it wasn't for the likes of her we wouldn't have prohibition today. The old cow. I got some good corn but it'll cost you a dollar a bottle.'

'A dollar! For corn liquor! That's highway robbery.'

'Then if I was you I'd go shop someplace else.'

'All right, all right.' I gave him the dollar.

'I got it hid outside. Come on.' He called back. 'Honey bunch, I'm taking some toilet paper to the cabins. Be right back.' He took me out past the shower bath to an old covered-up well with a wooden lid and a rock on top of it the size of a bushel basket. 'There ain't been water in this well for thirty years.' He lifted the rock, which looked heavy enough for two men, and removed the cover and about three feet down where the well was boarded over he had his bottles of corn whiskey neatly lined up. 'Lu, that's my wife, it's short for Lureen, don't know it but we make more money off the corn than we do the tourist trade. If she knew, she'd be wearing my balls for earbobs.' He took the cork out of one of the bottles. 'Taste it.' I did and half expected steam to come out of my nose. 'You ain't going to find better corn this side of the Mississippi. I stand behind the product.' He took the bottle and gulped down a big swig.

'Hey, that's my liquor!'

'Yup. And that's my commission. Now get the hell out of here before she sees us and wonders what's going on. That old woman don't miss a trick. I swear she got the eyes of a cat and the ears of a bat.' He covered up the well and replaced the rock. 'I'll have the shower water hot at six in the morning.'

What I knew I had to do, before we arrived in Hollywood, was teach the Angel to read. And write. At least his name. He had to be ready to sign those contracts with the moving picture studios. The only reading material I had in my car was an old copy of *The Police Gazette*, not exactly the perfect primer, but I figured words are words and it didn't much matter what they were saying as long as they could help him learn to read. So we stayed up late that night, stretched out on the bed, eating Aggie's ham salad sandwiches and drinking our cherry pop, mine liberally laced with the corn liquor, and reading about a chorus girl named Evalina who shot her boyfriend right between the eyes because he took pictures of her when she was naked, 'in the privacy of her boudoir', the article said, and sold them to some postcard company in Paris, France. There was a picture of her, with her clothes on of course, looking soulful and lost in her prison cell, and it was plain to see why anybody would want to take pictures of her in her birthday suit. She was a real beauty with what looked like blonde curly hair and eyes big enough to get lost in and I could have looked at her all night but by eleven o'clock I was beginning to see two of her from the whiskey and I decided it was time to turn in. The Angel had a good way to go before he could read but he did learn to recite the alphabet and he could recognize the letters and I fell asleep to the monotony of him chanting a . . . b . . . c . . . d . . . e . . . f . . . g . . . over and over and over again.

The knock on the cabin door awakened me.

'It's after six. The water's hot as it's ever going to be.' It was Vernon.

'OK, OK.'

'There's a piece of pine soap out there. Compliments of the management. I'd appreciate it if you don't leave any hairs on it. Bring your towel from the cabin.'

'Thanks,' I called.

'And' – it was Vernon's last order – 'don't run the water long or you'll run out of the hot and freeze your asses off.'

I was feeling a little hungover and didn't relish the idea of getting out of bed so I told the Angel to go and take his shower first.

'What's a shower?'

'A bath only you take it standing up. You turn the water on the same way you do the water in a bathtub.'

'I just had a bath yesterday.'

'Yeah, well you're going to have another one today. Enjoy it. We can afford it.' I told him where the shower house was and figured he understood because he didn't ask any questions and about a minute later I opened my eyes just in time to catch him walking out of the cabin stark naked. His wings weren't the only things that were showing.

'Hey, wait a minute. You can't walk outside naked like that.'

'I'm going to take the shower bath like you said.'

'But you can't walk around without any clothes on.'

'Why not?'

My head was hurting too much to deal with teaching him the concept of modesty. Besides, it probably wasn't in his nature, one way or the other, so I told him people would see his wings and know he was an angel and by then I had put the fear of God in him and he was convinced people knowing he was an angel wasn't such a good idea. He threw on his pants and shirt and before going out the door turned to me. 'It's a lot harder being an angel out in the world than I thought it was going to be. I'll sure be glad when we get to heaven,' and he went off to take his shower bath.

'Yeah, well, first we got a few stops on the way,' I said and rolled over.

*

From the time we left wherever it was we had spent the night until we stopped for lunch all I heard was the goddamn alphabet chant until I seriously thought maybe I'd opened a can of peas when I decided to teach the Angel how to read. In just one night it had become an obsession with him and mile after mile, no matter how hard I tried to change the subject, he wouldn't talk about anything else. The idea that he could put a name to a letter, that those little symbols all had their very own distinct sound, was downright magical to him. Occasionally, he'd worry about the doomed and beautiful chorus girl and markswoman, Evalina, but most of the time it was nothing more than the ABCs. I turned him off in my head just as easy as a person turns off a radio and daydreamed of Hollywood and the glories of being rich but when I tuned him back in he was still chasing the alphabet. It was just after we were back on the road, having had a greasy but filling lunch, that I thought of a way to stop the ABCs. lt was a big gamble and I knew I might have been jumping out of the frying pan and into the fire but I had to do something to put an end to the chanting so I decided to teach him a few songs. Anything was better than the alphabet. Well, I certainly jumped into the right fire. By the end of the day he had four songs in his repertoire. 'Bye, Bye, Blackbird', 'Blue Skies', 'Alexander's Ragtime Band,' and his favourite, 'Bill Bailey, Won't You Please Come Home'. I thought I had a pretty fast ear for music but he was remarkable. And in no time at all he knew the words. Of course, each song took a lot of explaining. 'Pack up all your cares and woe, here I go, swinging low, bye, bye, blackbird,' didn't make a lot of sense to him. It didn't make a whole hell of a lot of sense to me either but I did my best to explain. What's *ragtime*? Who's *Bill Bailey*? What's a *bugle*? What's a *fine-tooth comb*? What's a *honey lamb*?

There was no end to his questions. But it was all worth it because his voice was a rich baritone and the more familiar he got with the song the better it sounded. And the better he sounded the more certain I was that Hollywood was the perfect place for him.

'You really like to sing, don't you?' He had stopped for a few minutes to look at a farmer ploughing a field with a team of the biggest Clydesdales I'd ever seen.

He turned to me and his eyes had as much music in them as his voice. '*O come, let us sing unto the Lord: let us make a joyful noise to the rock of our salvation.* Psalms 95:1.'

'Amen.' I didn't think 'Alexander's Ragtime Band' was exactly singing unto the Lord but what the hell, it sure was a joyful noise. Especially when the Angel sang it. The world was in for a treat.

Because the Willys-Knight was in such shaky condition, I avoided the congested areas like around Chicago and the major highways so we weren't exactly zooming across the country. We sang our way, sometimes in perfect harmony, to just north of Bloomington where I got hungry. I knew the Angel was probably about ready to eat a bear so we stopped in a little roadside restaurant for supper. The name of it was Mac and Margie's. I won't forget the name of that place if I live to be two hundred. Stopping there was the single biggest goddamn mistake I ever made in my life. Well, one of the biggest. Not that there were so many places to eat that I could have shopped around. I hadn't seen a restaurant for miles. It was a plain little place with no decorations except for a picture of President Coolidge and a certificate of honourable discharge from the army neatly framed and hanging on the wall behind the cash register. There was a counter and five or six tables but there was only one middle-aged couple at a table in the corner and a fellow in a cowboy hat and boots sitting at the counter hunched over a cup of coffee. Behind the counter was a man and a woman. I presumed they were Mac and Margie. He was muscular and squat, somewhere in his mid thirties, and she was a tall woman who looked older, with a white streak down the center of her dark hair making her head look like a skunk.

'Sit any place you like,' said Mac and Margie headed towards us with menus.

'It's not on the menu but we have fresh catfish,' she said as we sat down. 'It's real good. Lightly breaded.'

'You like fish?' I asked the Angel.

'What is it?'

'It's good. You'll like it.' I smiled at Margie. 'We'll take the catfish. We don't need the menus.'

'He doesn't know what fish is?' Margie's pencil was poised over her order pad.

'Amnesia.'

'Oh, poor thing. I had an aunt who had amnesia once. Aunt Lorna. But hers would come and go. Every time my uncle Buck caught her doing it with one of the farmhands, well old Aunt Lorna couldn't remember who she was or where she was.' She laughed. 'Poor Uncle Buck was as thick as a brick. He believed her every time.'

While we were eating I noticed the cowboy turning to look at us every once in a while. He was smoking one cigarette after another and all through our meal Margie kept refilling his coffee cup. A couple of times when he looked at us he smiled and I smiled back but it wasn't until we were eating our lemon meringue pie that he came over to the table and I noticed he was much taller than he looked sitting down. He was an average sort of man, somewhere in his late twenties, with blondish hair and clear blue eyes.

'Hey,' he said.

'How you doing?'

'Mind if I join you?'

'No, but we're just about to leave.'

'My name's Kansas,' and he sat down.

'John and Michael,' I indicated the Angel who was so busy with a mouthful of pie he could only nod.

'You by any chance driving west?'

'Yeah, we are. Not tonight, though. We're about to look for a place to stay.'

'I just need a ride a few miles down the road. My car broke down and I been sitting here waiting to catch a ride back to it.'

'Oh, hell yes.'

'I appreciate it.' He smiled warmly.

'No trouble.' The Angel was scraping up the last of the pie. 'Come on before you lick the design off the plate.'

It was dark as pitch when we got back on the road again. The Angel sat in the back and Kansas sat up front next to me.

'What's wrong with your car?'

'I don't know. I'm not much of a mechanic. I came up this way looking for a garage but the guy in the restaurant said there's nothing near by. I'll sleep in the car tonight and look for somebody tomorrow.' He seemed a little nervous to me because he kept turning and looking through the back window.

'Where you from in Kansas, Kansas?' I asked.

'Oh, I'm from Minnesota. Kansas is just my name. I've got two sisters, Florida and Georgia and two brothers,

Maine and Oregon.' I expected more of an explanation of why all the kids in his family were named after states but he didn't offer any. 'Where you headed?'

'West coast.'

'Well, you got a long way to go.'

'I guess we do.'

'Is he your kid brother?' He turned to look at the Angel.

'My cousin.' It was the quickest and easiest way to avoid discussion since the Angel and I didn't look anything alike.

'He's kind of an odd duck, isn't he? Doesn't he ever talk?'

'He's a man of few words until you get him started.'

Kansas turned to the Angel and said, 'You're kind of odd, aren't you?'

'I am?' I could see the Angel in the rear-view mirror, smiling pleasantly.

'Innocent I think is the word,' I said before the Angel started spouting off Bible quotes about odd ducks. For some reason, I didn't like Kansas calling him odd.

'You're a big boy, aren't you. And I'll bet you're as strong as two men.' Kansas looked at me. 'He's strong, isn't he?'

'Yeah, I guess he is.' We rode along making small talk for a while but it was all disjointed, like he wasn't really paying attention to what was being said.

'I'm glad winter is over.' Kansas started bouncing his legs as if he was in a hurry to get somewhere.

'Yeah,' I said, 'I like the spring.'

'That coffee wasn't fresh. It was bitter.' I thought maybe that's why he was acting like a cat on a griddle. He had had too much coffee. 'How come you're going out West?'

'We've got relatives there.'

'I hate my relatives. Shit, I wouldn't go to the next town to see them, let alone clear across the country. You drive slow, don't you? Jesus, you guys will never get there.' His voice was getting louder as the conversation went on.

'Fast enough,' I answered. He was really beginning to make me feel uneasy because he seemed to be preoccupied with something and it was almost as if I could smell anxiety in the car. But I didn't know whose it was because I was feeling pretty damn anxious myself. I was getting a bad, sick feeling about Kansas and couldn't wait to get him out of the car. 'How much further?'

'Oh, I don't know. We'll get there soon as we get there.' He laughed too loud and too hard. 'It's just up the road a piece.' He started whistling to himself.

'I have to go to the outhouse,' said the Angel.

'Now?' I turned to look at him. 'Why didn't you go before we left the restaurant?'

'I didn't have to go then.'

'It's only been five minutes.'

'Let the kid go to the toilet if he has to,' said Kansas. It was more of an order than a suggestion and I didn't like his tone of voice because his breathing was rapid and shallow as if he was getting excited about something.

I stopped the car. 'Go on, but make it quick.' The Angel jumped out and ran into the bushes and as soon as he was out of sight Kansas reached down and pulled the biggest, meanest, sharpest-looking hunting knife I'd ever seen out of his boot and held it to my Adam's apple.

'I didn't know how I was going to handle the two of you. The kid was real considerate having to take a piss like that. Get out of the car.' I wasn't about to argue with a nervous man with a ten-inch blade pointing at my throat. 'Hurry up. I'm itching to stick this in something soft. Something like your throat.'

'I'm moving as fast as I can.' I got out and he slid across

the seat and got out right behind me. 'This car is a piece of crap. It's not worth stealing.' I was trying to stall him, to think of a way to save what was left of my three hundred dollars.

'It's better than no car at all.'

'Aw, come on. Can't we make some kind of deal?'

'Empty your pockets and throw everything on the seat.'

'You can't leave us out here with nothing.'

'I can do anything I want. I got the knife. If you don't do like I say I'll gut you like a Christmas turkey. And this knife is so sharp you'll be dead before you feel it.' He laughed. 'Now, don't be an asshole, do like I say and empty your pockets. And don't forget the roll of bills I saw when you paid the check.' For one second I thought about running away but the Angel would be coming back and who knew what Kansas was capable of doing with that knife. I threw everything I had on the seat and he jumped in the car and took off leaving me standing there in the dust. And just like that, in less time than it takes for a man to empty his bladder, every goddamn nickel of the money I got from Frank was gone. Everything I had in the world was gone, including my old Willys-Knight, my forged teaching certificate and my half-bottle of corn whiskey. Even Michael's angel dress disappeared into the night. And it all happened in no more than three minutes. The Angel came out of the bushes singing to himself as he buttoned his pants.

'Where's he going with the car?'

'You dumb shit!' I had to blame it on somebody. 'At least we would have stood a chance if you didn't get out of the car. There was two of us against one. And he was afraid of you because you're big. But no! You had to pee!'

'L . . . m . . . n . . . o . . . p . . .' He had no idea what was going on.

'And t . . . u . . . v . . . w . . . x . . . y . . . fucking z. That son of a bitch stole everything we have. Including the money. We've got no car and no money. Do you know what that means? You know what stealing is?'

'Let him that stole steal no more: but rather let him labour . . .'

'You quote one more word from the Bible and you'll be wearing my size ten shoe up your rosy red ass!' I couldn't believe it. One minute we have the world by the tail, money to burn, headed for Hollywood and fame and fortune, and the next we're stranded in the dark of night in the middle of Indiana without a pot to piss in. 'Don't talk to me for a while because I just might kill you. I'm not kidding. Go sit over there and don't say one single word until I calm down and figure out what we're going to do. And if you start on the ABCs, I swear to God I *will* kill you.'

'Can I sing?'

'No! You cannot sing. You can't even breathe.' He must have been getting used to the ways of the world, or at least my ways, because rather than shrink away in fear he just sort of ambled a few feet back off the road and sat down, waiting for me to cool off. I knew it wasn't his fault, but it wasn't my fault either. All I did was give the son of a bitch a ride. I was being a Samaritan for Christ's sake. But I should have known better. Just try being nice to somebody and see if it isn't the quickest way to step in shit.

It was damn near an hour before I relaxed enough to think straight. When I could take command and look at things objectively, with a clear head, I didn't know what the hell we were going to do. The Angel wasn't at all upset. And why should he have been? I was there to look after him. I was the one who had to figure out how to get us out of that mess. He was having a good time. In fact, he was enjoying sitting in the dark listening to the sounds of the night.

'We're going to have to hitch a ride to the next town and report to the police.' It was the first thing I said to him and as the words were coming out of my mouth I wondered if maybe the police were looking for me for kidnapping. It was possible. The little woman could have thought things over and reported me and the whole damn country could be looking for us. And, as good an idea as hitching a ride was, there hadn't been one damn car by since that bastard Kansas took off with everything I had in the world. 'And I'm going to have to call Frank and ask for more money. He'll probably die of apoplexy right there with the phone in his hand but what else can I do?'

'Can I sing now?'

'Well, why not? They sang when the *Titanic* was going down. And don't ask me what the *Titanic* is. It was a boat and that's all I'm going to tell you.' After about five choruses of 'Bill Bailey' I saw headlights way off in the distance coming at us. 'Don't you do anything. Stay right where you are and let me do the hitching.' As the car approached, I smiled and stuck out my thumb and tried to look every damn way but menacing. The driver slowed the car slightly, took a look at me and mashed his foot down on the accelerator leaving me standing there with my thumb in the air choking in a cloud of exhaust fumes.

'Can I try next time?' asked the Angel.

'What the hell do you know about hitching a ride?'

'I'd like to try, anyway. It looks like fun.' He was halfway through 'Alexander's Ragtime Band' when another set of headlights appeared.

'OK. You see what you can do. Remember, keep your thumb out.' He was getting all excited as the car came closer and I could see his wings twitching. Instead of putting his thumb out he just stood there waving, that broad innocent grin on his face, and I'll be damned if the car didn't come to a stop right next to us.

'Did I do it right?'

'Just get in the car.' It turned out to be an old Ford truck and we had to crowd in the front with the driver. It was too dark to get a good look at him but from what I could see in the spill of the headlights I thought he was a middle-aged man with dark hair.

'What in the world are you boys doing out here in no man's land?'

'We got robbed. Some son of a bitch took our car and everything in it. All my money. Every goddamn thing I own in the world.'

'No!'

'Yeah. Everything! I was giving the guy a lift to his car.'

'Do you know him?'

'No. Never saw him in my life. We were having supper and he came over to the table and asked for a ride.'

'And he left you stranded out here? These days you just can't trust nobody.' He sounded truly concerned.

'You can trust us,' said the Angel.

The man looked at him and smiled. 'Well, I'm sure I can.'

'We just want a lift to the next town,' I said.

'There's not much out here by way of towns. I'm on my way to Paradise.'

The Angel was on top of that in a second. '*And Jesus said unto him, Verily I say unto thee, To-day shalt thou be with me in Paradise*. Luke 23:43.'

'Not now, Michael, OK? I think he's talking about a different Paradise.'

'I believe I am,' said the driver. 'I mean the town of Paradise. It's no more than a flyspeck on the river.'

‘Is there a police station there?’

‘Oh, no. No, no, no, nothing like that. There’s nothing there except Dr Forepaugh. I’m taking him a load of wood for his cook stove. But he has a phone. My name is Ridge, by the way. Saladin Ridge.’

Well, Saladin Ridge wasn’t kidding when he said there was nothing in Paradise but Dr Forepaugh. There were maybe a dozen houses clustered together on the bank of the river but the Doctor was the only resident in the whole damn town. There wasn’t one other living, breathing soul there. Not so much as a cat or dog running through the dark streets as we pulled into town that night. It was downright eerie. And it turned out that except for Dr Forepaugh’s big old clapboard house, all the other buildings were empty and locked up. No, that’s not true. The church was open.

‘Saladin, please come in. Who are your friends?’ asked Dr Forepaugh when we arrived at his house. I noticed his shingle hanging next to the door, which read: Dr Mordecai Forepaugh, MD. He was an older man, tall, thin and aristocratic, with a neatly trimmed white moustache and sharp blue eyes that seemed to be lit from the inside. His face was as free from wrinkles as a baby’s ass. I explained what had happened and he showed me to the phone and gave me the number of the sheriff and I called. It was a chance I had to take, whether they were looking for me or not, just in case that son of a bitch had ditched the Willys-Knight someplace. The sheriff said not to hold too much hope but if he did hear anything he’d let me know. Then I called Aggie and Frank.

‘Hello?’ It was Aggie.

‘Greetings from Paradise, Indiana.’

‘Oh, John, I’ve been thinking about you all day. How are you?’

'More important, how are things there?'

'I picked out a piano today. It's the most beautiful piano in the world.'

'That's real nice.'

'And Squirrel got his pup. We answered an ad in the paper and he's the cutest thing you've ever seen. He's brown with white paws and a white diamond on his forehead. He's got feet as big as an elephant. He'll probably eat us out of house and home.' She laughed. I hadn't heard so much life in Aggie's voice since we were kids.

'That's good. That's real good.'

'He named the pup, Mike. After Michael.'

'I'll tell him. Listen, is Frank there?'

'Yes . . .' There was a slight pause. 'Is there any trouble?'

There was no use burdening Aggie when she sounded so happy. 'No, no. I just want to talk to Frank.'

Her voice was almost a whisper. 'He's been nice to me, John. Real nice. I don't know what happened but I want to thank you again. I can't tell you how different things are around here. And I don't know how long it's going to last. But it's real good.'

'Well, I'm glad to hear that, Aggie. Now put Frank on, will you?'

'Just a minute.'

I could hear some mumbling in the background then Frank came on the line. 'Yes?' His voice was wary.

'Frank, I hear things are going along just fine there.'

'You calling to check on me already?'

'No. No, that's not it. Can Aggie hear us talking?'

'No, she went upstairs.'

'I'm in big trouble here.'

'Well, it didn't take you long, did it?'

'It's not my fault.'

'It never is, is it? How many times have I heard you say that? Now, we made a deal and I'm sticking to it. And I am, goddamn it, I am sticking to the letter! Down to the smallest detail. I expect you to stick to your end of it, too.'

'But I got robbed.'

'Then you know how I feel.'

'Jesus, listen to me. Some cowboy named Kansas put a knife to my throat and took everything. Even the car.'

'Oh, come on, John, you can do better than that. What'd you do, lose everything in a crap game?'

'No, I mean it. He took every damn thing I have in the world.'

'I know what happened. You had time to think things over and decided you didn't get enough money out of me? Well, that's it. That's all you're going to get. Christ!' And then he did something I never expected in a million years. He cried. Right there on the telephone, Frank Orlansky cried. 'I can't live my life thinking that every time you want to you can gouge me. I'm not fucking made of money whether you think so or not.'

'Wait a minute. This is the last time. I promise.'

'No. Now listen to me. I'm going to take care of your sister and the kids the best I can. I'm going to try my damnedest to make life pleasant around here.' He was still crying. 'But I'll be goddamned if I'm going to live in fear of the phone ringing.' And, just like that, the son of a bitch hung up leaving me standing there with the receiver in my hand. I knew I was never going to get another penny out of old Frank. I couldn't do anything right. Not even blackmail.

'You look familiar to me,' the Doctor was saying to Michael when I joined them in the kitchen where they were sitting around the table having coffee. 'Are your parents from Paradise?'

'I'm afraid not,' I said. 'Michael's never been out of Pennsylvania and his parents were born and raised there, too.' I jumped right in because I didn't want the Angel to say he was on his way to heaven. Even Hollywood would be tough to explain to the likes of the Doc.

'Then you look like someone.' He smiled at Michael. 'It will come to me. I never forget a face.' He poured a cup of coffee for me. 'What did the sheriff say?'

'He'll call if he hears anything.'

'And I'm sure he will. In the meanwhile, you must be my guests.'

'Well, that's really nice of you. We have to accept your offer because we don't have any other choice.'

'It will be my pleasure. I don't have many guests. And I'm sure you'll be comfortable.' He refilled Saladin Ridge's cup. 'And you, Saladin, will you be spending the night?' It was the first time I took a good look at Saladin Ridge and realized he was Indian. His features were as clean and defined as a pencil sketch and his eyes as black as the Angel's. There was a pleasant little smile always playing around his full lips.

'No thanks, Doctor, Sunny's got a pulled muscle. I got to rub him down in the morning.'

'Sunny's his plough horse,' explained the Doc.

'Besides, you know Leila, she gets nervous when she's alone with the kids at night. I'll just sit a spell then unload the wood and be on my way.'

'If it wasn't for Saladin, I probably wouldn't eat. He keeps me supplied with wood for the stove. I'm very indebted to him.'

'Don't you believe a word he says,' said Saladin Ridge. 'Doctor's been taking care of me and my family ever since we came here. If anybody's indebted, we are.' He refused more coffee when the Doctor offered it. 'I'll just finish this and unload before it gets too late.'

Saladin Ridge went home and the Angel went to bed after we helped stack the wood outside Dr Forepaugh's back door. The Doc put us in a big, dark room with musty old furniture on the third floor and, after I saw to it that the Angel was settled, I went downstairs and the two of us sat in the parlour and had a glass of sherry, which I never did care for. But since my corn whiskey was gone it was better than nothing.

'He seems like a nice boy, your Michael,' said the Doctor as he closed the shutters.

'Yeah, I guess he is. A little green, but he's OK.' I told him the same story I had told Kansas, that the Angel was my cousin and we were off to the west coast to visit relatives. I filled in a few more details, saying he was off the farm and uneducated.

'How dreadful to lose everything you own.'

'Well,' 'I said, 'it wasn't a whole hell of a lot.'

'There's plenty of clothing around here so we won't worry about that. It might not fit perfectly and it may not be the latest fashion but we can make do. And Saladin and some of the others will help.'

'Well, that certainly is nice of you.'

'Do you like Haydn, John?'

'I don't know who he is.'

'Ah, then it will be my pleasure to introduce you to him. He's a composer. I prescribe Haydn for a headache. He has the extraordinary ability to put things in their proper place. At least for me and I suspect for anyone who will listen to him. I think his music has order with precisely the correct ratio of surprises. Life should be like that, don't you think?'

He smiled and the light in his eyes seemed brighter. 'Haydn always knows exactly where he's going. Do you, John?'

'I did before tonight.' I thought it was a queer kind of question. 'At least I always considered myself a person who knew where I was going.' The Doc wound up the Victrola and put on a record. I never did like high-toned music but sitting there in his parlour, surrounded by all that old furniture and all those pictures of stone-faced relatives staring at us, having a drink with the Doc, it sounded OK. I was afraid he was going to start asking a lot of other weird questions so I purposely shifted the topic of conversation. 'Saladin Ridge seems like a nice guy. He's Indian, right?'

'Oh, yes, Saladin is a Cherokee. Of royal blood. His people are from Oklahoma. He is directly descended from Little Carpenter, a Cherokee chief who fought for the American cause in the Revolution. Saladin is truly a prince of a fellow. A man couldn't ask for a better friend. He and his charming wife have a small farm about twenty miles from Paradise.'

'How come there's nobody here? I mean, except you?'

'Progress, John, progress.' He said it like he was talking about some kind of plague. 'Paradise had almost a hundred residents in its heyday. Back when I came here as a young doctor, scared to death that I might kill someone rather than cure them.' He laughed. 'That was a long time ago. Before the bridges were built. You see, Paradise was a ferry town. Before the bridges went in up and down river, the only way to cross for miles was on the Paradise ferry. We were famous in these parts and we had quite a thriving town then. Bustling, you might say. Quite a lovely little town, too. There was the Paradise General Store, Slout's Livery Stable, the First Community Bank and, of course, the hotel. Oh, yes, the Blue Moon Hotel. There were only six rooms but that was sufficient.' He chuckled. 'How peculiar! I'm talking about Paradise in the past tense and all the buildings are still here. I'm afraid I'm getting old. Anyway, the hotel was the centre of all the social activity in town. Oh, yes, and the restaurant was quite a gathering place. It was all under the management of the Comire family. They were here back when the first house was built. I think old Abel Comire named the town Paradise. His people were very religious. The last Mrs Comire came from a religious family, too. In fact, her brother, Sam Venable, Reverend Sam Venable, was the minister at the Methodist church and his wife, Lillian, was the teacher in our one-room school house. If it sounds a bit incestuous, I suppose it was.' He chuckled again. 'Paradise was quite a town in those days.' He poured more sherry for both of us.

'And you're the only one who stayed after the ferry stopped running? How come?'

'My patients. I couldn't leave them. I still have patients living on the farms. Not many but someone has to look after them. People like Saladin and his family. And someone has to look after Paradise, too. As she gets older, she needs taking care of just like any loved one. And I have a good deal of free time to do what needs doing. Once a week I clean the school and the church and before the Christmas holidays I always give the hotel lobby a sweep. And my patients help with the maintenance work.'

'Why?'

'Well, for instance, what if someone needed to stay at the hotel? Some traveller, perhaps. Yourselves, if Saladin hadn't introduced us and explained your plight.'

'Has that ever happened?'

'Not yet. But it could happen. It's in the realm of possibility.'

I started to think the doctor was living in his own little dream world. 'It's kind of spooky here when you drive in and there's not a light in any of the houses.'

'Not at all spooky. Comforting. If anything, there is something comforting about Paradise. Even in the dark.'

'Don't you get lonely?'

'Never. Loneliness never occurs to me.' I didn't believe him for a minute.

'But it's a dead town. A ghost town except for you.'

'Perhaps not.' He sipped his sherry then held up the glass to enjoy the light coming through the amber wine. 'I don't think Paradise is dead. She's resting . . . merely sleeping. But she'll awaken some day. Oh, yes, Paradise will wake up.' We sat for a while, not saying anything, just listening to the music and drinking the sherry until I started to get a pretty good glow on. I decided Dr Mordecai Forepaugh was a nice enough old guy but he definitely had a few screws loose in the reality department.

It was three weeks before I heard anything from the sheriff. I didn't know what the hell we were going to do without a car because I wasn't too keen on the idea of hitching rides for two thousand miles. Also, we were stony broke and even if we were able to get rides we didn't have a penny for food or a place to stay. Dr Forepaugh didn't have any money, either. When he was out of the house I looked every place he could possibly stash away some cash, in every drawer on every floor of the house, under the mattresses, in the cellar, in the sugar bowl and in every nook and cranny in his office and I didn't find a goddamn penny. He was as broke as we were. I did find a pair of gold cufflinks with a diamond in the centre of each one and a gold watch fob but there was no place to sell them so they weren't a damn bit of good to me. His patients, the few that there were, paid him with chickens and milk and canned goods and all kinds of other food. And they did chores for him and helped him look after Paradise. Saladin Ridge said someone always paid his phone bill and took care of anything else he needed cash for. Even medical supplies. Saladin Ridge wasn't the only man who looked after him but he was the only one who dropped by every few days to see if he needed anything. It seemed nothing was too much trouble for anybody to do for Doc Forepaugh. Not that he asked for much, it was just that everyone loved him so they'd do just about anything for him.

The Angel had taken a shine to the Doctor and followed him around like a puppy dog. I gave him strict instructions not to say anything about our plans, about going to Hollywood or heaven or any of it, and since I couldn't follow his every move, I had to take his word for it when he said he wouldn't tell. I did get a little nervous when, somewhere around the third day, the Angel said he had a surprise for me but I'd have to wait a while. He was cooking something up with old Doc Forepaugh but he wouldn't say a word about it. Neither one of them would. The Angel said they had sworn each other to secrecy and he was getting a big kick out of keeping me in the dark about it.

Towards the end of the week Saladin Ridge brought some cans of paint and I helped him do the trim on the house. I didn't particularly relish painting but since I was living in the man's home and eating his meals I thought there was no way to get out of helping. Besides, by then, I was so bored even work seemed interesting. The only pure pleasure I had had since arriving in town was wishing that son of a bitch Kansas would get the foot rot and syphilis and leprosy and every other curse of mankind that I could think of. Aside from that, I was going a little crazy. How many times can a person walk up and down the streets of a deserted town? It wasn't like I was going to bump into anybody or anything like that. Whatever charm the good doctor found in Paradise missed me by a mile.

'He never mentions anything about a family,' I said to Saladin Ridge when we were painting the banisters on the front porch.

'He doesn't have one. Not that I know of. He had two sisters, the Doctor is one of triplets, but they passed on a few years back. I believe they never married. They lived someplace in New England. From what the Doctor says, they were kind of eccentric. But I hear everybody in New England is.'

'Well, I don't know about *all* of New England but if Lowell, Massachusetts is an example they're pretty goddamn strange.'

'Dr Forepaugh comes from New England originally.'

'He never married either, huh?'

'No, he never married. And I think that's a pity. There was a woman he was interested in though. That was years and years ago. She left town even before the ferry stopped running. The story goes, her mother drowned in the river during a spring flood. Sometimes the river runs its banks and floods that whole lower part of town. Anyway, they say the mother was trying to save a neighbour's cat and she was swept away and it was two weeks before they found her body down river, all broken and twisted in the roots of a big oak tree. She was as naked as the day she came into the world because the river rocks tore all her clothes off. Folks always told the story of that lady with all the gruesome details and I had nightmares about her when I was a kid. By the way, the cat survived the flood. So folks said. Well, her husband, the father of the girl we're talking about, couldn't live here any more. You know, because he hated the river so. Word had it he took his daughter down south somewhere to live with a sister of his and that was the last anybody ever saw hide nor hair of the Hewlett family in these parts. That was her name. Hewlett. Rosella Hewlett. Least I think that's what it was. I know it was Hewlett but I'm not certain of the Rosella. As I said, this was all before my time. I just heard folks talking about her when I was a kid. They say she was a pretty girl, just about the prettiest girl that ever came out of Paradise. And Dr Forepaugh was sweet on her. And she was sweet on him, too. I always thought it was a pity the Doctor didn't have a family of his own. You should see how good he is with the little ones.'

'Did he have any girlfriends over the years?'

'Not that I ever heard of.'

'So, he never had a woman of his own. No wonder he's a little crazy.'

Saladin Ridge's black eyes clouded over and he put down his paintbrush. 'There's nothing crazy about Dr Forepaugh. You mustn't say things like that.' Even the perpetual smile disappeared from his lips.

'Now, hold your water. I don't mean anything disrespectful. But all these years, being alone. A man has needs. You know what I mean.'

'I don't know anything about the Doctor's needs. And neither do you.' His body tensed like he was getting ready for a fight. The man looked like he was made of iron and he was the last person I wanted to tangle with. 'Besides, he's not like other men. So don't you go judging him by the standards of other men.' It was plain to see he was madder than hell.

'You're right. I'm sorry. He's a fine, fine man and I

would never say anything mean about him. I apologize and I hope my apology is accepted.' He looked at me for a moment and then his eyes softened and the little smile returned. 'I shoot my mouth off sometimes when I shouldn't.'

'Apology accepted.' He shook my hand with a grip that could have cracked hickory nuts. 'Dr Forepaugh is . . . well, to me and my family and most of the folks living in these parts, Dr Forepaugh is a saint.'

'Well, I'm sure he is.' All I needed was to be living in the house of a saint. It wasn't bad enough I was travelling with an angel.

One night after supper, while I was lingering at the kitchen table over a cup of coffee and the Angel was doing the dishes, we started playing what had become his favourite game. Guess the surprise.

'OK, let's see.' I had already asked for every clue I could think of. 'Is it something to eat?'

'No, it's nothing to eat. What else?'

'Can I put it in my pocket?' This sent him into hysterics and he about fell over from laughter. 'I guess that means I can't put it in my pocket. Well, I don't know. You have to give me a hint.'

'No hints. Guess again.'

'Is it something I can sit on?' He laughed so hard he almost dropped a dish.

'What's so funny?' asked the Doc as he came in, carrying a large book. Just from the way he walked, I knew he was excited about something.

'Michael thinks it's the funniest thing in the world that I can't guess what the damn surprise is. He's going to bust a gut if he doesn't get to tell me soon.'

'Now, now, it won't be long.' He placed the book on the table in front of me. 'I told you I never forget a face. I knew Michael reminded me of someone.' He went to Michael and took him by the arm. 'Come over here and leave those dishes until later.' The Angel sat next to me. 'This is a wonderful book of pictures of Florentine art treasures and there are samples of the work of one of my favourite painters, Sandro Botticelli.' He turned up the wick on the oil lamp and flooded the table with light. 'Not only a favourite of mine but a favourite of the Medici, also. Don't *I* have good taste?' He chuckled as though he had told some kind of joke but it went over my head because I didn't know who the hell the Medici was any more than I knew who Botticelli was. 'Ah, Botticelli, a master of brilliant and iridescent colour. And composition. Oh, yes, what fluid and exciting composition! He was a student of Filippo Lippi, also of the Florentine School. Now, *there* was a bit of a scandal.' He was as excited as a kid and he looked forty years younger. 'You see, as a young monk, Filippo Lippi fell in love with a nun. Eventually the Pope gave them both dispensations in order to marry. Of course, the Medici had an enormous amount of power. Even at the Vatican. Believe me, it didn't hurt to have the Medici on your side.' He chuckled again. 'Ah, but I do so like the Renaissance. Such spirit. If I could have chosen the period in history in which I would spend my time on this earth, it would have been the Renaissance. And it would have been in Italy, of course.' That bright light was shining in his eyes and the Angel was looking at him as though he understood what the hell he was talking about. 'But I digress. We were talking about Botticelli.' He started to thumb through the book. 'I seem to have lost my place. I'm looking for a painting of the

Madonna called "the Virgin with Child and Angels". Art historians say Botticelli was approximately twenty-three when he painted it. Imagine that kind of genius. There!' He stopped turning the pages and pulled the lamp even closer, pointing to an angel in the foreground of the painting handing the baby Jesus to the Madonna. Well, I about went into shock. The angel was younger than Michael by some ten years but it was the dead spit of him. As handsome as Michael with the same perfect nose and strong chin. The same big, dark eyes and long curly brown hair. The similarity was enough to give a person goose bumps. There was Michael with full-blown wings and a gold halo. It was just plain creepy.

'Holy shit!'

'That's me,' said the Angel, pulling the book closer so he could get a better look. 'That's a picture of me in heaven, huh?'

I kicked him under the table. 'Well, it sure in hell looks like you. But don't be so dumb. How could it be you?' I couldn't believe my eyes. The more I looked at it the more it looked like him. 'Hey, Doc, when would you say this picture was painted?'

'Oh . . .' He thought for a moment. 'I'd say sometime between 1460 and 1470. Give or take a few years.'

'Jesus! That's before Columbus came to America.'

'Who's Columbus?' asked the Angel.

'Later.' I just kept looking from Michael to the picture, back and forth, and I still couldn't believe my eyes.

'The resemblance is remarkable,' said the Doctor, 'absolutely remarkable.'

'You don't know the half of it.' I was thinking about the Angel's wing things and I wondered if maybe he had shown them to the Doctor.

'It's not me, is it, Doctor?'

'No, of course not.' He patted the Angel on the head. 'It's merely a painting of someone who looked like you. Someone who lived several hundred years ago.' The more the Doctor said, the spookier it got. 'It's a painting of a little boy who modelled for Botticelli. A little boy who looked very much like you. It's just an amazing coincidence.' I wasn't so sure and I wanted to ask the Angel if he had any recollection of having somebody paint his picture. I knew it was crazy and absolutely impossible but I couldn't wait to get him alone so I could ask all the same.

'Can I have the picture?'

'You can't ask the Doc to take a picture out of his book!'

'Certainly he can. In fact, you may have the book. I've enjoyed it long enough, now it's time to pass the book along to someone else. And who better than the Botticelli Angel himself.'

That was it! It hit me like a ton of bricks. In Hollywood, Michael would be known as the Botticelli Angel. The Botticelli Angel! It already sounded like somebody famous. So who cared if nobody knew who the hell this Botticelli gink was? What a story it would make! Michael was the reincarnation of some kid who posed for a famous artist back in the fourteen hundreds. He was the grown-up version. He even had the goddamn wings. The public would eat it up. If they were so crazy about actors from other countries, foreigners like Valentino and Theda Bara and Greta Garbo, imagine how they'd feel about somebody from another century. They'd fall for it hook, line and sinker. I could feel that thing in the pit of my stomach, that feeling that lets you know something is right. I couldn't wait to get to Hollywood. Now all we needed was some money and a way to get the hell out of Paradise.

*

When we were both settled in our beds that night, just after I turned down the lamp, I asked the Angel if he remembered anything like having somebody paint his picture.

'That's not me. Dr Forepaugh said it's a boy who looks like me.'

'I just wondered,' I said and turned over.

'But,' he said after a few seconds, 'I think maybe I dreamed something like that once.'

'You did.' I could feel the goose bumps again. 'What was the dream?'

'I don't remember. My mother showed me pictures of what heaven is like all the time and she said I was in the pictures. Angels was in the pictures a lot of the times.'

'But do you remember somebody painting a picture of you? Did you sit still while some fella put paint on a canvas?'

'What's a canvas?'

'It doesn't matter. Did someone tell you to sit still while they painted your damn picture?'

'What are you getting mad at?'

'I'm not mad, goddamn it.'

'Well, you sure sound mad.'

'I just want to know if you remember.'

'What?'

'If some guy painted your picture.'

'Do you want me to say yes or no?'

'Just what you remember, goddamn it.'

'Maybe I dreamed it once. I don't know for sure.'

We were back to square one. 'OK. Just shut up and go to sleep.' I was ready to kill him.

'I didn't say my prayers yet.'

'Say them to yourself.' I heard him mumbling for a while, mentioning my name a few times and the Doctor's and

Aggie and the kids and Saladin Ridge and I think he even mentioned Evalina, the showgirl in prison for knocking off her boyfriend. He certainly gave God a load of shit to listen to every night. It was quiet for about ten minutes and I thought he was asleep.

'John?'

'What?'

'You want a hint about the secret?'

'No. I don't care about the stupid damn secret. Just shut up and go to sleep.' It was dark in the room and I couldn't see his face but I knew he was lying there with that stricken look and I started to feel guilty. That's one thing I always hated about the Angel. The way he could make me feel guilty. And when we met up with Celine, she could do the same damn thing. Make me feel as guilty as sin. The two of them. And the worst part of it was, I don't think they ever even tried. It must have taken me a good hour to fall asleep that night.

For the next few days, I couldn't get the painting out of my mind. I did my chores around the place and the Angel was off doing whatever he was doing with the Doc and all I could think of was Botticelli and the kid with the halo. I knew it was impossible but Michael had those wing things and the kid had wings and they looked so damn much alike. I wondered what Doc Forepaugh would say if he knew Michael had those things on his back? If he would still think it was just a remarkable resemblance? After giving it a lot of thought, I decided to have the Angel show him. He was the kind of man who, if I made him swear never to tell anybody, would stick to his promise. Guys like that are easy to spot. Probably because there are so few of them.

It was one night after the Angel had taken his bath and I was having my glass of sherry with the Doc that I told him.

'You swear you won't say anything to anyone?'

'You have my word. But, John, if you feel so strongly about whatever it is, perhaps you shouldn't tell me.'

'No, I want your opinion about something.' I called the Angel down. 'Michael's got some kind of weird growths on his back.'

'Yes, I know.'

'He showed them to you?'

'Oh, no. I could see there was some abnormality under his shirt but when I asked him about it he said he promised you he wouldn't say anything. He puts great store in what you think of him.'

'Yeah, well . . . he's just a dumb kid.' I didn't like to hear about the Angel putting great store in what I thought. Hell, we had only known each other such a short time. It just seemed like too damn much responsibility. 'Anyway, this is a little crazy but I have to ask you. Do you believe in God?'

'No.'

'You don't?' You could have knocked me over with a whisper. He was the kind of man I would have made a bet on believing in God. 'Of all the people I've met in my whole lifetime, I would have said you were the one who believed in God. You're not pulling my leg, are you?'

'No, I'm not. I don't believe in God.'

'How come you clean up the church and keep it open all the time?'

'In case someone needs it. God is essential to the very existence of so many people. If He wasn't, He never would have been invented.'

'Are you an atheist?'

'I don't really proclaim any particular ideology, but I suppose if I must categorize myself I'd have to say I am an atheist.'

'Then you don't believe in Adam and Eve and all that Bible stuff.'

'Wonderful stories. I dearly love to read the Bible. But as to an Adam and Eve in the garden, well, I believe there were many Adams and many Eves over the centuries. Men and women being the first to do something astounding. But I don't think God is a necessary component in any of their stories.'

'I guess that rules out believing people can lead other lives? You know, like some people have been around the track more than once?'

'You mean reincarnation? I think one life is all we get or *need*. It's such an extraordinary adventure. That's why we must make the most of it. Take advantage of every opportunity.'

'Oh, I agree with you there. I always try to take advantage of opportunities.' I knew we weren't talking about taking advantage of the same *kinds* of opportunities. The Angel came into the parlour wearing one of the Doc's old bath-robes. 'Hey, Michael, I know what I said about letting people see your wings but I think we can show them to Dr Forepaugh.'

He looked at me like I was betraying some kind of trust. 'Did you tell him I'm an angel?'

'Well, not exactly.'

He turned to the Doctor. 'John's an angel, too.'

'You are, John?' There was a sly little smile on the Doc's face.

'There's been a couple of women who thought so.' I laughed, trying to divert his attention from my angelhood. I didn't want him to think I was crazy and I sure as hell didn't want to get into the story of how Michael and I got together. 'Why don't you just show him your wings?'

'John says people are put off when they're around angels. Are you, Doctor?'

'Well, I don't know. I've never had the privilege of being in the company of an angel. At least not that I was aware of. You may be the first.' He smiled that warm, lit-up smile of his. 'But I don't think I could ever be uncomfortable with you, Michael. May I see?' His bedside manner was slick as slime.

The Angel let the robe fall off his shoulders and turned so Doc Forepaugh could look at his back. As soon as they were free the wing things started to move back and forth like they had been restricted and were aching to stretch themselves.

'Absolutely incredible.' The Doc was touching them. 'I've never seen anything quite like these.'

'They sort of make the coincidence double-barrelled, don't you think? You know what I mean, him looking like that kid in the painting and then having these things.'

'So, Michael, you're an angel. How do you know you're an angel?' He was looking at the place they were attached to the Angel's back.

'My mother said. I always been. She said the Lord gave her a gift and a trial in the same little package the day she birthed me.'

'I see.'

'What do you think?' I asked.

'Quite frankly, I don't know what to think. I suppose it's another example of man's infinite possibilities. Another of the countless inexplicable anomalies.'

'What's that?' The Angel was trying to understand.

'We'll talk about it later.' I didn't think he should be listening if the Doc was going to explain why he probably *wasn't* an angel. Him thinking he *was* seemed like money in the bank to me. 'Why don't you go on up to bed?'

As usual, he did as he was told. ''Night John, 'night Dr Forepaugh.' He pulled the robe over his shoulders and went upstairs.

'I know,' I said when he was gone, 'that him having any connection with that kid in the painting is really nuts but . . .'

'Oh, I understand. The coincidence and the similarity! Yes, yes. One could certainly allow one's imagination to run rampant.'

'What do you think those things sticking out of his back are?'

'Perhaps they *are* vestigial wings.' When he said that I thought maybe his atheism was starting to slip. 'But not the wings of an angel. Perhaps they are the product of some primal genetic memory. A memory that dates back to the time when we crawled out of the muck and had choices. When we were trying to decide whether to live in the water or walk the land. For that matter, whether to walk at all. Perhaps to fly or slither. To have scales or feathers. To have four legs or two legs. So many choices. Whether we'd lay eggs and patiently wait for them to hatch so we could experience the arrogance of reproducing what we considered to be our own wondrous selves, or to give live birth and have instant self-aggrandizement. Choices. Whether to be unisexual or hermaphroditic. I've often thought that was the case with so many so-called abnormalities. Children born with claws instead of hands, with both sets of genitalia, with webbed extremities. Children born blind or deaf. There *are* naturally blind fish, after all, and snakes evolved without the sense of hearing. Choices made, for whatever reasons, over the millions of millennia. Perhaps Michael's wings are some echo of that time when we were deciding whether we'd walk or fly.' He took a swig of his sherry. 'I know how fanciful all this sounds but to me, well, it makes as much, if not more, sense than the angel theory.' He smiled. 'Forgive my loquaciousness but I so rarely have the opportunity to talk to anyone and I'm afraid I take advantage.'

'Hey, don't apologize. It's interesting even though I was having a hard time keeping up with you.'

'Nonsense. I don't believe that for a moment. Don't underestimate yourself, John. And, please, don't underestimate me.' There was a little bit of a jab in the way he said that. 'Or Michael, for that matter.'

'Do you think he's dimwitted?'

'Not in the least. He's like someone newly born. He's very bright. Where has he been all his life?'

'Well, that's a long story. Too long.' And it was a story I was never going to tell him. 'Let's just say his people were real peculiar and let it be done at that.'

The Doc thought about it a moment. 'I hope you realize . . .' but the sentence drifted off. He must have felt he was getting too personal and he was a man who had trouble stepping over the line. 'Would you like some more sherry?'

'No thanks, I think I'm going to pack it in.' I didn't feel like talking to him any more. I just knew if we kept at it, he'd get tired of dancing around and start asking a lot of questions I didn't want to answer. 'All this philosophizing takes it out of a fella.' I put down my glass and got up to leave.

'I know this really isn't any of my business but I've become very fond of Michael and I'm concerned for his well-being. Where *are* you taking him?'

I wanted to say it really *wasn't* any of his business but instead I said, 'To California. I already told you.' That part was true so I could look him straight in the eye when I said it but I broke the connection when I said, 'To visit relatives.'

Doc Forepaugh was that kind of man. You couldn't look him in the eye and lie. And he knew I was lying, I could feel it, as real as cold rain on my skin, but I didn't want to get into any discussion so I tried to be reassuring. 'Don't go losing any sleep over Michael. I'm going to take real good care of him. I always have and I always will.' I thought the *always* would strengthen the cousin story. I started for the stairs. ''Night.'

'Goodnight, John.' That's all he said. But just in the way he said it I knew there was an accusation somewhere.

When I was in bed, lying in the dark listening to the slow even breathing of Michael across the room, I decided it was time to get out of Paradise because the Doc was getting suspicious and was going to forget his good manners and start asking too many goddamn questions. He was also getting too close to the Angel and I could tell he didn't trust me for shit. And who knew when the Angel would slip and tell him about Hollywood and me taking him away from his mother and anything else that came into his mind. It was all just a matter of time and I had to come up with a plan and soon. And I thought about the Doc's explanation for the wings and figured it was probably as good an explanation as I was ever going to get. I had never put much store in the idea of a God, anyway, and it was easier for me to deal with the Angel when I knew he was as mortal as me than when I thought there might be a possibility that he was some kind of heavenly something or other. It's one thing to dump some dumb hick when you don't need him any more and another to risk a bolt of lightning coming straight at your head because you dumped a real angel. But the face of the kid in the painting still bothered me and I knew the best thing was to get all of that reincarnation shit out of my mind before it started messing up my head and interfering with my plans for the future. So I did what had helped me forget my troubles since I was a kid, something I'm sure the Doc would have said was as primal as crawling out of the muck. I made myself think of pretty Millie Quick back in Lowell, Massachusetts, all soft and warm and smelling good, and I slipped my hand down inside my underpants.

The sheriff called the next day to tell me they found the Willys-Knight. Since we had been there almost three weeks, I had just about given up hope of ever seeing that old car again. It was discovered way the hell and gone off the main road by two kids going fishing and from what the police could figure, that son of a bitch Kansas ditched it when it ran out of gas and hitched a ride with some other poor sucker. What went through my mind right away was somebody buried in a shallow grave in the woods with their throat slit from ear to ear. I always thought what saved me from having that happen was the Angel just off in the bushes, taking a piss. That night, whether he knew it or not, he was my guardian angel. Except for having an empty gas tank, the car seemed to be in good condition but the sheriff didn't know if Kansas had taken anything. One of his deputies was going to bring it over to Paradise the next afternoon for me to identify and check over the contents. I didn't care what he took as long as I had the car and a way to get out of town.

The big surprise was revealed to me the next day when we were waiting for the deputy to arrive with the car. Saladin Ridge and I had scraped and painted the iron gate at the end of Doc's front walk and we were all having our lunch on the side porch, it being the middle of May and as warm and pretty a day as anybody could ask for. Mrs Ridge had sent along a big potato salad and tomato and bacon sandwiches and we were relaxing with our iced tea when the Angel made the announcement.

'Now, Dr Forepaugh?' His eyes were as big as an owl's.

'Now seems as good a time as any. Besides, if you don't do it now, you're going to have a seizure.'

'What's going on?' I asked.

'It's time for the secret.' I hadn't seen the Angel so full of juice since he danced in the aisle in Volkwein's music store. He started to go into the house. 'Oh, don't you move. Anybody. You stay there too, Mr Ridge.' He ran inside.

'Well, it's about time. He's about to drive me crazy.'

'I've been curious myself,' said Saladin Ridge.

'I think you'll be very impressed.' That intense shine was there in the Doc's eyes and I thought he was damn near as excited as the Angel.

'I'm ready,' he called from inside the house.

'Well, come on. Let's get this over with.'

He came out with the silliest expression I had ever seen on his face, hiding something behind his back. I thought he was going to sing or something the way he positioned himself in front of us but he stood there for a minute and then very slowly brought out a small book. He opened it and after clearing his throat he began to read.

'*I see the bird. The bird has a nest. I see the nest. The bird has eggs. I see the eggs.*'

'Well, I'll be damned! You can read.'

'I sure can,' he said dancing back and forth. 'There's lots more, too.' He turned a page. '*Nat has a hen. The hen has a nest. The hen has eggs. Nat has eggs. I see the hen and the eggs.*' He looked up. 'There's lots in here about Nat and a girl named Dora and a cow named Buttercup and all kinds of stuff.'

'The *Indiana First Reader* can be very exciting.' The Doc smiled and nodded to Michael.

'Are you surprised, John?' I couldn't have peeled the smile off Michael's face.

'I never in a million years would have guessed. Never. And I thought it was something I could sit on.' Michael roared with laughter. I turned to Doc. 'You're a teacher and a half, you are.'

'He's a wonderful student. And he paid for his lessons. Oh, yes, he certainly did. Every day when we went to the school house for our lessons, Michael helped clean up. Not only that! You know the old saying, something about teachers being taught by their pupils. Well, Michael taught me something, too. I can now sing "Bill Bailey Won't You Please Come Home" and "Alexander's Ragtime Band". And rather brilliantly, I might add.'

'Go on, Doctor, show him.'

'You want me to sing right now? I will if you sing with me.'

The Angel didn't need a bit of coaxing to sing. 'OK. And John can sing too. He taught me the songs. He's a real good singer.' He turned to me. 'You're a real good singer, huh, John?' He wasn't about to leave anybody out, he was just naturally too polite. 'And, Mr Ridge, if you don't know the song I'll teach you.'

'Well, thank you Michael, but I can't carry a tune in a hand basket. I'm a real good audience though.'

The Angel started to sing in his sweet voice and Doc Forepaugh joined right in.

> '*Won't you come home, Bill Bailey?*
> *Won't you come home?*
> *She moans de whole day long.*'

I chimed in for the second chorus.

'I'll do de cooking, darling,
I'll pay de rent,
I know I've done you wrong.
'Member dat rainy eve dat I drove you out . . .'

And when we were just hitting our stride the deputy pulled up in front of the house in the Willys-Knight.

Deputy Whitholder was what you'd call a man of few words and all business. He was short and fat and bursting out of his frayed uniform. 'Check the contents of the vehicle please.' His voice was nasal and sing-song. I did and discovered that that son of a bitch Kansas, obviously madder than hell because there was nothing of any value in the trunk, cut most of the clothes to shreds. He must have stabbed my old cardboard suitcase a hundred times. He even ripped up the angel dress. There were cigarette butts stomped out on the floor on the driver's side but otherwise the car was pretty much in the same shape as it was when Kansas stole it.

'I guess everything else is OK.'

'You're sure this is your car?' asked Deputy Whitholder.

'It's his car,' said Michael. 'I been in it before.'

'Yes, deputy, it's my car.'

'Sign here, please.' He shoved a clipboard in my face. 'And you owe the state of Indiana one dollar and twenty-four cents for gas. I filled the tank for you.'

'I'll take care of that,' said Saladin Ridge, digging in his pocket. I signed the form and handed it back to Deputy Whitholder.

'Now you have to drive me back to the station.' And he started for the car.

Saladin Ridge came to my rescue again. 'I'll take you in my truck. It's not far out of my way and I was about ready to leave anyhow.' The deputy didn't say a word, he merely redirected himself and got in the passenger side of the truck.

'Thanks, Saladin. I'll pay you back some day.'

'Well, don't go worrying about it.' He opened the truck door. 'When will you be leaving?'

'Tomorrow. First thing.'

'Already?' asked the Angel.

'We have to get on the road. We're way behind.'

'Well, you boys take good care of yourselves. And remember to stop by and see us if you come this way again. I hope the next time the circumstances will be different.' Saladin Ridge's smile broadened as he shook hands with the Angel and me. He told the Doc he'd be around to see him in a day or two and then got in the truck and took off down the street with Deputy Whitholder who was sitting there, staring straight ahead, anxious to get back to his office now that his mission was accomplished. The Angel was still waving long after the truck disappeared around the corner.

That night, after packing the clothes the Doc had given us in a box and an old suitcase, we had a special farewell dinner. He roasted a chicken one of his patients had given him and we had root vegetables and some of Mrs Ridge's special pickles and tapioca pudding. The Doc made toast for me to have with dinner because he knew I liked it so much. He was a very considerate host. He also cranked up the Victrola and played some Mozart for us which he said would energize us for the journey. As far as he was concerned, there was no better travelling music than Mozart.

After the dishes had been cleaned up, the Angel sat at the table with the Doc listening to the music and looking through the book of Florentine art treasures. He just couldn't get enough of it. I kept telling him he was going to wear the book thin if he didn't take it easy. Whether he gave a damn about any of the other paintings, I don't know, but it was a good excuse to look at the kid with the wings and the halo and speculate about who he was. The Angel had a fanciful imagination to begin with but when the Doc got in on it the two of them went nuts. They made up a whole life for the kid and talked about him as though they had known him. They even named him. Saladin. Because as far as they were concerned, Saladin Ridge was as close to an angel as any mere mortal was ever going to get.

I had more practical matters to worry about. Namely, what the hell we were going to do for money. We had a full tank of gas so at least we could get back on the road but that was it. On the pretence of checking to see if we had everything packed, while they were looking at the damned picture, I casually lit an oil lamp and went upstairs and got the gold cufflinks and the watch fob out of the dresser in Doc's bedroom. At least, when we got to the next big town, I could sell them and have some eating money. I could hear the Mozart playing and the two of them laughing downstairs and I thought to myself Doc Forepaugh was a nice guy and he had been good to us and maybe it was a lousy way to show appreciation but the goddamn jewellery was just lying in a drawer. It wasn't as if I was taking his last nickel or a crust of bread out of his mouth or anything like that. And he didn't even use the stuff. When I took it it was in exactly the same place it had been when I had first seen it weeks before so I thought it might as well be put to good use.

Two things happened before we took off from Paradise; one made me feel really stupid and one was just plain too much of a coincidence to be anything but weird. When our things were in the car and we were having a last cup of coffee with the Doc, he said, 'You're going to need some money for your journey.'

'Well' – I couldn't believe he was even bringing up the subject – 'it would help.'

'Then I suggest we go down to the bank and get some.'

'You have money in the bank?'

'Where else would I keep my money?'

It was too obvious ever to cross my mind. He kept the church open in case anyone needed to pray and he taught the Angel how to read in the one-room school house so it just followed naturally that if he had any money he'd keep it in the goddamn bank. An idiot could have figured that out! We left the Angel to wash up the cups and the Doc and I went down to the bank and on the way he said a few things I was hoping he wouldn't get around to before we left. Stuff about my responsibility and how much the Angel liked me and depended on me and how unfair it would be to do anything to disappoint or hurt him. He didn't actually come out and say my story about visiting relatives was a crock of shit but he let me know that he knew I wasn't telling the truth. I tried to laugh it all off but he made me feel uncomfortable as hell and I was glad when we got to the bank and his attention was focused on the money.

'I believe there's sufficient to get you wherever you're going,' he said as he opened the unlocked back door. I had visions of all this money sitting around getting mouldy, just waiting to make the trip to California clear sailing for the Angel and me. The bank was nothing but one big room with a single teller's window, a few desks and an old safe. Like everything else in Paradise, it was slightly dusty but it was obvious that somebody was looking after it. He went to the drawer at the teller's window and opened it and said, 'Help yourself.'

There was only one stack of bills and right off the bat I could see there wasn't much there unless they were all hundreds. When I counted it it came to thirty-four dollars. The Doc obviously hadn't travelled in the last fifty years if he thought thirty-four dollars was going to get us very far.

'I can't take all your money.'

'Why not? I have no use for it.'

'I'll just take a few bucks.'

'No, no. I insist. Take all of it. Really. I don't like the thought of you and Michael going hungry.'

'No, I can't.' I put the money back in the drawer, protesting as convincingly as I could. I was damn good at refusing money I knew I was going to get.

He took the money, folded it and put it in my hand. 'Now I don't want to hear another word about it.'

I thanked him as though he had given me a million dollars and as we were leaving and he was closing the back door he said, 'Now maybe you won't need the watch fob. I don't care about the cufflinks but the watch fob has sentimental value. It was my father's.' He even had a pleasant little smile on his face when he said it. Talk about getting caught with your pants down! I did the only thing I could do, what I always did when I was faced with a situation like that. I became the offended party.

'Watch fob! What watch fob? What cufflinks? Are you saying I took your watch fob and cufflinks? I don't know anything about them. I can't believe you're accusing me of stealing your jewellery. Doc, I have to say, I'm surprised that you could think something like that of me. What did I ever do to make you say something like that? It hurts me. It really, really hurts.'

He didn't buy it but he was too much of a gentleman to persist. 'I'm sorry.' It was an unenthusiastic apology. 'Perhaps I was mistaken.'

My next move, which usually worked, was to be sympathetic. 'Oh, I know how upset you must be. I mean losing something like that. Damn, there's nothing worse than losing something of sentimental value. If you want, Michael and I will help you look for it.' I had the best innocent expression I could muster. 'We'll stay until you find it.'

'That won't be necessary.' He wasn't buying any of my crap. I could tell. We started back to the house, walking along in silence. I thought about protesting a little more, or maybe being more sympathetic, but I figured it would be beating a dead horse. When we were about to turn the corner on Ivy Street, where the Doc's big old house sat, he took my arm and stopped me. 'You don't have to go, you know. You and Michael are more than welcome to stay here and live with me. I'd like that. I really would.' So much for his never feeling lonely.

For some reason, his invitation to stay made me feel worse than when he accused me of taking the goddamn watch fob and cufflinks. He knew I took them yet he was willing to forget it and overlook it and even offer me a place to live. The guy was really crazy.

'Well, thanks, but we got to move on. I mean, we already lost a few weeks. You know how that is when you're travelling. But I appreciate the offer.'

'If you ever change your mind, you are always welcome.'

'Thanks.'

We turned the corner and started up the street and there was the Angel standing at the kerb talking to a man, a woman and three kids. A beat-up old model T Ford was parked by the kerb loaded with all kinds of stuff, even an old rocking chair strapped on the roof. The Angel got all excited when he saw us and came running up.

'There's people here. They just came into town. They was asking me questions.'

The man, tall and thin as a sapling, with shabby clothes and an untrimmed beard that was starting to go grey, met us half way. 'You must be Dr Forepaugh. Michael told us you were here.' He extended his hand to the Doc. 'My name is Halsey. Amick Halsey.'

'It's a pleasure, Mr Halsey.' The Doc was as gracious as ever. He introduced me and we walked to the car where the woman was waiting with the kids.

'This here is my wife, Naomi, and here we got Joshua, he's our eldest, and Grace Ellen and the young one, Amick Jr.' We all exchanged greetings. You could tell the woman had been a beauty in her day, her features were soft and her eyes were tired looking but still pretty. The kids were scrawny and nondescript and the whole family looked like they hadn't had a good meal since the Flood. 'We didn't think we'd be able to find Paradise. It ain't on the map.'

'Well,' said the Doc, 'we used to be. They took us off several years back when the ferry stopped running and everybody left town. But we're still here.'

'I wondered,' said Amick. 'We just wanted to see it. I heard so much about it when I was growing up.'

'You heard about Paradise?'

'From my grandmother. She was born here in Paradise. Her maiden name was Hewlett. Rosella Hewlett.' The color drained right out of the Doc's face and for a minute there I thought he was going to pass out. 'Rosella! Good Lord.'

'Who's Rosella?' asked the Angel.

'Nobody you know,' I said.

'How is Rosella?' The Doc's voice was different, a little choked.

'She passed on a while back.'

'Oh, I'm sorry to hear that. She didn't suffer, did she?' He seemed to be truly concerned when he asked.

'Oh no, the Lord took her while she was sleeping. It was real peaceful like and she ain't never been sick a day in her life.'

'I'm grateful for that.' The Doc's eyes lit up a little and he smiled. I kind of wondered, since he didn't believe in God, whom he was grateful to? 'How often I've thought about her over the years.'

'Well, she never stopped talking about Paradise.' Amick turned to the wilted Naomi. 'Ain't that right, honey? Didn't Nana go on and on about Paradise?' Naomi smiled and agreed with Amick. 'You'd 'a' thought it was London, England or some fancy place like that to hear her talk. And she mentioned you quite a bit too, Dr Forepaugh. Ain't that right, honey?'

'Where are my manners? Please, come up on the porch and rest a bit. Have a glass of lemonade.'

'Dr Forepaugh makes the best lemonade,' said the Angel.

'Thank you, Michael.' The Doc turned to Amick. 'Do you have time?'

'All the time in the world. I'm looking for a job and a place we can settle. Ain't that right, honey?' I guess Naomi had to verify everything Amick said. We all started up the walk. 'I'm a blacksmith by trade. Where we was living folks started buying farm machinery, you know, tractors and the like, and they just don't use their horses no more. Looks like that's happening all over the damn country. Oh, excuse my language.'

'The farmers around here still use their horses. And

there's not a blacksmith for miles. This may be fortuitous. You may have come to the right place, Mr Halsey.'

'Amick. Just call me Amick.'

Everyone sat down and I slipped into the house and up to the Doc's bedroom and put the watch fob back in his dresser drawer. I stuck it under his shirts on the opposite side so he might think, even though he knew better, that maybe he was wrong about me taking it. I kept the cufflinks. What the hell, he said he didn't care about them and his thirty-four dollars wasn't going to go very far. And anyway, I figured since I put the watch fob back he kind of owed me.

By the time we left, the Halseys were settling in. There was no doubt about it. And I could tell that Amick Halsey, in his simple way, was as good a man as a person could ever expect to find and Naomi, just clearing the glasses away after they drank their lemonade, looked comfortable, like she belonged. The kids, shy as field mice, sat quietly in the shadows at first but the Angel and the Doc brought them around and they actually laughed out loud a few times. In only about three-quarters of an hour they looked like a family doing just everyday things. I know that's hard to believe but, like I said, I was going to tell the truth and that is the truth. If I hadn't known better I would have said those people had known each other for years. They all looked so ordinarily contented and at ease and the light was shining brighter than ever in the Doc's eyes.

I got the feeling that it was some kind of a beginning. That maybe Paradise was waking up from her long sleep.

'Remember what I told you, John,' he said, shaking my hand, 'consider this home and come back whenever you want.'

'Thanks, Doc. I might just take you up on that.'

'And, Michael' – he held the Angel close – 'you get John to teach you how to write.'

'I will. And I'll write a letter. Won't we write a letter, John?'

'That we will. Now get in the car, Michael. We'll never get to you-know-where.'

And we left Paradise behind us and headed west. The Angel didn't say anything for several minutes.

'It's funny, those people showing up like that.' I said it more to myself than to him.

'You think that was heaven?'

'No, it was not heaven. You think every place is heaven. All I can say is you're easy to please. I'll tell you when we get to heaven.'

'Well, it might be heaven. Least that's what I been thinking. And maybe Dr Forepaugh is God. Did you ever think of that?'

'What, that Doc Forepaugh is God? Well, if he is, he doesn't know anything about it.'

'Well, I think maybe he is God.'

'I hope not or I'm in bad trouble. I just stole God's cufflinks.'

Pleasant Mt Pleasant

For the first hour or so after we left Paradise, all our talk was about Doc Forepaugh. It wasn't easy for the Angel to tear himself away from what he considered, and rightly so, to be a good friend. Friends were new to him and he didn't want to part with any of them. His list was small but impressive. Aside from the Doc he had collected Aggie and Squirrel and Verna, Saladin Ridge and, by default, me. I thought to myself as he was talking about the Doc, that in such a short time he had more folks who cared about him than some people have in a whole lifetime.

That afternoon, after he put the Doc on the back burner and started reading his book, I learned more things about Nat and his girlfriend Dora and their cow named Buttercup than I ever wanted to know. Once he started, he hardly took his nose out of that *Indiana First Reader*. Nat had a friend named Tom and Dora had friends named Grace and May. Somewhere along the line they met up with a John which tickled the hell out of the Angel because he couldn't figure out how I got into his book. There was an elephant named Jumbo and Prince the horse. There was also a boy monkey named Dot and stories about ladybugs and mice, kings, parrots, robins and bees, and one of my favourites, Miss Pussy Willow. Try listening to that crap mile after mile and see if you don't feel like you're ready for the loony bin. He read them aloud over and over again until I damn near had them memorized. I tried to divert his attention by offering to teach him some new songs but, for the time being, reading was not to be replaced by music in his curriculum.

We crossed the mighty Mississippi at Burlington, Iowa and we weren't ten miles down the road when the Angel, taking a little break from Nat and Dora, noticed his first Burma Shave signs. Now that he was so big on reading, nothing with the printed word was going to escape his eagle eyes.

'*Within this vale*,' he read, haltingly, as we drove past the first sign and before he could ask what *within* or *vale* meant, the second sign came at us, '*Of toil and sin*', and I knew the way he read the word *sin*, that he realized it was a Bible word and it was all he needed. 'Sin! I know what that is.' It was like magic when he put words and ideas together and his face lit up with wonderment and the shock of recognition. He forgot the poem and went right for his quotes. '*All unrighteousness is sin*. I John 5:17. *How many are mine iniquities and sins?* Job 13:23. *Therefore to him that knoweth to do good, and doeth it not, to him it is sin.* James 4:17.'

'Hold it! Just hold it right where you are.' I was beginning to take some of that stuff personally, especially when it came to sin and knowing better but doing it anyway. I wasn't exactly sure how I felt about God and the Bible but I didn't have to believe in either one to recognize the discomfort of the shoe fitting. 'This has nothing to do with the Bible, OK? Those are just Burma Shave signs. It's just a little poem about a shaving soap.'

'Why?'

I should have known the questions would start. Being the

good teacher that I am I opted for a visual aide and put the car in reverse and backed up to the first sign. 'Now, I'm going to go real slow and we'll read the signs together and you'll see what I mean.'

We read the first sign, '*Within this vale*'.

Then the second, '*Of toil and sin*'.

And the third, '*Your head grows bald*'.

The fourth, '*But not your chin*'.

And, finally, '*Burma Shave*'.

I stopped the car and he just sat there staring at the Burma Shave sign for a minute.

'Burma Shave,' I repeated for no particular reason.

He was thinking hard enough to crack his brain and it occurred to me that he might be trying to remember a Bible quote about shaving soap.

'*Within this vale/Of toil and sin/Your head goes bald/ But not your chin.*' I put it all together for him.

'What's it mean?'

I seriously questioned the Doc's certainty of the Angel not being dimwitted. 'It means even if you go bald on your head you still have to shave the whiskers off your face. It's just a catchy way to get you to buy their shaving soap. It's advertising.'

A smile broke out on his face. 'It's just a catchy way to get you to buy their shaving soap!' Obviously, when it sank in, he thought my statement was brilliant enough to bear repeating. 'I think I like advertising. Let's go back and do it again.' His enthusiasm was directed at the goddamnedest things and even if he wasn't dimwitted I was sure he was crazy.

'OK, but just one more time.' So I did and he read it loud and clear and repeated it several times like he was memorizing Wordsworth or somebody like that.

'Can we do it once more?'

'No, we can not. Jesus Christ, we'll never get to Hollywood. Besides, we got the rest of the country to read Burma Shave signs. They're like horse shit, they're all over the place. Now, go on back to reading about Nat and his girlfriend.' But instead, he opened the book of art treasures of Florence and pretended to marvel at each one, oohing and aahing but transparent as window glass as he hurriedly riffled through the pages, just waiting to get to his favourite.

Spring was on the land and it was all as fresh and green as clover. We drove with the windows rolled down and the air was so rich and sweet I could taste it. I was humming my songs and the Angel was studying the picture of the kid who looked like him and I thought to myself, life is pretty goddamned good. We were on our way, breezing across the sun-clean Iowa countryside, heading straight into our great adventure and a new life right out of the *Arabian Nights* and even though we only had what was left of the thirty-four dollars, I was feeling on top of the world. I had been broke before, more times than I could remember, but never with such incredible prospects. In fact, I felt like those Old Timers must have felt bumping along in their covered wagons heading for the California gold fields. Of course, we were bumping along in that old Willys-Knight with nothing but the cufflinks to get us there but I knew something would turn up. Somehow it always did.

We weren't too far from Mt Pleasant when the Angel noticed the first poster announcing to the locals that the Cyril Blythe Comedians were going to be performing there for a week.

'It's a stage show,' I told him when he asked what the poster meant. 'It's actors up on a stage doing a show.'

'Like the moving picture?'

'Except these are live. You're right there with the real people. In the same room.'

'And they're singing and dancing?'

'Yeah, and talking and generally making fools of themselves.' I pulled over so we could read the announcement. 'Let's see what it says.'

> Glorifying the American Tent Stage Show. Each night a new play and five big vaudeville acts. See Cyril and Lydia. If you don't laugh, your bump of humor is a dimple. The first night comedy play, *Not Quite Married*, other comedy plays, *The Minister's Daughter*, *Wake Me When It's Over*, *Fancy Pants and Long Underwear* and *Any Day But Sunday*. We have gone from coast to coast and from Canada to the Gulf to bring to you the greatest array of entertainment ever offered under our beautiful tent theater. Children fourteen cents, adults twenty-five cents.

'Can we go see that show?' asked the Angel.

'Well, I don't know if it's even playing yet. Hell, I don't even know what date it is.' Paradise had been a place where one day was pretty much like the other and time didn't seem to matter at all. I had completely lost track. I wondered if Saladin Ridge and the Doc ever knew what day it was. 'We'll see when we get to Mt Pleasant.' It was as good a place as any to sell the cufflinks. In fact, I thought I'd probably make a better deal with some hick jeweller than if I waited until we got to a big city. And we had to stay somewhere for the night so why not there.

We pulled into town, as neat and inviting as any I had ever seen, with its brick streets and picture-perfect square with the band stand, watched over by the pristine, Victorian courthouse looking for all the world like a painting on one of those free calendars hardware stores give away at Christmas time. I drove around to try and get the lay of the place and I couldn't help but notice that everywhere I looked there were iris in bloom. On all the streets named after the presidents, Madison, Jefferson, Monroe, on Main St and Oak and Saunders, there were iris. The place was bursting at the seams with them. Every size and colour imaginable. It was like some artist had gone over the edge, splashing his paints and colouring up this practical mid-western town. In a real pretty way, the iris distracted from the orderliness of the place. But that was the only distraction. Everything else seemed to be exactly where it should be. Cars were neatly parked and the people on the streets looked scrubbed and healthy and purposeful like they all had someplace to go and something to do. Even the old men, sitting on the benches enjoying the sun, chewing over the problems of the nation and blaming the president and congress for everything wrong, looked like they were doing their designated jobs. They watched leggy beauties in filmy spring dresses saunter by, and I could just tell they were trying to jog their memories of other springs and other beauties long gone. When I look back, and think about those people in Mt Pleasant and people just like them all over the country going about their business like the life they knew was going to go on for ever, it's hard to believe the depression was just a hot summer away.

'Before you even ask,' I said to the Angel, who was enthralled with everything he saw, 'this is *not* heaven. OK? So you don't have to start any of that crap. This is Mt Pleasant, Iowa. It's just a town. But it is not heaven and God doesn't live here.'

'How do you know?'

'I just do, that's all.'

'You sure?'

'Don't start.'

'It looks real nice.'

'Well, let's see how nice some jeweller is.' I parked the car on Monroe Street and we walked along, nodding to the townspeople who for the most part didn't return the nods but merely observed us with suspicion and curiosity. We must have looked a little peculiar dressed in Doc Forepaugh's made-over duds so it was no wonder they were curious.

'Now, I'm going to do the talking in here,' I said when we came to a jewellery shop, its windows all decorated with white-paper wedding bells and black-crêpe-paper caps and gowns and spilling over with gifts for the graduate and the June bride. I took the cufflinks out of my pocket and polished them with my shirt tail before going in. There weren't any customers but a pretty young clerk, with apple cheeks and fine hair the colour of wheat and a bosom straining to free itself from her pink and white blouse, was cleaning the display cases. She looked up when she heard the tinkle of the doorbell.

'Can I help you?'

'How are you today?'

'Just fine, thank you. And you?'

'Right as rain.' I smiled my most dazzling smile which is my best feature and damn near always gets the women. 'A pretty young girl like you can't be the manager.' She blushed. 'Is he here?'

She flirted with me for one quick second, puffing her chest out ever so slightly, and moving all her body parts. 'Daddy,' she called to a man sitting behind the counter in the back, hunched over a watch, manipulating a tiny screw-driver as he looked at the guts through a jeweller's loupe.

'Huh?' He didn't look up.

'These men want to talk to you.' Her parts were still moving. 'Why don't you just go on back?'

'What do you want?' He was intent on the watch and couldn't take the time even to give us a passing glance. All I could see was the top of his head where he had what little hair was left wound around and around and plastered down in an effort to cover his baldness.

'You buy old jewellery?'

'Maybe I do and maybe I don't. Whatcha got?'

I held the cufflinks out to him. 'Heirlooms. Gold cufflinks with diamonds. They're old and valuable.' He finally looked at us with the loupe still in his right eye and his left eye looking meaner than an open wound.

'What's wrong with his eye?' asked the Angel.

'Nothing. He uses that to look at things.'

After a moment the jeweller removed the loupe and sat looking at us for what seemed like a long minute. His right eye was just as mean as his left. 'Let me see them.' He was scrutinizing me like I was some kind of bug that he was trying to decide whether or not to squash. I handed the cufflinks to him and he looked at them through the loupe and without raising his head said, 'Where'd you get these?'

'He stole them from God. Least *I* think he's God. John don't.' The Angel just smiled. As far as he was concerned, he wasn't saying anything wrong, he was merely answering a question.

The word *stole* did us in and I knew it the minute it was out of his mouth. I just wanted to take the cufflinks and get out of there. But first, I wanted to strangle the Angel with his own tongue.

'What the hell's he talking about?' asked the jeweller.

'Nonsense. He's just talking nonsense. He's not right in the head.' I said it confidentially, trying to validate myself and make it look like I was sparing the Angel's feelings and at the same time making him sound foolish.

'You're the one who said you stole them from God.' It wasn't argumentative, it was just a statement of fact. I did say it.

I smiled at the jeweller. 'It's an old Pennsylvania expression. *Stealing from God*. It goes way back. Oh, I don't know how far.' I was tap dancing as fast as I could. 'It's what you say when somebody dies and leaves you something in their will. You stole it from God. It kind of makes sense, doesn't it? I guess it's because the person is dead and in the arms of God and you get one of his possessions so . . . At least I think that's where the expression comes from.' With every word I spoke I was becoming a bigger and bigger bug and he just sat there, watching me grow. 'Maybe it was just an expression we used in *our* family. Maybe that was it. It doesn't make a whole hell of a lot of sense when you think about it, does it?' I tried to laugh it off.

'You're full of shit,' he said. 'What do you take me for? A couple of drifters coming in here thinking you can pull the wool over my eyes, why, I should call the sheriff!'

'The sheriff! Why? Now there's no need to do that. I'm just trying to sell my uncle's cufflinks.'

'Your uncle's cufflinks, my ass.' He looked at the Angel. 'Who'd he really steal them from?'

'Shut up!' I jumped in before he could answer. I turned to the jeweller. 'Just give me my cufflinks. I don't want to deal with a man as suspicious as you. A man who won't take another man's word. Give them to me.'

'What if you stole these from somebody right here in Mt Pleasant? What if the sheriff's looking for them right now?'

'What the hell are you talking about? We just pulled into town fifteen minutes ago. Give me my goddamn cufflinks.'

'Maybe I'll hold on to them until I can talk to the sheriff.'

'Are you out of your mind! You can't keep my cufflinks.'

'Sure I can. I got them right here in my hand. Come back tomorrow after I talk to the law.'

'You can't do that!' I couldn't believe it! The son of a bitch was conning me out of Doc Forepaugh's cufflinks. They were our little bit of security and besides, I didn't go to all the trouble of stealing them from the Doc just so some mean-eyed hick jeweller with a big curlicue on his head could steal them from me.

Just as nice as could be he said to his daughter, 'Mary Lou honey, call Sheriff Applegate for me, will ya?'

The last thing I wanted was a run-in with the law. There could have been a kidnapping and a burglary charge against me for all I knew. The Doc could have thought it over and decided against his benevolence and set the state police on my trail. 'OK. You call your sheriff and see if you don't make a damn fool of yourself. I'm coming back tomorrow. You bet your big fat ass I am. And I might just sue you for defaming my good name.' It was a weak protestation but it was all I could think of. I grabbed the Angel and headed for the door. 'Let's get out of here.'

'You come back and see us, you hear,' smiled Mary Lou as we left the shop.

I was so mad I was seeing blood. The Angel's! 'You *had* to open your big mouth, didn't you? You just couldn't stand there and let me do the talking like I told you. Now, because of you, we lost the fucking cufflinks. That son of a bitch stole our cufflinks and it's all your fault.'

'I just said what you said.'

'I told you to keep your mouth shut. Is that so hard to get

through your thick skull? Is it? Grow up, for Christ's sake. You're a man, you're not a goddamn kid! You don't have to say every stupid thing that comes into your feeble mind. I'm sick and tired of you acting like a baby. I'm sick and tired of *you*.' I took off down the street with him trailing behind me.

'I'm sorry, John.'

'Well, sorry isn't enough. Not by a country mile it isn't. You're on your own, buddy. I don't care about Hollywood or you or your fucking wings. I don't need you! You're more trouble than you're worth.' I tore open the car door and got in and he started to get in the passenger side. 'What are you doing? I told you, I don't need you any more. Don't get in this car.'

'What do you want me to do?'

'I don't care what you do. Go to heaven! Go to hell! I don't give a shit.'

'I won't do it again.' Tears as big as rain drops were welling up in his eyes, just about ready to spill down his cheeks.

'Yes, you will. You'll do it again and again and again. You'll just keep messing up my life. It's not worth it. And don't start crying, for Christ's sake. Men don't cry.'

'I won't.' He brushed away the tears.

'Stand clear of the door.'

'John, wait . . .'

I turned the key in the ignition and the car started. 'You've been nothing but a pain in the ass ever since I met you.'

'You're going to leave me here? What'll I do?'

'I don't know and I don't give a shit. Get a job. Take care of yourself for a change. Just get out of my life.' I put the car in gear and pulled away from the kerb. I could hear him calling after me and I could see him in the rear-view mirror, running behind the car with a look of panic on his face, but I didn't care. I stepped on the gas and sped down the street, damn near running over an old dog taking his time getting from one side to the other. The Angel and I were through and I wanted to get as far away from him as possible.

About ten miles west of town I stopped the car at a little café and had myself some toast and coffee. I was still so mad I could hardly swallow. There was a little woman, just an inch or two taller than the Angel's mother, working behind the counter. She had her hair braided and wound in buns over her ears and they looked like ear muffs.

'You should eat more than toast and coffee. A man needs something more substantial in his belly. Especially a big fella like you. I got three boys and a husband and I know. They eat like there's no tomorrow.'

'I'm not hungry.'

'You down on your luck? Is that it? What if I give you a nice big bowl of barley beef soup. No charge.'

The last thing I wanted was someone to be nice to me. I was enjoying my rage and I didn't want anything to detract from it or dilute it. I always thought people should respect a person when they're throwing a conniption fit and mind their own goddamn business and not try to be nice. It just shows good manners to leave a man alone at a time like that. 'What makes you think I need a handout,' I snapped.

'Well, excuse me for noticing but you're not exactly dressed in the latest out of the Sears and Roebuck catalogue. I haven't seen clothes like you're wearing since my grandfather was laid out and that was before I was old enough to talk.'

'I'm sorry I don't measure up to your sartorial expectations but if I want a bowl of your lousy barley beef soup I can damn well pay for it myself.' I didn't realize how loud I was getting.

'Well, do you want one or not?' she yelled.

'Yes, I do,' I yelled back even louder.

'Good!' She damn near made my ears ring.

I knew it wasn't her I was really carrying on about. It was the Angel. I had to go back into Mt Pleasant and get him, there was no question about it. Not because I cared what happened to him. I meant it when I said I was tired of having to look after him. If I wanted a kid I would've had one of my own. Hell, there had been plenty of opportunities. And for all I know there's a lot of fellows putting food on the table for kids they think are theirs but look just like me. I didn't have to be stuck with a grown-up kid like the Angel. But the truth was I needed the son of a bitch and I knew it. Without him I had no future and no prospects. And I couldn't think of any place to go. Hell, I couldn't even get a job as a teacher because that bastard Kansas had cut up my forged diploma when he wrecked everything else in the car just out of plain meanness. I was in a dark tunnel and the light at the end of it was a train heading full speed in my direction. There was nothing I could do but go back and find the Angel.

Of course, when I got back to the spot where I had left him, he was gone. I drove up and down the streets as slow as I could without causing an accident and there was no sign of him. All kinds of things began to go through my mind. As usual, my imagination ran out of control and filled every blank space in my head with the worst possible boogie men a person could conjure up. Like maybe he'd started asking people how to get to heaven and they thought he was crazy and he was already put away somewhere in some nut house, sitting in the dark corner of a padded room, trussed up in a strait-jacket, peeing himself Or maybe he told the police I took him from his mother and there was a nationwide intensive manhunt for me with a sizeable reward for my capture. Dead or alive. Or the Angel could have kept running after my car and been hit and he was lying in the Mt Pleasant hospital on his death bed with every bone in his body broken. Even his stubby little wings. I started wishing I had never been caught in that goddamn storm and stopped in Tamaqua, Pennsylvania when all of a sudden it hit me. I knew exactly where he was. The Cyril Blythe Comedians! It was the only thing he knew about in Mt Pleasant. I asked a tall skinny fellow with an Adam's apple the size of a pippin where I might find them and he directed me to the northern part of town, to the Ross lot, just off Maple Leaf Drive.

As it turned out, I was right. There was the Angel, smack dab in the middle of all the activity of putting the huge tent up. It was stretched out on the ground and a bunch of kids and some fellows who looked like they knew what they were doing were pounding stakes into the ground and tying ropes on the canvas. A short stocky fellow with legs as sturdy as tree trunks, who I later found out was Tigger Book, the boss canvasman, was overseeing the operation. There was already a kind of circus atmosphere. A Great Dane, all black and white splotches, was running around barking at everybody and a burro, tied to the back of a truck, was contentedly munching on hay, not paying a bit of attention to the hullabaloo going on.

The Angel was pounding stakes and I could see his muscles taut under his shirt and the slight fluttering of his wings. He was so intent on his work he didn't see me for a few minutes even though I walked right up to him and stood only a few feet away.

'That sledge-hammer looks heavy.' To tell the truth, I was nervous because I didn't know what he'd say or do after me cussing him out and running off and leaving him stranded like I did.

'John!' His face lit up like fireworks and he dropped the sledge-hammer and hugged me hard enough to squeeze the breath out of me, kissing me on the cheek and then jumping up and down, dragging me with him. It was as if I had been off in France or someplace, fighting in the trenches rather than just down the road having soup with a loud little woman with ear buns. He obviously held no rancour towards me and deep down I sort of wished he did because he made me feel peculiar and guilty and I hated that more than anything.

'Hey! Quit that. What's the matter with you? People are looking at us.' I pushed him away.

'I knew you'd come back for me.'

'You did, did you?'

'Yup. I did.'

'Well, you knew more than me. I had to think it over a good long time.'

'You had to come back.'

'Why?'

'You have my books in the car. My whole library.' I had told him his whole library consisted of two books. He thought repeating what I said was funny and started laughing. 'I'm real glad to see you. Real glad.' He started to hug me again and I stopped him.

'Don't go getting all stupid on me.' I had to admit to myself that I was kind of glad to see him, too.

'I did just like you said, John.'

'What?'

'I got me a job. That's what you said, wasn't it? Ten

dollars a week. Tigger gave it to me. That's Tigger over there talking to them kids.'

'Well, I'll be damned.' I couldn't believe it. 'Somebody actually hired you.'

'*Behold the hire of the labourers who have reaped down your fields . . .*'

'Don't start that Bible stuff. Jesus, you drive me nuts.'

'I'll bet Tigger'll give you a job, too.' He was so excited he was beyond being offended. 'He's real nice.'

'Ten dollars a week, huh? Slave labour. But it's better than nothing, I guess, until I figure out what to do about the goddamn cufflinks. That jeweller's got me by the short hairs and he knows it, the son of a bitch.' I looked in Tigger's direction and I saw a flash of colour out of the corner of my eye and when I focused on it I saw this young woman, picking her way through all that equipment, trying to stay upright on her high heels. It was Celine.

About Celine

First off, I have to say she was, without a doubt, the most beautiful girl I had ever seen. I can remember the moment I saw her like it was yesterday and the best way I can describe her is to say she looked like walking autumn. Her skin was all tawny and glistening and slightly sunburned and her short bouncy hair was red and gold and yellow, depending on how it caught the sun. It seemed like she was misplaced on that beautiful spring day, like she was walking through the wrong season. Her dress was a kind of ruffly clingy thing with big soft orange flowers printed on it and the breeze blew it tight against her body accentuating full breasts that didn't seem to be hampered by too much underwear and long legs with round thighs that promised a trip to someplace yet to be discovered by a mortal man. Sashaying past right before my eyes, was what I knew was the prettiest ass in the whole world, the girl out of every sinful dream I had ever had. She was heading towards Tigger Book and I noticed she had something white in her hand and she took a little nibble of it. I had to get closer to her so I took the Angel's advice and went to Tigger to see about a job.

'What do you think I should do?' she was asking Tigger as I approached.

'Tell Cyril right away. We open in a week.' He noticed me hovering near by. 'Yeah? What can I do for you?'

'My name is John Tree. I'm a friend of Michael, the one pounding in stakes over there.'

He looked me up and down. 'Where do you boys buy your clothes?'

'That's a long story.' All the time I had my eye on Celine and up close there was something not quite right about her, something more than being in the wrong season. 'I'm looking for work.'

'The whole world is looking for work. My name's Tigger Book and this here is Celine St Claire.' The name was as sensuous as she was and it echoed through my body and I could feel the little hairs on the back of my neck stand up. He shook hands with me and I just had to touch Celine St Claire so I extended my hand and she slipped the white thing into her pocket and took my hand and it was the first time we touched and I damn near heard music. She smiled and pulled her hand away and I noticed she had a slight overbite making her mouth look a little pouty and sensuous and as inviting as the apple in the Garden of Eden. And, right then, I saw what was off kilter about her. With all that rich, earthy colouring I expected brown eyes or maybe hazel but hers were a pale bluish-grey, the colour of a stormy summer sky. They were misplaced eyes. The wrong eyes in the wrong face. It was downright eerie and strange. But I was to find out that eerie-looking eyes were about the least strange thing there was where Celine St Claire was concerned.

'Hello,' she said in almost a whisper without really looking at me. She turned to Tigger. 'You have business to discuss with Mr Tree. I'd better go and tell Cyril.' She flashed her ghost eyes at me. 'It was nice meeting you, Mr Tree,' she said and immediately looked away.

'Oh, the pleasure was all mine.' I felt real twittery like I was going to giggle for no reason and make a goddamn fool of myself. As she walked away I noticed most of the men stopped working to watch her go.

'That is a woman and a half,' I said appreciatively.

'She's a nice girl.' There was a little bit of a warning in Tigger's voice.

'Yeah . . . well, I can see that.'

He didn't want to discuss Celine. 'I just can't take another man on. Sorry.'

'It's only for a while. Michael and I are on our way west.'

'Yeah, he told me. He's a likeable boy.'

'I guess everybody likes Michael.'

Tigger moved uncomfortably from one foot to the other. He was a man who clearly didn't like to have to say no to anyone. 'I wish there was something I could do but I got all the men I need. There just isn't enough money . . .' A little light came into his eyes. 'Hey, wait a minute. Just wait one darn minute. Celine,' he called and she stopped.

'Yes?'

'Come back here, will you?' She started back in our direction still picking her way carefully on those treacherous high heels.

'You're a nice-enough-looking fellow,' Tigger said to me. 'You ever done any acting?'

I figured, one way or the other, I had been acting every damn day since I popped my head out of my mother's womb. 'Sure. In high school and in college,' I lied. 'I was the star of the drama club. My teacher said I should have gone on the stage professionally.'

He kicked at the dust and said, 'Now, I don't know if this will work . . . I don't have anything to do with stuff like this, it's up to Cyril, but . . . you never know.' Celine walked up to us. 'You know that problem you were talking about. Well, maybe John Tree here could help out. You know what I mean, until Cyril can get somebody from Chicago. Why don't you take him to see what Cyril says.'

Celine looked at me then turned to Tigger. 'You think? Isn't he a little old?'

I was offended because I never thought of myself as too old for anything.

'You just never know,' said Tigger and Celine walked away with me following right behind her.

'Let me just tell my friend.' I walked along with her and the slightest bit of wind blew her perfume in my direction and I wanted to bury my head in her neck and breathe that fragrance until I suffocated. 'Michael, this is Celine.' It was the first time I said her name and I felt my mouth water as the word passed over my lips. I told him I was going with her and that I'd be right back.

'You sure you're coming back?' He got all nervous looking.

'Yes, I'm sure. I'm just going with her to see about a job. Isn't that right, Celine?'

'You're not running off and leaving me, are you?' He made a little move in my direction and I could feel Celine looking at me like I was some terrible kind of man who deserts his friends.

'No, I'm not going to leave you. Jesus!' I tried to laugh it off.

She reached out and touched his arm. 'He'll be back in a few minutes. Really, he will.' She smiled and the Angel relaxed and just like that I could see they made some kind of personal connection. Some kind of connection she certainly didn't make with me. Those big black eyes of his, so dark you couldn't even see the pupils, got all soft and she locked right into them and I could damn near feel an understanding between them and I had this queasy feeling in my stomach which it didn't take long for me to realize was a flash of jealousy. It was downright ridiculous because I had never thought of him as anything but a little kid. What did I have to be jealous of? Hell, he didn't even know he could use his cock for anything but peeing. But in that split second, with Celine's hand resting on his arm, I saw him not only as a man, and a tall, handsome man, but also as a threat, and I didn't like it one goddamn little bit.

'Come on, Celine. We better go.' I felt I had to get her away from him before the connection got any stronger.

'I'll be waiting right here,' said the Angel, all his apprehension gone. 'Me and the boys got a lot of work to do.' He was proud to be a working man who was part of a team and I didn't like that either because somehow it diluted my control over him and even if he wasn't aware of it, I was.

On the ride downtown where I was to meet Cyril Blythe, Celine didn't say much. She asked about the Angel and I gave her my cousin story which she seemed to accept without further questioning. A few times she turned her head away from me, pretending to be interested in something on the sidewalk and slipped the white thing out of her pocket and nibbled on it. I couldn't for the life of me imagine what the hell it was and I almost asked her but I thought that might be a little forward and I was doing everything I could to impress her. It had been a long time since that night in Lowell, Massachusetts when Millie Quick and I rumpled the sheets in Pinabaugh's boarding house before I hit the road for Pittsburgh and I was feeling all kinds of twitching in my private parts just sitting next to Celine in the car and smelling that intoxicating perfume. I already had big plans for us and I didn't want anything to mess them up.

'What's this acting job?' I asked. I figured I had a right to know at least that much.

'Our juvenile ran off with the dentist's daughter.'

'*Who* ran off?'

'Billy Cox. He played all the juvenile parts. You know, the young men. Cyril's going to have a fit. Not that it will come as a surprise to him.' All the time she talked to me she looked straight ahead, never once glancing my way. I was hoping she'd at least be curious. 'They say that girl's been after Billy since the company played Mt Pleasant last season. I just joined them this year. But I heard all about her. She followed Billy from town to town all summer long. And Billy did a tour of some farce in the winter and she showed up at almost every theatre. Lydia, that's Cyril's wife and the leading lady, said the dentist practically tied the girl down but it didn't do a bit of good. Can you believe that? Well, she finally hooked Billy which was no easy feat because he had more girls than you can shake a stick at. At least that's what everybody says.' She turned her face to the right and nibbled again.

'Where you from?' I asked, trying to keep the conversation going.

'Around,' she said vaguely as if she barely heard the question.

'I'm from Pittsburgh.'

'Uh huh,' she mumbled without showing a bit of interest.

'That's right,' I said. And the conversation was over.

Cyril Blythe wasn't quite what I expected. I thought an actor should look like an actor but he was so ordinary he could have been a farmer or plumber or anything else, for that matter. He was probably mid to late fifties, not too tall, not too stocky, just about as average a man as a person was ever likely to meet. But he was warm and easy, the kind of man that met everybody on equal ground. He was with the rest of the company in a hall on the third floor of the Union Building where they were rehearsing one of their plays. Celine had had the afternoon off so they were all surprised to see her when we walked in. After she introduced me she told them about Billy Cox running off and everybody got upset, especially Cyril, who started pacing up and down, and Celine said that Tigger had sent me over because I might be able to fill in for Billy until they got an actor from Chicago. Everybody looked at me like I was standing there stark naked and I wanted to run down those three flights of stairs and get the hell out of town.

'Where'd you come from?' asked Cyril.

'Just passing through.'

'You ever been on a stage?'

I told him the same story I had told Tigger about being a star in school.

'What plays have you been in?'

'*Uncle Tom's Cabin* and *Journey's End*.' It was the best I could come up with.

'My God, another amateur,' said a tall, thin woman with dyed ginger hair, big eyes rimmed with black and cheekbones like a skeleton. 'I'm surrounded by them.' Her voice was deep and cultured. She threw herself down in a folding chair by the window and lit a cigarette and I noticed her fingernails were long and painted the colour of blood. Her name was Amanda Wedgeworth and she was the character woman.

'Don't pay any attention to her,' said an older man with bushy eyebrows and a bulbous nose. 'She was in vaudeville on the Orpheum Circuit one season as a magician's assistant and she thinks she's Sarah Bernhardt. My name's Grayson Livingstone.'

'That's a laugh,' hissed Amanda Wedgeworth. 'Grayson my foot! It used to be Gray Livingstone, but he counted the number of letters in my name and added the *son* so his name would be longer than mine on the bill.' She took a puff of her cigarette, those long nails curling around her cheek. 'He's not only a minor talent he's also a minor human being.'

'Don't you two start,' said Cyril. 'We got a serious problem on our hands and I don't need you making it any worse.'

The two other people rehearsing were Lydia Noble and Carlton Kearney.

Lydia, who Celine had said was Cyril's wife, was much younger than Cyril. Maybe twenty years or so. Pale pink and white-blonde, she was as plump as a doll baby. Hell, she wasn't plump. She was fat. Short and fat and all smiles. She must have been at least sixty pounds overweight. There were little blue bows in her hair and dimples just about every place a dimple could be. Even her elbows. Her make-up was thick enough to scrape off with a trowel but she was just as pleasant as she could be.

'I think he'll do just fine,' she cooed to Cyril, looking my way as she took his arm. She wasn't being flirtatious or anything like that, she was merely trying to be reassuring to me and I appreciated it.

Carlton Kearney, who was the heavy, playing all the villains, was what I thought an actor should look like. He had a face you'd see on a coin, sculptured and dignified. His hair was greying and perfectly combed and everything about him was clean and in place. And for a man in what looked like his late forties he had a good body: broad shoulders, slim hips and a flat gut. This was a man who took care of himself. He probably never smoked a cigar or took a drink of hard liquor in his life. The odd thing was that, for someone who had every bit of good looks a man his age could want, there was something uncomfortable and withdrawn about him, something I spotted the minute I laid eyes on him. It struck me that for an actor he was kind of shy and distant. When he shook my hand he made very brief eye contact and then his focus sort of drifted to my nose and he let go of my hand like it was on fire.

'How are you?' he said warmly, but his discomfort was still there.

'Twenty dollars a week,' said Cyril. 'If you were a pro it'd be twenty-five but you don't have any experience. And, mind you, it's just until we get an actor out of Chicago. After all, we're a professional company.'

'Ha!' Amanda Wedgeworth blew a big cloud of smoke. 'That's a laugh.'

And the Angel Sang

And so, all of a sudden, I was an actor and the Angel was a canvasman. It should have been the other way around since we were on our way to Hollywood to make him a movie star but I didn't think I could push him on stage right then because he could barely read and he would have made every character sound like Nat and Dora, not to mention Buttercup the cow. For the time being it was fine. Money was money and we needed it. Christ, but we needed it! And I needed time to figure out how I was going to get the cufflinks back from that old son of a bitch in the jewellery shop.

As far as lodging was concerned, we had our choice of getting a room with one of the citizens of Mt Pleasant or sleeping on folding cots under the stage with the rest of the canvasmen and we chose sleeping under the stage because it was free. Cyril and Lydia and, as it turned out, Celine, stayed at the hotel. It was good business and it gave the impression of affluence.

The Angel was having the time of his life. Tigger said he was the hardest worker he had ever hired and, as usual, the Angel liked everybody and everybody liked him and also, as usual, more than once he asked me if maybe working on the tent show was heaven. He wasn't about to give up his search for heaven no matter what. He never said much about Hollywood. I suppose in his mind it was nothing more than a stopover on the Glory Road.

Well, I was *definitely* already in some kind of heaven because I spent my days with the delicious Celine. She didn't have a single movement, not the slightest toss of her head, that didn't stir something in me. I wanted her as deep down in my bones as I had ever wanted anything in my whole life. Not that it did me a whole hell of a lot of good. The more I was around her and the more I ached to touch her, the more indifferent she became. She damn near made me feel invisible. That had never happened to me before with a woman so, naturally, she was absolutely irresistible. From what I could pick up there weren't any other men in her life so at first I thought it was smooth sailing. But unless she was in character and we were rehearsing a scene she hardly talked to me and when she wasn't up rehearsing she was off in the corner, studying her lines and nibbling on the mystery white thing.

The plays were all about the same thing. Mostly a city slicker being bested by simple country folk. The stories and the costumes and settings were different but the message wasn't. Some were pretty good and some weren't very good at all. There was one thing, however, that was absolutely consistent. Me. I sure in hell was no actor. Stiff as a board, I stunk like a week-old fish. They were all nice to me, encouraging and pretending I was OK, but I knew what they were really thinking. I also knew that Cyril had put in a call to an agent in Chicago and as soon as they could find an actor, I was going to be just a memory to them. But since I got to do most of my scenes with Celine, secretly sneaking a sniff whenever I could, I didn't care. And the truth was, she wasn't much better an actor than me but she was so pretty nobody cared. Amanda Wedgeworth didn't like either one of us too much but then Amanda didn't like anybody. She was meaner than cat shit. Tigger Book said it was because the magician, the one she assisted on the Orpheum circuit, had married her but then run off with a pretty young fire-eater, just two weeks after the wedding. And Amanda never got over it. Whatever the reason, she didn't like anybody.

Carlton Kearney, as shy as ever, tried to give me pointers and every so often, when he'd get kind of excited about what he was saying about acting, he'd touch my shoulder or arm, then all of a sudden he'd pull his hand away, apologize and leave. I couldn't pay any attention to what he was saying because I was always waiting for that knee-jerk reaction. He was trying to be helpful, there was no doubt about it, but he was such a nervous wreck he made me nervous.

Grayson Livingstone, Amanda's arch enemy, who always had the slight smell of whiskey on him, turned out to be a good old boy, easy going and comfortable as a hound dog. After three wives, all actresses, and three divorces he had settled into being a bachelor with the occasional woman to spice things up. His landlady in Mt Pleasant for one. He always stayed with her when the show was in town. As he put it, at his age he just did it once in a while to prove to himself that he still could. He liked to read and said it was impossible to find a woman who was as interesting in bed as a good book. Especially when accompanied by a few shots of corn liquor. I suppose the Comedians were the only real family he had, especially Cyril and Lydia, and show business was his whole life. He was forever telling me I was going to get greasepaint under my skin and that I'd never get over wanting to be up there on the stage, parading around in front of the footlights. Well, I didn't say it to *him* but he was full of shit. He couldn't have been further from the truth if he tried. I hated it. It was embarrassing and stupid to get up in front of people and pretend I was someone else. Hell, I never even played that kind of make-believe when I was a kid. Not to mention saying words that were as dumb as anything I ever heard. I felt like a damn fool and that was just in front of the other actors. I hadn't even been up on a stage with an audience yet. I couldn't understand how a grown-up person could spend his whole life being an actor. It made no sense at all to me. However, I didn't let any of those feelings interfere with my plans for the Angel in Hollywood. It would be him up there on the screen making a jackass of himself, not me. I'd just be collecting my share of the loot and living the good life.

Cyril, who directed the shows and was the leading man, even though he was twenty years too old, was all things to admit I thought was a diamond until Grayson Livingstone told me it was a fake, used to impress the locals and make them think the Cyril Blythe Comedians were rich and famous. He also carried a roll of one-dollar bills with a hundred-dollar bill on the outside and he flashed that around town every chance he got. The truth was he was always worried about money and by necessity a penny pincher, but at the same time, if anybody needed a handout he was a soft touch. Every bum and drunk in town knew he was good for some change and Grayson said it was the same in every town they played. Cyril had a different and personal relationship with everybody in the company, from Lydia to Tigger Book to Tigger's girlfriend, Fern Pearl, the near-sighted, hook-nosed piano player who also ran the candy and souvenir concessions. He had that special knack of being close to everybody, right down to the last canvasman. Even with the Great Dane, Toby, and the burro, Little Texas, who didn't serve any purpose except for being pampered pets and eating like a couple of horses. And he seemed to have a very special relationship with Celine; suspiciously private and a little too dangerously intimate. At first, it about drove me crazy. They were always off together, whispering about something or other and sharing secrets. But at the same time, it was hard to believe there was something going on between them because, from what I could see, chunky little Lydia was the light of Cyril's life. As far as he was concerned she was the most beautiful woman in the world and he was forever telling her and she lapped it up like a cat laps cream. He had no idea she was too fat to play the leading lady roles because he was certain everyone else thought she was as beautiful as he did. And somehow, when she got herself squeezed into her dresses, corseted so much her neck disappeared and her eyes bugged out and her cheeks got fatter, she actually did look beautiful. Of course, it was that pleasant nature of hers, shining through no matter how fat she looked. She appeared to like everyone, even Amanda, who when Lydia wasn't within earshot, referred to her as the fat lady in the circus. I was sure Lydia knew how Amanda felt about her but it didn't make any difference. She was doing what she wanted with the man she wanted to be with and that was all that mattered. She loved Cyril as much as he loved her and she probably saw him as a glamorous leading man, not a paunchy middle-aged guy who was as undistinguished as a board fence. According to Grayson, who had been one of Cyril's comedians for more years than he wanted to think about and who was best man at their wedding, they were perfectly happy except for one thing. Lydia wanted a baby and try as hard as they did –

and from what Grayson said, they tried real hard – she couldn't seem to get pregnant.

There was one thing the Angel could do for his up-coming Hollywood career while we were a part of the Comedians. It was the one thing I knew he could do without making a fool of himself. He could sing. I told Cyril about his voice and we all got together on a break with Fern Pearl at the piano so Cyril could hear him.

'He better be able to sing in the key I play,' said Fern Pearl as she sat stiff backed at the upright, 'because it's the only key I know how to play in.'

'Fern doesn't read music.' Cyril was settling into a seat in the front row with Lydia. The rest of the company was scattered around the tent. 'But she can play any song she ever heard. She's a wonder.'

'Is this going to take long?' Amanda lit a cigarette. 'It's cutting into our rehearsal time and God knows, this little *group*' – the word almost exploded in her mouth – 'desperately needs it.'

'Why don't you try to relax for a change?' said Grayson Livingstone.

'Why don't you retire and drop off the planet?' hissed Amanda.

'Why don't you both shut up?' Cyril's word was law. They did shut up.

'Are you nervous?' I asked the Angel.

'Nope. Should I be nervous?'

'He's adorable,' said Lydia.

'The girls will go for him, that's for sure.' Grayson made a little clicking sound with his tongue.

'Even if he can't sing,' added Carlton who was sitting off to the side by himself.

Celine who didn't say a word was watching the Angel and smiling like a Cheshire cat.

'Well, let's get on with this. What are you going to sing?' asked Cyril.

'What should I sing, John?'

'What do you want to sing?'

'Can I sing "Alexander's Ragtime Band"?'

Without a moment's hesitation Fern started playing the introduction to the song and right away I noticed the Angel's wing things starting to keep time and I knew we might be in trouble. I hadn't thought about how much the Angel liked the sound of a piano and how uncontrollable his wings could be and I wasn't prepared to explain them to Cyril Blythe and the Comedians.

'Just a minute,' I broke in. 'I forgot to tell Michael something.' I went to him and put my arm around his shoulders so the wings couldn't move. 'Can I take him backstage and talk to him for a minute? It won't take long, I promise.'

'Oh, God.' Amanda shuffled around in her seat.

'Give them a minute,' said Lydia, taking Cyril's hand. 'We all know how hard auditions are.'

I grabbed the Angel and dragged him back to the men's dressing room. 'Take off your shirt, quick.'

'Why?' The Angel was completely confused.

'Your wings! The damn things won't stay still.'

'Oh, I'm sorry, John. I didn't even know they were moving.'

'Take off your shirt. Hurry up.' He did while I searched for something to use to bind down his wings. There was a towel covering the make-up at Grayson's place at the table and I tore it in strips, tying the pieces together and started wrapping it around the Angel's chest and shoulders, criss-crossing his back.

'I can hardly breathe,' he gasped.

'Tough shit. I don't care if you smother as long as the damn wings don't move. Now put your shirt on and let's get out there. You can't keep your audience waiting. And you sing just as good as you can. You hear what I'm saying?'

'Yes, John.'

'Like you did in the car and with Doc Forepaugh.'

'Why don't you sing with me, John?'

'No, no. You sing alone. They don't want to hear me sing. Besides, it's good experience for you.' We went back to the piano.

'Are we ready now?' asked Fern Pearl who was clearly annoyed, her fingers poised over the keys.

'Ready.' I sat next to Cyril and Lydia in the front row and I have to admit, even if the Angel wasn't nervous, I was.

He stood there, as unselfconscious as ever, a big warm smile on his face and his eyes shining, and just started singing.

> '*Come on and hear,*
> *Come on and hear,*
> *Alexander's Ragtime Band . . .*'

His voice, that rich, sweet baritone, soared, filling every corner of the tent and he sang with such obvious enjoyment, moving so naturally to the music, I could just feel the effect he was having on everybody.

> '*Come on and hear,*
> *Come on and hear,*
> *It's the best band in the land . . .*'

It was downright astounding. From the looks on all the faces we could have been sitting in goddamn Carnegie Hall listening to Caruso or somebody great like him. And I have to admit, I was proud of the Angel. Fern Pearl was so impressed she damn near stopped playing just so she could sit there and listen to him. He never sounded better and the more he sang the more he got into it and those actors just sat there in a trance. Even Amanda Wedgeworth, sour as she was, was mesmerized, with a smile on her face and the ash growing long and cold on her cigarette. Grayson and Carlton, I'm sure without even knowing it, rose to their feet as if sitting didn't give them enough of a good thing. Cyril had his arm around Lydia and they both had grins on their faces like they were listening to some kind of music they never heard before.

'They can play a bugle call like you never heard before,
So natural that you want to go to war;
That's just the bestest band what am, honey lamb . . .'

Tigger and the rest of the canvasmen and the kids who were always hanging around started drifting into the tent, standing in the entrances swaying to the music and just as caught up as everyone else was.

'Come on along,
Come on along,
Let me take you by the hand . . .'

And by the time the song was finished the Angel had quite an audience. For a split second there, when the music was over, nobody moved or clapped or said a word. And then, all hell broke loose. Lydia and Cyril were up hugging the Angel and everyone else was cheering and clapping, jumping around like they lost their minds. I looked over at Celine and she was all curled up rocking back and forth and munching away on the white blob. It was like some gleeful thing a kid would do. The Angel hit a nerve deep down in everybody who heard him sing, there was no doubt about it. And I was surer than I had ever been before that Hollywood was the only and perfect place for him to be.

Fern Pearl spent the next few days teaching the Angel some new songs. After his impressive audition he didn't do too much more work as a canvasman because Cyril knew he had something special and he started advertising around town. And I started being a manager. First thing, I thought the Angel was worth more than ten dollars to Cyril so I asked to have his salary doubled. We negotiated and I settled for fifteen dollars a week. It didn't seem like too much but what the hell, it was a fifty per cent increase. And there was an excitement to the negotiating. I knew how much Cyril wanted the Angel to sing the vaudeville in the intermissions and Cyril knew that I knew and that put me in the position of top dog. It was an unusual place for me, one I was hardly ever in in my lifetime. It felt damn good to be there, too. Then I wanted some decent clothes for him so Cyril dug out an old tuxedo and some pants and a shirt and Lydia altered them. They were a little on the small side but they still looked a hell of a lot better than Doc Forepaugh's old duds. When he was being fitted I had to be careful nobody saw him with his shirt off so I did the measuring and told everyone he was so modest he got upset if anyone saw him without clothes. They bought it but I know they thought there was something real strange about us.

'My mother was a seamstress,' said Lydia, smiling as she

was working at letting the pants of the tuxedo down. 'She used to do piece work for the actors when they came through town. We lived in Grand Rapids. She also rented rooms to them for extra money. Oh Lord, we always needed extra money because my father never made very much. He was an inventor.' She chuckled and took a minute to rest her eyes. 'Least that's what he called himself. What he was, really, was a handyman who made gadgets.' She laughed out loud. 'You should have seen some of that junk. One of my favourites was an automatic bread-slicer and -server.' She was laughing uncontrollably and could hardly get the words out. 'It sliced the bread and then this little gadget was supposed to hand you the slice. I'll never forget that suppertime when he tried it out. First off, it was so big there was hardly any room for food on the table. Then, when it sliced the bread it crumbled it so there was no slice for the machine to hand you. My mother said it was the best breadcrumb-maker she had ever seen. She laughed so hard she almost wet her pants. He was always a good sport about being laughed at. He had to be because most of his inventions were like that. There wasn't a day that went by that he didn't think he was going to invent something that would make us millionaires. Poor Daddy. He always had his head in the clouds. But he was kind and loving and my mother just thought the sun rose and set on him. We all did.' She went back to her sewing. Her fat little fingers, dimpled at the knuckles, looked like they really knew what they were doing with a needle and thread. 'That's how I met Cyril. He rented a room from us. Yes, he did. I was fourteen the day he walked up on the porch and knocked on the door and I thought he was the handsomest man I had ever seen. I fell in love with him the first time I clapped eyes on him. I really did. That night, as I was getting into bed, I told my mother that I was going to marry him some day and she told me to stop being so foolish and to go to sleep. When I was lying there in the dark I actually made plans for my wedding. That's the truth. And two years later, when I was sixteen, I did marry him. That's how I became an actress.' She bit off a thread. 'There, that ought to do it. You're going to look like a fashion plate, Michael.'

The Angel took to all the attention like he was waiting for it his whole life. And, when he wasn't learning songs or having people fuss over him or having clothes remade, if Celine had the time, she was teaching him how to write. He had school notepads that he kept with the rest of his library and a person would have thought they were made of gold. Celine and the Angel were becoming closer and closer and I didn't like it one little bit. Not that there seemed to be anything between them, of a sexual nature I mean. I just didn't know what the hell was going on. I guess they were more like brother and sister. Like little kids playing together. As much of a woman as Celine was, and it was plain to see without a second glance that she was enough woman for any man, there was something childlike about her. The same as the Angel. And I suppose him being so simple and naive appealed to her. But there sure in hell was nothing about *me* that appealed to her. I did everything I could short of standing on my head in front of the courthouse to get her to notice me but she wouldn't have any part of it. She made me feel like a fungus or something. However, that didn't keep me from trying and getting more and more frustrated every day. But it was almost as if she was afraid of me. Whenever I came around she clammed up and hardly looked at me but as soon as I walked away the two of them started talking and laughing like it was me they were talking about and that just irritated the shit out of me. It made me edgy and I started resenting the Angel but at the same time, because he was getting so close to her, I found out things about Celine I never would have known. Like, for instance, what it was she was always chewing on.

'Tell me something,' I said to the Angel one night when we were getting ready to slip under the stage and go to bed. The rest of the canvasmen were in town and we had the place to ourselves. 'What does Celine think of me?'

'She never said.'

'She doesn't mention me at all?'

'Just to say you seem to look after me real good. She said that once.'

'Does she like me?'

'She never said.'

He was starting to get on my nerves. 'Well, what the hell do you two talk about all the time?'

'Stuff.'

'What stuff?'

'Just stuff.'

'What's that white thing she's always chomping on?'

'Plaster.'

'Plaster! What are you talking about?'

'It's a big old hunk of hard plaster. She likes to take little bites of it. She also eats wood and wallpaper. Least that's what she told me. But it's a secret so don't you tell nobody.'

I could hardly believe my ears. 'You're making that up.'

'I am not. It's a big old hunk of plaster.'

I knew it had to be the truth because the Angel just didn't have it in him to lie to me. He's one of the few people I ever met who wasn't capable of lying. 'Christ! Plaster and wall-paper! Is she crazy?'

'No, she's not crazy. She's real nice. And she's real good

at teaching me how to write. I can do the alphabet and my name and your name and her name. C . . . E . . . L . . . I . . . N . . . E.' He made the letters in the air with his finger. 'Pretty soon I'll be able to write a letter to Dr Forepaugh and Mr Ridge.'

'Plaster, for God's sake.' He was rambling on about writing letters and she was eating plaster. The shock almost made me dizzy. 'I never heard of anybody eating plaster. And wallpaper!'

'She says she especially likes the glue on it.' He smiled like he was talking about mustard on a sandwich. 'Promise you won't tell nobody. She asked me not to but I reckon I can tell you anything. Angels can tell each other anything. Can't they, John?'

'Plaster and wood and wallpaper! I never heard anything so crazy in my life. Does Cyril know she's eating that shit?'

'Maybe.'

'They put people in the nut house for doing crazy stuff like that.'

'Why?' He didn't seem to think there was anything particularly wrong with it. 'If it tastes good to a person why shouldn't they eat it?'

'Who the hell eats plaster, for Christ's sake?'

'You ever try it?'

Well, I couldn't get through the night thinking about Celine eating all that crap. As if it wasn't bad enough my dream girl didn't give me the time of day she also carried around a piece of plaster and ate it. God! I had always heard that people in show business were different but this was pushing it to the limit. If only old Doc Forepaugh was around I thought, he might have had some kind of explanation like way back when we were just amoebas we used to get nourishment from eating stones and twigs and things. Better yet, he might have had some kind of cure because I was sure it had to be a disease. People just don't eat stuff like that. The truth of the matter was, thinking of her eating wallpaper paste and wood took the fun and excitement out of wanting to get her in bed. Well, hell, it would give any man pause. Even though that excitement, the idea of lying next to her, the both of us naked as eggs, touching and kissing and rubbing all the right places, had been a sustaining force since the day I saw her picking her way across that field in her high-heeled shoes. Breaking her down, so to speak, had become a dream, like some people dream of climbing the Himalayas or going over Niagara Falls in a barrel or crossing the Sahara desert. Although, truthfully, I never could understand why the hell anyone in their right mind would be stupid enough to want to do any of those things where you had a damn good chance of getting yourself killed. But Celine had become my Niagara Falls and I wanted to go over her any way I could and I didn't want anything to interfere with that dream. Especially something as weird as her eating plaster, for Christ's sake.

Opening night finally came and I managed to get through it without some paying customer demanding his money back. The first play of the week was a farce called *Not Quite Married*. We were all running in and out of doors and everybody was mistaking everybody else for the wrong person and it was just as silly as could be but the audience thought it was wonderful. The opening show was always fancy dress where the ladies wore evening dresses and the men formal wear. Lydia was squeezed into enough ruffles to decorate a bandstand and when she made her first entrance all the women in the audience sighed and oohed at such a beautiful creation. And when Amanda made her entrance, all slinky and sophisticated in a tight black dress, and finally Celine, in her favourite colour, orange, with her perfect shoulders and arms, cool and bare, looking good enough to eat, well, those ladies thought they were in Paris, France, on the rue de something-or-other watching a fashion show. I must admit, I cut a pretty neat figure myself in my tails – they didn't have a tuxedo to fit me – and my hair all slicked back, shirt-front starched as stiff as a board and a fake ruby flashing on my finger. But I still felt like I was making a fool of myself and being all dressed up didn't help my acting one little bit. However, there was a surprising advantage to being an actor that nobody had ever called to my attention. When the intermission came, the actors walked through the crowd selling boxes of candy and I discovered that the young girls, sitting there all dolled up in their fanciest clothes, were very impressed with me. Maybe it was the make-up, giving me bigger eyes and rosy cheeks and redder lips, making me look like a corpse ready for the grave. Whatever it was, those girls couldn't get enough of me. They didn't give a shit that I was a lousy actor. I was an *actor* and that was enough for them. And the one that stood out, the one that seemed to appreciate me the most as I walked through the crowd selling my boxes of treats, the one who looked the ripest with little yellow flowers stuck in her yellow hair, was Mary Lou, the daughter of that son of a bitch of a jeweller. By the end of that week in Mt Pleasant, I had pretty much given up the idea of ever getting my cufflinks back because he knew he had me by the balls but I was going to make him pay one way or the other or drop dead trying. I just didn't have the foggiest idea how. I had thought of burning down the jewellery shop but it was attached to buildings on both sides and I might have burned down all of the centre of commerce in Mt Pleasant. Somehow I didn't think a single pair of cufflinks warranted that. But I had to get revenge and it wasn't until I saw little Mary Lou sitting there in that audience, smelling of innocence and giving me the eye, that I knew what I was going to do. And I was ready for it. Ready and needy seeing as how Celine had me in a constant sweat and didn't seem at all interested in doing anything to cool me off. I smiled broadly at Mary Lou and she smiled back at me and I don't know what she was thinking but I was thinking it had been a long time since I had been with a girl with her cherry still intact and I was going to take it and give her the ride of her life to boot.

'How are you, you pretty thing?' I slipped her a box of the candy kisses and told her she didn't have to pay her ten cents for it. Indebtedness was always a good start with a woman. Getting them to feel like they owed you was half the battle. 'Maybe we could get together some night after the show?'

'Maybe.' She smiled and her face flushed a bit. 'I'll be at every show.'

'Well, so will I,' I said, making a little joke, and she laughed. 'How about tomorrow night?'

'OK.'

'It's not going to upset your parents, is it? I mean you going out with an older fellow?'

'You can't be that much older.' She unwrapped one of the kisses and slipped it into her mouth and the way she did it, real slow, like she was doing something obscene with it, was just about the hottest thing I had ever seen. 'Besides, they won't know anything about it. They're in Davenport visiting my Uncle Pee Wee and his new wife.'

'What about your sisters and brothers? They might see us together and tell your parents.' I had to know if there was anybody else in her house.

'I don't have any sisters or brothers. It's just me.'

Jackpot. My mind started flashing pictures and I could feel the twitching starting in my drawers. Not only would I get revenge on that son of a bitch, there was a good chance I'd get it in the very bed the bald turd slept in. 'Then tomorrow night it is, little darling.' I flashed her another smile and moved on, selling my candy.

Well, if I thought I had an effect on the ladies in the audience, it was nothing compared to the Angel. He sang his first song after the candy-selling was done and before the second act started. It was called a specialty act. He was in his tuxedo and Lydia had put a little bit of make-up on his eyes and lips and Celine had trimmed his hair just a bit and it was hanging loose and she'd put a blue wildflower in his lapel buttonhole. When I saw him, finally all put together, I thought to myself, there's no question about Hollywood loving him. America, Canada, England, the rest of Europe and any other damn place in the world where they showed moving pictures. He was something else to look at and with his hair hanging down he looked even more like the grown-up version of that kid in the Florentine art book. I had put all that out of my mind, for the sake of saving my sanity, but seeing him all prettied up I just couldn't help thinking of it. The creepy chills went right up and down my spine. I had tied his wings down and helped him get dressed but I didn't really take the time to give him a good look until he was standing in front of the mirror, and I was adjusting his tie. He sure looked like the Botticelli Angel to me and I wanted to say something about it but he seemed to have buried all that once we got involved with the show and I didn't want to start it going through his head again. He was as excited as he had been the day he told me his big secret, that he could read, on Doc Forepaugh's side porch. In fact, it looked like he had that same light in his eyes, that light that Doc Forepaugh always got when *he* was excited.

'I don't see why you don't sing with me, John. We could be real good singing up there in front of all them people.' He didn't have any idea how good he was.

'I act alone, you sing alone. That's the way it works.' I took one last look at him. 'Now get out there. Fern Pearl's at the piano.' I thought a little something from the Bible might cheer him on. 'Don't forget to make a joyful noise.'

'Sing aloud unto God our strength; make a joyful noise unto —'

'You don't have time for that now. Fern's playing your introduction. Go on.' Lydia and Cyril were standing right behind me and Celine and Grayson were with Amanda and Carlton in the wings on the other side of the stage. Tigger and all the canvasmen were scattered around watching, too.

'Nice and loud,' said Cyril as the Angel stepped on the stage, 'just the way you did it the other day.'

'Break a leg, honey,' whispered Lydia who took my hand and squeezed it.

He walked to the centre of the stage, just as he had rehearsed, as fearless as ever, gave a little wave to Fern Pearl and smiled at the audience and I could hear a kind of purr ripple through the crowd. He was singing 'Alexander's Ragtime Band' for his first song and when the stone-faced Fern Pearl, smiling like an idiot for a change, gave him the nod, he just opened up and sang out and it was everything I expected. I looked out at the audience and they were in the same kind of trance the actors had been the day he sang for them in the empty tent. That same magical kind of look was on every face as though they were hearing something they never expected to hear in this lifetime. And I got the chills again, thinking to myself that maybe it *was* something extra special, that maybe he *was* an angel. I shivered and shook the thought right out of my brain.

There was no swaying to the music, no movement at all going on in the crowd. They just sat staring and smiling. But the Angel was moving. The music was in every part of his body, just as natural as his blood, and he couldn't stop what it was doing to him any more than he could have stopped his blood flowing and I was glad I had tied down his wings or they would have burst right through his tight tuxedo jacket.

When he finished his song, I thought the applause and whooping and shouting was going to tear the tent at the seams. The Angel just stood there beaming and I swear to God, as true as I'm putting all this down on paper, it was like he was radiating a special kind of yellow-white light. Whether anybody else saw it or not I don't know, but it was there, there was no doubt about it. I looked at Lydia but she wasn't seeing much of anything too clearly because of the tears in her eyes. Cyril had a tear or two, too and he wasn't doing a thing to hide them. From what I could see of Celine and the rest of them across the stage, I had a feeling maybe they were seeing something strange because they all had peculiar looks on their faces. It was the goddamnedest thing, something beyond the reach of anybody in that tent was happening and I would have bet good money that not a one of them could put a name to it. Fern Pearl started playing the introduction to the second song, 'They Didn't Believe Me', a new song she had taught the Angel, and everyone quieted down like they were sitting in a church. All we needed were the stained-glass windows and a pipe organ. The Angel planted himself and his face took on a different look, almost mysterious, and he started.

'And when I told them how beautiful you are
They didn't believe me,
They didn't believe me.
Your lips, your eyes, your cheeks, your hair
Are in a class beyond compare,
You're the loveliest girl that one could see!'

Fern Pearl's accompaniment suddenly sounded like a damned symphony orchestra. She was so carried away she was playing chords she didn't even know existed. Maybe they didn't for all I know. This time the Angel didn't move a muscle, he focused his eyes in a way that looked like he was singing privately to every person there. Peeking out front I could see there was a whole tent full of women who believed every word he was singing. The men looked like they were believers, too, for that matter. The Angel had them all right in the palm of his hand. I had never heard him sing a slow song except for little bits when Fern Pearl was teaching him and I could hardly believe that that inexperienced kid could put so much meaning into such a pretty romantic song. Hell, he had never even kissed a girl.

'And when I tell them,
And I'm certainly going to tell them
That I'm the man
Whose wife one day you'll be . . .'

Across the stage in the shadow of the wings damned if Amanda wasn't standing there with Grayson's hand on her shoulder. I'm not lying. And she wasn't raising hell either. In fact she was smiling and I thought she looked sort of pretty and I could see what a truly good-looking woman she must have been when she was younger, back when she was that magician's assistant, before she turned sour. Celine was nowhere to be seen but Carlton was still there, looking as handsome as a Greek statue, half hiding in the shadows, dabbing at his eyes every once in a while. It beat all hell out of me why everybody was all teary. It wasn't like the Angel was a cripple who suddenly got up out of his wheelchair and started walking, for Christ's sake. It was just him out there singing. Granted he was singing better than anybody I had ever heard but still, it was just singing. I wondered what had happened to Celine when all of a sudden I got a whiff of that tantalizing perfume of hers and I turned and she was right next to Cyril holding his hand. It seemed the Angel's magical singing was working a charm on everyone so I thought it might be a good time to get close to Celine but when I went and stood next to her, I'll be goddamned if she didn't move to the other side of Cyril so there'd be a barrier between us. I started to think maybe I smelled bad or something because I couldn't win for trying with that girl. Lydia slipped her fat little arm around my waist and held on to me while the Angel went on with his song. I felt she knew how much I was smitten with Celine. When I think back, the way I was always mooning after her, I suppose everybody knew it.

> '*They'll never believe me, they'll never believe me,*
> *That from this great big world*
> *You've chosen me.*'

No doubt about it, the Angel was the hit of the evening. I don't think the audience paid too much attention to the rest of the play after he sang.

*

'You could have any girl in that tent if you wanted her,' I said when everyone had left the dressing room and I was taking the binding off his wings.

'Aw . . .' He fidgeted around, embarrassed as he always was when I came anywhere near the subject of sex.

'There wasn't a dry pair of panties in the house when you finished singing your song. I'm not kidding you.'

'Hurry up and get those rags off, John. My wings are itching.' He was changing the subject and I knew it. We had had a few discussions about men and women and doing it and he kind of knew about it but it was in terms of the chickens he looked after when he was home and his mother was selling eggs to keep them alive. I told him that chicken love and human love weren't exactly in the same category. As curious as he was about everything else he seemed to know all he wanted to about that particular subject. And if I forced the issue he started quoting his Bible and that drove me crazy and usually put an end to the conversation. 'Scratch right between them, will you?'

'You're going to have to do it sooner or later. Hell, boy, you're full grown, it's about time you started getting some use out of that pecker of yours. If you don't, it'll just rot and fall off.' I scratched between his wings good and hard and he made all kinds of satisfied sounds.

'You always say things like that,' he laughed. 'Fall off,' he repeated. 'That's a good joke.' It was a measure of how he was catching on to the world the way he didn't take me as literally as he always had.

'It's not a joke. You got to get a little pussy. And I'm not talking about a cat and you know it. And don't start the Bible stuff, either. I think I've heard all those quotes by now, anyway.'

He changed into his work clothes and neatly hung up the tuxedo. 'They liked me tonight, didn't they, John?'

'You're a crazy person, you know that?' I said, knowing the conversation about him and sex was over. 'Yes, they liked you. I never in all my life saw people like a singer so much.'

'*And all the people came up after him, and the people piped with pipes, and rejoiced with great joy, so that the earth rent with the sound of them*. I Kings 1:40.'

'Well, I didn't hear any pipes but I was sure I heard the earth renting a little.'

He smiled happily and sat himself down so I could get the grease paint off his face. 'Celine liked my singing, didn't she?'

That annoyed me. 'Everybody liked your singing, OK? Jesus!'

'But Celine liked it special, don't you think?'

'What in the hell is it with you and Celine, anyway?'

'She's teaching me how to write.'

'I know that. Christ, that's all you talk about.' I spelled Celine in the air with my finger, mocking him. 'I know she is teaching you how to write.' I rubbed hard getting the red off his lips.

'Why are you getting mad, John? Did I do something bad?'

'Just shut up. I can't get this crap off your face if you keep on jawing at me.' And that's all it took to start that guilty feeling. That rolling in my stomach that came on like a sudden gas attack. It was some kind of an affliction and it was all the Angel's fault. All I did was yell at him a little. Sometimes he really was a pain in the ass.

Mary Lou and the Way West

I had to put my date with Mary Lou off a day because the following afternoon about the worst thing that can happen to a tent show happened. There was a storm, which in itself isn't too bad but this was a storm with a powerful wind and wind is the mortal enemy of the tent. That morning there were a few clouds to the west that nobody was paying any attention to when all at once, like an express train rushing through a local stop, the storm hit. There was thunder and lightning as fierce as I'd ever seen and rain pelting down so hard the ground didn't have time to absorb it and before anybody knew what was happening, everything flooded. But that God-awful wind was the worst part. It wasn't a tornado but it was as close as I ever want to get to one. Of course, the show was cancelled, which hit Cyril real hard in the pocketbook but there wasn't anything he could do about it. In that part of the country nobody in their right mind went out if there was even the possibility of a tornado.

The whole company showed up at the lot to help tie everything down. Tigger Book took over as the boss man and directed every move with the efficiency of Alexander the Great commanding his armies. The first thing the canvasmen did was throw a rope, called a belly band, over the top of the tent. That was to keep it from blowing away altogether. And then all the poles were double staked and tied with extra lines. Luckily there was a rain before the wind hit so the water tightened up the canvas but there were still pockets of water that had to be dumped out of the roof of the tent. That was my job. I had a flat piece of board attached to the end of a pole and every place I saw the rain accumulating I had to push up and dump it out. My arms were so goddamned sore I thought they were going to fall off. The Angel was in the dressing rooms with Lydia and Amanda and Celine covering the costumes and putting the trunks and stuff up on boards to keep them out of the flood. I got a look at Celine, all wet, with her dress sticking to her like a second skin, outlining everything I wanted to touch, and I could hardly keep my mind on my water dumping. The Angel told me later that it was while they were running around trying to keep everything dry, with all the roaring of the wind and the flashing of the lightning and the thunder reverberating, that Lydia announced she was finally going to have a baby and the three women hugged each other and started jumping up and down and shrieking like there wasn't even a damn storm tearing up half of Iowa. Even Amanda, the old prune face, was overjoyed for the good fortune of the 'fat lady in the circus'.

Toby, the Great Dane, thought all the hollering and racing around was a big old game and was running in circles, barking and having a hell of a good time, covered from head to paw with mud and enjoying every bit of it. And Little Texas, the burro, who was tied to the back of one of the Model T trucks, was scared shitless every time the lightning flared and the thunder crashed and he kicked and pulled and finally broke loose of his tether and took off for town like he was running in the Kentucky Derby. Cyril said to let him go because there wasn't a car on the road so he'd probably be perfectly safe until the storm was over and we found him. There was the danger of him tearing up some citizens' flower gardens if there were any flower gardens left after the wind but, as Cyril said, 'Fuck 'em.' Between him and Tigger, everything that could be done was done as fast as was humanly possible and the only thing left to do was wait out the storm. We huddled in the trucks, listening to the raging of the wind and the hard beating rain. I tried to find the truck Celine was in but I couldn't. The Angel was nowhere to be seen either and it crossed my mind that the two of them were cosying up by themselves someplace maybe doing a lot more than reading lessons. Of course I knew better but since I saw him on stage with all the women going crazy over him the last thing I had was good sense where he and Celine were concerned. I was flat-out jealous of the time he spent with her and when it comes to jealousy, good sense is about the last consideration. And, to make matters worse, I was stuck in the back of a truck with Fern Pearl, a couple of smelly canvasmen and, right next to me, weird Carlton Kearney.

'You know your way around a tent in a storm, don't you,' I said. I had noticed he was doing the work of two men when we were all running around in the thick of it. The rain was hitting the roof of the truck so hard I practically had to yell at him.

'I've been there many times before. We all have. We just do our share.'

'Yeah, well, you were pretty damned impressive.'

'Your *boy* was certainly impressive. Last night, I mean,' he said, his face so close to my ear I could feel his breath.

'He's not my boy.' I tried to move away from him a bit but I was already squashed up against Fern Pearl. 'He's my cousin.'

'I didn't mean to offend.' The knee-jerk reaction was there in his voice and I thought to myself, you poor bastard, why don't you just try and relax for a minute or two, and I realized I wasn't doing anything to help him relax by snapping at him so I tried to make up for it by agreeing with him. 'He *was* pretty impressive, wasn't he?'

'It's none of my business,' he started in his apologetic way, 'but you know what I'd do if I were you?'

'What?'

'As soon as the actor gets here from Chicago, I'd take my cousin and hit the road for Hollywood, California.' He surprised me so much by bringing up Hollywood I turned to face him full on. 'I mean it. I shouldn't be saying this because Michael is money in the bank for Cyril. Oh yes, he is. And Cyril knows it. But I wouldn't think twice about going west. That boy is a natural for the talking pictures. Especially since they're making musical pictures now. A voice like his doesn't come along every day, you know.'

A flash of lightning lit up his face and it was amazing. Soaking wet, with his hair stuck to his forehead he looked like an entirely different person, unafraid and as enthusiastic as a kid. It's funny how much a person changes for the better when you know they see things the same way you do.

'Hollywood,' I said as if the idea had never crossed my mind. 'You think he'd stand a chance out there?'

'No doubt about it. So young and good looking and with a body like that. And he's a sweet boy, too. He is, he's a very sweet boy. And it comes across the footlights. I never saw an audience react like they did when he was singing. He's a very sweet boy.'

'Well, he isn't sweet all the time. He can be ornery as an army mule when he wants to be,' I lied. And right then, it crossed my mind that old Carlton might be interested in the

Angel and it was a hell of a lot more than his singing that he might be interested in. No wonder he called the Angel my *boy*! He probably had visions of the two of us rolling around in bed doing all kinds of things. If he did feel that way it explained a whole hell of a lot. Especially why he was so aware and strange about casually touching me. My automatic reaction was to move away from him and I damn near crushed Fern Pearl.

'What on earth are you doing?' she growled.

'Sorry, Fern Pearl.'

'You're hogging all the space.'

'Yeah, well . . . sorry,' I repeated. And then I had an idea. I let myself ease back in Carlton's direction and relaxed a bit. 'What you were saying, about me taking Michael to Hollywood, that's a pretty damn good thought. I wonder why it never came to me?'

'Well, I guess it occurred to me because I've been in the business so to speak for a lot of years now. It came to mind the very first time I heard Michael sing. It's a good idea, John. It really is. If I were young, I'd head for Hollywood, that's for sure. And I can't sing worth a damn.'

'Well, you're not that old. A good-looking fellow like you would probably stand a real chance of making it big out there. You keep yourself in fine shape and you've got a really good speaking voice, too. Seems you'd be a natural for the silver screen.' I didn't know exactly what I was heading for but I had a feeling the right thing to do was to grease him up. And it was easy to do because it was all true. He was good-looking and he had a fine voice. And I didn't feel I had anything to worry about, it was the Angel he was interested in, not me.

'Well, it's nice of you to say that but I couldn't go even if I wanted to. I have responsibilities.'

'A wife and kids?' I said, shocking myself at the very idea of it.

'No, no. My mother. Yeah, I look after my mother in the wintertime.'

'Your mother?'

'She's all alone. I kind of look after her. I have been for years.'

'That's a tough break. Can't she look after herself?'

I could feel he wanted to talk about it but instead he said, 'You don't want to hear all this.' He pulled back into himself for a minute just waiting for a little encouragement.

'Sure, I do. It's interesting.' I kept thinking the poor bastard probably never got a chance to talk to anybody. By his own choice by the looks of things. He was always off by himself, almost as if he was trying to be invisible. I never saw him have a conversation with a single person since the day I joined the Comedians. And, besides, with the storm whipping itself into a frenzy, I wasn't going anyplace. It helped pass the time.

'She lives in Kansas City.' He talked close to my ear as though he didn't want anyone else in the truck to hear, not that they could with the rain on the roof of the truck and all that thunder. 'My aunt Dottie, my mother's younger sister, comes and stays with her in the summer while I'm doing the shows. She's a widow from Kalamazoo and she's real active in her church in the winter and she doesn't like to be away from the congregation. I don't think faith in God has anything to do with it, she's just afraid she'll miss something.' He laughed and it surprised me because I didn't think old Carlton had the sense of humour of a door knob.

'Is your mom sick?'

'She says she is. Ever since I can remember. I never remember a time when there wasn't something wrong with her.'

'That's too bad.'

'The truth is, I don't think she's *ever* really been sick. She just said she was to keep me around. My brothers – I have three – all married and moved away.' He thought about things for a minute and I suppose he couldn't handle the possibility that he might be guilty of disloyalty. 'Maybe she *has* been sick all these years. I don't know. It doesn't matter any more.' He trailed off. 'Where's your mother?'

'Shacked up with a Polack insurance salesman someplace.'

'I wish mine was.' He laughed again. 'My mother shacked up!' That killed him and he really started laughing.

'What's so funny?' asked Fern Pearl.

'Nothing in particular. Just a little joke between Carlton and me,' I answered. Carlton was still chuckling to himself at the idea of his mother shacking up. 'Where's your old man?'

'Dead. A long time, now. We never saw much of him when he was alive. He was a travelling man. Sold ladies' foundation garments. Corsets and girdles and things like that. Mother said he didn't like us very much. But I don't think that was true. I think he liked me and my brothers but he didn't like her. I heard them fighting once and he asked for a divorce but she said she'd never give him one. Then, when I was a sophomore in high school, I found out why he didn't spend any time with us. He had a lady friend just a couple of towns away. Fact is, he had a whole family. I have a half-brother and -sister I never even saw.'

'Your old man was a bigamist?'

'Oh no, I don't think he ever married that woman. But maybe. I don't really know.' He shook his head in quiet disbelief. 'I remember once waking up in the middle of the night thinking I should hate him because of what he was doing. I mean living with that other woman. But I didn't. I didn't hate him at all. Instead I realized how much I loved him and how much I wanted to be a part of that other family. I imagined them all together, laughing and having a good time. We never laughed in our house. I don't think my mother, ever in her life, laughed.' He sat back, kind of spent, like he had said more in those few minutes than he had ever said in his life. 'Crazy what a person remembers.'

And I thought to myself, this poor bastard has spent his whole life wanting things he couldn't have.

'*You* should go to Hollywood,' I said, really meaning it. 'And I'm not shitting you, either.' Anything to get him away from that old bitch of a mother of his.

'No, that's out of the question. Anyhow, it's way too late. But not for you and Michael. You're young and you've got all the good years ahead of you. Seriously, you should go.'

'Well, it's not that easy . . .' and then it came into focus, the reason I had thought it was a good idea to be nice to him. Money. I didn't care what he thought Michael and I were doing. 'We're kind of hurting in the cash department.'

'I have a little money saved. I could loan you some and you can pay me back when you get to California.'

'Hell, I couldn't take your money. You don't even know me.'

'Yes, I do. And I'd like to do it.'

'No, no, no.' I figured a few more seconds of stalling him would do it.

'Really I would. It'll make me feel like I'm helping Michael. I never made any kind of move or took a risk in my whole life, so you and Michael can do it for me.'

'You're an actor! That seems like a pretty risky move to me.'

'I'm an actor because a cousin of mine knew Cyril and he

took me on as a kid and I just stayed. If I had had to do it on my own, believe me I never would have. Let me give you the money.'

'Well, Michael would sure look good up on that screen. That face of his is pretty near perfect. But you know that, don't you? Imagine that smile up there for everyone to look at. You're right, Carlton, Hollywood is the perfect place for him. It's one hell of an opportunity. Yeah, and it *was* your idea.'

'I could let you have a hundred dollars.'

'A hundred dollars! That's a lot of money. Lord, a hundred dollars!' It was twice as much as I expected him to offer. My protests were very convincing. 'I couldn't take a hundred dollars.' Why was it that I could act better face to face with a man when I was trying to take advantage of him than I could up on a stage in front of a bunch of strangers? I never did figure that one out.

'A hundred dollars it is and I won't hear another word about it.'

He sounded like a happy man and I was glad I could be a party to making him feel that way. 'Well as long as you're twisting my arm. I'll pay you back.'

And just like that as suddenly as it had come up, the storm was over. The sun started to come out right off the bat and I was going to be one hundred dollars richer. If it hadn't been for that storm, if old Carlton and I hadn't huddled in the truck, he never would have told me the depressing story of his miserable little life and I wouldn't have had a hundred dollars. I always say, you have to be in the right place at the right time. Even if it's in the back of a dirty old Model T truck in the middle of a tempest. Just as Doc Forepaugh said, you have to take advantage of every opportunity in this life because you only get one shot at it.

That's the bottom line. Of course, you have to be smart enough to recognize the opportunity when it presents itself. I guess it's all in the game and the way you play it.

The next day when we were drying out and getting ready for the show that night, there was nothing but talk of Lydia being in a family way. Those fat little cheeks of hers must have hurt from all the smiling and Cyril looked as though he had grown at least three inches taller. The storm was soon forgotten. It was natural, a fact of life, something that just happened and to talk about it would have been a waste of breath. But Lydia's pregnancy, also natural, also a fact of life, also something that just happened – almost – was the biggest news since World War I ended and it put new life and energy not only in Lydia but in the whole company.

Carlton was a little on the peculiar side when I first saw him that day. It was a mixture of embarrassment for having confided as much as he had in me and, at the same time, the recognition of some slight connection between us, some little intimacy that nobody but the two of us knew about. He actually blushed when I said hello but he smiled, too, hinting at a friendship that he imagined but really didn't exist. I didn't know what in hell was going through his mind when he took me aside and it made me a little nervous but, true to his word, he slipped a roll of bills into my hand and then, whispering something about not saying a word to a soul, he went on about his business, checking to see if anyone had seen us.

Mary Lou and I met after that night's show and I'm here to tell you, the storm, with all its raging and thunder and lightning, was nothing compared to what happened when the two of us got together. She waited for me in front of the tent while I got out of my costume and make-up. The Angel had been a smash hit again with his singing and word had got around and there was standing room only for the show. I had told him I was going to be away for a few hours and for one split second he got that scared look in his eyes like I was abandoning him or something but then he realized that he had made plans of his own anyway. Plans with Celine, plans that didn't include me, which didn't come as any big surprise. She was going to work with him on writing a letter to Doc Forepaugh and Saladin Ridge. And, he told me, if that letter was successful, he was going to write to my sister Aggie and Verna and Squirrel. Writing a letter to his mother didn't seem to be a consideration. Not that I wanted him to in case we were being looked for by every officer of the law in the entire United States of America. But he never talked about his mother, not since he told me about her reading the Bible to him, and my curiosity got the best of me.

'How come you never mention writing a letter to your mom?'

'I wouldn't do that.'

'Why not?'

'I don't want to disappoint her.'

'How in hell would a letter disappoint her?'

'She thinks you and me went to heaven. That's what you told her, John. That you were taking me to heaven.' It wasn't an accusation. Once again, it was merely a statement of cold, hard fact. 'Remember? That means a lot to her, me going to heaven. I'll just wait till I get there, then maybe I'll write her a letter.' It was one of those times when I was convinced he was a total idiot. He smiled. 'It won't be that long now, will it? Besides, I'll be a better letter-writer by then,' and he laughed. I didn't know whether it was his way of forgiving me because I lied to his mother or what. I did know things were going on in his head, things that for someone as simple as he was were pretty complicated, and things that I wasn't privy to. Things he didn't seem to want to talk about. I wondered if he was letting me know that he knew I had kidnapped him but I wasn't in the mood to discuss it so I went back to the matter of the letter to Doc Forepaugh.

'Where are you going to write this letter to the Doc and Saladin Ridge?' I asked as we were leaving the dressing room.

'At the hotel. In Celine's room. She's got a real nice room, John.'

'You've been in her room?'

'Well, sure.' He said it like every man in Mt Pleasant had been in her room. Every man except me, of course.

'Son of a bitch!'

'Are you mad?'

'No, I am not mad.' I could have killed him.

'Well, you sound mad. You are mad, aren't you?'

'No.'

'Can you give me a lift to the hotel?'

'No. The walk will do you good.' If he was going to spend time in Celine's room it sure in hell wasn't going to be with any help from me.

'Where do you want to go?' I asked Mary Lou as we were getting into the Willys-Knight.

'Well, it's such a nice night and the moon is so pretty and full and I never saw the sky so twinkly with stars and I thought we could just relax in the glider on our front porch and have a root beer.' She looked like a picture in an advertisement for some complexion soap. 'I have some of the latest records and we can wind up the Victrola. I think there's nothing nicer than a cold root beer on a warm night. Mama makes the best root beer in Mt Pleasant.'

I could think of a few things nicer than a cold root beer and I had every intention of introducing sweet Mary Lou to at least one or two of them. 'Sounds real nice,' I said, thinking also that I would have preferred a real beer or a whiskey rather than one of Mama's homemade root beers.

The house was a big square yellowbrick with white trim and a white picket fence. Sturdy is the word that comes to mind when I think of it. As we came up the walk I could see, from the spill of the porch light, the iris in bloom in the front yard and bright red geraniums in pristine white urns edging the steps. It was all as clean and neat as the rest of Mt Pleasant. Another picture from another calendar and the perfect setting for someone as wholesome and tasty as Mary Lou who for some reason kept reminding me of a breakfast cereal.

'You just relax on the glider and I'll get the root beer.' She was the gracious hostess with a smile on her pretty lips and a little bit of blush in her apple cheeks.

'Do you mind if I use your bathroom?'

'It's right at the top of the stairs.'

'Thanks,' I said and went up the dark wood-panelled stairs to the second floor. I didn't have to use the bathroom at all, I just wanted to get the layout of the place and I figured I might just do a little shopping for some jewellery while I was there. And where would be a better place to find some jewellery than right in a jeweller's house? Besides, that son of a bitch owed me. And if any trinkets came up missing, Mary Lou wasn't about to tell her daddy that I had been in the house so I was safe on that score. The first bedroom I came to looked like the parents' room with its big double bed covered by a quilt and everything as neat as a pin. Fast as I could I went to the dresser and started going through the drawers but I couldn't find a single damn piece of jewellery. Nothing but underwear and stockings and socks all perfectly folded and tidy as the rest of the house. I had to be missing something. I was in a jeweller's house, for Christ's sake! I looked in the wardrobe and behind the pictures on the wall just in case there was a safe but I couldn't find a thing. Mary Lou must have given the Victrola a few cranks because I could hear music downstairs. As quietly as I could I moved down the hall to the next room which was all pink and white and obviously Mary Lou's and checked through all the crap on the dressing table but there wasn't even one goddamn necklace or bracelet. It didn't make a bit of sense to me.

When I got downstairs, Mary Lou was on the glider holding two tall glasses of root beer and somebody on the Victrola was singing about finding a million-dollar baby at the five- and ten-cent store.

'Here you are,' she said, handing me the glass.

'Thanks.' I took a swig and it was so goddamn sweet I thought my teeth were going to fall out. 'Umm, this is good.'

'It's such a pretty night, don't you think?'

'As pretty a night as I've ever seen.'

'You ever see so many stars in your whole life?'

'Yeah, there's a lot of them.' But I didn't want to talk about the stars. I wanted to find out about the jewellery. 'Isn't it kind of dangerous, leaving your front door open all the time?'

'Everybody in Mt Pleasant leaves their front door open.'

'What with your father being a jeweller and all. I mean, people could break in and steal stuff.'

'They'd be wasting their time if they came here to steal jewellery. There isn't any.'

'You and your mother don't . . . ?'

'Mama was raised an Old Mennonite. She's from Ohio. Of course, she left the church when she met and married my father. But she holds on to a lot of the things she was taught as a girl. The old ways, if you know what I mean. She doesn't believe in wearing jewellery. She doesn't like me wearing it, either. I just never did and I don't miss it. We don't even own any. The fact is, Mama doesn't allow it in the house. Besides I help out in the shop so much the last thing I'm interested in is jewels. I guess it's like people working in candy stores. It gets kind of sickening after a while.'

Well, I should have expected it. If there was one house in the whole fucking world belonging to a jeweller whose wife and daughter didn't own any jewellery, not a necklace, not a bracelet, not a damn rhinestone, that would be the house *I* would plan to steal from. I was starting to think there was a serious defect in the way I went about doing things. And I was also starting to think that all my bad luck was, in a peculiar way, proof of some kind of God. Of course, the God I was conjuring up would have to be on the perverse side and flat out one mean son of a bitch if my life was any kind of testament to His existence because, there was no doubt about it, He was trying to do me in at every turn. A weaker man than me would have given up a long time ago.

'Penny for your thoughts,' cooed Mary Lou.

'Take my word for it, they're not worth a penny.'

'You're not drinking your root beer.'

'I'm not real thirsty for root beer. You wouldn't have a drop of whiskey around the place, would you?'

'Whiskey! Oh, no. Mama doesn't . . .'

'. . . allow it in the house,' I finished the sentence for her.

'Yeah. Sorry.'

'That's OK.' I was beginning to lose interest in everything.

Even Mary Lou's cherry didn't seem like such a prize. 'I think maybe I should be running along. It's getting kind of late.'

'We just got here.'

'I know but . . .'

'Come upstairs for a minute. I want to show you something before you go.'

All that day I had been trying to think of how I was going to get her upstairs and here she was inviting me and I just wasn't in the mood any more. Sex was mixed up with jewellery in my mind and having one without the other didn't seem right somehow. But I thought maybe seeing a bed in the same room with Mary Lou might sort things out and put them in their proper perspective and it had been one hell of a long time since I bedded Millie Quick and got run out of Lowell, Massachusetts. 'All right.'

She led the way up to her bedroom and when we were inside she turned on the little light on the night stand and closed the door. She stood looking at me for a few seconds and then reached down and took the hem of her dress in her hands and pulled it up to her chin and she wasn't wearing a single goddamn thing under it. I noticed right off the bat that she was a natural honey blonde. 'I went to the show like this, no underwear,' she squealed and before I could say anything she had the rest of her dress off and was standing there as naked as the day she was born, all milky white and delectable with high round breasts and dusty-pink nipples already hard and set for action. At first, I was speechless. It wasn't quite what I expected from sweet little Mary Lou. In fact, I had quite a complicated strategy planned to get her out of her clothes and her standing there in her birthday suit kind of threw me off centre. It was like watching Dr Jekyll turn into Mr Hyde right there in front of my nose. But I recovered when she started running her hands up and down her body and moving seductively in my direction. 'I'm all wet just thinking about you,' she said in a low growl. I was about to show my appreciation by saying what a pretty picture she was but in a second she had her lips locked on mine and her tongue halfway down my throat and she was tearing at my clothes and in the time it takes to blink an eye she had me stripped to the bone and sprawled out on the pink ruffled bedspread. She knew how to undo a man's pants buttons faster than I did and right then and there I reckoned that my plan for revenge, my dream of taking the cherry of the daughter of that son of a bitch of a jeweller, was nothing more than that. A dream. No question about it. Mary Lou probably hadn't had one since kindergarten.

The next half-hour was heaven, the realization of every fantasy I had had about Mary Lou since she agreed to meet me after the show. But the following three hours were hell. I was rubbed, pulled, jerked, sucked and ridden until I thought I was going to be cockless if we didn't stop. I tried to get away from her but I was burning down fast and she was young and agile and everything we did, every wild exploration with tongues and fingers and toes, seemed to recharge her and she always managed to catch up with me no matter how hard I tried to escape. We did it in her room, her parents' room, the hallway, the bathroom, the kitchen, on the staircase – perilously – and right smack dab in the middle of the iris bed in the back yard. She was every man's dream turned into the worst possible nightmare. I'm here to tell you she was great at doing everything she did but it would have taken the Confederate Army to satisfy her. And I was only one lone, little soldier. When I finally said no more and surrendered I think she was disappointed because she was just getting warmed up. I don't know what she was used to getting from those Iowa farm boys but if they were satisfying her then to a man they were a hell of a lot better than me.

'You want to rest a while?' she whispered in my ear as we were sprawled out on the Persian rug in the living room.

'Oh, God,' I gasped, trying to get my breath.

'We can dribble chocolate syrup all over each other and lick it off.'

'I don't think so, Mary Lou. I don't have a lick left in me.'

'You just lay there and let me do all the work . . .' And her hand started down my belly.

'Don't,' I said, managing to gather enough strength to stop her. 'Don't touch anything. Every part of me is inflamed and hurting and right on the edge of being for ever inoperable.' Extreme as that may have sounded, at the time I was sure it was true.

'Oh,' she whimpered, disappointed. 'You don't like me.'

'I do. I like you a lot. But I have to go while I can still walk. *If* I can still walk, I mean.'

'You're no fun.'

'Mary Lou, I have been *fun* with you longer than I have ever been *fun* with *anyone* in my entire life. I'm not kidding, there is a possibility that I may be permanently impaired. I don't know if I can make it up the stairs. Will you go and get my clothes?'

'You really want to leave? Is there something you'd like me to do? Something I didn't do?'

'No. Oh no, no, no. No, there's nothing you didn't do. In fact, there's nothing else *to* do. Not a thing in the world. I can't think of anything we missed.'

'Then why are you leaving?'

'Because I'm feeling very old and if I don't leave I might

die right here on the living-room floor. And how are you going to explain that to your mother and father when they get home from visiting Uncle Pee Wee?'

'You can't go unless you promise to meet me after the show tomorrow night. My parents won't be home for another three days.' Her eyes were aglow with the plans she was making for me.

'Oh, God!'

'Promise.'

'Mary Lou . . . '

'You better promise.' She took my left nipple in her teeth and I had no doubt she had every intention of biting it off if she didn't get her way.

'OK, I promise.' I would have promised to overthrow the government just to get out of that house and away from her.

'And you better keep your promise, too.' There was a nasty little threat in her tone of voice.

Every bone in my body was aching as I crawled under the stage to my bed. All the canvasmen were asleep but the Angel heard me and sat up.

'Hey, John.' He yawned and stretched. 'You're awful late. You have a good time?' he asked.

'Shut up.'

'What did I do?'

'Nothing. Just go to sleep.'

'I wrote my letter,' he whispered. 'It looks real nice. I told Dr Forepaugh and Mr Ridge about us being in the show business and all about singing up on the stage in front of all them people and about Celine and Cyril and Lydia . . . ' His litany went on and on, including the Great Dane and Little Texas. 'But how do I send it to him?'

'Dr Forepaugh, Ivy Street, Paradise, Indiana, I guess.' I wasn't in the mood for discussing addresses. 'Christ, it's not as though the postal service is going to mix his mail up with anybody else's. There's nobody in the town but him. Now go to sleep. I'm so tired it hurts to talk.'

'I had a real good time writing it. Celine and me were eating sandwiches and lying on her bed –'

'Will you shut up. You're going to wake everybody.' I didn't want to hear about him lying on a bed with Celine. In fact, the last thing I wanted to hear about was a bed. Any bed.

'She said it's a real good letter.' He whispered even louder.

'Are you deaf or something? I said to be quiet and go to sleep.'

He was so full of the letter he couldn't stop himself. 'I'll tell you all about the rest of what I said tomorrow.'

'OK, you do that.'

'And you can tell me all about what you did tonight.'

'Oh shit,' I said as I rolled over on my bruised and battered private parts.

The next night as I walked through the audience selling my candy, there was Mary Lou looking all fresh faced and rested. When I came up to her she smiled and moved her knees back and forth ever so slightly which I'm sure was a signal that she was underwearless.

'I'll meet you out front,' she said and rolled her tongue over her lips.

'Mary Lou, I don't think . . .'

'You promised.' Her eyes were fierce and she set her jaw in a bulldog lock.

'Yeah, but I still hurt.'

She grabbed my arm and pulled me aside. 'You promised. You be there or else.'

'Or else what?'

'You'll see if you're not there.'

It crossed my mind that it might be a good idea to fix up the Angel with Mary Lou. It was long past the time when he needed a little experience in that department but when I gave it a little thought I knew I couldn't wish her on my worst enemy. 'I won't be any good to you.'

'Be there.'

'Mary Lou, you're a beautiful girl and there's nothing I'd rather do than spend another wonderful night with you but be reasonable.'

'I said, be there.'

Sweet little Mary Lou had turned into a bushel basket full of rattlesnakes but even so, there was no way I could be chased around that house for another three hours. Besides, I wouldn't have been able to get it up if she had held a gun to my head. 'No. I will not be there. I'm sorry but I can't. And that's my final word.'

'Well, let me give you *my* final word.' Her eyes got small and mean. 'My daddy will be home in two days and when I tell him you took advantage of me . . . that you raped me, well, if I were you I wouldn't be anywhere in the state of Iowa. And Sheriff Applegate is my daddy's best friend. Ever since first grade.' Her eyes got even meaner. 'You ever see how we slaughter pigs?'

'Raped you! Jesus Christ, if anybody got raped, it was me. I probably won't be able to have any children because of you.'

'I don't care about you or your children. I'm warning you.' She took a box of candy, and smiled as evil a smile as I had ever seen. 'Like I said, be there.' She waved to somebody in the audience as she returned to her seat, just as sweet as apple pie.

The rest of the performance was nothing but a blur to me. There was no way I could have done it with Mary Lou that night. Hell, I couldn't have done it with Celine and she was the woman I wanted more than anything on the face of the earth. I didn't know if Mary Lou would do what she threatened, tell her old man and the sheriff, but I did have images of a pig being slaughtered and it gave me a very queasy feeling in the pit of my stomach. It was impossible for me to concentrate on what I was doing up on that stage but, seeing as how my acting was nothing to shoot off rockets about, I don't suppose anybody noticed. Finally, when the show was over after what seemed like a couple of lifetimes, I had the Angel check and see if Mary Lou was waiting for me out front. Of course, she was. She waited damn near an hour. Every few minutes he'd come back and report that she was still there. He didn't know what was going on but I think he liked the intrigue. I guess he thought it was some kind of game because he seemed to be tickled and could hardly hold back his laughter. It may have been funny to him but it sure in hell wasn't to me. I felt like I was walking with one foot on either side of a giant razor blade. When she left, I went to bed, still exhausted from the night before and I slept fitfully, dreaming of being eaten by a blond-haired monster, piece by piece and bit by bit. I woke up about three o'clock in the morning, sweating all over and wishing I was miles away from Iowa and Mary Lou. It wasn't twenty-four hours before my wish came true.

At the show the following might I peeked through the curtain to see if Mary Lou was in her usual seat but she wasn't. I looked all over that audience but I didn't see her anywhere in the tent. I figured she had given up on me and I felt a huge weight lifted off my shoulders. However, it only lasted until the first intermission when the Angel was singing, 'My Blue Heaven' and I overheard Cyril talking to Lydia and Celine. I was sitting in the dressing room and they were on the other side of the canvas partition.

'I don't know exactly what it's about,' said Cyril. 'But Tigger Book says Sheriff Applegate's been hanging around asking a lot of questions.' Lydia made a funny little exasperated sound.

'Now, Lydia, don't go getting yourself upset,' said Celine. 'Not in your condition.'

'Shush' – it was Cyril – 'there's no point in anybody getting upset. We don't even know what it's about.' They moved away and I couldn't hear anything more.

My mind started doing cartwheels. Not only was it possible the police were looking for me for kidnapping the Angel or maybe stealing Doc Forepaugh's cufflinks, now they could have been after me for rape! It was possible that I was quickly becoming one of the ten most wanted criminals in the country. The Angel and I had to hit the road as soon as we could.

'Get your things together during the third act,' I said to him when he finished singing. 'We're leaving.'

'When?'

'Tonight. After the show.'

'Tonight! Why?'

'We have to. I'll explain it to you later. And don't say anything to anybody.'

'Aren't we going to say goodbye?'

'We can't.'

'Sure we can.'

'Goddamn it, do what I tell you. Don't tell anybody we're leaving.'

'Can't I even tell Celine? I have to tell her.'

I knew just how he felt. 'All right, but you have to make her promise not to say anything.'

'She's real good at keeping secrets.' I wondered what other secrets they had. 'And you should tell Cyril. He's been real nice to us, John. It's not right that we just go away and don't say anything to him. Everybody's been real nice but Cyril's been special nice.'

He was right, of course, I was leaving Cyril in the lurch. Not only was he losing his juvenile, not that I was such a big loss, but he was losing the Angel, too, and he was what people were paying their good money to see and hear. 'OK, I'll say something to Cyril. But that's all. You hear me? Not another word to anybody else.'

When I said something to Cyril, after the show, he already knew we were going. A tent show was no place to try and keep a secret.

'I'm not asking you boys why you're taking off in the middle of the night. That's your business and I don't want to know anything about it.'

'I'm sorry to leave you holding the bag like this.'

'Oh, Tigger can fill in for you. He doesn't like it but he's done it before. Of course, nobody can replace Michael. I had high hopes for him, I can tell you that. The boy has something very special. It's not just the singing, either. I can't put my finger on it but he makes something happen to people. I never saw anything like it in all my years in the business and I've been doing this since I was four years old.'

'I just want you to know we're thankful for what you did for us.'

'How you fixed for cash?'

'We have a little.'

He took his famous roll of bills out of his pocket and peeled off the hundred. 'That's the best I can do. It's the beginning of the season and what with expenses and all, I haven't stashed anything away yet.'

'You don't owe us this much.'

'Take it.'

'I appreciate it.' I didn't tell him Carlton had given me the hundred. I shook his hand. 'You say goodbye to everybody for us.'

'Yeah, I will.' I started to walk away and just as casual as anything he said, 'Celine said she'd be all packed and ready to go in half an hour.'

'Celine!' I almost tripped and fell. 'What are you talking about?'

'Didn't Michael tell you? She's going with you.'

'What?'

'Yeah, she decided to go with you.'

It was too much for my brain to absorb all at once. My first thought was having Celine in the car with us all the way to California. What could be better than travelling clear across the country with the most beautiful girl in the world? It was almost too good to think about. But the big question that instantly sprang to mind was, why? Why in hell would Celine be leaving the Comedians and taking off in the middle of the night to go wherever it was we were going? She didn't even *know* where we were going. It certainly wasn't because she was so crazy about *me*. We still barely spoke. So, it had to be because of the Angel. There *was* something going on between them. There had to be. It was the only explanation. And it was a hell of a lot more than letter-writing lessons.

'Why would Celine decide just like that to take off with us?'

'Well, she's young and you know women. I guess she wants a little adventure in her life.'

'How are you going to get along without her?' It seemed to me he was being awfully casual about her leaving.

'Fern Pearl will take over until we get somebody. But that's not your problem so don't you worry about it.' I would have liked getting a look at hook-nosed, flat-chested Fern Pearl in Celine's costumes.

'Celine's real partial to Michael,' I said hoping he'd tell me if he knew there was anything going on between them.

'You better hurry,' said Cyril, ignoring me, and he patted my shoulder. 'Good luck, John.' And that was the last I was to see of Cyril for a good while.

The Angel was waiting for me with our stuff in the Willys-Knight just as we had planned.

'Why didn't you tell me about Celine going with us?'

'I didn't have a chance to. It's good, isn't it, John? You like Celine, don't you?'

I grabbed him by the shoulders and looked him straight in the face. 'Are you fucking her?'

He winced as though he was in pain and those black eyes of his turned even blacker. 'John, don't talk bad like that about Celine.' He shook his head, not believing I even asked the question. 'Why do you ask me a question like that when you know it's not true?'

'Then why the hell is she going with us? That's what I'd like to know.'

'She just said she'd go along when I said goodbye to her. She got real excited about it. That's all. I thought you'd like her going with us to heaven.'

'Did you tell her about all that crap?'

'No. But once I said we were going to Hollywood sometime. I told her it was a secret and not to tell nobody.'

That was it. She wanted a ride to Hollywood. Well, at least that made sense. She was prettier than any girl I'd ever seen in a movie. But I still couldn't figure out why Cyril was seemingly so accepting of the idea. She could have waited to go to Hollywood when the season was over. 'Get in the car before somebody sees us and starts asking questions.' And just as I was sliding into the driver's side I saw Carlton down by the tent entrance, standing in the shadows watching us. Word did travel fast. The poor bastard wasn't even going to say anything, he was just going to watch us start off on the adventure he always wanted and would never have. 'Hold on a minute,' I said to the Angel, 'there's somebody we have to say goodbye to.'

'Who?'

'Carlton. See him over there?' The Angel got out of the car. 'I want you to be especially nice to him because he's been real good to us. When you say goodbye, hug him and give him a kiss on the cheek. OK?'

'Well, sure.' We started towards Carlton.

'Hey, you going to hide in the shadows or are you going to say goodbye?' I said as we approached him.

'I wasn't spying on you,' he said apologetically. 'I didn't want to say anything because I know your leaving is supposed to be a secret and you're trying to get out of here as fast as you can and I didn't want to hold you up.'

'Well, something's come up.'

'You don't have to explain anything.'

I extended my hand to him. 'We're not in such a hurry we can't say goodbye.' He took my hand and held it for a quick moment before dropping it. 'Thanks again. I mean it. You're a life-saver.'

'You know how to get in touch with me if you need anything.' He turned to Michael. 'You remember that, if you ever need anything.'

'I will,' smiled the Angel.

'Say your goodbye, Michael.'

'Yeah, Mr Kearney, it was real nice meeting you.' He threw his arms around Carlton and held him close and kissed him on the cheek just as I told him to do. For a moment, Carlton stiffened and froze but then he made a strange little catching sound in his throat and relaxed and returned the hug and I knew, if I could have seen his eyes, they'd be glowing.

'Come on,' I said. 'We've got to hit the road.'

'I'll be thinking about you,' said Carlton as we walked to the car. 'And tell Celine I said to take care of herself.' Jesus, everybody knew everything. I half expected the whole town to be down by the court house to see us off with a brass band and coloured balloons. The Angel waved a couple of times and we got in the car and pulled away.

'Tell everybody we said goodbye,' the Angel called.

I could see the figure of Carlton as he disappeared in the rear-view mirror and I thought to myself, well, I can forget the one-hundred-dollar debt to old Carlton. I just gave the poor bastard the closest thing he'd probably ever have to a sex life. That was worth at least a hundred dollars.

Celine was waiting with her suitcase in front of the hotel. I expected to see Cyril and Lydia with her but she was all alone. She was wearing the orange-flowered dress she'd worn the first time I saw her. When I pulled up, the Angel got out and took her bag.

'It's all right, isn't it?' She was talking to me through the open car door.

'Yeah, sure it's all right. Get in.' But instead of getting in next to me she climbed in the back seat. 'You can sit up here if you want.'

'This is fine. I like the back seat.' Probably because she could sit back there and chew on her plaster without anybody knowing about it.

The Angel got up front with me. 'Here we go,' he said, pulling his door closed. And just as the car moved away from the kerb I noticed two figures in the window of the hotel. I couldn't see who they were exactly but one was a short, fat woman and the other was a man of very average stature.

There wasn't a single solitary soul on the streets of Mt Pleasant as we drove through the town past the silent bandstand and empty court house and westward into the night. Not even a damn cat or dog prowling around. And as we headed out into the countryside, with nothing but the illuminated highway coaxing us along, I didn't feel the same exhilaration I usually felt when I was moving on to something new. It was there but it was all mixed up with a lot of other feelings: the unexpected joy of having Celine with us; the panic all of a sudden of being on the lam and the fear of having every goddamn law officer in Iowa and the rest of the country on our tail; and the dumbest feeling of all, the nagging jealousy I felt towards the Angel because Celine was so partial to him. And there was something else. Something that gave me the creepy chills and was almost too strange to think about. The lonely notion that there was no one left in the whole world but the Angel, Celine and me and we were three people who were just passing through, heading hell bent for leather for something that none of us wanted but that there wasn't a goddamn thing we could do to keep from happening.

How I Got My Revenge

We went clear across Iowa and into Nebraska before we stopped to do any serious resting. I felt like the devil, in the form of Sheriff Applegate, was right behind me, nipping at my rear end. Other than the obvious advantage of having Celine along, that is, just to look at her, she could also drive the car which was a real blessing because I was trying to put as much distance between me and the enemy as fast as I could. We took turns spelling each other and napping and occasionally stopping to get something to eat at some little roadside joint until the next night when we hit the Platte Valley and decided to look for a place with honest-to-God beds.

When I was at the wheel, most of the time Celine sat in the back and the Angel sat with her and if he wasn't reading the Burma Shave signs, which he was particularly partial to and just about went nuts whenever he saw them, one of us was reading from his library which had doubled in the short time we were in Mt Pleasant. Along with his *Art Treasures of Florence* and the *Indiana First Reader*, he now had a dictionary, a gift from Celine, and a new book from over in England, *Precious Bane*, that Fern Pearl had read a dozen times and had given to the Angel as a remembrance of the first night he sang. Some of the words in *Precious Bane* were too much for the Angel so Celine, who turned out to be a hell of a lot better book-reader than actress, and I did most of the reading. Nat and Dora and Buttercup and the rest of the cast of the *Reader* were replaced by the hare-lipped Prudence Sarn and her mean brother Gideon, pretty Jancis, the wizard Beguildy and the not-to-be-forgotten hero and weaver, Kester Woodseaves. It was slow going because every two minutes whichever one of us was reading had to stop to explain something to the Angel or some word would kick off a Bible quote that we had to wait for him to impress us with. And the language was almost foreign sounding at times because a lot of it was written in dialect but once we got into it we couldn't wait to find out what Prue was up to next. Maybe everything on a long car trip gets more intense because the world becomes the few feet of space you're stuck in but we got so caught up in the story that pretty soon we all started talking like the characters in the book. Caterpillars, and they were all the hell over the place every time we stopped, became 'butterflies-as-is-to-be' and lakes became 'meres' and all birds, no matter what kind they were, became 'rooks' even though I'm sure there isn't a single damn rook in the whole of America. But what a time we had reading that book! I will take the story of Prue Sarn and her son of a bitch of a brother, Gideon, to my grave because from Iowa to past the Rocky Mountains it was about the only thing I heard. And if the Angel liked a certain part, we'd read it over and over again. Every once in a while we might get a break while the Angel read from the dictionary or we'd sing a few songs but most of the time the three of us were in Shropshire, England, suffering all the shit the gang at Sarn Mere had to live through.

Even in the confines of the Willys-Knight Celine stayed as indifferent to me as ever. She was so easy with the Angel, always chuckling and touching and sharing something I couldn't even put my finger on. The only thing we shared was the reading of the book. Sometimes I felt like an outsider or a parent sitting alone in the front seat, driving two kids who had secrets they'd never share with me. The crazy thing was, the more time I spent with Celine the less I felt I knew anything about her. She was the woman I wanted to go to bed with more than I wanted to breathe and up to the time we left Mt Pleasant that was all I cared about. But now I wanted to know more. More than that she was a not-so-good actress who ate plaster and crap like that and wanted to go to Hollywood. One thing I did find out right away was that she paid her own way. She was adamant about that. I tried to pick up the check in the first restaurant we stopped to eat in but she insisted she pay her share. Hell, it was only breakfast and the whole bill was less than a dollar but when I went to pay for it she damn near made a scene. She paid for her own meals and places to sleep, too. And for half the gas the old Willys guzzled up. I don't know how much money she had because she wasn't flashing it around but however much it was, she was paying her own way and there was no question about it.

Another thing I discovered about her was that she was smart. She was a high-school graduate who for sure should have gone on to college. There was no question about that, either. One day when we were driving along the Platte River and taking a break from the book because the Angel had fallen asleep, we had our first real conversation. Just between the two of us.

'Did you notice,' I said, just to make small talk, 'there aren't any big boats on the river.'

'It's too shallow.' She had that information right at tips of her fingers. 'And in the early spring it floods.'

'How do you know stuff like that?'

'From school. I liked geography.' She was nibbling back there, I could tell by the way she talked.

'But I never even heard of the Platte River before we drove into this valley.'

'The Oregon trail followed this river and the Mormon trail.'

'How do you know so much?'

She chuckled a little. 'Where'd you go to school?'

'Pittsburgh, Pennsylvania.'

'Then you probably learned about the Ohio River and the Allegheny and the Monongahela.'

'Yeah, we did. But how'd you know about them?'

'I told you, I liked geography. It was my favourite subject. How many of the major rivers of the world can you name?'

I hated car games but I was talking to her and I would have stood on my head behind the wheel just to keep the conversation going. 'Oh. Jesus, I don't know. Math was my subject.'

'I bet you can name more than you think. I'll tell you what, I'll name one then you name one, OK?'

'Sure, why not?'

'Let's see. All right, the Mississippi.'

'I knew you'd say that. The Ohio.'

'The Rio Grande,' she snapped back.

I could tell by the new sound in her voice that she liked competition. 'Ah, let me think. The Amazon.'

'The Nile.'

And I couldn't think of another goddamn river. She used up all the good ones. 'Give me a minute.'

'You're kidding! We haven't even started yet.' She had really come to life.

'I told you math was my subject. Let me think for a

minute.' I knew there were thousands of rivers in the world for Christ's sake, but I had to dig deep to come up with another one. 'OK, I got one. The Danube.'

'The Thames,' she shot back.

There wasn't an unnamed river running through my head. All I could do was wade through the ones we had already mentioned. 'I give up.'

'You can't. Not so soon.'

'I can't think of a single goddamn river. I give up.'

'This is too easy. What about the Volga, the Congo, the Niger, the Ganges, the Shannon, the Murray . . .'

'The Murray? Where the hell's the Murray?'

'It's the longest river in Australia.'

'Oh, well, if I had known we could do rivers in Australia . . .'

'Oh sure.' And she laughed. It was loud and spontaneous and free. I had never heard Celine laugh before except for the little chuckles she shared with the Angel. But now she was laughing out loud and I was the one who made her do it. I actually made her laugh and I got this almost light-headed feeling. I looked back at her with the Angel's head resting on her shoulder and she looked more beautiful than ever. The wind was blowing her red hair all over her face and she had a sweet smile and she looked like a painting. One of those paintings of a woman that you just know the artist loved to distraction. So much so he had to put her down on canvas so men for the next dozen centuries could see the woman he had had in his lifetime.

'You really know your rivers.'

'I loved school.' All her defences were down and her voice was warm and easy and relaxed. 'I truly did. In the summer, when we had our vacations, I was the only kid in town who couldn't wait for school to start up again. The other kids thought I was crazy. I went to a one-room school house for the first eight grades. Our teacher was Mr Biddermuth. Mr Vladimir Biddermuth. He was born right there in Michigan and his mother named him Vladimir. Imagine what poor Mr Biddermuth had had to put up with from the other kids. She was reading some story when she was pregnant and named him after one of the characters. I was so in love with Mr Vladimir Biddermuth I could hardly talk when he called on me to recite. He was real short and balding and he had the thickest glasses I had ever seen but I thought he was a Greek god. I only wanted two things out of life when I was a kid. I wanted to grow up and become Mrs Vladimir Biddermuth and I wanted to be a teacher just like him.' She fell silent for a moment. 'I graduated the top of my class.'

'That's pretty damn good.'

'Of course, there were only seven kids in my class. I don't tell that to too many people.' She laughed again.

'Your secret is safe with me.'

'I wonder where Mr Biddermuth is today?'

I thought of telling her I had been a teacher but she would have started asking questions like where did I go to teachers' college and I wasn't about to tell her I was a fake so I didn't say anything about it. But I had to keep her talking. Her new voice was washing over me like cool water. 'You ever think of going to college?'

'Two girls from my school did go. Alice Anderson and Greta Rose Hayes. They were cousins.'

'As smart as you are, you should have gone.'

'I got married.' And I heard a little sound in her voice like the life was going out of it. Almost like a full stop to the sentence and before another word was spoken I knew our conversation was about to end.

'I didn't know you were married.'

'Well, I'm not any more.' The old protective shield was there, hard and impenetrable.

'What happened?'

'I don't want to talk about it. I think I'll take a little nap.'

And with that our conversation was all over. I could see her face in the rear-view mirror and I knew she was locked away because the mask was back.

'Can I go in the water, John?' The Angel and I were sitting on the banks of the Platte trying to cool off in the shade of some big old cottonwood trees. It was midday and hotter than hell and Celine was off in the bushes doing her business. We were watching some minnows nibbling at a dead bug in the shallows and dragonflies were buzzing around keeping an eye on us.

'You mean swim? You'll have to take off your clothes and Celine will see your wings.'

'Can't we tell her we're angels? I'd sure feel a lot cooler if I could take my shirt off and get in that water. And I'm sure she don't care if we're angels.'

'Doesn't. *Doesn't* care if we're angels.' We were working on the Angel's grammar. It wasn't easy keeping all the secrets we had. It was a problem I had been thinking about since we started off from Mt Pleasant. Aside from the Angel's wings, there was the matter of why we took off in the middle of the night like that on the spur of the moment so to speak. Nothing had been said about it, one way or the other. Celine never asked and I never offered any kind of explanation. She must have known it had something to do with the Law, though, being as smart as she was. What I couldn't figure out was why, if she knew we were running from something or somebody, she took the chance of riding off with us the way she did? And I still couldn't figure out why Cyril didn't do more to stop her. That was a very puzzling matter to me. There was a hell of a lot that was being left up in the air without any discussion. But the Angel's wings were something that had to be dealt with and I knew it. Since we were all so close together she was bound to find out sooner or later anyway.

'I'll tell you what,' I said to the Angel, 'you go for a swim and I'll tell Celine about you. But I'm not going to say anything about me being an angel, too. OK?'

'Why not?'

'Well, I think one angel is enough of a shock for a person to endure. You know what I mean? Having two angels around might be too much for her.'

'You know, you might be right about that, John.' He was dead serious and his brow knitted like he was making a decision that would change the course of history. 'Two angels just might be too much for a person to endure.' I noticed that when the Angel liked a word he repeated it, planting it in his own vocabulary.

'Go on. Go for a swim.'

'I never been swimming before.'

'Well, just splash around. Be careful and test the waters. And stay out of the deep part.'

'I will.' He took off his shoes and socks, shirt and pants and slipped his drawers down around his ankles.

'Now just hold on there,' I said. 'Keep your drawers on. You want Celine to see you naked? What in hell is wrong with you?'

'I don't see what difference it makes,' he said, pulling his drawers up. 'Adam and Eve were naked in the Garden of Eden.'

'Don't start on the Bible, OK? Besides, I don't give a shit

about them. You're not Adam and Celine's not Eve. Now go on, get your ass wet. We have to be hitting the road soon and I don't want you dripping all over the car.' He waded out to the middle of the river, some thirty feet or so, to where he was about hip deep and started splashing water up all over himself. His wing things stretched and fluttered and looked like some independent creatures that had rested on his back and were having as good a time as he was.

'Come on in, John. It's so nice and cool. It feels real good.'

'I'll just watch you from here.' The truth of the matter is I never learned to swim and being anywhere near water scared the hell out of me.

Celine came out of the bushes. 'Hey, Celine,' he called, 'look at me. I'm swimming.'

'I see you are,' she said. She stared at him for a minute. 'What are those things on his back?' she asked.

'Well, that's something I have to tell you about.'

'Come on in,' said the Angel.

'Maybe later.' I motioned to Celine to sit next to me.

'I knew there was something wrong with his back,' she said. 'I just knew it. I could tell by the way his shirt fit. What are those things?'

Well, I was in a real puckersnatch. How much of the truth could I tell her? I wasn't about to say I kidnapped the Angel. Christ, that would have scared the hell out of her, thinking she was travelling across the country with a kidnapper. I thought the cousin story was a good start and I had already told everybody that and they seemed to believe it. I also didn't think it was a very good idea to say I had stolen Doc Forepaugh's cufflinks, especially since she knew all about him because she helped the Angel write the letter. Nor did I want to say anything about Mary Lou and the rape that never happened. Jesus, if I told her all that stuff she'd be thinking I was a kidnapping rapist. So I decided to concentrate on the Angel's crazy little mother and nonexistent coal miner of a father. Celine was wide eyed as I described how the little woman read the Bible to him so much he memorized it and how she dressed him up in his angel dress on rainy nights waiting for the heavenly messenger. Of course, I didn't say *I* was the messenger. There was a real problem telling her all that because I didn't want to lie any more than I had to so I left a lot out and was as vague as I could be about the rest of it.

'. . . and she always told him he was an angel because of the growths on his back and the family sort of goes along with it. To make him feel better about having those wing things. You know what I mean? It's kind of a game we play. Deep down he really doesn't believe he's an angel.' I didn't think she'd ever believe he really *did* think he was an angel! 'Don't go thinking he's dimwitted or anything like that, though. He's far from it.'

'Oh, I think Michael's as smart as can be. Look how fast he learned how to write. It's a crime he didn't go to school.'

'His crazy mother thought the kids would be too hard on him. At least she was sensible about that.'

'And you looked after him ever since he was a little kid.' She said it, not me.

'Well, he wasn't really a little kid . . .'

'And you're taking him all the way to Hollywood . . .'

'With a voice like his it seemed like the right thing to do. And he's not educated to do anything else. I thought it was worth a try.' I didn't say I planned to make a million dollars off him before we parted company.

'He is kind of like an angel, isn't he?' She smiled as we sat watching him splash around. 'If I was born with growths like that on my back I'd want to think I was an angel, too.' The defences were down again. Compassion is a powerful tool when it comes to knocking over walls. 'I wondered why you were so good to him,' she said, looking at me like she had never seen me before. 'He's really lucky to have a cousin like you. I mean somebody who'll look after him. You must love him a lot.' There was something in those pale grey eyes, just the hint of a connection that only lasted a split second but it was there long enough for both of us to be aware. I felt some wonderful kind of ripple go through my body. And at the same time, deep down where it always started, I felt that goddamn guilt that I didn't seem to have any control over.

'Aren't you going to come in?' The Angel was jumping up and down.

'I'll just watch.'

'Come on, John,' said Celine, standing up and unbuttoning her dress.

'You go on. The shade is cool enough for me.'

She stepped out of her dress and started into the water in her slip. 'Oh, John, you really should come in. This is wonderful.'

'Watch me, I can go under water.' The Angel took a deep breath and disappeared and I felt like I was going to smother waiting what seemed like ten minutes for him to resurface. He sprung up out of the water and shook big droplets from his long hair. The wing things shook themselves dry, too.

'Don't do too much of that underwater shit,' I yelled, 'you can't swim.'

'*I* can,' called Celine as she got closer to the Angel. 'I'll teach you, Michael.' And for the next hour that's exactly what she did. Like everything else, he learned right off the bat and was swimming like a damn slippery eel in no time at all. He kept asking me to come in but no amount of coaxing was going to get me in moving water. I confined my water sports to the shower or the bathtub and sometimes I was afraid I was going to drown there. They were hooting and hollering and I laid my head back and looked up into the dense green of the cottonwoods and watched the acrobatics of a couple of squirrels going crazy chasing each other. I felt as peaceful as I had ever felt in my life. It was one of those few moments in a lifetime when everything seemed to be right. Someone could have come along and said I could have anything I wanted in the world and at that moment I wouldn't have been able to think of a single thing. But I knew it wouldn't last. Nothing that good ever does. I dozed off for a few minutes and when I woke up the Angel and Celine had moved down river about ten feet and were taking a break from their swimming. They were standing there talking to each other, silhouetted against a stand of willow trees, their hair slicked back and what little clothes they were wearing stuck to their bodies so they looked as naked as statues. The sun was sparkling off the water all around them, lighting them all silver and gold and I thought to myself, it would be hard to find two more perfect people in the world. So what if she had an overbite and the wrong coloured eyes and was secretive and ate plaster and he had a couple of questionable growths on his back and acted like an idiot sometimes and could be a pure pain in the ass. I started to feel a queer uncomfortable something that I couldn't put my finger on and it annoyed me. Later that day, riding along in the Willys, thinking about them swimming and having such a hell of a good time, I realized what it was. All those peculiar things about them that annoyed me, all those imperfections so to speak, seemed to make them even more perfect. It didn't make a goddamn bit of sense.

'Come on, you two. Get the hell out of the water and dry off. We've got to get going.'

'You should come in, John.' The Angel didn't want to give it up. 'You don't know what you're missing.'

'Maybe I don't but get your ass out here, anyway. We've got to hit the road.'

'You can be such a grouch,' said Celine and they started wading towards me, splashing each other.

There are a few times in every man's life when something so unexpected and impossible, so out of the ordinary and the realm of probability happens, that when it does he can hardly believe it. I suppose I've had more than my share. Meeting up with the Angel for one and Celine for another. What are the odds of a man, in his entire lifetime, running into a fellow with wing-like things growing out of his back? Most likely a zillion to one. Except for some of those old ginks with the funny names in the Bible who kept bumping into angels, I'm probably one of the few people in the world it ever happened to. And how many men get to meet the woman they have spent thirty years lovingly and lustfully creating in their minds, in the all-too-perfect and exquisite flesh? Me and a few of those fellows who painted pictures of their women, I expect. It would seem that those two improbabilities should be enough for any man. But I was blessed beyond belief. There was one more, so unexpected and impossible it took me a few seconds to believe my eyes. And it happened just before we left Nebraska and headed down into Colorado, right after the Platte forked into the North Platte and the South Platte. We followed the South Platte for a while and stopped for the night at some travellers' cabins done up to look like teepees, about fifteen miles past the town of Ogallala. It was called the Pawnee Village. Of course, no self-respecting Pawnee would be caught dead within a hundred miles of the place. It was a white man's version of a village and an insult to the Pawnee and all the other plains tribes. The teepee cottages were dirty white and falling apart with painted junky made-up Indian symbols and fake cactus along the paths. And there was a totem pole back near the outhouses, big and ugly with the damnedest cross-eyed birds and shit like that painted in bright colours. As far as I knew, totem poles were only carved by the coastal tribes of the northwest. What the hell would a Pawnee have to do with a damn totem pole? No question about it, it was a crummy place but I will remember it for ever, as some people remember great and famous landmarks like monuments and shrines and places where presidents are buried because it was, and will always be, a place of unsurpassed personal triumph for me. Impossible and improbable as it might sound, in that crappy teepee village, we ran into that son of a bitch, Kansas. And I got a taste of revenge and I'm here to tell you it was sweeter than I ever imagined it could be. Goddamn, but it tasted good.

Celine and the Angel and I checked in just before dark and there wasn't a car in the parking lot. She got a teepee for herself and the Angel and I shared one. The inside of the teepees was as bad as the outside with bed sheets more grey than white and mouse footprints in the dust on the dresser but we decided to stay because it was the first tourist rentals we had come to for several miles and we were getting ass weary and hungry. Besides, we all needed a rest from the troubles Prue and her folks were having at Sarn Mere. She had just saved Kester – an animal lover from the word go – from a vicious dog that had him by the throat by sticking the dog right in the heart with a carving-knife and we were all exhausted from the harrowing experience.

The food in what they laughingly called a restaurant looked as though it was capable of causing plague. We should have got the hint when we got there and there was no one in the place but a tall skinny waitress doing a crossword puzzle. But food was food and whatever they had to offer filled up the holes in our stomachs and we were grateful for that. The toast, which I always asked for, was made from homemade bread and I have to admit was admirable. I also have to say the butter was sweet and fresh and the strawberry jam was perfection. But everything else we ordered was almost unrecognizable as something edible. The Angel, who never complained about anything, especially where food was concerned, thought everything was delicious and asked for a second piece of the custard pie which I would have sworn had flies baked into the surface. We were all relaxing with our coffee, talking about heading into the Rocky Mountains and Celine was trying to trap me into playing a game of 'great mountain ranges of the world' when I saw an old faded Ford pull up to the office and a man in a cowboy hat get out and go in. I only saw him in the bright light outside the office teepee and right away he looked familiar. However, since Kansas was the last person in the world I ever expected to see again in this life, at first it didn't even occur to me that it was him. It didn't register until he disappeared through the office door and then, like a bomb going off inside my head, I knew it was that son of a bitch.

'Holy shit!'

I startled Celine. 'What's the matter?'

'Kansas!'

'What are you talking about?'

The Angel was so involved in his fly-specked pie he didn't pay any attention to me.

'Nothing. Let's pay the check and get back to our teepees. Right now.'

'What's the big rush?' asked Celine. 'I haven't finished my coffee.'

'And I want another piece of pie. It's real good.'

'Just finish the damn pie and let's get out of here. You too, Celine.'

'Don't talk to me that way,' she said, getting her back up. She was not a woman to be cross with.

Well, all I needed was to have to argue with them! Kansas had a knife. And a big, mean knife that I remembered very well as anyone would who had had it stuck up against his Adam's apple. And he was crazy. A crazy man with a big knife was someone to be reckoned with. I didn't want to confront the son of a bitch because if he was as nervous as he had been in the Willys-Knight who knew what he might do if he felt cornered. The fact of the matter was, I didn't want Celine or the Angel to get involved at all. They would only complicate things. I just wanted to have a little time to figure out what I was going to do. And I knew I *was* going to do something. There was no way in hell I was going to let Kansas off the hook.

'Please, let's get out of here. *Please*. OK? I'm sorry I snapped at you,' I said to Celine. 'I'll explain everything in the morning. I will. I promise. Please trust me.'

'Honestly!' Celine wasn't happy but she and the Angel got up. I threw some money on the table and told the bored waitress who was erasing something in her crossword puzzle and swearing to herself to keep the change and we went out the door and around behind the office and hightailed it to our teepees. We said a quick goodnight to a confused Celine and I pushed the Angel down the path to our teepee and got inside just as I saw the office door open and Kansas walking out with the manager. I held the curtains closed except for a slit and watched them go to a teepee just down the path from us. They went in and after a moment the manager came out and went back to the office.

'What are you looking at?' asked the Angel.

'Nothing, just go to bed.'

'Aren't we going to do some reading, John?'

'No. We're leaving early in the morning and you need your sleep.'

'I'm not tired, John. I'd really like to do some reading.'

'Not tonight, goddamn it. Now get in bed and go to sleep.'

'Don't you want to know what happens to Prue?'

'No. I don't care. Just go to bed.'

'What are you so mad about?'

'I'm not in the mood for this shit. I mean it, go to sleep.'

He got out of his clothes and got in the bed. 'Are you going to get some sleep, John?'

'Later. I got some thinking to do.' The Angel rolled over and I stood guard at the window watching Kansas's teepee. All kinds of things went through my mind, the first being to slip in in the middle of the night when I knew he was asleep and take the knife out of his boot and stick it in his heart just like Prue had stuck the carving knife into the heart of the vicious dog. But somehow that didn't seem bad enough for Kansas. He would have died before he knew what hit him and I wanted the satisfaction of knowing that he knew I was responsible for whatever happened to him. What I really wanted to do was scare him shitless. I wanted him to know what it felt like to be threatened the way he'd threatened me. I wanted him to know that feeling of powerlessness and the numbing fear of being seconds away from what could be the end of his life. I suppose I also wanted to pay him back for all the people I had imagined the son of a bitch had robbed. People who would never have the opportunity of accidentally catching up with him the way I had. It must have been hours before it hit me, and then, like magic, it all became crystal clear and I knew exactly what I was going to do. He hadn't been to the outhouse since he checked in. It was something he was going to have to do sooner or later.

By then, I could hear the slow even breathing of the Angel and I knew he was sound asleep so I left, quietly closing the door behind me, and I noticed all the lights were out in all the teepees except for the one Kansas was in. I crept over and looked in the window and he was stretched out on the bed reading a magazine. He was wearing his boots. The son of a bitch probably slept in them. As quickly as I could I went to the car and got the tyre iron out of the trunk and I went back and hid in the bushes next to the outhouse. The moon was high and full and lit up the teepees so they looked eerie and clean and bright. Even though I was hidden I was sure anyone walking up to the outhouse could see me. My heart was pounding and I was shivering and sweating at the same time. It seemed like a few days before I saw the door to Kansas's teepee open but it was probably only about a half an hour. I watched him get bigger and bigger the closer he got to me and I was afraid I was going to throw up and give myself away but I took some deep breaths and got control of my nausea. He was only a few feet away from me and my heart was pounding so loud I was certain the whole state of Nebraska could hear it. And then I did it! Just as he put his hand on the door knob of the outhouse I sprang up from the bushes and before he knew what was going on I whacked him on the head with the tyre iron and he fell in a heap without making a single goddamn sound except for the wind escaping him. At first I thought I had killed him but I saw him breathing and I couldn't fight the sick feeling any more and ran to the bushes and vomited up my disgusting meal.

When Kansas came to I had him tied to the totem pole without a single stitch of clothes on. Not even his precious boots. With his big pig-sticker of a knife I cut up his shirt and pants and used them and his belt to bind his hands and feet and gag his big mouth. It took him a few minutes to come around fully and a few more to realize he was tied and gagged.

'I thought you were going to sleep the night away,' I said, just as pleasant as I could be. His body, in the moonlight, was paler than the underside of a frog and his already tiny little dick was starting to disappear up into his belly as he realized what was happening to him and the panic set in. He looked at me and I could see right off the bat, by the flash of terror in his eyes, that he recognized me. 'I bet you have a terrible headache.' He struggled and tried to scream but I put the knife to his throat. 'I wouldn't make too much of a fuss if I were you. If you do, I'll gut you like a Christmas turkey. Does that sound familiar, asshole? It's what you said to me just before you made off with my car and my three hundred dollars and every other fucking thing I owned.' He stopped struggling and looked at me with such horror in his eyes I thought I was going to burst out into song. 'You look like you're about to shit yourself,' I said and he groaned and tried to say something and I just had to know what it was. 'I'm going to take the gag off on the condition that you don't make a sound. You're going to keep quiet. Just as quiet as a little mouse. You understand me, Kansas? Otherwise I'm going to slit your throat from ear to ear and the only sound you'll be able to make will be a little gurgle as your blood bubbles out. Just nod your head if you agree to my terms.'

He nodded his head and I took the gag off. 'What the hell are you doing?' he said, wide eyed, trying to pull loose.

'No, no, no.' I pushed the point of the knife into his throat. 'No talking. Unless, of course, I give you permission. Now, what am I going to do with you? I already went through your pockets and all I found was twenty-two dollars and change. That doesn't come close to paying me back. Not by a country mile it doesn't. Your boots are probably worth something but you know what? I tried them on and they don't fit me. They won't fit my friend, either, his feet are a hell of a lot bigger than mine. Seems they won't do anybody any good, so . . .' I picked up the boots and started slashing from top to bottom and, with lips pressed together so he wouldn't scream, he groaned in agony as he watched me cut them clear through until they were just strips of leather hanging off the high-heeled soles. All the while I was doing it, with great enjoyment I might add, old Kansas was having a fit, struggling to get loose and just wearing himself out but not saying a word.

'You can talk if you want to but keep it real quiet.'

'Those were my boots,' he said, like a little kid who had just had his favourite toy smashed. 'I loved those boots.' There were tears in his eyes.

'Now, that takes care of your clothes and your boots. Oh, by the way, I have your car keys in my pocket.' He looked like he was going to have a stroke. 'You know, I read somewhere that cowboys are so tough they shave with a knife like this. They don't even use soap and water. You think that's true? Why don't we find out?'

'What the hell are you going to do?'

I held the knife close to his chest. 'If I were you I'd be real still. I'm not very good at this and I don't want to slip and cut you . . . fatally. You know what I mean?'

'Oh, shit!' he whimpered.

'You got a lot of hair on your chest for the poor excuse for a man that you are. Maybe we should start there?'

'Oh, shitty ass rat fuck!' The panic in his voice was music to my ears.

'Now, don't you move and don't you make a peep or I just don't know what I might do.' And I shaved, without the benefit of soap and water, a big path of hair off his chest, right down to his belly button. I know if he could he would have been screaming his head off because I did a lot of skin nicking as I went. It wasn't as easy to shave with a dry knife as those cowboys would like people to think. In fact, when I finished, he looked like someone had dragged him chest down over some barbed wire.

'It hurts,' he whispered.

'I guess it is possible to shave with one of these things. A little Burma Shave might help though, right, Kansas, old pal? Now, we're not quite through. But don't worry 'cause there's not too much left to do.'

He was looking a little faint. 'No more, please.'

'Remember when you said this knife was so sharp it could kill me before I even knew you had stuck it into me? You remember that? You don't have to say anything, just nod if you remember.' He nodded, feebly. 'Do you think you'd feel it if I cut your balls off?' A peculiar glaze came over his eyes and he made a sound that was desperate and indistinguishable. I thought he was going to pass out. 'Don't you dare pass out on me, you son of a bitch. I'm not through with you yet.' He came back to life a little. 'I'd never cut your balls off even though I'd like to. But . . .' And I let the 'but' hang in the air for a minute while he imagined every possible horrible thing I could do with a knife. 'But I think I will circumcise you.' With that, his eyes rolled back in his head and he passed out and his bladder let go and he peed all over his feet and his legs. It was a moment of spectacular triumph that I would have liked to have shared with the world but instead I did a little silent war dance around the totem pole and his limp, urine-covered body. It was another one of those times in my life when I thought there just had to be a God.

I hated to leave old Kansas but he was out cold and the fun was over and I knew we had to get away from there before somebody had to answer nature's call and found him. I gagged him so he couldn't raise holy hell when he came to, then I ran to Celine's teepee and told her to get ready because we were leaving. I made some excuse about getting on the road before sun-up and she was so dazed she didn't even put up an argument. Before going to the Angel I slashed the tyres on the old Ford Kansas had driven up in and while I was doing it wondered whose car it was. When I shook the Angel to wake him, he didn't quite know what was going on but he got up and we gathered our things together.

'I'll be ready as soon as I go to the outhouse,' said the Angel.

'You can do that on the road.'

'Why?'

'Because I said so, that's why.'

'You mean I can't even go to the bathroom?'

'You heard me. Let's go.'

'Sometimes I just don't understand you, John.'

'So don't try. Now, come on.'

We met Celine at the Willys-Knight.

'This seems awfully early, John,' she said as we were piling in.

'The earlier the better,' I said, and we left the Pawnee Village in our dust.

'What was all that about last night? I mean, why were you in such a rush to get us out of the restaurant?' She yawned.

'It was nothing. Forget it.'

'I feel like I haven't had any sleep at all.' She was snuggling down in the back seat.

'Me, too,' the Angel yawned.

'That's funny,' I said. 'I have never ever felt better or more rested in my life.' And I started singing 'Bye, Bye, Blackbird' and almost immediately the two of them were sound asleep in the back seat as we headed for Colorado.

It was somewhere between the state line and Denver that I pulled over alongside the South Platte. Celine and the Angel were so dead to the world they didn't even hear me get out of the car. I went to the edge of the river and as hard as I could I threw the knife. It landed with a big splash and I envisioned it sinking down into the weeds and muck, lost to the world for ever. And that son of a bitch Kansas was right there with it.

'Green gravel, green gravel, the grass is so green!
The fairest young lady that ever was seen.
I'll wash you in milk, and dress you in silk,
And write down your name with a gold pen and ink.'

'I always think of you, Celine, when I sing that song,' said the Angel. He had taken to singing little songs he memorized from *Precious Bane*. Of course, he didn't know the melodies so he made them up and when we weren't reading we'd get a little concert of his Shropshire songs. He sang them so often Celine and I learned them, too, and most of the time we'd join in. Now, when I think back, they almost seem like the little songs I grew up with. It's the goddamnedest thing, after a certain age and passage of time, so much of what happened in the past gets all jumbled together and it's hell trying to sort out what happened and when it happened. No wonder a lot of old people seem so damned confused. They're trying to figure out what happened in their lives and it probably isn't making any sense at all to them.

One of the Angel's favourite songs from *Precious Bane* was:

'A vargin went a-souling in the dark of the moon.
A soul-cake! A soul-cake!

O give it me kindly and give it me soon.
A soul-cake! A soul-cake!
The young man he looks from his window so bright.
Here's a vargin come wailing in the dark of the night!
Now what'll you give me for a soul-cake, my maid?
My body, my body for a soul-cake! she said.'

He sang it over and over again until his melody seemed to be the only possible one that fit the words. Celine and I even harmonized with him and we were pretty damn good, too. Of course, those first few days after we left the Pawnee Village I was ready to sing at the drop of a hat. All I had to do was picture that son of a bitch Kansas tied to the totem pole as pale as chalk in the moonlight, his cut-up boots on either side of him looking like some kind of leather flowers blooming on the altar of his humiliation and I was the happiest man on the face of the earth.

The Angel never paid too much attention to the words of those little songs until one day when we were starting up into the Rockies with beefy overblown clouds coming from out of nowhere and rolling around the snow caps like they were looking for someplace to settle. The Willys-Knight was huffing and choking like an old man with pleurisy, when suddenly the Angel stopped in the middle of the song and after a few seconds of looking perplexed he asked, 'What's a "vargin" anyway?'

'The same as a virgin,' said Celine. 'It's the way they say it in the part of England where Prue lives.'

'Somebody who's never done it,' I added.

'Done what?'

'Had sex, you idiot.'

'Don't talk to him like that,' Celine scolded. 'I hate it when you do that.' She was always coming to the Angel's defence when I mouthed off at him.

'Oh, I know that word,' he said and I could see it coming a mile away. 'It's in the Bible.' I always knew by the look in those black eyes of his.

'Don't start with the Bible virgins.' His quoting was like fingernails on a blackboard to me. It just drove me crazy. 'The list is probably endless, for Christ's sake, and you'll be quoting till the cows come home.' He didn't say a damn word but I could see he had a head full of virgins just screaming to get out.

'A virgin,' he said, turning the word over in his mind.

'Yeah, a virgin. Like you. Like you're going to be for the rest of your life if you don't do something about it.'

'Oh, John . . .' It was his dismissal of any talk concerning his sex life.

'Oh, John, yourself,' I said and we rode along in silence for a minute or so. Big drops of rain started splattering on the windshield.

'Are you a virgin?' he asked Celine, flat out like he was asking her the time of day. I looked in the rear-view mirror to see what her reaction to the question would be and she sort of smiled and chuckled and looked at me for a split second like she was telling me not to be embarrassed by the Angel.

'You don't ask people questions like that,' I said. 'Jesus!'

'Why not?'

'It's OK.' Celine took a deep breath. 'I was married.' Talking about it was obviously a trial for her. There was a clap of thunder and a flash of lightning and the sky cracked open and the rain came down like somebody pulled the plug out of a cloud. It was a storm that made the one in Mt Pleasant seem like a sun shower. There is nothing as awesome as Mother Nature acting up in the mountains with clouds rushing around the black sky like they're out to do no good and thunder, the kind that puts cannon fire to shame, echoing off the cliffs. Lightning lit up the ridges like they were on fire and the rain was so hard I couldn't see a damn foot in front of me so I pulled the car over to the side of the road and we just waited it out. It was as good a place as any for the Angel to find out that Celine had been married.

In one of our short discussions of the facts of life, before he squirmed out of it and moved on to another subject, I had managed to explain to the Angel that marriage and sex went hand in hand so that answered the question of Celine's virginity but he wasn't at all prepared for the fact that she had ever been hitched in the first place. 'I didn't know that,' he said with all the amazement of someone hearing for the first time that the world was round. 'Where's your husband?'

'Well . . .' She hesitated for a moment. 'He's dead.' That answered a question I had had in my mind ever since she told me she had been married.

'He's in heaven?' The Angel's face brightened. 'He's in heaven, isn't he?' The thought of anybody getting to heaven damn near made him giddy.

Celine dug the hunk of plaster out of her pocket and, hiding it behind her hand, started nibbling. She just sat there not saying a word but I could see the tears welling up in her eyes. She wasn't nearly as secretive about her nibbling but she never actually did it right out where I could see it and it was never discussed. I supposed it was to remain just another in the long list of little mysteries. But it was the first time I had seen her with the plaster in several days. She let her head drop down and the last thing I wanted to see was her crying so I changed the subject.

'Why don't we all sing a song? We have to wait here a bit

until the rain lets up so it'll give us something to do. Celine, you pick one you like and we'll sing.' She wasn't in the mood for singing, there was no doubt about that. I thought to myself she loved that dead husband of hers the way I wanted her to love me and I felt uneasy about it. Her mood was as dark as the clouds passing over pissing down on us, and she didn't say a word.

'I'll pick a song,' said the Angel.

'No, maybe we'd better play a game instead of singing.' I was trying to think of something to cheer up Celine and take her mind off the man who I was just naturally jealous of even though I never met the poor bastard. What I really wanted to do, instead of playing games, was to ask her all about him, how they met, when they married, what happened to him and things like that. I didn't like the thought of any man but me being with her. I hated competition. Especially dead competition. 'How about "great mountain ranges of the world"? We never did get around to playing that. What do you say, Celine?' She didn't answer me. 'I'll start. The Rockies.' I was hoping that competitive spirit of hers would pull her out of her despair but she didn't say anything. 'Come on, there must be a hundred mountain ranges. You're good at geography. Don't forget you graduated the top of your class. You didn't know that, did you, Michael?'

'You did, Celine?'

'Ask her how many were *in* her class,' I said, trying to make a joke, but no amount of coaxing was going to get her to climb out of the black hole she was in, thinking about the past, so I gave up and told the Angel to sing us a song which he did without thinking twice about it. 'Bill Bailey, Won't You Please Come Home', as I recall. Probably in an effort to cheer Celine up and I remember thinking it might not be such a good selection. Especially if her late husband happened to be named Bill.

We must have been there for three hours waiting for the storm to play itself out. There were times when I was certain we were going to be struck by lightning because there didn't seem to be any end to the ferociousness of it. The Angel sang for almost an hour, going through his repertoire a couple of times, but Celine never joined in. She was off in some miserable private hell, mourning, and there didn't seem to be any way to rescue her from it. Finally, the two of them fell asleep as if they didn't even notice the thunder blasting through the mountains. I sat there, my head resting on the seatback, hoping I could get a little shut-eye, but I had too many questions about Celine's husband going through my mind so I just stared at the stains on the ceiling of the car with my imagination going crazy. By the time the storm passed I had a vision of him firmly planted in my mind. He was taller than any man in the history of the world and his shoulders were broader than Samson's. He never in his life had a pimple or wind or bad breath. He was handsome and generous and wise and kind to animals and little children and he was way ahead of the pack when it came to being a good lover. In fact, after a woman had him, she never ever wanted another man. I hated his dead guts.

The mountains were taking their toll on the poor old Willys-Knight. It was boiling over more and more and I had the feeling that any time it was just going to explode all over the road. It was a serious concern because, even though I am a lot of things, I am no mechanic. All I know about cars is you turn the key in the ignition and step on the accelerator and it takes off.

We had decided to go south through Colorado to New Mexico and then west into Arizona so we could visit a while at the Grand Canyon. I didn't give a damn about seeing it because I was sure it was nothing more than a big hole in the ground but Celine had always wanted to go there, being the geography-lover that she was and, since there was no sign of any lawmen pulling us over and trying to pick us up and haul us off to prison, I thought we could relax and take our time. Besides, I was enjoying driving through the mountains, sharing the warm days and cool nights with Celine and the Angel and Prue and Kester and the rest of that crowd. I told the Angel, when we had a private moment together, not to bring up the subject of Celine's late husband because it upset her too much and even though he couldn't understand why the thought of somebody being in heaven should be so sad-making he promised and, as usual, was true to his word. And as long as we avoided that subject, Celine was as happy as Christmas morning.

'The Rocky Mountains are the spine of the continent.' She was always throwing in things she remembered. Educational things like that. If anybody was born to be a teacher, Celine was. 'I read that someplace when I was just a little kid. Funny the stuff that sticks in your mind, isn't it? The backbone of America! That's pretty impressive, isn't it?'

'Real impressive,' said the Angel. 'My, oh my.' And I could just see, by the look on his face, that he was storing away the information along with the word 'impressive', which he mumbled to himself several times, rooting it in his memory. He was like a damned sponge, learning every minute of the day. It was no wonder he knew the whole Bible by heart. And geography was something new and exciting to him. As we toodled along through the mountains, his job was being the navigator, following a Rand McNally Auto Trails Map we had picked up at a gas station and as we passed any little point of interest he made sure we didn't miss it.

'This here's the Sawatch Range of mountains we're going through. It says so right here on the map.'

'All part of the Rockies,' wondered Celine. 'So beautiful.'

I thought it looked like a lot of nothing.

'There's lots of mountain ranges around here. How about this one? The Sangre de Cristo Mountains,' he said, murdering the Spanish.

'That means "the blood of Christ".' Celine knew everything.

The Angel looked up and before I could stop him said, '*Now in Christ Jesus ye who sometimes were far off are made nigh by the blood of Christ*. Ephesians 2: 13.'

'Now why did you have to go and do that? We were having such a nice time doing our geography lessons and you had to bring in the damn Bible.'

'Well, Celine said the blood of Christ –'

'I know what she said. Just read the mountain names if you don't mind.'

Celine chuckled and the Angel went on with his points of interest. He just about did cartwheels when we'd actually come to a town we had been aiming for. There was the name of that town on the map, in those tiny letters that he had been looking at for maybe a hundred miles, and before he knew it we were driving past the 'Welcome to' sign and he just couldn't believe it. Of course, there was the problem of him getting us lost more often than not and Celine getting a big kick out of it and laughing her head off and making me madder than hell. We saw parts of the Colorado Rockies that even eagles haven't seen and every time we'd come to some dusty, pebbly, dead-end road that wasn't on the map and had never had a white man anywhere near it before us, Celine would have a fit of laughter. The Angel tried to figure out where we made our wrong turn by shifting the map in every possible direction, studying it like all of a sudden it was going to make sense and Celine would laugh even harder and before I knew it I was laughing right along with her. Those were good times for the three of us. Damn good times. But trouble was waiting just over the next mountain.

The Willys-Knight died not too long after we hit New Mexico. It hissed and wheezed and just couldn't take any more of the strain and after one last shudder it gave up the ghost. I did what I usually did when it broke down. I kicked the tyres several times, cussed it out and just stood there like an idiot.

It was just an hour or so after the Angel announced that we had gone through the Raton Pass. 'It says A. 8790. What's that mean?'

'That's the altitude,' said Celine in her best school-teacher voice. And that's when it happened. The old Willys just upped and quit.

'What's wrong with it, John?' asked the Angel.

'How the hell do I know? Do I look like Henry Ford?'

'Maybe if we wait and let it cool down completely it will start,' said Celine, just as calm and in control as could be. 'Just relax.'

'Relax! Don't you know a death-groan when you hear it? It'll take a miracle to get this old rattle trap to come back to life.'

'*And when he thus had spoken, he cried with a loud voice, Lazarus, come forth* –'

'I'm warning you . . .'

Celine saw I was ready to explode. 'I don't think you should do any Bible-quoting. Not right now, Michael. It doesn't seem to be the right time. Maybe we should sit in the shade of the car and read a little while we're waiting for it to cool down.'

'How the hell can it cool down? It's hotter than a griddle out here. It's not supposed to be hot in these mountains. We'll probably be overcome by the heat and die and when they find us there'll be nothing left of us but a few grease spots on the road and picked-over bones. The buzzards are probably starting to circle already.'

'Maybe they are and maybe they aren't,' said Celine. 'I have no way of knowing what the buzzards are doing. But I do know you're not making things any easier by carrying on about bones and the like. Talk about looking on the dark side of things! Good Lord! You can do what you want, but Michael and I are going to sit here in the shade.'

And that's exactly what they did. But instead of *Precious Bane*, the Angel got out the Florentine art treasure book and told Celine whatever he remembered the Doc saying about Botticelli and he said he wasn't sure if he had ever had his picture painted but that the likeness between him and the little angel in the picture gave me the creepy chills and he didn't understand that at all. Celine, who had heard it all before, went along with what she thought was the Angel's little game, played every now and then to justify the wing things growing on his back. I was not in the mood for listening to all that stuff about the painting because it still *did* give me the creeps, and aside from that I didn't know what the hell we were going to do. We were stranded and I seemed to be the only one who was worried about it one way or the other.

We were there for hours with nothing more than the runny-nosed cattle wandering by wondering what the hell we were doing in their territory. Not a single goddamn car passed. It was like we were on a road that had yet to be discovered by the rest of the motorists in the country. But it was right there on the Rand McNally map, just as plain as could be. Every once in a while, even though I knew better, I tried to start the old Willys but it was dead as a doornail.

In mid-afternoon, when the sun was high and hotter than a son of a bitch, an Indian man, old as time, with a face that looked like it had been the model for the craggy mountains, came ambling by, sitting comfortably on a paint horse, leading a small flock of dark brown sheep. A black-and-white dog, as thin as a wisp, kept the sheep in a tight little tangle without so much as a yip. Walking about fifteen feet behind the man on the horse was a woman, probably as old as him, with skin the colour of a saddle, wearing a long skirt as blue as the sky. Her eyes disappeared in her leathery wrinkles and her hair was the same colour silver as the belt she was wearing. I was never so glad to see strangers in my life. The old man reined the horse in right next to the car and the woman stopped and they looked at us as though we were some kind of weird curiosities and I'm sure we were looking at them exactly the same way. I told them the Willys had broken down and I asked if they knew of a mechanic in the neighbourhood and they listened politely, not saying a word and then, without so much as a twitch of the horse's nose, moved on. It was like they stopped to look at something out of the ordinary on the side of the road, a dead lizard or a smashed crow, and once they got their fill of gawking at it they were bored. I called after them but they just kept going and I realized they probably didn't understand a goddamn word I said.

'We have an Indian friend,' said the Angel as they left. 'Mr Ridge. He lives in Paradise and he's a real nice man.' But they didn't even turn around. 'You'd like him a lot.' His voice faded as we watched the dog take the flock off the road, followed by the horse and rider and the brilliant blue of the withered old woman's skirt.

'Now what the hell do we do?' I asked myself out loud.

'We push,' said Celine.

'Push!'

'That's right, we push.'

'Push where? The next gas station could be clear across the goddamn state. Are we supposed to push all the way to Arizona?'

'If we have to, yes.'

'Hey, that's a good idea, Celine.' The Angel was all for it.

'It is not. We'll kill ourselves pushing this damn car.'

'You don't know' – Celine was trying to work up my enthusiasm for her suggestion – 'there could be a gas station just around the next bend. Or maybe there's a long, long hill and we could coast all the way to the bottom of it where there's some big town.'

'That's right, John. There could be a hill and we could coast.' The Angel loved repeating what he thought was a good idea.

'The hill could be going up, too, you know. Besides, there's no big town on the map,' I said, looking at the ever-present mountains in the distance.

'That's right.' Celine was like a snake oil salesman just getting warmed up. 'But what if there is a town? And what if there's a hill and the hill does go down? And at the bottom of that hill there's a gas station? And in that gas station there's a mechanic who specializes in fixing Willys-Knights?'

'I think the heat is getting to you.'

'Seriously,' she said, 'what if?'

'Yeah, John, what if?' The Angel was getting all excited.

'With my luck the gas station will be closed and the mechanic will be on vacation.'

'But what if he isn't? What if instead of sitting here until we're just grease spots and bleached bones we push the car to someplace where we can get it fixed? What about that, huh?'

'It's crazy thinking we can push the car . . .'

'Well, Michael and I are going to do it. You can come along if you want to.'

'What are you talking about? It's *my* car.'

'We're stealing it. Come on, Michael.' Her hair was sticking to her sweaty, sunburned face and she looked like a kid trying to talk a couple of other kids into doing something daring.

'All right.' I gave in. 'You get in the car and steer.' She did a little dancey kind of skip as she opened the door and got behind the wheel. 'But we're just going around the next bend in the road. I mean it, that's all. Jesus Christ, I'm as crazy as you two are.'

She released the brake and the Angel and I started pushing. It was like a big game to him. He sang his songs about 'vargins' and 'green gravel' and 'the fairest young lady that ever was seen' and I sweated until I thought there wasn't a goddamn drop of moisture left in my body. I didn't have enough spit to lick my lips. We pushed around the next bend and the next and the bend beyond that and cattle watched us like we were some big old dinosaur moving down the road and I was cussing and fuming and just when I was about to give up, Celine screamed.

'It's the longest damn hill I ever saw. Come on, hurry up and get in the car.'

We scrambled up on the running board and got in and I had my first real look at the hill and she was right. It stretched out ahead of us, as straight as a ruler, for what looked like miles. Not that it was the steepest hill in the world but it went down and that was all we needed. Celine let the car go and the breeze rushed in and felt as cool and fresh as water. She started hooting and yelling and the Angel joined in and before I knew it I was yelling my head off, too. The three of us, just screaming for the sheer joy of screaming as we barrelled down the hill heading for who knew what?

We must have gone a couple of miles when Celine, like a sea captain at the wheel of a schooner looking for land, let out a screech. 'What's that?'

Way off in the distance, where it looked like the hill ended and the road flattened out, there was a cluster of small buildings looking forlorn and forgotten.

'A damn ghost town.'

'Are you kidding?' She was all smiles, mostly because her suggestion paid off. She was definitely a woman who was partial to winning. 'Don't you know Xanadu when you see it?'

'What's Xanadu?' asked the Angel, all caught up in the frenzy of the moment.

'In Xanadu did Kubla Khan
A stately pleasure dome decree . . .'

'It's from a poem.' Even I knew that much.

'It's the most beautiful city in the world, Michael.' She pointed to the sun-bleached houses that were getting closer and closer as we sailed down the hill with no sound but the wind rushing by. 'That's Xanadu right down there.'

'More like a bunch of goddamned outhouses.'

'Oh, John, you don't even know Xanadu when you see it. That's too sad to even think about.' She was so full of herself.

Well, I'm here to tell you Xanadu didn't live up to its reputation in any way, shape or form. There was a little sign reading, 'You are entering Mesa Vista, New Mexico, population 7.' I looked around but since I didn't know a mesa from a butte, I didn't know what the hell the *vista* those seven people were supposed to be looking at. There were just the same old, ever-present mountains off on the horizon. Not a single solitary resident of Mesa Vista was anywhere to be seen. There were a couple of houses and a gas station with what was meant to be a little restaurant connected. Just past the sign announcing the seven citizens was a small graveyard, surrounded by a knee-high, peeling, black wrought-iron fence with a few lopsided tombstones. There was a vegetable garden, untended and already going to seed behind one of the houses, and clean laundry was flapping on the line: children's clothes and a woman's underthings and men's drawers, so I supposed there was a family living there. Two old dogs, too lazy and bored to do much more than look at us, were half dozing in the shade of a spindly aspen tree and a goat was nosing around in a pile of junk looking for something to eat while chickens pecked their way in and out of the garage. A cat was curled up in a window of the house, leaning against a flowerpot with a plant that looked like it had been dead for years. There may have only been seven people in the town but the animal population was booming.

'I told you it would be a ghost town,' I said after we looked around the garage and found nobody.

'There's somebody looking at us from the window in the house. I seen them move.'

'You *saw* them move. Not *seen*.'

'Either way, there's somebody in there looking at us.'

I took a step or two towards the house and called and after a little bit a pregnant young woman holding a baby came out on to the porch. There was a kid about four tagging along, holding on to her skirt. She had long black hair and looked to be Mexican or maybe Indian.

'You want gas?' she asked with a little bit of an accent.

'What we need is a mechanic,' I said, walking towards her.

'The old Willys died on us.' The Angel was being helpful. 'Just up and died on us.'

'My husband is sleeping. He doesn't like it when I wake him up.'

'Well, what time does he get up?'

'Another hour maybe.' And she started into the house, the little kid right behind her.

'Lady,' I called, 'can we get something to eat in the restaurant?'

'No,' she said, without even so much as giving us a glance, and went into the house.

'I'll be goddamned!'

'We have to wait. That's OK,' Celine wasn't about to get her feathers ruffled by anything or anyone. 'We'll just wait. At least we got the car to a garage. We should be thankful for that.'

I found a faucet and we all had a drink of warm rusty-tasting water then joined the dogs in the shade of the aspen. Just like the woman with the baby said, in about an hour the front door opened and a giant of a man, as blond as the woman was dark, started across the yard towards us.

'I have to get my beauty sleep every day.' He smiled, flashing crooked teeth. 'I'm Sven.' He looked like a Sven. In fact, he looked like he just got off a Viking ship. The Angel was big but Sven had at least four inches on him.

'Am I glad to see you. My name's John Tree.' I introduced Celine and the Angel and told him about our predicament with the car.

'Well, I'll take a look at it' – he scratched his head – 'but Margarito is the man who fixes the cars around here.' All the time he was talking he was eyeing Celine.

'He's not sleeping, too, is he?' I asked.

'Yeah, but no amount of sleep is going to improve his looks.' He laughed as he walked over to the garage door and shouted, 'Margarito! Get up! We have customers.' I couldn't imagine where Margarito could be sleeping in there because we had looked around and didn't see anybody. Sven turned back to us. 'Where you folks headed?'

'California.'

'Oh,' he said. 'You got a long drive ahead of you.' It was all directed at Celine who I could tell was beginning to feel uncomfortable.

'I don't like the Willys-Knight.' The voice came from the garage; leaning in the doorway was a dark man wearing dirty bib overalls. His hair was as long as the Angel's and blacker than midnight and he was almost as big as the Viking.

'These folks are on their way to California,' said Sven. He turned to us. 'This is my brother-in-law, Margarito.'

'You going to California in that piece of crap!' He had the same accent as Sven's wife. 'You must be *loco*.'

'Well, maybe.' I tried to laugh it off. 'Will you take a look at it?'

'Sure. I got a lot of work to do but for you, *señor*, I'll put it aside.' There wasn't a goddamned vehicle in sight except for an old truck parked behind the garage. 'And for such a pretty *señorita.*' He smiled at Celine who was holding the Angel's hand. 'Let's look at it.'

He and Sven pushed the car into the garage and I followed. Celine, wanting to get away from the ogling of Sven and Margarito, took the Angel back to the shade of the aspen. When Margarito lifted the hood, I stood with the two of them looking at the motor like I knew one hose from the other because that's what men are meant to do. Look at motors like we know what the hell they're all about. It's a natural something we're supposed to be born with, right along with testicles and the ability to grow whiskers. Without question, motor-looking is just a thing that men do well. I must have been deprived at birth because I didn't give a shit about looking at motors but I knew I could never openly admit that to anyone, especially another man, so I usually faked it for a while.

'Well,' I asked after a minute or two of the reverence, born of just being in the presence of a motor, 'what do you think?'

'Well . . .' Margarito took his cap off, ruffled his hair and put the cap back on.

'Well . . .' agreed Sven, scratching his chin as they both stared at the motor for another long minute.

'I think you need a new car, *señor.*'

'Looks bad. Real bad,' said Sven, shaking his head like a doctor saying there was no hope.

'You can fix it, can't you?'

'We'll have to see, *señor*. But it'll cost you.'

'How much?'

'There's no way of telling till we give it a good once-over.' Sven yawned, bored with the preliminaries of the business deal.

'We have to have a car, for Christ's sake.' I figured it

couldn't cost more than ten dollars and I still had well over a hundred from the money we left Mt Pleasant with. 'Go ahead.'

'I don't like people hanging over my shoulder when I work.' Margarito smiled. 'You know what I mean?'

'He's a temperamental artist,' laughed Sven.

'Oh, sure. I'll wait outside.' I started to leave. 'The restaurant's not open, huh?'

'Three years now. Nobody to look after it. My wife keeps popping out kids. I don't know what the hell's wrong with her. Anyway, I'm too busy to be messing around with a damn restaurant.' Sven yawned again, still trying to wake up from his beauty nap.

'I'm real hungry, John,' said the Angel when I joined them stretched out in the shade.

'Well, you're just going to have to stay hungry for a while. There's nothing to eat here.'

'How long's it going to take?' Celine was pushing her hair up, trying to get some breeze on the back of her neck.

'They're taking a look.'

'It shouldn't be too long,' she whispered, leaning over. 'It's not like they're overworked.'

'To hear them talk you'd think they were the only garage in downtown Pittsburgh, for Christ's sake. That Margarito acts like he's doing us a favour just looking at the goddamn car.'

'Well, why don't we enjoy the rest. Get a little sleep maybe.' She turned to the Angel. 'It'll take your mind off your empty belly.'

And that's what we did. We laid back and with nothing but the occasional sound of something metal crashing in the garage, and Margarito or Sven swearing, we all fell asleep.

It was some time later when I felt the shadow deepen on

me and I opened my eyes to see Sven standing there, staring at Celine's legs.

'Is it fixed?' I said, sitting up.

'Yeah, it's fixed. Come on, I'll show you. It's damn near good as new. I told you Margarito is an artist.'

We all went into the garage and did some more motor-looking. Even Celine stood there staring as Margarito did his talk about this part and that part, explaining what he'd had to do to get the old Willys going, and I had the feeling she understood what he was talking about a hell of a lot more than I did. It was Greek to me. The Angel smiled pleasantly and nodded in agreement, as he always did when people were talking about things that were way over his head. Sven didn't say much except every once in a while when he'd fortify Margarito's claim that it was a 'bitch of a job'. Personally, I didn't give a damn. It was running and that's all I cared about.

'How much do I owe you?' I asked.

'Seeing as how we like you folks, we're going to give you a bargain. Fifty dollars even and we'll call it a deal.'

'Fifty dollars!' I couldn't believe my ears. 'Fifty dollars! I could buy a whole new fucking motor for fifty dollars.'

'Hey, watch your language in front of the lady.' Sven smiled at Celine and she looked away.

'Fifty dollars is highway robbery. You might as well have a mask on and a gun in your hand.'

'Are you accusing us of cheating you, *señor*?' Margarito took a step in my direction.

'No, but the whole damn car isn't worth fifty dollars.'

'Pay the money, John,' said Celine.

'Yeah, John.' The Angel backed her up as usual. 'Pay the money so we can go someplace and get something to eat.'

'I'm not going to pay fifty dollars to have a car fixed. Hell, that's damn near a down payment on a house!'

'I've got money if you need it.' Celine touched my arm. 'Let's pay and get going.'

'Let me handle this, OK?' It was a tone of voice Celine didn't like and I knew it but I didn't want the Viking and the Aztec knowing she had any money. I didn't have a good feeling about them at all. 'Take Michael outside and wait. I'll be right there.' She did it but she wasn't at all happy about it.

'Fifty dollars,' said Sven when they were gone.

'I'll give you twenty-five.'

Sven laughed. 'Fine. Margarito, you think you can undo half of the work you did?'

'I think maybe I can.'

'Wait a minute. Twenty-five is better than nothing, isn't it?'

'Oh, sure, *señor*. It's better than nothing but not as good as fifty.'

'And we got the keys to the car.' They were both being as pleasant as could be and I was standing there, knee deep in shit again.

'I never heard of anybody paying fifty dollars to get a car fixed. Jesus!'

'You want to try for double or nothing?' Sven smiled. 'You a gambling man?'

'Well, yes, but . . .'

'OK. I'll flip you for it. Double or nothing. Heads you win, tails we win. What do you say?' He took a coin from his pocket and started flipping it.

I never could resist the possibility of getting something for nothing. The coin went sailing, shining in what little sunlight managed to come through the dirty window and I thought to myself, That coin has my name on it. I had that feeling in the pit of my stomach. That feeling that tells you there's no way you can lose.

'Double or nothing,' said Margarito, tempting me. 'You got a fifty-fifty chance here. *Sí*? The odds are as much in your favour as they are in ours.'

'OK. But let me see the coin.'

'Sven, I don't think he trusts us.' He turned to me. 'That's not nice, *señor*, not to trust people.'

Sven flipped the coin to me. 'Go ahead, take a look.'

It was a regular two-and-a-half-dollar gold piece, the Indian head on one side and the eagle on the other. I could even see the date: 1914.

'I'll flip,' I said.

'No, no,' Sven held his hand out for the coin. 'There's two of us and one of you. And it's my gold piece. I'll flip but you can choose which side of the coin you want.'

I tossed the coin to him. 'Heads.'

'Heads it is.'

'No, wait a minute. Tails. I want tails.'

'Whatever you say.' He played with the coin, dropping it from one hand into the other. 'You sure you want tails?'

I didn't know what the hell I wanted but I was sure I was going to win the toss so it didn't matter which side of the coin I chose. 'Yeah, tails. Tails it is.'

'Tails it is,' echoed Margarito.

'Here we go,' and Sven flipped the coin high into the air and it spun around and seemed like it was never going to come down. He caught it in his left hand and slapped it down on the back of his right hand. 'Let's see what we got.' He lifted his hand. 'Well, well, well.'

'What?'

'Looks like you owe us a hundred bucks.' He showed it to me and it was heads.

'Jesus Christ!' I couldn't believe it. One hundred dollars! Almost everything the Angel and I had. I couldn't understand it because that feeling was there, strong as it had ever been. I just had to win. 'How about two out of three?

'I don't think so,' said Sven. 'We won fair and square. You owe us a hundred bucks.'

'Son of a bitch.' I started pacing up and down. There had to be some way out of paying them all that money.

'Hey,' said Margarito, 'we're not bad guys.' He turned to Sven. 'Are we, Sven? How about we give him another chance?'

'What do you mean?'

'Yeah, what do you mean?'

'One more flip. Double or nothing again. What do you say?'

Before I could say anything Sven jumped in. 'We could lose a hundred bucks. I don't think we should do it.'

'Let's give the guy a break.' Suddenly Margarito was on my side. 'Come on. If it was you, you'd want another chance, wouldn't you?'

'Well . . .' Sven hesitated.

'Yeah, you'd want another chance, wouldn't you,' I said. I didn't even stop to think that if I lost I'd be out two hundred dollars. That is, two hundred dollars I didn't even have.

'I'm a sucker,' said Sven. 'I'll do it.' He looked annoyed. 'You want tails again?'

'Heads this time.' I couldn't lose twice in a row. But at the same time, what were the chances of tails coming up again? Fifty-fifty. It was all fifty-fifty, no matter how I sliced it. 'No. Tails. I'll take tails again.'

'You sure you want tails again?'

'Well . . .' I could feel the sweat running down from my armpits and I had a bitter metallic taste in my mouth. 'Yeah, tails. Tails.'

'Tails. Right.' He flipped the coin and it seemed to go even higher and slower and this time when it came down, Margarito grabbed it and smashed it down on his left hand.

'This just isn't your day, *señor*,' he said, showing me it was heads again.

I felt like someone had knocked the wind out of me. 'Oh, shit.'

'Sorry,' smiled Sven.

'You want to try one more double or nothing, *señor*?'

'No.' I didn't even have to think about it. 'Christ, I don't even have the two hundred dollars.'

'Your girlfriend said she has some money.'

'I don't want to take her money.'

'But you owe us two hundred dollars.' Margarito started to crowd me. 'I don't like people who make a deal and then pull out. You know what I'm saying?'

'There is one way . . .' Sven was smiling. 'We could go back to what you originally owed us, the fifty dollars, I mean, and you can work off the rest. Well, not you exactly . . .' He was leering at Celine who was with the Angel petting the goat. I knew the Angel and I were no match for those two big bastards so I wanted to get away from there as fast as I could before they got any more ideas about Celine.

'I'll give you the two hundred dollars,' I said as I walked out of the garage. I counted the cash I had on my way over to Celine and the Angel and it came to 132 dollars. That included bills and coins, every bit of money I had in the world.

'Well?' Celine shaded her eyes from the sun as she looked at me. 'Did you pay them?'

'I need sixty-eight dollars.'

'Sixty-eight dollars? What happened? I thought they wanted fifty?'

'Yeah, well, I need sixty-eight dollars. You have that much?'

She looked at me for a couple of seconds and I guess she figured out what happened – I mean that I did something to mess up – and without saying a word reached down into her bosom and pulled out a wad of bills. She counted out the sixty-eight and handed them to me and I saw she only had a few bills left. I felt so damn guilty taking her money I didn't know what to do.

'I'll pay you back,' I said. 'I mean it. I really will.' And I meant it more than I ever meant anything in my life.

She smiled and said, just as nice as could be, 'Don't worry about it.'

'Can we go now, John? Can we go and get something to eat? I don't like it here.' The Angel had had his fill of Mesa Vista and I knew just how he felt. I knew those bastards had cheated me somehow but I'll be damned if I could figure it out. If I could have beaten the shit out of myself I would have. How the hell could I have been so stupid? They took me for every goddamn penny I had. But I was smart enough, seeing as how big they were, not to accuse them of anything. Besides, there was Celine to think about. They had their eyes on her and I was sure it wouldn't have taken too much for them to go after her.

As I was backing the car out of the garage, Sven, who was counting the money, said, 'You're not mad at us, are you?'

'Fair's fair, *señor*.' Margarito was walking alongside the car. 'You know what I'm saying? It's a gamble. Hey, *vida* is a gamble, no?'

I was in too much of a hurry to get out of there to give him any kind of argument about his half-assed Spanish philosophy. 'Yeah, right. That's what I always say. *Vida*'s a gamble.' I backed up to Celine and the Angel. 'Hurry up, get in.' I wasn't even thinking about the money then. I just wanted to get Celine away from Sven and Margarito. As she stepped up on the running board I could see them both looking at her ass.

'What's the big rush?' Sven was laughing.

'Why don't you stick around. We could make a party. You like a party, *señorita*?'

'I like parties,' said the Angel, all smiles.

'Shut up.' I put the car in gear and we pulled away.

'Come back any time, *señor*.' Margarito grabbed his crotch. 'You too, *señorita*.'

'Yeah, any time.' Sven waved with the money in his hand as we left the yard and hit the road.

Not one of the three of us said anything or looked back. I didn't even want to think about Mesa Vista because deep down I had the feeling that if we hadn't got away from there as fast as we did, there might have been three more graves in the little Mesa Vista cemetery without even the lopsided tombstones.

The Biggest Mistake of All

Celine didn't say anything. She didn't ask what I needed the extra money for or what went on in the garage and she didn't lose her temper. All she did was tell me we only had seven dollars left. Seven dollars and we had over eight hundred miles to go. That was a little less than a dollar every hundred miles for the three of us for food, lodging and gas. I thought I was going to throw up as we moved down the highway, leaving Mesa Vista behind us, and I would have too if I had had anything in my stomach. But we hadn't anything to eat since breakfast. There wasn't a single solitary thing to throw up. I knew the Angel was hungry because he ate like a damn bear but he sensed something was wrong and didn't say a word about it, making me feel like a bigger shit than I already was.

I wasn't in the mood for talking and Celine knew it and came to my rescue by sitting in the back with the Angel and reading what was left of *Precious Bane*. Prue's brother, Gideon, turned out to be even a worse son of a bitch than he *had* been in the beginning of the book. I was feeling so down on myself it was a kind of comfort to hear about somebody worse than me. Funny how that can make you feel a little bit better about yourself To begin with, pretty little Jancis got pregnant and Gideon wouldn't marry her, and then his mother got sick and wasn't any help on the farm and the doctor said she might linger for ten years, feeling poorly and bedridden, so the bastard poisoned her. His own mother! With foxglove tea. I stashed that bit of information away in case I ever had to knock someone off. Apparently it had a hell of a kick. He did the old lady in with just one strong cup. Needless to say, our Prue was sick with grief. But that was only the beginning. Jancis had the baby and walked into the mere and drowned the both of them. Prue laid mother and baby out in white and covered them with flowers and it was sadder than hell. And as if that wasn't enough for Prue to have to deal with, Gideon starts feeling guilty and goes nuts. I identified strongly with that seeing as how it was my fault that we were going to wither up and die of starvation before we got to California and I was already feeling guilty enough to go crazy myself. Well, Gideon, who goes completely around the bend, rows the boat out into the centre of the lake and slips into the deepest, coldest water and commits suicide. It was just one thing after another for poor Prue. His body was never found because it was too deep to drag for him. Of course, being scared to death of water as I am, I had this image of him floating down there in the dark water with a few shafts of light coming down and it gave me the creepy chills even though I thought it was a fit ending for the bastard. But that wasn't all of it. Not by a long shot it wasn't. Prue sells all the stock and decides to give up the farm and old Grimble, the troublemaker who owned the dog Prue stabbed in the heart to save the life of her beloved weaver, accuses Prue of murdering her whole damn family and gets the village all worked up into a tizzy and they all think she's a witch. That's too much for Prue and she passes out. Well, who wouldn't? And when she comes to, she's tied to a chair at the end of a long pole and being dunked in the mere. I guess that's what they did to witches in those days.

'She didn't do nothing wrong.' The Angel was beside himself worrying about Prue.

'*Anything*. She didn't do *anything* wrong,' I corrected him.

'Well, she didn't.'

'Go on, Celine, what happened next?'

Well, there wasn't anybody about to help her and just when it looked like all was lost who should ride up on a horse, big as life and twice as handsome, but our weaver and hero, Kester Woodseaves. He told old Grimble to go to hell and challenged him to a wrestling match but Grimble was too much of a coward so Kester ends up wrestling Huglet, another village bully and pure pain in the ass. Of course, Kester wins by pitching Huglet into the muck and mire of the mere and while the whole village is laughing at Huglet, Kester takes Prue up on the saddle and the two of them ride off together. But Prue doesn't think she's good enough for the weaver, him being the best-looking fellow in all of England and her having a harelip and she tells him to find a prettier girl. Not on your life, says Kester, I've got my own little piece of Paradise right here in my arms. It was something like that. And then he kissed her long and hard and off they went to live happily ever after. Celine and the Angel dissolved into tears and I have to admit I had a lump in my throat, too. Christ, if anybody ever deserved a happy ending it was Prudence Sarn.

Listening to Celine read was a nice diversion but when the story was over and she stopped, the reality of our situation came back to me and I knew there was no Kester Woodseaves who was going to ride up and save my ass. Believe me, at that moment I would have run off with him. Hell, I would have run off with *Gideon* for that matter. Anything to get away from what was happening to us.

*

When we stopped to fill up the gas tank we decided to stay the night in the free campground next to the station because it had toilets and a shower bath. We had been pretty easy with our money, staying in nice places – except for the Pawnee Village, of course – but that night we had to sleep in the car. There was a nice little restaurant, all clean and bright, where several travellers were dining, and where the Angel and Celine had coffee and a piece of pie. I had coffee and toast. I wanted to blow the money and eat because in our situation we might just as well have been broke with something in our bellies. What the hell were we going to do with a few bucks? But Celine insisted we hold on to as much as we could. The Angel didn't say a word but I noticed him looking at the food being delivered to other tables with the same kind of hungry longing a fat person on a diet looks at a piece of chocolate cake. It occurred to me that the Angel was growing up. He wasn't the same kid, responding to everything with the very first thought in his head, as when I first met him. He was thinking things through a little bit more, figuring out what he should or shouldn't say and I admired him for that. But the food problem didn't get any easier when we left the restaurant and went to the campground to turn in because there were people cooking over open fires and there is no smell in the world more tantalizing than outdoor cooking. The greasy, sizzly smell of meat and the earthy aroma of potatoes burning in the coals and the smell of coffee perking away, the all-time greatest smell there is, was enough to drive us all out of our minds. It was too dark to read and besides, Celine was kind of read out, having finished *Precious Bane*, so we tried our best to get comfortable in the car and not pay attention to the hunger pangs and just go to sleep. I thought some talk about more pleasant times might relax us so I brought up the good life we were going to have in Hollywood.

'First thing we do, when you two are movie stars, is get rid of this old clunker of a car and get us a big red sports model. Or one of those imported motor cars with all that chrome and custom-made leather seats.'

'Will we be able to eat anything we want, John?'

'Anything at all. Any time we want to.' Celine wasn't joining in, but then, she never did when we talked about Hollywood. She never ever mentioned becoming a movie star. 'What do you want, Celine? What's the first thing you want when you're rich?'

'Oh, I never think of things like that. It's just a lot of pipe dreams.'

'John says dreaming is half the fun of getting there. Don't you, John?'

'I certainly do.'

'That's hard to believe,' she said. 'He didn't even recognize Xanadu when he saw it.' She sounded sad and I wished I could have seen her face.

The Angel and I did a little more talking about the good times ahead of us but without Celine joining in it fizzled out and we all grew silent. Celine and the Angel were in the back seat and I was trying to find some way to stretch my legs in the front. The odd thing was, there we were, on the verge of starving to death and for the first time in several days, all I could think of was making love to Celine. It was the nicest thing I could fill my mind with, I suppose, and I wanted to be in the back seat with her holding her in my arms, telling her everything was going to be all right. Alone, of course. If the Angel hadn't been there I *would* have been in the back seat with her. I was past jealousy at that point but there were a lot of times when I was downright resentful of him being there. Especially when I thought of the good times Celine and I could have been having. The truth was, however, except for being a whole lot friendlier to me, things hadn't really changed between us. We did have those few moments of connecting with one another but for some reason she would stop it, guarding herself. It was as automatic as Carlton's knee-jerk reaction when he accidentally touched a man.

We could hear people singing someplace in the campground and here and there the fires lit up the canopy of trees and it was all warm and friendly but I started to feel like one miserable son of a bitch. The Hollywood talk didn't do a thing to cheer me up. Nor did wanting Celine and not being able to have her do me a bit of good. I didn't know if she and the Angel were asleep or not because they never said another thing and their eyes were closed but I knew I wouldn't be able to sleep a wink. There was too much on my mind. Most of all that I had fucked up again and I didn't know what to do about it. The only good thing I could think of was that I *did* get Celine away from Margarito and Sven before anything happened to her. If anything *would* have happened. Maybe I was just looking for some little something to feel good about. Either way, it wasn't putting food in our mouths.

After about an hour I was so restless I got out of the car as quietly as I could and took a walk around the grounds. By then, the fires had died down and the tents were quiet and all I could hear were some loud snores and the night sounds of insects and other little critters. Way off in the distance I heard a howling which I guessed was a coyote. It made me feel lonely, like a train whistle in the night makes me feel lonely, no matter where I am or who I'm with. Mr Coyote didn't sound at all happy and I knew just what he was going through.

*

The next morning we started out for the Grand Canyon with clean bodies if nothing else. We all took shower baths because we had no idea when we'd have the opportunity again. After a breakfast of toast and coffee, my favourite but sparse pickings for the Angel and Celine, who had as big an appetite as the Angel in the morning, we headed out. The Angel was back at his post as navigator and Celine resumed telling us interesting things she remembered from school. They were doing their damnedest pretending that everything was just the way it should be and I truly admired them for it.

'You know the strange thing about the coyote,' she said after I told them I had heard one howling the night before, 'on good years, when there's going to be plenty of prey, they have big litters of pups but on years when the game is going to be scarce they don't have nearly as many. Isn't that interesting?'

'Well, it sure is,' said the Angel. 'Don't that beat all!'

'And scientists have no idea how they regulate the size of their litters. I read that in a nature book once. It just amazed me.' She knew I was still feeling bad about losing the money and she tried to engage me in conversation the way I had with her the night before, talking about Hollywood. 'Isn't that amazing, John?'

'Well, it sure is. It's the goddamnedest thing I ever heard.' I did my best to work up some enthusiasm for the coyote information but I couldn't so I just let them go on about this and that while I tried to map out some kind of plan in my mind. I did hear the Angel read a few Burma Shave signs and Celine tell us what she knew about the Indians and wildlife we were probably passing but most of the time my brain was too busy to pay any attention to them. Hard as I tried, I couldn't come up with anything short of robbing a bank but that was hard to do when the only weapon I had to threaten anybody with was a pretend gun made out of my finger. I *did* think it would have been easier if I had been alone. Not because we had to share the little bit of money we had left but because I would have been able to do more. It wasn't easy trying to do something underhanded or illegal when you were stuck with an extra set of consciences. Both good.

'It's almost a mile to the bottom of the canyon,' said Celine, as we stood at Yavapai Point lookout, 'and it's all because of the Colorado River running through here for millions and millions and millions of years.'

'That scraggly little string of a river! Goddamn, it's hard to believe.'

'We're really in heaven this time, aren't we, John?' The Angel's eyes looked like they were going to fall out of his head and I didn't have an answer for him because I was feeling we were about as close to heaven as we were ever going to get.

'Not quite, but pretty near.'

'It's beautiful.' Celine couldn't get enough of it.

I certainly had to eat my words about the Grand Canyon being nothing more than a big hole in the ground. They didn't call it *Grand* for nothing. It was about as fantastic and magical as anything I would ever see in my lifetime and I knew it. Just the size of it alone reduced me to no more than a speck of dust and for the time being made all my problems seem pretty damned insignificant. Celine had tears running down her cheeks and I knew just how she felt. It was all too perfectly unimaginable. Ravens floated on the winds, squawking and making a hell of a racket echoing off the canyon walls and there were pillars of stone rising up with such grace they rivalled any damn Gothic cathedral in the world. They were painted colours of brown and grey and red and every other earth colour there is. For some reason, I thought of Doc Forepaugh talking about the colours in the Botticelli paintings. That light in his eyes would have been shining bright as a lighthouse if the Doc'd had a gander at the Grand Canyon. It was crazy but for a minute I kind of missed the old man and wished he had been there to share all that wonder with us. I think places like that were made especially with people like Doc Forepaugh in mind.

Here and there, there were still patches of snow catching the sunlight and reflecting like pools of water, and clouds, like sea foam, passed over making shadows that moved like some kind of giant hand.

'*Hath not my hand made all these things?* Acts 7:50,' said the Angel as if he was reading my mind. I was too impressed with all of it to be annoyed by his quoting.

'It does make you think of God, doesn't it?' Celine was wiping her eyes.

'And the ocean,' I said. 'I don't know why but I keep expecting to hear waves. I suppose it's just so damn big. It's true, I get the same feeling I get when I'm on the shore looking at the ocean.'

'*Whatsoever the Lord pleased, that did he in heaven, and in earth, in the seas, and all deep places*. Psalm 135:6.'

'Amen,' said a heavyset man standing right behind us. I hadn't even heard anybody come up. He wore rimless glasses that made his eyes look like they were too close together and he had on a long canvas duster and a cap. He was as big as a house. With him was a spidery-looking woman, skinny arms and legs with black hair, cut square across her forehead and just below her ears. She had as much make-up on as Lydia wore but it was smeared and the lipstick was running into little creases around her mouth. After taking a drag on her cigarette, she smiled at us, showing slightly yellowed, tobacco-stained teeth.

'Quite a sight, isn't it,' said the man.

'It surely is,' smiled the Angel. The woman nodded to him.

The man started to read out loud from a marker. All about caves and monoliths and stalagmites and petroglyphs, Hopi mesas and Navajo Indians and Ponderosa pines. All kinds of stuff that I wasn't the least goddamn bit interested in but Celine and the Angel were listening to every word. I was willing to admit to the majesty of the place and how every minute, as the sun moved, it all changed but I wasn't about to fill my mind with all the *liths* and *glyphs* and that kind of crap. I liked the simple version of what Mother Nature had to offer. When the man finished reading he offered some information of his own. Like that the river, which looked like a little old creek from the rim of the canyon, was actually as wide as a football field in some places. Celine and the Angel loved all that.

'My name's Floyd Wilburforce,' he said after a while. 'This is my wife, Vilma.' The skinny lady nodded but didn't say anything. 'Where you staying?'

'We haven't decided yet.' I tried to sound like a regular tourist.

'We're at the Ridgecrest Lodge. Beautiful place, isn't it, Vilma?' Vilma smiled and nodded and took a drag of her cigarette. 'It was built about the same time as the Tovar. The Tovar is the oldest lodge here, you know. Built in 1905.' Floyd was one of those guys who was full of facts. The kind of man who you just knew memorized the mileage between places and kept track of how many miles he got to a gallon of gasoline. Vilma never said a single goddamn word. Not that he ever gave her a chance to. She just looked at us and smiled and every so often, seemingly for no reason at all, Floyd would turn to her and nod his head and she'd nod back as though they were agreeing on something. Floyd went on with his facts and figures until I could see the Angel's eyes glaze over with boredom and even Celine started to lose interest.

'Well, we better find ourselves some place to settle for the night. We'll be seeing you.'

'Don't forget, we're at the Ridgecrest. Really a beautiful place. I'm sure you'd like it there.' Vilma nodded in agreement.

'We might take a look at it.' We started for the Willys.

'We'd like to see you again.' It seemed like Vilma, without saying a word, was encouraging Floyd to keep the conversation going.

'Well, I'm sure we'll bump into each other.'

'By the way, we're from St Louis. I'm in porcelain fixtures. Toilets, sinks, the like.' He took a few steps in our direction. 'Where'd you say you were from?'

I hadn't said anything. 'Pittsburgh.'

'I do a lot of business in Pittsburgh. Maybe you've seen the name. It's Wilburforce. It's in fancy black scroll on toilet bowls all over America.'

'I think maybe I have,' I said. I wanted to say that not only had I seen it but on many occasions, when I had a few too many drinks, I aimed at it.

Vilma looked like she was giving Floyd another nudge. 'Maybe we should arrange to meet? Tonight, perhaps?'

'We know where you are. Once we get settled. We'll see.'

He took another couple steps in our direction. 'Whatever you do, don't miss Ooh Aah Point. At sunset. It's everything people say it is. Could be we'll see you there this evening? Maybe we should make plans.'

'Well, we're not settled. We'll see what happens.' I figured Floyd was so bored with Vilma, or vice versa, that they would have asked the devil himself to spend time with them just for the change.

'And from Hopi Point you can see Isis Temple. Believe me, it's a sight you'll never forget.'

'I'll just bet it is,' I called to Floyd. Then I whispered to Celine and the Angel, 'Let's get the hell out of here before he tells us how tall he is and how much he weighs.' Celine laughed as we got in the car.

'Don't forget, we're at the Ridgecrest,' he called. 'We'd really like to see you again.' I waved as we pulled away.

Vilma and Floyd stood looking at us for a long time as we drove down the narrow road edging the Canyon and I could see that Vilma *could* talk because she was saying something to Floyd.

Of course, there was no question about our looking for a place to spend the night. We were going to stay in the car again in the public campground because I hadn't figured out how to get any money. But money or no money we had to eat something so we went to the Ridgecrest to get some lunch. The parking lot was full of shiny touring cars and the old Willys-Knight looked dingy and sorely out of place next to them. So did the three of *us*, for that matter. People were walking around dressed in clothes that were probably the latest thing for the traveller. Women wearing riding pants and boots, some of them looking ridiculous with asses the size of a barn, and men looking even dumber in their plus fours and argyle knee socks wrapped around legs as spindly as a chicken's.

'What are they all dressed up for?' asked the Angel.

'Halloween, but they don't know it.'

Inside the Ridgecrest, which was elegant and clean as a hospital, with wide staircases and chandeliers and enough stuffed animal heads on the walls to wipe out half the wildlife population of the state of Arizona, there was a regular fashion show going on. Celine couldn't take her eyes off the passing parade. Some of them looked like they were going to start singing cowboy songs and the rest looked like they were ready to board an ocean liner. I guess fashion was half the fun of going on vacation.

A waitress, all starched in black and white, showed us to a table in the crowded dining room. I ordered my usual toast and coffee. The truth of the matter is I was past being hungry. I felt a little light headed but I also felt like I had more energy than I had ever had in my life. It was a very weird sensation. But I knew Celine and the Angel should eat something. And what the hell difference did it make? We were damn near down to flat broke. Holding on to whatever change we had didn't make a bit of difference as far as I was concerned. I insisted they each order a sandwich. Well, I should have known better. Nobody *insisted* with Celine.

'We'll order one sandwich and Michael and I will share it.'

'But . . .'

'But nothing. We have to watch every penny.'

'That's right, John. Every single penny.' The Angel would have agreed with Celine if she had said there was no such thing as electricity.

'An egg salad sandwich, please.' She smiled and handed the menu back to the waitress who had been standing there smiling through our exchange. Egg salad was the cheapest thing on the menu, I guess. 'Now' – she folded her hands on the table as if she was the head of the board getting down to business – 'we have to make a plan. I've been thinking about it and the only option we have is to get some kind of jobs.'

'That's right,' said the Angel.

'Jobs! What the hell kind of jobs can we get? There's nothing around here.'

'There are hotels and lodges.' Celine had obviously been giving this some serious thought. 'There must be all kind of jobs we could do.'

'You know how little these jobs pay? We'll be here for ever trying to save enough to get going. We're on our way to Hollywood, for Christ's sake. I don't want to be a goddamn busboy.'

'Well, then don't. But I'm going to ask about a job.'

'Me, too,' the Angel smiled. 'I *like* working, John.'

'You don't know what you're talking about.'

'You have any better ideas?' I could hear that competitive thing in her voice.

'Give me a little time.'

'We don't have time.'

'That's right, John. We don't have time.' The Angel was leaning towards me with his hands folded the same as Celine.

'Did you ever once in your life try thinking for yourself?' He was beginning to get on my nerves. And then, I had what I thought was a reasonable solution to our problem. 'Hey, why don't we check into the hotel. Like any other tourists. We'll have a good night's sleep, order room service and eat till the damn food comes out our ears. Think of a good night's sleep in real beds.'

'And how are we going to pay for it?' She already knew the answer.

'We don't. We get up early in the morning and pretend we're going to watch the sunrise. That's a big thing here, isn't it? Sunrises and sunsets. Then we get in the car and take off.'

'I couldn't do that,' said Celine.

'You mean and not pay any money?' The Angel was just putting it all together. 'We couldn't do that, John.'

'You just keep out of this, for Christ's sake. Just keep your big mouth shut unless you have a better idea.'

'Don't go picking on Michael because you're backed into a corner.'

'What corner? I come up with a perfectly good plan and –'

'I just couldn't do it. That's all there is to it. It's like stealing.'

'So?'

'I'll look for a job.'

'Me, too, John.'

'Jesus!' I knew there was no point in wasting my breath on them. She was a strong-willed woman and the Angel would have messed things up some way so I just gave up. 'I'll think about the job business,' I said, starting to give in but not wanting to.

'You do that.'

We spent the rest of the meal in silence with me cracking my brain to come up with an alternative to work that wasn't so obviously underhanded. Celine watched the stylish ladies gliding by and the Angel drooled over at all the food passing him. I couldn't think of a thing so before we left the table I agreed to look for a job. No question about it, it was against my principles but what else could I do?

'OK, we'll see if they have a personnel office here,' I said.

'And descend on it in a group? I don't think that's a very

good idea.' She was taking over as captain of the ship. It was goddamn mutiny. 'One of us will try here and the other two will go to other lodges. We'll stand a much better chance that way.'

I wasn't about to argue because I knew it was a waste of time. 'Fine. Tell me what to do and I'll do it.'

'You don't have to start pouting.'

'Yeah, John, don't pout.'

'You shut up. I'm getting tired of you echoing everything Celine says.' I turned to her. 'Tell me what you want me to do and I'll do it, goddamn it. And I'm not pouting.'

'Yeah, sure.' She smiled. 'All right, John, you try here and I'll drive around and drop Michael off at one of the other places and we'll see what happens.'

'Fine. I'll meet you here. Out front on the terrace, later this afternoon.' We walked out to the lobby and as Celine and the Angel were leaving he ran back to me.

'You wait and see, John, I'm going to get me a job and we won't have a thing to worry about. You just wait and see. We'll be able to eat anything we want.' Then he put his arms around me and hugged me and kissed me on the cheek like he was going off to war or some damn thing.

'Will you stop that,' I said, pushing him away. And he ran to join Celine, laughing. He knew how to drive me crazy and was having fun with it.

I asked at the desk where the personnel office was and a tall, pimply-faced, college-boy type, so full of energy and good cheer he made me sick, directed me to the rear of the second floor. As I walked up the stairs, I had the feeling that the moose and elk, hanging on the walls and staring straight ahead with their filmy glass eyes, were laughing at me. When I found the office, there was a handsome blonde woman who looked to be in her early forties sitting behind a desk stirring a cup of coffee hard enough to wear out the spoon.

'Can I help you?' She was mercifully less cheery than the college boy with the pimples.

'I was wondering if you had any jobs.'

She looked at me for a quick moment. 'What do you do?'

I thought there was a little bit of an invitation in her voice so I smiled my most dazzling smile. 'Anything you have in mind, pretty lady.'

I was mistaken because she gave me a look that let me know she wasn't inviting me to anything and she wasn't at all interested in my smile, dazzling or otherwise. Her eyes narrowed and she said, 'I asked you a question. What do you do?'

'Work. Hell, I don't know. Do you need a waiter? I can be a waiter.'

'We have the Harvey Girls waiting tables at the Ridgecrest. It's a tradition. I'm afraid you don't qualify.'

'You can bet I don't, pretty lady. Not by a long shot.' I tried to inject a little sexual innuendo hoping I might still be able to break her down. I knew she picked up on it right away so I sat on the edge of her desk.

'What are you doing?'

'Getting comfortable. You mind?'

'Get off my desk.' And I did. There was no breaking this woman down. She meant business. 'This conversation is over. There are no jobs available at this time. Or in your case, any time. Good-day.'

'What did I say?'

'Nothing. I'm busy. I said, good-day.'

'I was just trying to be friendly.'

'I know what you were trying to be. Get out of here. You're making a fool of yourself. Out. Now.'

'OK, OK. Don't get your bowels in an uproar, for Christ's sake!' I went to the door. 'What you need is a sense of humour.' The phone rang and she picked it up, dismissing me with one last mean glance. 'Bitch,' I said, not loud enough for her to hear but loud enough to make me feel like I had the last word.

I went down to the lobby, not knowing what I was going to do next, and this time I was *sure* all those dead animals were looking and laughing. I picked up a newspaper someone had left on a settee and sat down. Since we left Mt Pleasant we hadn't seen a paper and for all I knew we could have been at war or some goddamn thing. I sat there trying to read but before I knew it, my night of trying to get comfortable in the car took its toll and I fell asleep. It was a heavy sleep, deep as a coma for over two hours, and when I woke up from it it took me almost fifteen minutes to really come to. I felt drugged and at the same time the hunger caught up with me and I could have eaten one of the guests prancing around the lobby in their fancy duds. I was feeling nauseous when I went out to the terrace to see if the Angel and Celine had come back but they weren't there. Seemed like they were gone for a hell of a long time and I started to worry about them. People were coming and going and I watched them for a while hoping I could forget my hunger but I knew I had to put something in my stomach or I was going to pass out. There was this strange feeling of walking on cushions every time I took a step and I thought I was going to pitch forward right on my face. At that point I didn't give a shit about holding on to the little money that was left. I had to eat and that was all there was to it.

There weren't many people in the restaurant when I went in. I took a seat and when the waitress came I ordered an egg salad sandwich without even looking at the menu. And coffee because I knew she'd give me free refills. When she delivered the sandwich I forced myself to eat it slowly, savouring every bite like it was Christmas dinner but it didn't even make a dent in the hunger. But at least I didn't feel like I was going to faint any more. After the third cup of coffee, when I was feeling a little shaky from the caffeine, I paid the check and as I was leaving the restaurant I passed a table where one of the guests had left a whole dollar as a tip. It looked like a thousand dollars to me so without thinking twice I checked around and when I saw no one was looking I picked it up and slipped it in my pocket and hurried towards the door. Floyd Wilburforce was standing there watching me. He had seen me steal the tip, I just knew it.

'Well, hello there.'

'Mr Wilburforce.'

'Are you staying here at the hotel?'

'We haven't decided yet.'

'I see.' He looked around and after a moment said, 'Come with me, I want to talk to you.' He led the way to the same settee I had fallen asleep on. 'Sit down.'

I knew he had seen me. 'What's up?'

'I saw what you did. Taking the money off that table, I mean.'

'So, what are you going to do? Report me? I'll put the goddamn dollar back.'

'Take it easy, boy.' He was talking down to me, like he was in control because of what I had done. 'Did I say I was going to report you?' He looked around the lobby again. 'It's just a dollar.' He smiled and his little eyes disappeared in his fat face. All of a sudden he reminded me of my brother-in-law, Frank. 'You and your friends are broke, huh?'

'You might say that. I lost all our money.'

'Well, that's too bad. Maybe I can help. I'd like to if you'll let me?'

'Why do you want to help us?'

'We like you kids. Vilma and I, that is. We said that after you left this morning.' He patted me on the knee. 'How'd you lose your money?'

And I told him all about Sven and Margarito and he listened, shaking his head and making little sounds with his tongue like he was amazed at the treachery of the human race. 'And so I've got about two dollars left. That's it.'

'Hard luck. That's what I call it, hard fucking luck.'

'Christ, I'll say.'

'Well, I've got a little proposal for you.'

'At this point, I'll go for anything.'

'That's good.' He looked around for the third time to make sure there was no one standing near by. 'Vilma and I have been married for a long time. Thirty years next June. Lord, where does the time go? Anyway, we were always a very loving couple. You know what I mean. Loving. We couldn't get enough of each other.'

'Well, that's real good. Nice.' I didn't want to think about the two of them wrestling around in bed but if he was having a good time talking about it that was fine with me as long as it led to some money.

'Well, to make a long story short, seven years or so ago I had me a couple of surgeries. Serious surgeries . . . I don't want to go into any detail but they were serious. I'm lucky I'm here. The trouble is, since then, I haven't been any good to Vilma. In that department, I mean. You know what I'm saying? Some of my plumbing doesn't work the way it used to.'

'You mean you can't get it up?' I started to feel peculiar because I knew what was coming next.

'That's it. I can't get it up. And Vilma is a woman with urges. She always has been. Strong urges and needs that I can't do much about. So, for the past few years when she sees something she likes in a fellow, I make an arrangement with him . . . financial, of course . . .'

'Christ!' He wanted to pay me to screw skinny old Vilma! I don't know what thoughts were going through my mind when I sat down to talk to him but screwing his wife certainly wasn't one of them. Now, I have to say right here that sleeping with another man's wife had never been a problem for me. Hell I'd probably still have been teaching school in Lowell, Massachusetts if I hadn't been caught with Mrs Millie Quick and drummed out of town. The truth is I always thought adultery was good for all parties concerned. *I* didn't have to worry about getting serious and the *woman* had a good time and, from what they usually said, it spiced up things at home for the *husband*. But the difference between the Millie Quicks of the world and Vilma Wilburforce was that with the Millie Quicks, I usually did the picking. The thought of tearing up the sheets with the spider woman, yellow teeth and runny make-up and smelling of tobacco, wasn't exactly a dream come true. But then I thought of the first time I ever had a woman. It was in Akron, Ohio in a whorehouse, I was sixteen and the woman was old enough to be my mother and she had a front tooth missing and she smelled of whiskey and cheap perfume. The only way I got through it was to keep my eyes squeezed shut and pretend I was doing it to Emily MacCaffrey, a girl I went to school with who was my inspirational fantasy every time I played with myself. I thought, we are as broke as broke can be, I guess I can squeeze my eyes shut with old Vilma.

'Well,' asked Floyd, 'what do you say?'

'I'm thinking about it. How much?'

'Twenty dollars. That's a lot of money when you're broke.'

'Yes, it is,' I said but I was thinking it was just a drop in the bucket when your name was on most of the goddamn toilets in America. 'One hundred dollars and I'll do it.'

'Oh, I guess I didn't make myself clear. It's not you Vilma wants. It's the young fellow. She likes them young.'

Well, it never occurred to me he was talking about the Angel. It surprised me so much I got a little light headed. 'Michael! He's just a kid. He's never even been with a woman, for Christ's sake.'

'Oh, Vilma will like that. We've found her a couple boys like that before and just the thought of her being the first makes her real happy. Boys like Michael aren't as easy to find as you might think.'

'Michael! No, I don't think so.'

'I'll give you the hundred dollars.'

'The hundred dollars was for me, I'll do it. She'll be satisfied. Believe me, I never had any complaints.' Mary Lou, the only exception, went through my mind but that was a different situation altogether.

'Nothing against you' – Floyd shuffled his bulk around on the settee and I could hear the frame creak – 'but Vilma has her heart set on the other one. Michael. And I always try and give Vilma what she wants. What can I do? I love the woman. How about a hundred and twenty-five?'

All I needed was for someone to start bargaining and I was a goner. 'How about two hundred?'

'A hundred and fifty?'

'Two hundred. Two hundred dollars and nothing less.'

'Can you speak for your friend? I mean, are you sure he'll do it?'

'He does what I tell him to do.'

'Then, two hundred dollars it is. I never paid that much for anybody. That's more than most men make in a month. I guess I'm just a fool in love where Vilma is concerned. You drive a hard bargain.' He put out his hand to shake. 'For how long?'

'For two hours. Take it or leave it.'

'I'll take it.'

'It's a deal.' And as I took his fat hand to shake it I knew I was making a big mistake.

'Seven o'clock tonight in our room.'

'How come so early?'

'We're very conservative people. We don't stay up late.'

'You're not going to be there, too, are you?'

'Of course. We're taking a big chance. What if some guy got rough and wanted to do something to hurt Vilma. I'd never forgive myself. I'm always there.'

'Christ, that's disgusting.'

'I just watch. Don't worry, I don't do anything strange, if that's what you're worried about.'

I needed a reason to get out of it and suddenly, the Angel's wings came to mind. 'Listen, there's something unusual about Michael. He's got these things growing on his back. They're growths. On second thought, I don't think Mrs Wilburforce would like him. I think we'd better call off the deal.'

'What kind of growths?'

'Well, they're like an extra set of hands coming out of his shoulder blades. It's kind of weird and they're ugly. Truly, they are ugly. Let's just forget it.'

'Vilma might like that. One boy had two pairs of nipples and she was partial to him. And he wasn't nearly as good looking as your Michael, either. A deal's a deal.' His eyes got mean and any trace of a smile left his face. 'Seven o'clock,' and he gave me the room number and got up to leave. 'By the way,' he said, digging into his pocket, 'here's twenty dollars. I'll give the rest to Michael. After.' He threw it on the settee next to me and I had the feeling it was because he had such contempt for me he didn't want to risk actually touching me. 'Get yourself something to eat. And get something for your girlfriend and Michael, too. He's going to need his strength.' He started to walk away. 'Two hundred dollars! That boy better be worth it.' He waddled across the lobby and disappeared up the wide staircase, the animal heads watching his every step. He didn't look back once. He was a man who had just transacted some business and that was that.

Well, it was almost an hour before Celine and the Angel showed up. An hour in which I went back and forth and back and forth thinking about what I had done until my head was spinning. I must have walked up and down that terrace a thousand times. On the one hand, I knew I couldn't tell Celine before it happened or she would have called the whole thing off because she'd be mad as hell. She was such a mother hen where the Angel was concerned. Women can be vicious as hell when it comes to protecting their own. And they make so much out of everything. Especially where love or sex is concerned. But, I told myself, it was none of her business. It was just something between the Angel and me. Just between men. And it was time he got laid, for Christ's sake. Hell, he was damn near twenty years old. It wasn't such a big thing. I did it with that whore in Akron when I was a hell of a lot younger so why couldn't he stick it to old Vilma? And the bottom line was we needed the goddamn money. It wasn't like he was doing it for fun.

We were starving to death and this was a way out. It was the least he could do for me after all I had done for him. Maybe if we had had some other options it would have been different but we didn't. Two hundred dollars would get us to Hollywood with money to spare. And, I *did* offer to do it myself! It wasn't like I was expecting the Angel to do something *I* wouldn't do. It was no big thing. Just something men do and he was way behind schedule in that department. I told myself that over and over as I did my pacing and by the time the two of them came walking up from the parking lot I almost had myself convinced that what I was going to ask the Angel to do wasn't anything to worry about.

'Any luck?' asked Celine as she came towards me.

'Not really. I'm not a Harvey Girl.'

'Well,' said the Angel, full of himself and bubbling over, 'I maybe got me a job, John. It's true. Carrying luggage at the Hopi House. It's a real nice place. Real nice. I have to go back to see the man tomorrow.'

'He did better than I did.' Celine looked tired. 'Seems as though the whole country needs work. At least that's what they told me every place I went.'

'They were very nice to me. They gave me a meat sandwich and a glass of milk. Free, John.'

'I bet you're still hungry. How'd you like a pot-roast dinner with mashed potatoes and gravy and all the pie you can eat?'

'I'd like that. I really would like that.'

'What's going on?' asked Celine, suspiciously.

'I'm taking you two to dinner.' I took the bill out of my pocket and held it up. 'Twenty whole dollars.'

'Where'd you get twenty dollars?'

'The tooth fairy! What difference does it make. I've got it so let's get something to eat.'

'We should save that . . .'

'Not this time. This time we're going to eat. And I don't want to hear another word about it. There's plenty more where this comes from.'

'Twenty dollars!' The Angel was astounded.

'Come on. Let's eat.'

We weren't at the table in the restaurant twenty minutes before Floyd and Vilma Wilburforce came in and sat at a table clear across the room near the window. I was certain they knew we were sitting there but they never once looked our way or nodded or acknowledged us in any way whatsoever.

'There's the people we saw today,' said the Angel.

'Yeah, I see them. Now eat up.'

I ate, as hungry as I was. but I didn't really enjoy it. Celine didn't say much, partly because her mouth was too full of food to talk and partly because she knew I wasn't about to tell her where I had got the money. The Angel made things worse for me because he kept telling me how everything was going to be fine when he got the job at the Hopi House and I didn't have anything to worry about. He was making me feel guilty before I even did anything. It was about half past six when we finished eating so I kept stalling, drinking enough coffee to float a battleship, until it got closer to seven. The Wilburforces got up and left the dining room, again without the slightest hint that they even knew we were there and when I saw by the big clock that I couldn't put it off any longer, I paid the check and we left.

'Will you wait for me out front,' I said to Celine when we were in the lobby. 'I want to talk to Michael alone for a minute. I won't be long.'

'What's going on?' asked Celine.

'Just men talk.' I tried to smile and make it sound like a trivial matter. 'I'll be right out.'

'There's something going on here.'

'One minute and I'll be there.'

She wasn't smiling when she left.

'What's the secret, John?' There was nothing the Angel liked more than a secret or a surprise. Well, I certainly had a surprise for him.

'I want you to do something for me.'

'Anything.'

'You know those people we met? The Wilburforces? They liked you.'

'They did?' He thought about it for a second. 'Well, I liked them, too.'

'Good. That's good because they want to spend some time with you.'

'What for?'

'Because. Because they like you. And they're going to give you money. A lot of money.'

'Just for spending time with them? Are you and Celine going to be there, too?'

'No, they just want to spend time with you.'

'That's really nice, isn't it, John, but why can't you and Celine be there?'

'Because they don't want us there, that's why.' He wasn't understanding any of what I was trying to say. 'You'll have to do some things . . .' I was having trouble looking him in the eye so I turned my head away.

'What things?'

'Things.'

'What things?' There was a change in his voice as he repeated his question. 'Why aren't you looking at me, John? What things?'

'Christ, I don't know. Just things. It's a lot of money. Just think about that part of it. It'll get us all the way to Hollywood.' I started to walk him towards the stairs.

'I don't think I want to do this.' There was a little bit of panic sneaking into the way he was talking as we started to climb.

'Grow up, for Christ's sake. I've done a lot for you, haven't I? Haven't I?' He nodded. 'You're goddamn right I have. Looking after you all the time. Even when you were a pain in the ass. I still looked after you. I never let anything bad happen to you, did I?'

'No, you never did, John. And that's the truth.'

'Well, I'm not going to start letting anything bad happen to you now. So don't get all crazy on me. Anyway, it's time you grew up.'

'I think I know what you're talking about. I know what that means when you say it's time I grew up.' His face went white.

'It's fun. You'll have a good time.'

He wasn't at all convinced. 'Please don't make me do this.' The look on his face was the same as it was on the streets of Pittsburgh when I yelled at him that first time. Like he wanted to run but he didn't know where to go.

'We don't have any other way. We're broke and we're going to starve. Can't you get that through your thick head? It's only for two hours. That's all. Just two hours and all our problems are over. Don't you see?'

'I'll work. The Hopi House said they might have a job for me. I'll work hard. I'm a good worker. Tigger Book said I was one of the best he ever hired. I'll give you all the money I make. You know I will.' We reached the top of the stairs and I had to take his arm to keep him moving.

'And how much do you think they'll pay you? Fifteen dollars a week? How much?'

'I don't know.' He was pulling against me.

'This is two hundred dollars. One hundred dollars for

each hour. Christ, the President of the United States doesn't make that much money. Come on.' I yanked him along the hallway. 'The man only wanted to pay twenty dollars and I got him up to two hundred. Two hundred! Now, I don't want to hear any more about it.' We were at the door of the room.

'Please, John. Please.'

That scared-rabbit look that I hated was on his face and I wanted to take him by the hand and run out of there but I knew we were stuck if he didn't go through with it. Instead, I pulled him close and whispered. 'Stop it. Be a man for Christ's sake. You hear me. Grow up and be a man.' I knocked on the door. 'Now, you do what you're told.' I was shaking as much as he was. 'Hey, it'll be fun. Relax and enjoy it.'

The door opened and Floyd was standing there.

'Well, right on time. Come in, Michael, come in.' He smiled broadly, the piggish eyes disappearing. The Angel looked at me one last time, his eyes pleading with me, but I pushed him in the room and pulled the door shut and hurried down the hall and stairs and out the front door.

Celine was standing with her back to me some fifty feet away. I leaned on the building fighting to get control of my breathing. I kept telling myself that it wasn't a terrible thing. Fellows had to do it a first time and what difference did it make how or where they did it? He was making too big a thing of it. And because of him I was, too, for Christ's sake. I told myself it was OK. We'd get the money and get the hell out of there and it would all be forgotten. *And* the Angel would have something funny to tell his grandchildren. We'd all be laughing about it in a day or so. I kept telling myself that but I have to admit, deep down I didn't believe a word of it.

When I had fooled myself enough to regain some kind of even breathing I went to Celine.

'Come on, we're going to see the sunset at Ooh Aah Point.' I took her arm and started walking her to the car.

'Where's Michael?'

'We're going to meet him later.'

'Where is he?'

'Busy. There's nothing to worry about. We'll see him later.'

She pulled away from me. 'Busy doing what?'

'Jesus, you're going to laugh about it. No, I mean it. You truly will.' I took her arm again. 'Come on.'

'Stop pulling at me. Why won't you tell me what's going on?'

'Because he wants to tell you. He wants it to be a surprise.' Anything to shut her up. 'Now let's go before the goddamn sun goes down.'

She followed reluctantly to the car.

'I know what it is,' she said after a few minutes. 'Of course. He's going to sing, isn't he? You fixed it for him to sing tonight.'

'No, I didn't. That's not it.' I wished it had been.

'Yes, it is. You are so sneaky. Tell me. I swear I'll act surprised. That's it, isn't it?'

'No, it isn't.'

'Oh, you!' She laughed. 'You big liar. That's where you got the twenty-dollar bill. He's going to sing. I know he is. You might just as well admit it. Lord, I can keep a secret. I may not be the best actress in the world but I know how to act surprised.' And, for the first time since I had met her, she slipped her arm in mine and held close, as casually as if she had done it a hundred times. I wanted her to touch me more than I wanted my heart to beat and yet, when she did, all I could think about was the Angel and the way she was going to react when she found out what the hell I had done and I almost threw up my dinner.

We watched the sunset from Ooh Aah Point and for all the attention I paid it we could have been watching the moonrise on the goddamn planet Pluto. Celine, convinced she was going to hear the Angel sing and that he was getting paid to do it, was the most relaxed I had seen her since we left Mesa Vista. She talked about the beauty of the sun and sky and canyon while she held my hand and I just felt sicker and sicker. There were couples all over the damn place hugging and kissing and sharing the marvel of the moment and all I wanted to do was jump into the fucking canyon and never be heard from again. I suppose that was because I knew that if Celine had known what was going on she'd have pushed me in. I *did* think of running back to the hotel and calling the whole thing off but it was too late for that and besides, no question about it, we needed the money.

'There has to be a God,' she said after about an hour when the sun was showing off and colouring the sky all pink and orange and purple. 'Don't you think there has to be a God?'

I certainly was in no mood to think about God because in my mind *God*-thinking led directly to thinking about the possibility of retribution, accountability and damnation. 'Let's not talk about stuff like that, OK?'

'What would you like to talk about?' She was leaning on me, looking at me with those pale grey eyes of hers. It was the warm, comfortable look that people who care about each other share. But at the same time there was something else. Something I tried to put my finger on but it was as slippery as a bar of soap. It was all around us as real as life itself, and I had the feeling that I could have reached out and grabbed a handful of whatever it was. *Jesus Christ*, I thought, *I'm in love with her*. I wasn't even sure what being in love felt like but I knew I was in love with her. *And I think she loves me*. And it all changed in that one goddamn second. It wasn't that I just wanted to go to bed with Celine. That wasn't nearly enough. I wanted everything two people could have together. I wasn't even sure what *that* meant but I knew I had to have it. She smiled as though she was reading my thoughts and agreed with me and I kissed her and I knew by the way she returned the kiss that she wasn't in the least bit surprised. The sunset didn't matter any more, and the Grand Canyon didn't matter. Nothing mattered but Celine and me. At that moment, not even the Angel mattered.

'I have to tell you something,' she said without looking at me. 'Something I've been wanting to tell you but I didn't know how.'

'You can tell me anything.'

'This is difficult.' She walked away from the rest of the people and looked out over the canyon and I went to her.

'Celine . . .'

'My name isn't Celine St Claire. It's Lily. Lily Blythe. Well, it was Lily Blythe before I got married.' Her hand went into her pocket and clutched the bit of plaster. 'Cyril's my father.'

'Jesus!'

'Everyone on the show knows. It's a wonder someone didn't slip and tell you.'

'Why's it such a big secret?'

'Oh, God, this is so hard.' She took a breath and turned to me. 'My mother died when I was three and I went to live with my grandmother Blythe in Michigan. She raised me.

She was a strict Methodist and it wasn't easy but she did her best and I loved her. And I got to see Cyril a lot. I really didn't have any complaints as a kid . . . Well, I told you all about school and Mr Vladimir Biddermuth. I guess it was a happy time for me.' I didn't know what all this was leading to but I wanted her to get to the part that was so hard to tell. 'Anyway, when I was in the tenth grade I fell in love with Will Van Gulik. Oh, God, he was the boy of my dreams, handsome and amusing and I just thought the sun revolved around him. And when Will fell in love with me, well, I thought I was the happiest girl in the world. Two years later, the weekend after graduation from high school, Will and I were married. I became Lily Van Gulik. His father was a miller, Van Gulik's Mill, and Will worked there and stood to inherit the business one day. We were the perfect couple with the perfect future.'

'But he died,' I said.

She looked at me for a long minute, touched my face and said, 'Yes, he died. But he died because I killed him.'

'Jesus Christ.'

She pulled her skirt up in the back and rolled her stockings down and showed me three scars like three white circles on the back of her thigh. 'Those are burns from a cigar.'

'Will?'

She nodded her head. 'And that was the least of it.'

'The son of a bitch.'

'After we were married for about a year he turned mean. He drank a lot of corn liquor and spent most nights out with his friends. By then, I was glad when he was out of the house. But when he came home he was always in a bad mood and he'd start a fight over something . . . any little thing, and before I knew it he was either beating me up or raping me or both.'

‘Why the hell did you stay with him?’

‘A lot of reasons. For one thing, nice girls didn’t get divorced. At least not where I grew up. And I didn’t want my marriage to fail. I know how stupid that sounds, but I didn’t. Besides, I didn’t have any place to go.’ I thought of my sister, Aggie. She used almost the exact same words when I asked her why she stayed with Frank. ‘And he kept promising he’d change. After a fight was over and he sobered up he’d be so loving and contrite, he’d cry and carry on and say he’d make it up to me . . . and he always made me feel like I caused the fight. That everything that was wrong was my fault. I was a kid, what did I know?’

‘I’m sorry.’ I tried to put my arms around her but she pushed me away.

‘Let me finish.’ Tears welled up in her eyes and she had to wait a minute to get control. ‘I got pregnant. Oh, Lord, I was so happy about it and so was Will and for a time everything was fine. I was really happy. Then, one night, he came home drunk and for no reason at all started hitting me and I tried to run but he grabbed me and somehow, pushing me around the kitchen, he knocked me down the cellar stairs and I lost the baby.’

‘Oh, Christ.’ This time when I put my arms around her she let me hold her and she cried.

‘I lost my little baby. It died before it even had a chance to live. And I knew it right away. I was sure, the minute I hit the floor in the cellar, that the baby was dead.’ She was crying so much I could hardly understand what she was saying. ‘I never even knew if it was a little boy or little girl. My baby died right there on the cold cellar floor and he stood at the top of the stairs and watched it happening and I swore I would make him pay for it. I swore I would kill him.’

'You should have taken a gun and blown the bastard's brains out.'

'I would have. I would have shot him if I'd had a gun. And I wouldn't have had to think twice about it, either.' She cried even harder.

'There now. Try to calm down,' I said, rocking her in my arms. 'It's all right now. Just calm down.'

But she kept on crying. 'I don't even really have red hair,' she said.

'What?'

'This isn't my hair colour.' And for some reason, that struck me funny and I laughed. 'What's so damn funny?'

'I don't know. Just the way you said it. Out of the blue like that. It sounded funny. What colour's your hair?'

'Light brown. Just plain old brown.'

That explained her misplaced eyes. 'Lily with the light brown hair.'

'I guess it did sound funny, didn't it?' Her face was all tears and her nose was running like a dripping faucet so I pulled out my shirt-tail and wiped her off 'I pushed him off the roof and he broke his neck,' she said, trying to control her sobs. 'I broke his neck and I was glad.'

'That was too good for the bastard.'

'I didn't know how I was going to do it but all I could think of was killing him because he killed the baby. And then, one day after a rain storm when he was on the roof trying to fix a leak, he asked me to bring his tool belt up to him and as I was climbing the ladder, I knew I was going to push him. It was early in the day and he was already drinking and half drunk and looking for a fight by blaming me for the leaks. I got off the ladder and he was bending over on the edge and as I went to him, without batting an eye, I swung the belt as hard as I could and hit him on the back of his head and he fell off the roof and broke his neck. I stood looking down at him as he twitched and squirmed in the mud, slowly dying and making ugly little animal sounds, and I was never happier.' She was still fighting her sobs. 'Never happier,' she repeated. 'Anyway, I told the police it was an accident and they believed me except for Kyle Hayes. I told you about his sister, Greta Rose Hayes, one of the two cousins who went on to college from Mr Biddermuth's one-room school house. Well, Kyle Hayes was Will's best friend and he was new on the police force and he was suspicious. He kept making little remarks to me about the way Will died. Remarks that in a roundabout way made it sound like I was somehow involved. He couldn't prove it and he knew it. But he'd never give up on me so I told everybody I was going to a job in Florida and I disappeared and dyed my hair and became Celine St Claire. Cyril gave me the name.'

'And everybody knew about it?'

'Not that I killed Will. Lydia knew. And Grayson and Tigger Book. But the rest of them thought I wanted to go into show business and changed my name so it wouldn't be the same as Cyril's.'

'Why did you decide to leave with us all of a sudden like that?'

'Because the sheriff was asking questions about me. Tigger told Lydia and Cyril.'

Everything was starting to make sense. 'I thought he was asking questions about *me*. About me and Michael.'

'And when you decided to leave, well . . .'

'Weren't you taking an awful chance? I mean, if you thought we were running from the law, didn't it worry you?'

'Michael did nothing but tell me how good you were to

him. I knew whatever you had done that made you take off like that couldn't have been too bad. So did Cyril. In fact, it was Lydia and Cyril's idea. They told me to go with you. I didn't care where you were going.'

'I'll be goddamned.' And right there on the rim of the damn Grand Canyon, in the last fading light of the day, I told Lily Blythe Van Gulik Celine St Claire the whole truth about me and the Angel. All about Lowell, Massachusetts and Millie Quick and getting kicked out of town and how I found the Angel in the storm and took him away from his crazy mother and how, in a theatre in Pittsburgh, I got the idea to take him to Hollywood and make him a moving picture star . . . Everything. I even told her he thought he really was an angel. And he thought I was an angel, too. That gave her a laugh. One thing I didn't tell her was about Mary Lou. That was a minor incident she really didn't have to hear about. And, while we were standing there confessing to one another, I didn't tell her where the Angel was, and what he was doing.

'I'm glad I told you,' she said when I was finished. 'You don't feel I'm a bad woman . . .'

'I wish I had been there so I could have killed the bastard for you.'

She kissed me. 'I feel a thousand pounds lighter,' she said, slipping her arms around my waist and holding me. 'Don't you?'

'Not quite.' I didn't know how I was going to get to tell her what was happening to the Angel. 'What time is it?'

'What time does Michael sing?'

'He's not singing. I told you.'

'You are terrible,' she said, taking a poke at me. 'If he's not going to sing then what's going on?'

We had just stripped ourselves as naked as we were ever

going to get but I didn't know what to say. I wish it had been as easy as saying I pushed some guy off a roof and broke his goddamn neck. There would have been nothing to that. 'Well, when I tell you you're going to laugh.' It was a feeble attempt at minimizing what I had done and I knew she wasn't going to laugh, for Christ's sake, she was going to be mad enough to kill *me*. 'It's nothing to make a big fuss over. Just a thing fellows do.'

'Tell me.'

'Maybe later. What time is it?'

She looked at her watch. 'Quarter till nine.'

'Come on, let's get back to the Ridgecrest.'

She slipped her hand in mine, just as natural as could be, and we started towards the car.

'Wait here,' I said when we were in front of the lodge. 'I'll get Michael.'

'I can't wait to find out what's going on.'

'Yeah, well . . .' I could have waited about a hundred years.

I went inside and up to the room and knocked. I don't think I ever had a sicker feeling in my life. The door opened right away and the Angel was standing just inside, like he had been waiting there, and the minute I saw him I knew I had done something worse than I expected. Something I'd be sorry for for the rest of my life. At first his head was down and his hair covered his face, but he reached up and brushed it away and when he looked at me I could see the light was gone from his eyes. 'I did what you said, John. Here's the money.' He put the bills in my hand and walked past me into the hall. I had let him down, betrayed him, and we were both aware of it. Whatever the Angel and I had had between us was gone for ever.

'He was a very good lad,' said Floyd Wilburforce who

followed right behind the Angel. He stepped outside the room and pulled the door shut behind himself. 'Very good. Vilma liked him. Vilma liked him very much.'

'I'm glad you got your money's worth.' Christ, how I hated him.

The Angel walked along the hall and stood leaning against the wall, his back to us.

'More than our money's worth. He's quite a boy. In fact, I'd like to talk a little business. We'd like to buy him.'

'What the hell are you talking about?' I was getting sicker by the moment. 'Buy him! What do you think this is? Slavery? You can't buy and sell people.'

'Don't be naïve,' said Floyd. 'And don't get so fucking high and mighty with me, either. Most everybody's for sale one way or another.'

'Well, Michael isn't for sale.'

'What the hell are you talking about! Of course he is. You sold him to me for two hundred dollars, didn't you?' And, just like that, I punched Floyd square in his fat wet mouth and sent him crashing through the door. I heard Vilma scream, the only thing I ever heard out of her mouth, and I went to the Angel and grabbed him and went down the stairs through the lobby and out the door.

'Come on,' I said to Celine, 'get in the car.'

'What's the matter? What happened to Michael?'

'Just get in the car.' The Angel got in the back and Celine got in with him.

'What happened?' she asked as we drove away.

'Nothing,' I snapped. The Angel was looking out the window. 'We'll go to one of the other hotels and check in and get a good night's sleep.'

'I want to go to the campground,' said the Angel. 'I want to go and shower.'

‘What’s going on here?’ Celine was angry.

‘You go to a hotel,’ said the Angel. ‘I want to go to the campground.’

‘Will somebody tell me what the hell is going on?’

‘All right,’ I said, ignoring her. ‘We’ll go to the campground. Jesus Christ!’ I would have done anything the Angel asked.

‘I want to know what happened. Michael, tell me, please.’ But he didn’t say anything and we rode to the campground in silence. I parked near the showers and the Angel got his towel out of the trunk and went in and I went with him.

‘Are you going to be OK?’ I asked.

‘I’ll be fine, John. Fine.’ He stood there for a minute not taking off his clothes. ‘Turn your back, please. I want to get into the shower.’ Never once in all the time that I had known him had he been shy about taking off his clothes. It just wasn’t in his nature to think there was anything wrong with it. Now, all of a sudden, he didn’t want to be seen naked.

‘I’m sorry, Michael. I’m sorry.’

He looked at me for a moment and half smiled. ‘I know you are, John.’

‘I really am, goddamn it.’

‘I know. And I forgive you. Can I take my shower bath now?’

‘I’ll wait outside,’ I said and hurried out. I didn’t know if I was going to cry or get sick but I never in my whole life felt lower than I did at that moment. And the bastard said he forgave me and that made it worse.

Celine was near the car walking up and down, frantic to know what the hell was going on. ‘What happened to him? You tell me right now!’

‘All right, all right! He fucked Vilma Wilburforce. You

satisfied? For two hundred dollars.' I couldn't look at her and I started off not knowing where the hell I was going.

'You arranged the whole thing, didn't you?' she asked, following close behind me. 'You set it up.'

'Yes, goddamn it, I set it up. Didn't you hear what I said? It was two hundred dollars.'

'You son of a bitch!' She spun me around and slapped me across the face so hard that for a minute there I thought I was going to black out. But she didn't hit me hard enough and I wanted to tell her to do it again and again. To push me off a roof and break my neck.

'Celine . . .'

'Don't,' was all she said.

'Listen to me.'

But she went to the car and got in the back seat and slammed the door.

It must have been an hour before the Angel came out of the shower house. All that time I walked around the campground feeling like the biggest fuck-up who ever lived. How was I ever going to make it up to him? And what about Celine and me? After trusting me the way she did, telling me the dark secret of her life, what was going to happen? I loved her and I thought she loved me but after what I had done, how could anybody love me?

The Angel got in the back seat next to her and I got in the driver's side. She tried to put her arms around him but he smiled and pulled away.

'We have money for a hotel,' I said.

'I don't want to stay here.' There was no anger in his voice, it was merely a statement of fact.

'Where do you want to go?' I asked.

'Let's just keep moving,' said Celine.

'Fine. If that's what you want.' We pulled out of the campground and headed for the highway to Los Angeles in complete silence. I didn't know where else to go. We drove all the way down through Kingman, Arizona and crossed the state line and went into California at Needles in the early hours of the morning and still no one said anything. Not even when we stopped for gas or to use a toilet. It was as though we were all in separate little prisons, moving through space and I knew there wasn't a goddamn thing I could do to get us out of them. And, worse yet, I was the architect of the prisons. When we drove through the Mojave desert, as stony and bleak as a dead star, I tried counting jack rabbits and coyotes and the occasional bobcat, lit up by the stark brightness of the headlights, just to get my mind off the problems but when the count got past a hundred I quit. Every once in a while I'd see a snake stretched out on the road and try as hard as I did to avoid them, I ran over a few and it upset me but it didn't do any good to say anything to Celine and the Angel because they wouldn't answer. I felt as isolated as I would have if I had been in the middle of that desert all by myself. Celine dozed once in a while but the Angel never slept. He sat staring at the blackness of the night and I wondered what terrible things were going through his mind. Whatever happened to him in that hotel room, I would never know but I didn't even want to think about it.

Just before sun-up, when the desert barely started to have a chilly glow, I heard him singing to himself in a small voice. I had to strain to hear but there was no mistaking what he was singing.

> '*A vargin went a-souling in the dark of the moon.*
> *A soul-cake! A soul-cake!*

O give it me kindly and give it me soon.
A soul-cake! A soul-cake!
The young man he looks from his window so bright.
Here's a vargin come wailing in the dark of the night!
Now what'll you give me for a soul-cake, my maid?
My body, my body for a soulcake! she said.'

Sister Glory Love and the Angel

Hollywood was so sunshine bright and white it was damn near blinding. We arrived about two o'clock in the afternoon and the air was warm and seductive, thick with a mixture of the smell of jasmine and car fumes. There was a paleness about the place, like it had been bleached, accented by the fiery reds and purples and pinks of the bougainvillaea, all the hell over the place, spilling down walls or climbing up fences. It was palm trees and orange trees and avocado trees growing right in people's yards, and motion picture palaces the likes of which I couldn't even imagine growing along Hollywood Boulevard. And looking at the hills, north of the town, all white houses and red-tiled roofs, it looked like a travel poster for some kind of cruise in the Mediterranean. The streets and sidewalks were jammed, traffic everywhere you looked, and the streetcars were packed with people coming and going, people I imagined all trying to get into the pictures.

As soon as we arrived in town I picked up a copy of the *Los Angeles Times* and went through the classified ads for places to stay and we found one that very afternoon. I say *we* but *I'm* the one who found the apartment. Celine and the Angel still weren't talking to me very much or to each other for that matter so there was no discussing where we were going to stay. The old Willys-Knight was as silent as a tomb. We rented an apartment on Wilton Place, just south of Sunset Boulevard. It was a white stucco block of a building with no distinguishing features at all, that looked like dozens of other white stucco blocks in the neighbourhood. There were six apartments upstairs and six down, all off wide central hallways. The landlady Mrs Entwhistle who was English and anywhere between seventy and a hundred and ten years old, called them apartments but what they really were was one big room with a kitchenette and a bath. But they were nice. I don't want to give the wrong impression. They were nice and clean and furnished as well as any transient rooms like that could be and she agreed to bring a third daybed in *and* the price was right and that was all that mattered.

Mrs Entwhistle, she told us to call her Hermione but we never could, was tall and fine featured with skin that never ever let the sun touch it. As soon as she went out into the light of day a tattered old parasol, which she left just inside the front door, was up and protecting her from any damage the sun might do. Her hair was about the same colour red as Celine's and probably came out of the same bottle. I never did figure out how that old dame made any money because she was forever giving her tenants food and half the time they didn't even have the money for their rent. Most of them were young would-be actors and she was in heavy competition with other landladies in the neighbourhood to have one of *her people* make it big in the moving pictures so she looked after them all as though they were her own kids. She and Mr Entwhistle, who had been dead since before the New Testament was written, never had any children of their own. It was all Mr Entwhistle's fault because, according to her, 'he never quite got the hang of sex. In fact, he was never very good at it at all.' She always said he had been *connected* to the Royals but she never said what the connection was. King George, a particular favourite of hers, not only because he was king but because, as she put it, 'he had the good sense, during the big war, to drop all of those silly German titles and change the name of the royal house from whatever absurd name it was to a respectable name like Windsor', was enshrined on her wall and got fresh flowers every damn day. She was British through and through but she never wanted to go back to live in England because she loved the madness of southern California. 'In England,' she was fond of saying, 'we have our charming loonies. Our beloved eccentrics whom we all adore and hold near and dear and would go to war to protect. But in America, and especially California, people are truly and enthusiastically mad, motivated by lust and greed and several of the other better deadly sins. It's infinitely more exciting.' When I got to know Mrs Entwhistle a little better, it occurred to me that she would have been a good woman for Doc Forepaugh to meet. She liked long-hair music and reading and art books and that kind of stuff and she was also partial to a nice glass of sherry of an evening. And, if the truth be known, a couple of tea cups of bootlegged gin during the day. I know, because I shared quite a few with her. Doc Forepaugh would have liked Mrs Hermione Entwhistle. I liked her a whole lot. She was a damn good friend to Celine and me during the dark days that followed our arrival in Hollywood.

'I'm going to take a walk and look around the neighbourhood.' It was our first night and the Angel had washed up and put on a clean shirt.

'I'll go with you,' said Celine. I guess she didn't want to be left alone in the apartment with me.

'No thanks, Celine. I'd like to do it by myself.' He turned to me. 'Is it OK, John, if I do that?' It was the first time since we left the campground at the Grand Canyon that he directed anything to me.

'Whatever you want. It's nice and cool now that the sun went down. You sure you don't want company?'

'No thanks.' He smiled. 'I want to go alone.' And he walked out the door and left Celine and me standing there, staring in opposite directions. It was so goddamn awkward I didn't know what to do.

'Are we ever going to talk?' I said, finally.

'About what?'

'About anything. Everything. I made a big mistake. How many times can I say I'm sorry, for Christ's sake?'

'Not enough.'

'What do you want me to do, kill myself?'

'That might be good for starters.'

'Jesus.'

'I'm going to wire Cyril for some money and then I'll get a place of my own.'

'I have money.'

'I don't want any of that money.' Her tone was vicious. 'I'd like to take Michael with me. That is, if he *wants* to go with me. It's up to him. Meanwhile, I might have to stay here for a couple of days if that's all right with you.' She was being the captain of the ship again but this time it was only her own ship.

'Whatever you say.'

'Thank you.'

'You're welcome,' I said and went into the bathroom and showered. While I stood there, the water running down my body, thinking about Celine and what we had shared at Ooh Aah Point, I hoped the Angel had had better luck washing himself clean in the shower house than I was having. No amount of lather was doing the trick.

We didn't talk any more that night until about ten-thirty when he still hadn't come back from his walk.

'I'm going out to look for him.' I slipped my shoes on.

'I'll go with you. '

'No, I think it's better if one of us stays here.' She didn't put up an argument. 'In case he comes back, I mean. He might not understand if we're both gone. He panics.'

'Yes, I know.' She said it as if she was pronouncing my goddamn death sentence.

'I'll be back . . . whenever.' And I left.

I was fighting hard to keep my imagination in check as I walked up one street and down the other for over two hours. Guilt was making the possibilities of the Angel's fate a thousand times worse than anything I had ever imagined before. It was crazy because the three of us could have enjoyed being there together so much. If the daytime was seductive, the nights were downright sensuous. The jasmine was even stronger smelling at night and I could almost feel the scent sticking to my skin. And, the damnedest thing, there were birds singing like there was no tomorrow. I had never ever heard birds singing at night before and I stopped a fellow passing by and asked him what they were.

'You're new in town, aren't you?' He was dark haired and smiley and good looking and I guessed he was trying to get into the pictures along with everybody else in town. 'From back East?'

'Pittsburgh.'

'Yeah? I'm from Philly. Those are mockingbirds. Sometimes when you're trying to sleep they drive you nuts.'

'Thanks.'

'Take care.' And he moved along. 'Good luck,' he called. I guess he thought I was trying to get into the movies, too.

Music was coming from radios and Victrolas and people were sitting on the stoops or porches, talking and laughing or maybe playing cards and everything seemed peaceful and orderly, the way it should be except that the Angel was lost or worse.

I got back to the apartment sometime before one in the morning and he hadn't come back and Celine was sick with worry. For the time being a truce was called between the two of us and without thinking of the possible consequences we got in the car and went searching for the Hollywood Police Station. I didn't give a shit if they locked me up for kidnapping, rape or high treason as long as we found the Angel.

'What can I do for you?' said a sergeant at the desk when we walked into the station. He was a trim man with plastered-down hair and a waxed moustache and a nose as big as a moose's. His name tag read *Sgt Lucky*. He folded the corner of the page of the *Saturday Evening Post* he was reading and, putting it aside, gave us his full attention.

'Our friend is missing.'

'He went for a walk and he didn't come back,' said Celine. 'Something's happened to him. I know it has.'

'How old is this person?' he asked, leaning over to us.

'Almost twenty. I think. Maybe he is twenty.'

'Well now, he has a right to stay out late if he wants to, don't you think? He's a man.'

'You don't understand. We just arrived in Hollywood today. He's not the kind to go wandering off by himself. He just wouldn't do that.'

'Well, he's probably out seeing the sights.'

'He's very innocent,' said Celine. 'He's very sweet. He's not like other people . . .'

'Are you saying he's simple minded?'

'No,' I said. 'He's just different. For Christ's sake, something's happened to him. Just take our word for it.'

'Calm yourself, mister. And I'd appreciate it if you didn't take the name of the Lord in vain. I don't appreciate that kind of talk. Now, let's get a little information and see what we can do.' He took a form out of the drawer and methodically picked up a pencil and started asking questions. 'What's his name?'

'Michael.'

'Michael what?'

Celine and I looked at each other. The Angel didn't have a last name that I ever knew of. 'Tree,' I said. 'Michael Tree. He's my cousin.' Celine didn't say anything. I answered the rest of the questions as truthfully as I could and when he came to distinguishing marks I told him about the wing things.

'Like hands, you say, growing out of his back.' Sgt Lucky looked a bit bewildered. 'Can he move these hands?'

'Yes,' I said, not knowing what the hell that had to do with anything.

'Hmm. Moveable hands on his back. That's interesting.'

'Or maybe little wings,' said Celine. 'I mean that's sort of what they look like.'

'Wings! Well, we won't have trouble identifying him, will we? If he ends up in the hospital or the morgue, I mean.'

Celine and I weren't speaking when we got back to Wilton Place. Not because of what had happened to the Angel at the Ridgecrest, at least as far as I was concerned, but because of what was going through our minds. I had already thought about hospitals and morgues before Sgt Lucky mentioned it, when I was walking the streets of Hollywood.

We stretched out on the daybeds across the room from one another and when I went to turn off the light, Celine told me to leave it on. Just in case the Angel came back when it was still dark. I didn't sleep a wink and I'm sure she didn't either. We both stared at the ceiling listening to the mockingbirds singing their damn hearts out.

And it was that way for the next two weeks. We checked with the police several times a day as well as the hospitals. Celine put an ad in the *Los Angeles Times*'s personal column. *Michael, please come home. We love you. John and Celine*. There was no response. Mrs Entwhistle helped us make up signs and we plastered them all over the goddamn neighbourhood describing the Angel and asking anyone who might have information about him to call us on her phone number. Celine and I didn't have one. I tried to think of where in hell he could possibly have gone and after the first week I called Doc Forepaugh and my sister Aggie. I didn't tell either one of them what had happened, I just said he had wandered off and we didn't know where he was. They hadn't seen hide nor hair of him. I realized it was a mistake as soon as I made the calls because it upset them no end. But even though he was upset, Doc Forepaugh did his best to reassure me that everything was going to be all right and he took the number and said he'd call if he had anything to report. He'd have Saladin Ridge and Amick Halsey keep an eye out for the Angel. He said 'Amick Halsey' so casually that I knew he was now a part of the Doc's life and I was glad for that. And Aggie said she and the kids would pray for the Angel. They talked about him all the time. She also said they were happy, that Frank was being good to them and that Squirrel's dog was growing inches by the day. And she thanked me again for whatever I had done to change Frank. It was all good news but it didn't do a thing to cheer me up.

Celine called Cyril to see if maybe the Angel had found his way back to the show but they had seen no sign of him either. Cyril had wired some money to Celine but because of our crisis there was no talk of her moving out. For the time being, anyway. We slept across the room from one another, when we could sleep, with the light burning, waiting for the Angel to show up.

It was Mrs Entwhistle who, by chance, discovered where he was. She had gone to the market, parasol in hand, and on the way back 'a young person with the eyes of a bloody fanatic' stuck a leaflet in her hand which she had intended to throw in the trash as soon as she got home. She would never think of littering the street. As she tried to balance her groceries and her parasol she shifted hands and the leaflet caught her eye. All she saw were the words: The Botticelli Angel, and she started running back to the apartment house. We had told her about *Precious Bane* and when she borrowed the Angel's copy she saw the rest of his library, including the *Art Treasures of Florence* and we told her about the Angel being the dead spit of one of Botticelli's angels.

Celine answered the loud knocking at the door and there stood Mrs Entwhistle, gasping for breath. 'I think I know where your Michael is.'

'Where?'

'Look at this, my dears.'

'Sit down, Mrs Entwhistle. Let me get you some water.' Celine took her to one of the daybeds.

'Read that,' she said, handing me the leaflet.

A lousy drawing of an angel, wings outstretched, covered the page and printed over it was a message:

The Church Of Heaven On Earth Invites You To Witness An Ascension. Share In The Miracle Of Jesus Christ As He Welcomes The Botticelli Angel Back To His Heavenly Home Once Again. Let Sister Glory Love Show You The Light And The Way To Have All That Heaven Promises Right Here On Earth. Peace And Prosperity In The Name Of Jesus. Communion. Healings. Brotherhood. Music By The Reverend Lester Tittle And The Gloryettes. Free Admission But Generous Donations In The Name Of the Lord Gratefully Accepted To Aid In His Work Being Accomplished, With No Monetary Recompense, By Sister Glory Love And Her Acolytes.

And it went on to give the address, the time and the date. It was Saturday night at seven-thirty. The following night.

'It has to be Michael,' said Celine.

'You're goddamn right it does. How the hell did he get mixed up in something like that?'

Mrs Entwhistle said the church was in a warehouse area in downtown Los Angeles and told us how to get there. 'That Glory Love woman is in the press quite a bit of late. Seems she and that other woman, that Aimee Semple McPherson person, are fighting to get the souls and pocketbooks of the same idiots.'

'How are you feeling?' asked Celine.

'Fine dear, just fine. Don't fret about me. I'll have a cup of tea and that will put me right in no time.' And she was off to have her gin and Celine and I went to the car and headed for downtown Los Angeles.

The traffic in Hollywood was nothing compared to downtown. Cars were bumper to bumper, narrowly missing streetcars that had people hanging on with hardly any footing. The streets were mobbed with businessmen and shoppers bustling around and jostling each other so much they almost looked like they were fighting. We found our way to the church because Mrs Entwhistle's directions were right on the button. She had been quite a motorist before her eyes started to fail her and she gave up her driving licence for fear of causing an accident. Mr Entwhistle never drove, she said. He took the driving test several times but failed. Seems there were a lot of things Mr Entwhistle never got the hang of.

There was no mistaking the church. Christ, a blind man could have found it. The sign, reading *The Church Of Heaven On Earth*, was at least twenty feet tall. And under that was a slightly smaller sign, *Sister Glory Love*, and in smaller letters yet, *Handmaiden Of The Lord*. The building, a huge, ramshackle wooden place, looked like it probably *was* a converted warehouse. It looked like it had been painted recently, a light blue, but it was a slap-dash job with splotches of old white paint showing. Celine and I went through the big double doors under the sign and the goddamn place looked twice as big from the inside. There must have been seating for three thousand people. There were large windows on the side walls and up at the far end, opposite the door, there was a huge stage, all draped with white material, and in the centre of the back of the stage there were banks of lights about thirty feet across that went clear up to the ceiling, which was probably about three storeys high. There was a pulpit, also draped in white, and to the right of the stage there were rows of seats facing the audience. It was the damnedest church I'd ever seen. A little old man, all twisted and bent over, with the face of a gargoyle, was cleaning between the rows of seats.

'I'm looking for Sister Love,' I called.

'Around the side. A white building. She lives there. It's the office, too. She won't see you, though.' He went back to his sweeping.

We found the building and went into an anteroom and were stopped before we even took two steps by a big man in a white shirt and white short pants and white socks and shoes. He looked like a muscle man in a carnival.

'Peace and prosperity in the name of Jesus,' he said in a kind of salute. 'I'm Brother Kyle.'

'Yeah. Same to you, brother. Look, I want to see Sister Love.'

'She doesn't see people who haven't arranged for an audience.' He smiled, flashing teeth that looked like they could bite through iron. 'Requests should be made by mail.' Over his shoulder I could see a door marked *Private* hanging slightly ajar.

'I have to see her.'

'I'm sorry.' His smile got broader.

'It's about Michael,' said Celine.

'Who?'

'The Botticelli Angel,' I said. The door opened and two other muscle men, looking exactly the same as Brother Kyle, white shirt, white shorts, white socks and shoes, and they even had the same haircuts, suddenly came out of the office.

'What about the Botticelli Angel?' Brother Kyle perked up and stopped smiling.

'He's my cousin. We want to see him.'

'I don't think that's possible.'

'Bring them in here,' shouted a raspy voice from inside.

Brother Kyle, annoyed, led the way and the other two brothers parted and stood on either side of the door like a couple of beefy bookends.

The room was painted a blood red and had white drapes and white furniture and white beaded lamp shades and looked a hell of a lot more like the lounge room in a movie-set whorehouse than the office of a church. There were enough potted ferns and palms for a goddamn funeral parlour and curled up on one of the two sofas was a small fluffy white dog that stood up and yapped at us when we came in.

'Shut up, Grace,' said Sister Glory Love as she came out from behind a long white desk with papers scattered all over it. 'Brother Duane,' she said to one of the bookends, 'take Grace inside, please.' Brother Duane snatched up the dog and they were gone through a door behind the desk in two shakes of a lamb's tail. Sister Glory Love got her way when and how she wanted it. That much was clear to see. Well, I'm here to tell you she was quite a sight to behold. Not at all what I expected. I don't know for sure what I *did* expect but it certainly wasn't a woman six inches taller than me with a face like Abraham Lincoln. For a handmaiden of the Lord, she sure got short changed in the looks department, no question about it. That was a face that only the Lord could love and even He'd be hard pressed. She was probably in her early forties, all made up and wearing something an Arab might wear. A long white gown, turban, the works. All in all, Sister Glory Love was one ugly-looking woman.

'Peace and prosperity in the name of Jesus,' she said in her gravelly voice. She smiled but her eyes were as wary and mean as a snake's. 'Aren't you a handsome couple? You must make babies. Lots and lots of babies. You really must. John and Celine, right? Michael has told us all about you.'

'Where is he?'

'He's where no harm can come to him. Rest assured.' She

tilted her head to the side as if she'd just said something that would end the conversation happily for everyone.

'I want to see him.'

'Why?'

'I want to see if he's all right.'

'He couldn't be better. Don't worry about it.' Her eyes narrowed and her voice got deeper. 'He's well taken care of.'

'I want to see for myself.'

'Why can't we see him?' asked Celine.

'Did I say you couldn't see him? Did I, Ceeeline?' Sister Glory Love hissed the *Ce* right in Celine's face. 'Did I say that, darling?'

'Then where is he?'

'Brother Teddy,' she said to the other bookend, 'would you tell Michael he has guests, please?' And, just like that, Brother Teddy was gone through the door behind the table. 'Sit down,' she said, dropping into an overstuffed chair. Celine and I sat on the sofa vacated by the hairy little Grace.

'How did he get here?' I asked.

'Fate, my darling, fate. One of my recruiting acolytes found him wandering the streets. Lost, I might add. Lost. Lonely and lost.' The words lonely and lost almost did her in and she let her head drop for a moment as if she was trying to get control of herself and at the same time waiting for the words to affect us as much as they did her. It only took her a second or two and her head popped up. 'Now.' She crossed her legs and smoothed the gown. 'Who are you, really? Michael never said you were a cousin. You're not his cousin, are you? Michael thinks you're an angel. Are you an angel? I somehow think you're not, John. Tell the truth and shame the devil, darling.'

'We're friends of his,' said Celine.

'You must have been so worried!'

'We want him to come home with us.'

'Do you? Then, by all means, when he comes out, darling, ask him to go home with you. Jesus will tell him what to do. He tells us all what to do. He whispers in our ears every moment of the day. Some of us have to learn how to listen.'

'Well, Jesus won't tell Michael what to do. *I'll* tell him what to do, goddamn it.'

'Please,' said Brother Kyle, 'no profanity in the presence of Sister Love.'

'It's all right, Brother Kyle. The Lord forgives and so do I.' She smiled and leaned back. 'I wondered when you'd show up. I mean, one doesn't misplace a splendid animal like Michael and not *look* for him, does one? By the way, what are those marvellous things growing on his back? Non-believers might call them deformities but in Michael's case I think they're a gift from God. He says they're wings. Isn't that sweet? Wings!' Clearly, she didn't think they were wings. 'What are they really?'

'I don't know what they are. Some kind of growths.' I wasn't in the mood to discuss the Angel with her. I didn't like her and I wanted to get him and get the hell out of there.

'Well, wait until you see what we've done to enhance them for the ascension. It's marvellous. We've fashioned the most gossamer wings you've ever seen, of fine wire and chiffon, stitched by the tiny, tiny fingers of four very talented Chinese women, light as a feather and eight feet long and they fit over those little stubs of his and he can actually move them. Like real wings. It's the most amazing thing!'

'You're sticking fake wings on him?'

'John, your perception is skewed. Think of them as enhancements. The Lord can use all the help He can get when it comes to saving souls. Don't you think?'

'What the hell are you doing to him?'

'It's not what we're doing to *him*, it's what he's doing for the *Lord*. Oh, darling, wait and see. You *are* coming to the ascension, aren't you? It's going to be spectacular. If I were you I wouldn't miss it for the world.'

'Where is he?' I was getting tired of her.

'Patience. Patience. It's a virtue, darling. By the way, I think it's absolutely charming that he thinks he posed for Botticelli. And maybe he did. The Lord works in wondrous ways, doesn't He. An angel actually painted by Botticelli, come back to earth to do whatever angels do when they come back. It gives me goose bumps to think of it.'

And just then the door opened and the bookends returned with the Angel. He was dressed all in white, the same as the rest of them. But he still had his long hair.

'John!' He came to me and hugged me, then hugged Celine. 'I'm so glad to see you.'

'Are you all right?' Celine held him close.

'You've had us worried sick. Christ!'

'Watch your language,' said Kyle.

'Why don't you shut up?' I said and Kyle made a move in my direction.

'No, no.' Sister Love motioned him away.

'Come on. Let's get out of here.' I took the Angel by the arm but he pulled away.

'I can't leave, John. I'm going to heaven tomorrow night.'

'Jesus Christ!' He believed it.

'But they want you to go home with them,' said Sister Glory Love in an oily voice.

'Come on,' I insisted, 'let's go.'

'I can't,' he said to me. Then he turned to Sister Love. 'I don't have to go with them, do I?'

'Of course not, darling. You can do whatever you want.' She turned to me and smiled. 'He'd like to stay.'

'Listen to me, this is crazy. You're not going to heaven. They're making a fool of you.'

'Please, Michael, come with us.' Celine was pleading.

'You're free to go if you wish, Michael. Darling, I'd never hold you against your will. Never, ever.'

'Come on, for Christ's sake. Let's get out of here.'

'I can't, John. I'm going to heaven. That's why we came to California, isn't it? To go to heaven?'

'No, goddamn it, we came to get in the movies. That's all. In the fucking movies.' Sister Glory Love, offended by my language, covered her ears.

'I told you to watch your language,' threatened Kyle.

'All that heaven stuff was just crap,' I said to the Angel, trying to convince him. 'Just a load of crap.'

'I don't want to be in the moving pictures, John. I don't want to sing any more. I just want to go to heaven. Sister Glory Love is sending me there tomorrow night.'

'Michael, please,' said Celine with tears in her eyes. 'Please listen to us.'

'Oh, Christ, Michael. You're not an angel. Do you hear what I'm saying? I'm not an angel, either. I'm just a man and so are you. And you're not going to heaven. This is all shit! I lied to you about taking you to heaven and I'm sorry. It was a way to get you to come with me. And she's lying to you, too. These people are only using you. The way I used you. Listen to me! They're going to stick fake wings on you, for Christ's sake. Don't do this. Please. You'll only get hurt again. These are bad people, Michael. They're evil.'

'*The Lord shall deliver me from every evil work, and will preserve me unto his heavenly kingdom.*'

'Who said that, darling?' Sister Glory Love was winning and she was enjoying every minute of it. 'Matthew? Mark? Or one of the other boys?'

'II Timothy 4:18.'

'Such a gift! I wish I could do that. The congregation is so impressed with the Bible, especially when it's right at the tips of your fingers.' She turned to me. 'Now, I think Michael needs his rest.'

'Michael! Shit! Please . . .'

'Don't worry about me, John . . .'

'*Michael* . . .' It was a cry from Celine's heart.

'Take him back to his room, brothers.'

The bookends went to the Angel and I tried to stop them but Brother Kyle had my arms pinned behind my back before I knew it and I couldn't move.

'Let go of me, you bastard.'

'Will you be here tomorrow night?' asked the Angel as they were leading him away. 'I'll see you . . .' And they went through the door and closed it and the Angel was gone.

'Let him go, Brother Kyle.' He released his grip on my arms. Celine came to me and I held her. 'You can leave us alone.' And Kyle was gone.

'I'll get the police, goddamn it.'

'Why?' Sister Glory Love smiled and shook her head as though she was having trouble understanding me. 'Michael is here because he wants to be here. You heard him. He wants to help us with a little demonstration that's meant to bring sinners into the arms of Jesus. Who does it hurt if he thinks he's going to heaven? No one. In fact, everyone who comes to the services here thinks they're going to heaven. Don't we all think we're going to heaven? Well, don't we, darling? Isn't that why the faithful come here in the first place? To be told they're going to heaven when their life is over? That's what religion is all about. We tell you what you want to hear. That's our job. In the name of Jesus, of course.' She was getting a little fired up. '*I* tell you even more. *I* tell you you can have anything you want before you even *get* to heaven. And I believe it's true. The Lord loves His children.' She was sounding more and more like a preacher every minute. 'The Church of Heaven on Earth is the church of what you want to hear. You want a new job? Car? House? Pray. Glory's way, of course. Jesus shows me the way. You want to be cured of some vile and disgusting disease? Pray. Jesus wants you well. You know He does, darling. You want to jump out of your wheelchair and dance a jig? Pray. Glory can do it. Glory and the Lord, of course. We have a covenant, Jesus and I. Whatever you want, you'll get if you pray to God through Sister Glory Love. And if you don't get what you pray for, well it's clear to me that God has other plans for you. He has plans for all of us, you know. Remember, His eye is on the sparrow.'

'Let us have Michael. Please,' said Celine.

'Oh, darling *Ceee*line, nothing's going to happen to your Michael. We're going to stage a little ascension, that's all. It's not the first one, you know.' She chuckled. 'That was a little joke. The Lord has a wonderful sense of humour, by the way. Michael will come out on stage and show off his wings and the congregation will believe he really *is* an angel because, darling, they want so desperately to have some proof that there *is* a God. Faith alone doesn't do it for most people, I'm sad to say. So I have to convince them. That's my mission and Michael is helping me with my mission. He's a gift from God. A heavenly gift. A man with wings! What better proof than an actual angel, and a divine angel at that, shyly wafting his pristine wings while the choir is singing about going back to the Promised Land as only coloured gospel singers can? Wait until you hear them. Then, while the crowd is working itself into a frenzy, our angel will get into an invisible rigging' – she looked heavenward, overwhelmed by what was about to come next and then dropped her eyes and said confidentially – 'for even miracles need help sometime, darling. They do, believe me when I say they do. Well, Michael will be strapped into the rigging that will take him up and up and up and when he gets to the top, heavenly lights will flash, blinding the faithful, and while they're enjoying their miracle, Michael escapes along a scaffold. The crowd thinks he's in heaven and hundreds, perhaps thousands are brought back to Jesus. Isn't a slight bit of legerdemain excusable when thousands of souls are saved?'

'What a bunch of bullshit!'

'But Michael?' said Celine. 'He thinks he's going to heaven.'

'He'll understand when I tell him the Lord has other plans for him. He will, he's very sweet. And I can honestly say that one day he *will* get to heaven. We all know he will. If he doesn't, none of us will.' She smiled as if that made everything all right. 'So when the ascension is over, Michael is all yours. I won't have any use for him any more. He will have fulfilled his destiny in the name of the Lord.'

'You bitch.'

'I'm sorry you think badly of me. I'll pray for you. God forgives you. He truly does.' Everything on her face smiled but her eyes. 'And so does Glory Love, darling. So does Glory Love. This audience is over.' And she turned and disappeared through the door behind the desk.

*

That night, when Celine and I lay in our separate beds, thinking about the Angel, I turned the light off for the first time since we arrived in Hollywood. There was nothing for us to talk about because neither one of us knew what the hell to do but wait until the service was over the next night and bring the Angel back with us. Never in my life did I ever feel so goddamn helpless and impotent. There was no way to save the Angel from the humiliation and disappointment he would feel. No way at all. What made it worse was knowing I hadn't saved him from humiliation when I could have. The only comfort I had was that at least we'd have him back with us.

Sometime in the middle of the night I heard Celine crying. I wanted to go to her and take her in my arms and hold her but I knew better. I was the last person she'd want to hold her.

'Can I get you something?'

'No.'

There was another very long silence except for the occasional sob. 'Are you going to be all right?' I finally said.

'I don't think so. I don't think any of us are going to be all right ever again.'

There was nothing to say because I agreed with her.

The next day, Celine, Mrs Entwhistle, who insisted on going, and I were there at four in the afternoon, waiting in the queue to get front seats when the doors to the church opened. We weren't the first in line, either. There were already about fifty people there with lunches and thermos bottles, like they were on a damn picnic or something.

It was hotter than hell and Mrs Entwhistle shared her parasol with Celine and her flask of gin with me.

'Little sips,' she said, 'will help us endure. Believe me, I would never have got through Mr Entwhistle's funeral without my flask. Actually, by the time he was lowered into the ground, I was quite drunk. Friends told me I laughed out loud once or twice. Mr Entwhistle would have liked that. He always enjoyed a good laugh. It was one of the few things Mr Entwhistle did very well. Laugh. And that's such an endearing quality.'

By five o'clock, there must have been a thousand people in the line and by six, hundreds more than the church could accommodate. I did think the crowd looked a little inbred, like they were all the products of brothers and sisters or at least first and second cousins. There was a separate section for the sick and infirm. They got to wait in the shade while the rest of us cooked and when the doors finally opened at six-forty-five, they went in first. Wheelchairs and people on crutches and stretchers paraded by and they were the healthiest-looking bunch of sick people I'd ever seen. I also noticed most of them were on a first-name basis with Brother Bill and Brother Alex who ushered them in ahead of the rest of us. These new brothers, cut from the same mould as the three we had met the day before, were dressed in white suits, white shirt, white tie, shoes, all white with a red rose in their buttonholes and identification tags. These guys were even bigger than Kyle and the bookends.

After the lame contingent were in and settled the rest of us were allowed to enter. The closest we could get was the fifth row because the first four rows were reserved for the folks who were there to be cured. Sister Glory Love was right when she told us it was a production not to be missed. There were more white drapes on the stage than there had been the day before: big billowy ones hung from the ceiling, put there, I was sure, to camouflage the Angel's escape route. Flowers were everywhere and there were enough candles burning to light up downtown Los Angeles. It was already hotter than hell and all those candles only made it worse. All the big windows were open but it didn't seem to be cooling things off the slightest bit. By the time everybody settled down they were glistening with sweat and we hadn't even got to the ecstasy part.

'This promises to be even better than I expected,' said Mrs Entwhistle, passing me her flask. 'Have a sip, dear, gin activates the cooling mechanism of the body. It's absolutely essential to survival in India, I'm told.' She turned to Celine. 'You really should try some, my dear.' But Celine didn't like the taste.

Sister Glory's acolytes – there must have been twenty-five of them – were passing collection baskets while we were all waiting for the show to begin. At exactly seven-thirty, Revd Lester Tittle and the Gloryettes appeared, all dressed in bright blue choir robes, and filed into their places to the right of the stage. The accompanist, a woman of mountainous proportions, sat at the piano and the lights went down and the crowd quieted. In just a few minutes it was still enough to hear a whisper.

'Peace and prosperity in the name of Jesus,' boomed the voice of Sister Glory Love over the loudspeaker, full of promise and salvation and a warmth that was as slippery as she was, and there was a thunderous reply repeating, 'Peace and prosperity in the name of Jesus, peace and prosperity in the name of Jesus, peace and prosperity in the name of Jesus', so damn loud the seats vibrated. The frenzy generated by the miracle they were expecting to happen right before their eyes was as thick and heavy as the heat. A spotlight hit Revd Tittle and after another roar from the crowd he turned to the choir, nodded to the accompanist and they were off and running with 'Roll Jordan, Roll'. The rich, strong voices filled the place with music that came from every pore of the singers' bodies. They rocked back and forth and clapped and sang with such sheer joy that nothing in the whole world existed but them and their message. They went on to sing several other songs, all about Jesus and faith and promises and crossing rivers and climbing mountains and laying down burdens and sin and forgiveness.

'Aren't they marvellous,' shouted Mrs Entwhistle, getting with the spirit of the singers. 'Absolutely marvellous.'

By the time Revd Tittle and the Gloryettes were finished, the crowd would have eaten each other if Sister Glory Love hadn't made an appearance. As the lights came up on the stage, all of the acolytes, gleaming in their white suits, were lined up, their heads thrown back and their arms outstretched to heaven.

'And now, brothers and sisters,' came a voice over the loudspeaker, 'here she is, the handmaiden of the Lord, Sister Glory Love!' Well, the Gloryettes started singing again and the congregation started screaming and shouting and, I swear to Christ, it was enough to make a stone-deaf man even deafer. The acolytes parted and retreated like chorus boys in a musical show, one hand behind their backs and the other pointing to the centre of the stage where a staircase was emerging through the drapes from the back wall. Coloured lights lit up the staircase and at the top, in silhouette, with her praying hands clasped in front of her, was Sister Glory Love. Everyone, including several of the cripples who weren't supposed to be able to stand, and Mrs Entwhistle who was slightly drunk and completely carried away by the dazzle of it all, jumped to their feet and started screaming.

'Did I tell you Mr Entwhistle and I once went to Paris on holiday? We went to the Folies-Bergère,' shouted Mrs Entwhistle. 'Wasn't quite as entertaining as this, as I recall. And not nearly as vulgar.'

Sister Glory Love was dressed in the same kind of Arabian outfit except this time it was all gold and her turban was covered with jewels. The acolytes went up the stairs on either side of her and as she slowly descended she took their hands, one by one, until she was on the stage. All the time the congregation was screaming like a bunch of crazy banshees. The bookends, Duane and Teddy, led her to the pulpit as the staircase disappeared back through the curtains and the adoring followers jumped up and down shouting their anthem, over and over, in unison, 'Peace and prosperity in the name of Jesus'. Duane and Teddy withdrew and Sister Glory Love raised her arms and the crowd fell silent and sat down like someone had turned off their motors. She stood looking at the crowd without saying a word, smiling that Abe Lincoln smile of hers, making fleeting eye contact with the blessed, and finally she started talking.

'I love you all,' she said and her head dropped as it had in the office when she was talking about the Angel being lost and lonely. 'Brothers and sisters, I love you,' she mumbled. Then her head came up and she smiled. 'And Jesus loves you. He does, oh, yes, He does, He does, He does. He loves you. He told me he did. He said, "Glory" – that's what He calls me – "Glory, I want you to tell my people how much I love them. Didn't I love the multitude when they were hungry and I gave them the loaves and the fishes? Didn't I do that for my children? And at Cana, didn't I change the water to wine in order for my children to carry on with their wedding feast? Didn't I do that, Glory?" That's what He said to me. "I want my children to have everything . . ."' And she started spouting the philosophy of the church of what you want to hear. Just as she had said, the members of her congregation could have anything they wanted. Jobs, women, men, good sex, cures, vacation trips, whatever, it didn't matter because it was all there for the asking. All they had to do was donate money, lots of it, and pray along with Sister Glory Love and it was theirs. She had a few good Bible quotes about riches, like: *The rich man is wise in his own conceit*, and *By thy great wisdom and by thy traffick hast thou increased thy riches and thine heart is lifted up because of thy riches*, and my favourite and the most outstanding, *The crown of the wise is their riches.* Riches brought the biggest cheers from the crowd. They wanted to hear all about the riches they were being told were their legacy. And the Bible was as good a way as any to convince them they all had whatever they wanted coming to them. I didn't think she was nearly as good at Bible-quoting as the Angel because I knew he probably could have done a hundred quotes on either side of the riches issue. Listening to him when he *did* quote I learned that the Bible covered all bases, pro and con, and had something to say about everything. There wasn't a thing you couldn't prove or disprove, good, bad or indifferent, by quoting the Bible, and Sister Glory Love was pretty good at it.

After her sermon, which was interrupted about a hundred times by shouts of 'Peace and prosperity in the name of Jesus' by overcome followers, there was another round of spirited songs by the Gloryettes. Sister Glory Love sat on a little white throne on the stage when they were singing and looked like she had gone off to the other world for a visit until they finished. Her head was back and, aside from her knee, which she couldn't keep from bouncing in time with the music, she looked like she was in a goddamn trance. I suppose that was in preparation for the next item on the agenda: miracle cures.

The Gloryettes got to take a little break during the curing. With them singing, it was too hard to hear the list of complaints of the people carried and pushed up on the stage by the acolytes. Cancer, arthritis, blindness, deafness, venereal disease, sinking feelings, dropsy, barrenness, homosexuality, heart flutters, warts, stutters and canker sores were all treated and miraculously cured on the spot. As was heavy smoking and drinking. Sister Glory Love touched the afflicted on the forehead and shouted for Jesus to do his job and, just like that, He did. Some of the afflicted passed out or went into some kind of convulsions before they were cured, and when they did the congregation felt more like they were getting their money's worth and hooted and bellowed until Jesus just *had* to do something. I think Celine was frightened by it all but Mrs Entwhistle was having the time of her life. All I kept thinking about was the Angel and what must be going through his mind while he waited for his moment of departure. It came right after the healing was over but not before the acolytes went through the audience with their baskets and, while everyone was fired up, cleaned them out.

Sister Glory Love went back to the pulpit and with an enraptured look on her ugly face told her followers that the miracles they had seen so far that night were nothing compared to what they were about to see. 'The Angel Michael, called the Botticelli Angel because, on one of his former visits from heaven, he actually posed for the famous painter, Botticelli. Over four hundred years ago.' There was a murmur of wonder and appreciation from the crowd. 'You've all heard of Botticelli, haven't you?'

And while they all lied and shouted 'yes', Mrs Entwhistle leaned over and said indignantly, 'My Great-aunt Mary, they've heard of Botticelli!'

'Tonight,' continued Sister Glory Love, 'the Botticelli Angel is going back to heaven. Yes, he is. Going back to the arms of our Lord and Saviour Jesus. And he's leaving right here from this stage.' There was another roar from the crowd. 'Remember, Jesus loves you, He does, He does, He does. And I love you. I do, I do, I do.' She reached out her hands. 'Feel the love coming from my fingers into your bodies. Feel it, taste it, wash yourselves in it, sisters and brothers, and ask Jesus for anything you want. He'll give it to you. He will. Ask for it while you witness the Angel Michael ascend into heaven. Ask Jesus during the miracle.'

Celine took my hand. 'I'm scared, John.'

'It's going to be all right,' I said, but I was scared, too.

'Brothers and sisters, the Angel, Michael.' The lights went out and a spotlight lit up the drapes and the staircase started to emerge again. The Gloryettes started singing.

'I got a robe up in-a that Kingdom,
Ain't-a that good news.
I got a robe up in-a that Kingdom,
Ain't-a that good news.
Gonna lay down this world,
I'm gonna shoulder up-a my cross,
Gonna take it home to my Jesus, ain't-a that good news.'

The staircase came through the drapes and the Angel was standing at the top of it with a silver cape over his shoulders covering his whole body. There was no sign of the wings. He looked as deadly serious as I had ever seen him and as soon as she saw him Celine started to cry. He walked down the stairs while the choir sang more and more fervently and when he got to the bottom and stepped on to the stage the staircase disappeared and the bookends came out of the wings and stood just behind him. The crowd was applauding and shouting and just when it seemed like it couldn't get any louder the bookends took the cape off the Angel and, like magic, the huge wings sprang to life. He stood there in little more than a loin cloth moving the wings back and forth, then slowly turned so the congregation could see how they grew out of his back. Sister Glory Love was right when she had said it was the most amazing thing. Dozens of people fainted. Or at least pretended to. The acolytes looked after them. The scary part was that Michael looked so happy. And why shouldn't he be, I thought? This was what his crazy mother had been preparing him for all his life. Only once, in all the hoopla, did he glance our way but I couldn't be sure if he saw us or not. He walked to the edge of the stage and then went back and forth so everyone could get a good look at his wings, then the bookends led him to the back wall and the bank of lights that were rolled into place after the staircase disappeared. The bookends left and the Angel turned to face the audience and somebody back there hooked him up to some kind of harness that we couldn't see. The Gloryettes went from singing about the robe to a crown to a Saviour but it was still good news.

And suddenly, the Angel started to ascend. His eyes were looking heavenward and he was smiling and his arms were outstretched and I thought the building was going to blow apart from all the noise. Celine was crying uncontrollably and Mrs Entwhistle was shaking her head at the wonder of it all. The Angel slowly went up, as smoothly as if he really was ascending by some heavenly power, and when he was about forty feet off the ground, it happened. One of the wires in his wings hit a light and sparks flew. There was a hush over the audience but whoever was hoisting the Angel couldn't see what was happening and kept pulling him up and there were more sparks. All the time, the Angel kept smiling. Then the lights started flashing and everyone was blinded and I knew everything was going wrong because it was all happening too soon. Sister Glory Love screamed for the acolytes who came on stage and when they saw what was happening, ran behind the drapes. The Angel stopped ascending but by then the drapes behind the lights were on fire. There must have been a hundred lights going off and on, making it almost impossible to see what the hell was happening, but I could see that one of the Angel's wings was ablaze. By then, people were yelling 'fire' and running for the exit. The lame and the cripples in the wheelchairs got up and started to fight their way towards the back.

'Get Mrs Entwhistle out of here,' I said to Celine as I pushed my way through them trying to get to the stage. The lights kept flashing and I could barely make out what was going on but I did see Brother Kyle grab Sister Glory Love and head for the exit. He was punching people, trying to get them out of the way, yelling for the other acolytes to come and help but it was every man for himself. The Angel was still hanging there and, when I could get a glimpse of his face, he still had that enraptured look, like he was totally unaware of what the hell was happening. The fire was spreading and people were screaming and I started to climb up the bank of lights thinking maybe I could release the Angel and get him down. Pieces of drapes in flames were falling around me and the metal bars the lights were attached to were already hot enough to burn. As I climbed, I was behind the glare of the lights and I looked up and saw the Angel's other wing catch fire. I started calling to him but he didn't even look at me. The stupid son of a bitch thought he was going to heaven and that's all he cared about. I got closer and closer to him and just when I was close enough to touch his foot I heard a noise like a loud ripping sound and the bar I was holding on to started to fall and I went with it. The last thing I remembered was the crashing sound of the lights hitting the stage and then everything went black.

I came to in the ambulance on the way to the hospital. I didn't know where the hell I was at first but the whining of the siren and the antiseptic smell that almost made me sick to my stomach brought things into focus. Celine and Mrs Entwhistle and a pretty young nurse with dark curly hair were with me. There was an oxygen mask on my face so when I asked about the Angel, Celine couldn't hear me. She leaned over and I tried to talk louder but I passed out again.

The Church of Heaven on Earth was no more. Strange as it was, parts of the stage area where the fire started survived but the rest of it burned to the ground and Sister Glory Love and her boys were out of business. The papers were full of pictures of her, remorseful and distraught with smudges of dirt all over her ugly face, and pictures of the blaze, one of the worst in the history of Los Angeles, and for days it was headline news. City Hall was under the gun because there had never been a fire inspection or permit granted and the inference was that Sister Glory Love had bought off the Fire Commissioner. An investigation was under way. Several people were hurt trying to get out of the building and whatever was left of the Church organization was expected to face hundreds of law suits. But the miracle was, according to the police, no lives were lost. No bodies were found. None. Not a single goddamn one. So the question was, where in the hell was the Angel? Some of the spectators were quoted as saying that the moment the sparks started flying, they saw him ascend through the ceiling and into heaven. Even though his ascension, the rigging and the whole phony business was exposed and explained by some of the acolytes who were trying to save their own asses, several of the faithful told the press they saw a miracle. Well, the press had a field day with that. For a few days, the Botticelli Angel was as famous as Rudolph Valentino had been, but the public was fickle and their appetite for the sensational had to be satisfied and, in no time at all, the question of the disappearance of the Angel was replaced by juicier, more recent murders or disasters or mayhem. Sister Glory Love faded away, too, but every once in a while there'd be a letter in the press from one of her irate followers accusing her of being everything from a charlatan to a whore. Of course, I agreed with every one of them.

I was in Queen of Angels Hospital for two weeks. Mrs Entwhistle paid all my expenses and wouldn't allow me to pay her back. Not one red penny. There were burns on my hands and on my chest and a small burn over my left ear. But they were minor and the doctors said there'd be little or no scarring. I did have serious problems from smoke inhalation and that's what I was being treated for. I was told by Dr Stickley, a specialist in treating burn victims, who was as jolly as a Salvation Army Santa Claus, that I would probably have problems with my lungs for the rest of my life. Celine or Mrs Entwhistle visited me every day and spoiled me rotten. They never came together because one or other of them always stayed at home in case the Angel showed up. There was always that possibility. The vigil started again and Celine slept with the lights on.

There were times, when Celine was visiting me and we

were alone in the room, I'd wake up from a short doze and she'd have her hand on my arm and there'd be tears in her eyes. I never said anything because I felt I had no rights where she was concerned but I never loved her more and I knew, in spite of everything that had happened, that she loved me. There was no need for words. We both knew it.

I was almost out of the hospital when I found out that it was Celine and Mrs Entwhistle who saved my life. They hadn't left when I told them to, no surprise where Celine is concerned, but instead followed me up on the goddamn stage. They were calling to me all the time I was climbing but with all the screaming going on I couldn't hear a thing. When I was knocked out the two of them dragged me off the stage and up the aisle and, halfway to the door, one of the acolytes picked me up and carried me outside just before the roof caved in. We were damned near the last people out. When I asked about how much she saw of the Angel, Celine said there was too much smoke on the stage for her to see anything so she had no idea what happened to him.

When I was released, I was told to take it easy and rest for a while but we'd be running out of money soon so I started looking for a job. Celine and I decided that one of us should always be in the apartment, just in case the Angel came back, so I got a job working nights in a bagel bakery and she started working in a Mexican restaurant on Sunset Boulevard during the day. There were a few hours when we overlapped but Mrs Entwhistle took up the vigil then. She was convinced the Angel was alive and well and would walk in the door one day. So was I. I did think he might be hurt, though. I had visions of him all bandaged lying in some county hospital or burned so bad he didn't have any ears left or suffering from amnesia and not knowing who the hell he was but I also knew how easy it was for my imagination to get out of control so I tried to put all that out of my mind and waited for the day when he'd come back. Celine wouldn't talk about it much but there was a part of her that believed he went to heaven. I could tell. Or maybe it was a part of her that, if he couldn't come back for whatever reason, *wanted* to believe he went to heaven. There were times, when things looked particularly black and I doubted whether we'd ever see him again, that even *I* wanted to believe he went to heaven. But until we found out something, anything, all our plans were in the frame of reference of Michael's return. We'd go to the beach when Michael came home. We'd go to Palm Springs when Michael came home. We'd go to the Hollywood Bowl when Michael came home. I didn't give a shit if we did any of those things but I did want him to come back. More than I ever wanted anything in my life.

By the end of September, when we had been there over three months, we had to face the fact that the Angel probably wasn't coming back and neither one of us wanted to stay in California. It just seemed to get more painful being there as each day went by. We had exhausted every goddamn possibility. We were in the personal column in the *Times* every week. We never stopped putting up our signs, only now it was in a different neighbourhood every time we went out. We called the hospitals and the morgue religiously, and looked at dead bodies and sometimes just pieces of dead bodies and mental people who were found wandering and didn't know who the hell they were. There was a very *un*glamorous side to Hollywood and we spent most of our time in every goddamn corner of it. We asked enough questions of the police to drive them crazy and they went over every bit of information and evidence they had with us at least ten times. They were very patient and understanding but they got tired of seeing us show up at the station house. The only thing they said that gave us any hope at all was that they found a door backstage in the small piece of the building that wasn't razed, a door that was always locked, wide open. That was it. That and the fact that there was no body, which they thought was a pretty significant indication that he was still alive. They weren't at all interested in the idea of his actual ascension into heaven. Celine tried to get a compassionate reporter on the *Times* to start a campaign to find out what happened to the Botticelli Angel but he was yesterday's news and the reporter couldn't get his editor interested.

And so, at the end of October, we finally gave up hope and left Hollywood and headed back East. We hated saying goodbye to Mrs Entwhistle, who by then was a part of the family. I loved her more than I had ever loved my own mother. She tried to give us money but I refused. Christ, there was no way I was ever going to pay her back for everything she had already done. Not that she expected it or would have accepted it.

'I'll be here, my dears, in case he comes back. You have nothing to worry about on that score. And I'll make sure there's a light on at night.' She hugged Celine and wished her well. 'And you,' she said, 'dear boy, look after her.' She put her arms around me and when her cheek was next to mine she whispered, 'You did everything you could. Pay attention to an old woman who knows what she's talking about. Now get on with your life.' And she gave me a bottle of gin to see me off. She was standing at the kerb in front of the house, holding her parasol and waving as we drove off. All I could think of was that there was something wrong with always moving on and leaving the people I cared about behind.

It was the morning of October 28. I can never forget that date because the next damn day, the stock market crashed and the world started to crumble.

After the Angel

When I started writing this I said some people still blame me for what happened to the Angel. Now that I've put it all down on paper I realize I'm the only one still blaming me. Celine never says anything. Nor does Aggie or Doc Forepaugh or Cyril and Lydia. And if they *think* it, they're all the best goddamn actors in the world because they never let on and it's been over five years. I am my own accuser. I guess that will go on for as long as I live.

Celine and I were married by Justice of the Peace Wiley Mountain, in Tucumcari, New Mexico on October 30, 1929. She became Lily Tree on the official records but she was and will always be Celine to me. Mrs Wiley Mountain, Pinkie to her friends, was our witness and she loaned Celine a bouquet of paper flowers to hold. She also played the piano and sang 'Oh, Promise Me', worse than I had ever heard it sung in my life. The woman never even came near hitting any of the notes. Their dog, Geronimo, which couldn't have weighed more than ten pounds, humped my leg through most of the wedding ceremony. Our honeymoon night was spent in the Starlight Tourist Haven which was a private home with one room to let to travellers. The owners, Frances and Chooch Coyle, opened a bottle of homemade red wine and after a toast to our future we went off to our room which was right next to theirs. Without a doubt, Celine and I were made for each other. Until that night, I had no idea what it was like to hold the one person you're meant to have in your arms for the rest of your life. It was goddamn wonderful. We made the sweetest, warmest, best love in the history of the world to the loud and contented snoring of both Frances and Chooch Coyle.

Celine got her teaching certificate in Pittsburgh. It wasn't easy for her because she could only take a course here and there when we could afford it. That's why it's taken her damn near five years to graduate. When we first got back to Pittsburgh after Hollywood, Frank and Aggie put us up for almost a year until we got a little place of our own. They really put themselves out to make room for us because aside from them and the kids, there was that dog of theirs, Mike, who had free run of the house and took advantage of everyone and was, just as Aggie had said, as big as a horse. He was a lovable mutt and everyone, including Frank, was crazy about him. Frank, though he never liked me, gave me a job in the butcher's shop to pay for our room and board and even gave me a little salary. It was a sacrifice for him to do that; the depression hit him as hard as it did everyone else. Cyril sent us a little money whenever he could but times were tough for everybody, especially the farmers who didn't have any spending money and the tent show suffered.

We moved into a tiny apartment on the South Side, just a few blocks from Aggie and Frank, after our first kid was born. Prudence Tree came into the world about eleven months after we were married. She's as beautiful as her mother, with the same soft brown hair and ghost eyes, and she's as smart as a whip. At four, she can already read the *Indiana First Reader* so I get to hear about Dora and Nat and their cow named Buttercup all over again. She's sitting right here next to me, pretending she's writing a letter to her make-believe husband. She calls him John which I think is a great compliment to me. He's been working way off in California as a policeman and she hasn't seen him in two years, she tells me, and she's writing to inform John that she's going to have a baby. Won't John be surprised! Prue has been having a baby every day since about a year ago when her little brother, Michael, was born. Even as I write these last words, he's crawling around, dusting the floor and generally getting into things he shouldn't and making a pain in the ass of himself.

I wanted to finish this so I'm watching the kids while Celine's out putting the last of our stuff in the Willys-Knight. Hard as it is to believe, the old buggy is still running. Margarito and Sven may have been a couple of cheating bastards but whatever they did to the Willys I haven't had a bit of trouble with it since we left Mesa Vista. As soon as the Willys is all packed, the four of us are heading for Paradise. Celine is going to teach in the school house which is being refurbished by Saladin Ridge and Amick Halsey and a few of the other men from the new families in town. There are six families altogether and fifteen kids for the school. Paradise has awakened just as Doc Forepaugh said it would. I don't know what the hell I'm going to do there. Maybe open up the Blue Moon Hotel? I suppose the real reason we're going to Paradise, aside from the fact that I couldn't think of a better place to raise kids *and* Doc Forepaugh is there *and* the town needs a teacher *and* they're not going to get one any better than Celine, is that if there's one place on this green earth that the Angel would come back to it would be to Paradise. For Christ's sake, he already thinks *God* lives there. And, unlike Celine, who now thinks the Angel did go to heaven when the church caught on fire, I think he *will* show up one day. In fact, I'm *certain* he will. I have that feeling deep down in my bones, that feeling that lets you know you're right about something.

Celine and I hardly ever talk about her late husband. When we do, it's just a passing reference to the terrible accident he had falling off that treacherous roof. But that's life, accidents will happen. Oh, yeah, she doesn't eat plaster any more. At least I don't think she does. I haven't seen her do it and I know she doesn't carry it in her pocket. Not since before we left Hollywood. The closest I've seen her come to anything like that was one day when she was chewing on a pencil. But, hell, everybody chews on pencils.

There's just one more thing that I have to put down here. Just in case there's something to this idea of the Angel living all those lives and going to heaven and then coming back every so often, to pose for paintings or whatever, when I give little Michael his bath, and I like to do that, I check very carefully to see if there's any hint of things growing on his back. There's a part of me that keeps thinking I'm going to discover little wing buds starting to sprout. But, so far, nothing. He's just as healthy and fat and normal as any little baby could be. I just wish I could explain why, when Celine has the eyes of a cloudy summer day and my eyes are as blue as an ocean on a picture postcard, the baby's eyes are as black as midnight. It's the goddamnedest thing!